Praise for *A Rogue's Pleasure*

"For a sexy, romantic ride through the Regency era, *A Rogue's Pleasure* more than delivers. Hope Tarr's enchanting debut will sweep you back to a world of dashing lords and daring ladies, providing twists enough to keep your heart racing and your hand turning the pages. This first novel is more than just a promise of great things to come, it's a gem in itself. Robbery and abduction, seduction and romance—this book's got it all."
—Elaine Fox

"What a wonderful read. *A Rogue's Pleasure* [has] all the makings of a great novel: vivid historical detail, vibrant characters, and a fast-paced adventure—everything I look for in a historical romance."
—Victoria Lynne

"Wonderfully written! This is an impressive debut from a bright new author. Readers will devour it."
—Cathy Maxwell

I0669445

A Rogue's Pleasure

Hope Tarr

J
JOVE BOOKS, NEW YORK

This is a work of fiction. Names, characters, places, and incidents are either the product of the author's imagination or are used fictitiously, and any resemblance to actual persons, living or dead, business establishments, events, or locales is entirely coincidental.

A ROGUE'S PLEASURE

A Jove Book / published by arrangement with the author

PRINTING HISTORY
Jove edition / November 2000

All rights reserved.
Copyright © 2000 by Hope Tarr.
Author photo by Image Pro Inc., Sarasota. FL.
This book, or parts thereof, may not be reproduced in any form, without permission.
For information address: The Berkley Publishing Group, a division of Penguin Putnam Inc., 375 Hudson Street, New York, New York 10014.

The Penguin Putnam Inc. World Wide Web site address is http://www.penguinputnam.com

ISBN: 0-515-12951-8

A JOVE BOOK®
Jove Books are published by The Berkley Publishing Group, a division of Penguin Putnam Inc., 375 Hudson Street, New York, New York 10014. JOVE and the "J" design are trademarks belonging to Penguin Putnam Inc.

PRINTED IN THE UNITED STATES OF AMERICA

10 9 8 7 6 5 4 3 2

Acknowledgments

It is often remarked that it takes a whole village to raise a child. Much the same can be said for the collaboration that carries a manuscript from inception to bookstore shelf. First and foremost I thank my agent, Jenny Bent, for her encouragement and patience while waiting for the book to be "born," and my editor, Cindy Hwang, for her gentle guidance in bringing the manuscript to its final "adult" form.

I also extend my heartfelt appreciation to my husband, Earl Pence, and to my friend and fellow author, Lisa Arlt. Steadfast and fearless souls, they each plowed through the first primitive manuscript draft in its entirety without complaint. Others whose wise counsel found its way into these pages are my critique partners and fellow writers Jane Sevier Sanchez, Elizabeth Fedorko, and Vicki Burgess. I am particularly indebted to Jane, who tackled the Prologue and first chapter more times than I'm sure either of us would care to count.

I extend very special thanks to my mother, Nancy Tarr, for her unflagging love and encouragement throughout the years. Most especially I appreciate her repeated assurances that, yes, of course my book would sell!

More special thanks go to my husband, Earl. In addition to serving on the front lines as my reader, he has been my friend, confidant, and soul mate.

Lastly, I thank Palmer Christian Bassich for his help with interpreting early nineteenth-century military stratagems and weaponry.

Historical Notes

The Peninsular War was fought from 1808 to 1814 on the Iberian Peninsula of Portugal and Spain—the Allied Forces of Great Britain, Spain, and Portugal pitted against France and her conquests. The catalyst for the conflict was Napoleon's invasion of Portugal on November 30, 1807 in retaliation for that country's refusal to comply with his trade embargo against Great Britain. He next invaded Spain in the Spring of 1808 and set his brother Joseph on the throne. The Spanish and Portuguese peoples appealed to Great Britain for support in ousting the invaders. The first 9,500 British troops, led by Sir Arthur Wellesley (the future Duke of Wellington), landed in Portugal in August 1808. The Peninsular War had begun.

The Campaign's bloodiest battle was fought on May 16, 1811 at the deserted Spanish town of Albuera. There, on a mud-soaked patch of land little larger than a rugby field, more than 37,000 British, Spanish, and Portuguese slogged it out against 28,000 French. Sir Lowry Cole, commander of the British Fourth Division, finally resolved the deadlock. Urged on by twenty-six-year-old Major Henry Hardinage, he counterattacked on his own initiative. The Allies lost nearly 6,000 men, the French an estimated 7,000.

The French withdrew first, enabling the British to claim victory albeit at a price. When Wellington received his general's grim dispatch, he reportedly declared, "This won't do. It will drive the people in England mad. Write me down a victory."

In *A Rogue's Pleasure* the hero, Anthony Grenville, assumes Hardinage's role as the bold visionary behind Cole's counterattack. But heroism exacts a toll, inflicting wounds that cut deeper than flesh and bone. Wounds that only the truest of loves can heal . . .

To Earl, with all my heart

Prologue

Not even the roar of exploding cannonballs could drown the anguished pleas of the wounded languishing on the corpse-littered field. Some of the wretches called for water, some for their mothers, and some simply for death. Standing on the low ridge, Anthony Grenville studied the carnage through the lens of his spyglass. Squinting through rain and gray-black smoke, he forced himself to view the battlefield dispassionately, as if it were a chessboard and the dead and dying merely rooks sacrificed to win the match.

The fighting had begun just before eight that morning when Soult's French forces attacked the British Allies to the right instead of to the east as the English had anticipated. Mayhem ensued, a grim slogging match with volleys at close range. Neither side would cede defeat even after a torrential downpour rendered many of the muskets unfireable.

Rainwater slid off the front flap of Anthony's felt shako so that he was looking out through a waterfall. Cursing, he took off the hat and shook it just as his fellow rifleman and best friend Peter came up beside him.

Peter pulled off his own headgear and wiped his freckled forehead with the mud-spattered sleeve of his dark green jacket. "How's it looking, *Captain*?" He grinned, apparently not yet tired of teasing Anthony over his recent promotion.

But the past forty-eight hours without sleep had stolen

what little capacity for humor Anthony still possessed. And grief over the loss of their friend, Stephen, to malaria the month before made it almost impossible to smile.

He passed Peter the spyglass. "Here, see for yourself."

Predictably Peter's smile turned into a scowl. "Bloody, bloody hell." He handed the telescope back to Anthony and pulled a silver flask from the haversack he wore slung over one shoulder. "Sweet Jesus," he exclaimed around a mouthful of port, "what can Cole be thinking? If we hold back much longer, we're all done for."

Anthony exhaled. Their division commander, Sir Lowry Cole, was a decent sort but, like many staff officers assigned to the Peninsula, he lacked the boldness of a born leader. If Cole didn't make his move soon, they'd end up trapped, their alternatives being to surrender or to stand and be massacred. Had they really abandoned Badajoz the day before and marched through the night only to come to *this*?

His frustration, fueled by a week of spoiled food, spotty sleep, and stupid command decisions, roiled. "Something has to be done," he muttered, more to himself than to Peter. "Someone has to get to Cole, make him see that continuing to hold back isn't prudence; it's suicide."

Peter snorted. "Someone who doesn't mind spending the rest of the war clapped in irons."

This time Anthony smiled. *At least I'll face the firing squad in one piece.*

Scanning the melee below, Anthony spotted Cole's gold-trimmed cocked hat. Already the enemy's cavalry was breaking through. The general, withdrawing his sword from the rib cage of a French dragoon, apparently did not see the Polish lancer charging toward him.

"Sir, look out!"

Anthony threw his spyglass aside. Ignoring Peter shouting for him to stay back, he ran down the incline and into the open field. Sword drawn, he shoved Cole aside and parried a deadly lance thrust aimed at the general's skull. Before the trooper could launch a second attack, Anthony seized him by the collar, yanked him off his horse, and threw him to the ground. Avoiding the frightened eyes, Anthony neatly severed his foe's jugular.

Sickened, he turned back to Cole. The general had a gash on his forehead; otherwise he appeared unharmed. Anthony helped him to the periphery of the field where a crumbling stone wall provided temporary shelter from the enemy's artillery.

Sir Lowry pulled a lace-edged handkerchief from his pocket and mopped his brow. "Well done, Grenville. I owe you my life."

"I'll settle for a word with you, sir."

"You have my attention, Captain."

Anthony braced himself. What he was about to suggest was tantamount to inviting a court-martial.

"Sir, it is my belief that we shall all be dead men ere nightfall if we remain here as fodder for Soult's powder."

"Our orders are to hold and let Soult make the first move." Cole's face was set in stubborn lines, but his eyes mirrored his uncertainty.

"With all due respect, sir, I believe that to follow those orders is suicide. If Soult manages to hold onto the right much longer, it's only a matter of time before he cuts us off from the roads to both Badajoz and Valverde."

"You've a keen eye, Grenville, and a keen mind along with it." Cole's expression was world-weary. "What do you propose?"

"A counterattack to drive them back over the river. 'Tis a risk, to be sure, but if we fail at least we die fighting like men."

Cole hesitated. "Very well. Spread the word among the other company commanders. I'll give the order to move out as soon as they have their men in position."

The next hours sped by like the whizzing artillery. Reality transmuted to the pelting rain, the metallic tang of blood, and the blinding haze of gunpowder. Anthony tried to keep an eye on Peter, fighting nearby. His friend was peerless with a rifle but his swordsmanship left much to be desired, and he had a bad habit of forgetting to watch his back. An expert swordsman, Anthony covered him as best he could, although his own sword arm was cramping dangerously.

He'd just gutted a French *fusilier* when a sudden burning sensation scored his bicep. At first he thought he was having a muscle spasm, then he looked down. Wetness seeped through the powder burn below his shoulder. The blood turned the green fabric a muddy brown but, despite the liberal flow, the bullet had missed the bone and made a clean pass through the sinew. He was about to give thanks for his narrow escape when a second shot struck him above the right knee, knocking him off his feet. He landed facedown on the sodden ground less than a foot away from the slain Frenchman. Fighting nausea, he dragged himself up on his elbows, the grass beneath him slick with blood. His blood. He thought of the truncated limbs he'd seen stacked outside surgeons' tents, and fear clawed his insides. He closed his mind to the image and forced himself to concentrate on how to avoid being trampled.

The closest cover was a pigsty nearly a yard away. White-hot lightning streaked down his injured leg, and his arm burned as though someone held a brazier to it, but he had to try. Gritting his teeth, he dragged himself toward the wooden enclosure, his progress measured in inches and sweat streaming his face. He gave a cheerless laugh. Crawling on his belly in the mud hardly seemed in keeping with the dignity of a future earl, but life, even the prospect of life as a one-legged cripple, suddenly seemed very precious.

He was halfway to the sty when a horse's hooves thundered toward him. He looked up. The French *cuirassier* charged, the braided horsehair queue of his helmet lashing the air. From several yards away, Anthony could see the blood lust blazing from the cavalryman's eyes.

One last, longing glance at the pen. Not a prayer of reaching it in time.

Not a prayer.

Dear God, I don't want to die. Not here. Not now. Not like this.

Saber raised, the cuirassier whooped his triumph. Anthony slumped to the ground. A few paces away, a horse reared, then shrieked. Curses in French, then a man's scream melding with a sickening thud.

Anthony felt the rumble in the soaked soil pressed beneath his cheek. The coarse brown grass was a far cry from the verdant meadowlands of England, but with a little imagination . . .

I hope you're a skillful swordsman, Frenchman.

Anthony closed his eyes and waited for blackness to overtake him.

Chapter One

*R*obert, kidnapped!

More than an hour after Chelsea Bellamy spotted the black-edged letter lying amidst that morning's post, her hands still shook. As did the rest of her. Sitting in the center of her canopied bed, legs tucked beneath her voluminous black skirts, she scanned the dispatch yet again, searching the elegantly penned words for some clue she might have overlooked.

> *My Dear Miss Bellamy:*
> *I have your brother. I've plucked the lad from the London Road like an overripe plum to be my guest for the month. The price of my hospitality—and his release? Five hundred pounds to be delivered by you at midnight on the thirtieth.*

Five hundred pounds! A fortune. Biting her bottom lip, she forced herself to read on.

> *Come alone to the church of St. Mary-le-Bow in East London, place a satchel with the money on the first pew, then leave. Proceed directly to the Rutting Bull Tavern. Young Robert will join you there within the hour. Fail to obey even one of my instructions, so*

much as show this letter to another living soul, and
you will be signing your brother's death warrant.

Palms damp, Chelsea refolded the crisp, cologne-scented
foolscap and dropped it into her lap. Could it be a ruse?
Might Robert be aboard his ship bound for Lisbon, safe for
the time being from kidnappers and Boney's Butchers alike?
She doubted it, but she'd write to the War Office in London
anyway. Surely someone there would be able to tell her
whether or not he'd reported to his duty officer?

Until she received a reply, she must assume the note was
genuine. As it must be, for how else could Robert's signet
ring have gotten inside? An intaglio "B" worked in onyx and
ancient gold, it hadn't left Robert's middle finger since the
vicar had removed it from their father's stiff hand.

Tears burned the backs of her eyes. *Oh, Papa, if only you*
were here to advise me. But she could imagine what he'd
say. *Cogito, ergo sum. I think, therefore I am,* she translated
aloud, a wistful smile playing about her lips. A great admirer
of Descartes, Richard Bellamy had reared his only daughter
to believe that there was no problem in the universe so vast
that a properly exercised intellect could not master it. Over
the past year she'd been called on to put the French philoso-
pher's maxim to the test more times than she cared to count.

Beginning with the carriage accident that had claimed the
lives of both her parents the autumn before. Then a drought
had ruined the corn crop. Robert had been in his second year
at Oxford, and Chelsea had scrimped to pay his tuition. That
he had rewarded her efforts by being sent down for behavior unbecoming a gentleman—a schoolboy prank involving
a feisty goat placed in a professor's bed—had exerted a particularly depressing effect on her usually formidable spirit.
And when he'd announced his intention to use the last of
their money to purchase a commission in an army regiment
bound for Portugal, they'd quarreled bitterly.

"Christ, Chels, I'm off to London in a week." Robert, eyes
wounded, crossed the library toward her. "I know you're not
happy about it, but won't you at least wish me Godspeed?"

Barricaded behind their father's desk, she mounted her

defense. "Don't blaspheme," she spat, her own eyes brimming. "And no, I won't wish you Godspeed, bon voyage, or anything else. Not when it's bullets and cannonballs you're rushing to meet."

She'd even refused to attend his farewell assembly. Everyone in Upper Uckfield between the ages of nine and ninety had turned out to bid farewell to their local hero. Even now, with guilt twisting her throat so taut she could barely swallow, she didn't think she could have borne it. An entire evening of their neighbors ruminating over every detail of Robert's impending departure—date, time, travel route—like cows chewing their cud.

She released a shaky breath. Date. Time. Travel route. Everything someone would need to know to plan an ambush.

Could Robert's kidnapper be one of their neighbors? The prospect chilled her, and she hastened to dismiss it. They had no enemies to speak of and, even if they had, their straightened circumstances were common knowledge. If the kidnapper lived among them, surely he—or she—must realize that five hundred pounds was a fortune to her, nearly as unreachable as moonstone and almost as dear.

But not as dear as Robert.

No, this mischief was the work of a stranger, some ne'er-do-well who'd passed through Upper Uckfield just as preparations for Robert's departure were underway. A nineteen-year-old who made no secret of his plans to travel to London alone, a sister left behind to fend for herself—Robert and she would seem easy marks. And, while Upper Uckfieldians didn't hesitate to gossip among themselves, most would be loathe to admit to an outsider that their leading family was worse off than the proverbial church mouse.

Perhaps she should ignore the kidnapper's injunction and appeal to the parish magistrate? Of all people, John Minnington should know if any suspicious persons had visited the hamlet of late. Nibbling on her bottom lip, Chelsea weighed the risk. Unpopular with both his tenants and neighbors, Minnington was appointed magistrate only after Chelsea's father resigned and no one else came forward to fill the vacancy. In the course of his tenure, he'd shown himself to be both incompetent and lazy. Chelsea wouldn't entrust her horse to the blunderbuss let alone Robert.

That decided, she turned to her principal dilemma—how to raise the ransom? Twirling Robert's ring about her thumb, she finally concluded there was no help for it. She would swallow her pride and bespeak a loan from her neighbor, Squire Dumfreys.

The prospect was far from appealing on several counts. Stubborn, self-reliant pride was the bane of the Bellamys, and Chelsea had inherited it in full measure. But pride was not the only reason she was reluctant to ask for money she had no idea of how or when she could repay.

The owner of the adjacent estate, Dumfreys had been a frequent guest at Oatlands for as long as Chelsea could remember. A bachelor with a fondness for children, he had played the honorary uncle to Chelsea and Robert. It was during her sixteenth year that he changed toward her. Although she wanted to believe that his frequent touches and compliments conveyed nothing more than avuncular affection, his behavior over the past year put flesh on the bones of her suspicions. On his last visit he'd cornered her in the library, and she felt certain he meant to kiss her. Fortunately her maid-of-all-work appeared at the door, and Chelsea seized the excuse to slip away.

But Robert's life was on the line. If she were to save her brother, she would have to put both the Bellamy pride and her misgivings about the squire aside. Her decision made, she rose and crossed to the wardrobe, the hem of her bombazine mourning gown rustling on the bare wooden floor.

Having long ago learned to live without the luxury of a lady's maid, she pulled her dove gray riding habit off its peg and dressed quickly. Then she picked up her brush from the dresser and stepped in front of the mirror. Even after braiding and pinning her waist-length hair into a prim coronet, the red-gold strands shimmered as if ablaze. Scowling at her reflection, she picked up her bonnet and put it on. The effect was like snuffing a candle flame, and Chelsea felt relieved. Some folk might admire red hair, but she considered the color more affliction than boon. For one thing, people were forever testing her to determine whether or not she possessed the redhead's fabled volatile temper, which she did—in abundance. Far too often she had been goaded into displaying it.

The last time she lost control was the morning of Robert's departure for London. She'd known it would likely be a year or more before she saw her brother again, assuming he survived the French soldiers' bullets and the malaria sweeping through Wellington's Peninsular Army. Yet she'd wasted their last precious moments together upbraiding him for his past irresponsible behavior. Now guilt stabbed at her.

Unless she could raise the ransom, she would never be able to retract those scathing reproaches. Never have the chance to put her arms around Robert and tell him that, in spite of everything, she loved him. Choking back tears, she slipped the folded message into her pocket. Her baby brother was in grave danger, and she would do everything in her power to save him.

"Chelsea, my dear, come in." Squire Dumfreys rose from the desk and hurried to where Chelsea stood in the study doorway.

She bit her lower lip. "I hope I'm not disturbing you."

"Nonsense. This is an unexpected pleasure."

The squire was tall and distinguished, his dark hair shot with silver at the temples. In his early fifties, he still attracted his fair share of admiration from matrons and maids alike. Ordinarily, expert tailoring disguised his tendency toward portliness, but the afternoon was warm, and he had removed his jacket. The bulge at his midriff strained the buttons of his embroidered waistcoat.

His hand slid to her shoulder as he guided her to the camelback sofa. His eyes, however, slid a good deal further until she felt as though she stood before him stripped to her shift.

"How charming you look. You've blossomed into a woman this twenty-first year, and a beautiful one at that."

"That is very kind of you." Fighting the urge to flee, she sat and untied her bonnet strings.

"May I offer you some refreshment? A glass of ratafia, perhaps?"

Chelsea set the bonnet aside and smoothed her hair. "No thank you. I do not care for anything." Heart hammering, she watched him pour himself a glass of port. "I'm afraid I've come to ask a favor."

He strolled toward her, glass in hand. "My dear child, I've always told you that if I can ever be of any assistance, you have only to ask."

"Perhaps you had better hear me out first."

Bypassing a pair of leather chairs, he sat next to her, his shoulder brushing hers. Fear frissoned through her.

He leaned closer and patted the top of her hand. "Nonsense. Now tell me, how can I help?"

"I need to borrow . . ." she drew a bracing breath " . . . five hundred pounds."

His smile slipped. "That is a great deal of money." He cleared his throat. "May I ask why you require such a sum?"

She hesitated, twisting her hands in her lap.

"You aren't in some sort of trouble, I trust?"

"I-I'm afraid I can't tell you that." Realizing how rude she must sound, she rushed on, "It would only be a loan. I promise to repay you with interest after the next harvest."

"This loan . . . it wouldn't happen to be for that young scamp Robert, now would it?"

She studied his face, wondering how she had betrayed herself. "How did you know?"

He chuckled, once more the indulgent uncle figure of her childhood. "Robert would not be the first young officer to be lured into deep play by an experienced card sharp. Did he get into trouble after he bought his commission?"

Chelsea exhaled in relief. Praying she could carry off the deception, she bowed her head. "Robert is having . . . er . . . difficulties, I'm afraid." It was, after all, the truth.

His smile was sage. "Young men will sow their wild oats. 'Tis inevitable. You must not be too harsh with Robert for a first offense."

Her throat tightened. "No, I suppose not."

"Very well, my dear, you shall have your five hundred pounds." His tone was beneficent, his smile benign. "I shall contact my solicitor directly. It should take only a few days for him to remand the sum."

Tears gathered in her eyes. "Oh, thank you. Thank you, sir. You shan't regret it, I promise."

"I'm sure I shan't. But not another word about repayment. All this sordid talk of loans and interest dishonors me. I fully intend on making you a present of it."

She turned to him, shamefaced in the presence of such generosity. "Oh no, you are too good to us. I couldn't possibly accept."

"But you must." He raised a hand to stem her protests. "It gives me great pleasure to assist you." He drained his glass, then set it aside. "In fact, Chelsea, you have always given me the greatest pleasure."

Her stomach tightened. "Sir?"

"You were such a delightful child. I can see you even now. Such a pretty little thing. Those big, turquoise eyes of yours, so innocent, looking up into mine." Laying a hand on each of her shoulders, he drew her closer before she could move away. "Your child's hands, so soft, so small, reaching up for me to take you in my arms."

The benevolent mask fell away, revealing the stark desire beneath. His hand slid down her arm, enfolding her cold fingers in his clammy grasp.

"Do you remember how you used to perch on my lap, letting me stroke your hair while I read to you?" He carried their linked hands to his face, stroking her knuckles down his smoothly shaven jaw. "Oh Chelsea, it's been an eternity since I've felt your hands on me, since I've been able to kiss and fondle you as I once did."

A sense of unreality descended, as though Chelsea's true self had separated from her body and stood watching from the safety of a shadowed corner. *This can't be happening. This must be a dream, a nightmare.*

His glassy-eyed gaze fell to her breasts. "Even in that hideous riding habit, your beauty shines forth like a beacon to rescue a drowning man at sea. Only you can save me, Chelsea. *Save me!*"

Turning over her hand, he pressed his wet lips to her palm. The touch of his mouth returned her to reality. Fright churned her stomach in queasy waves.

"Squire Dumfreys . . . please." She struggled to pull free. "You mustn't say such things."

"Oh, but I must. If I keep the words locked inside me any longer, I shall burst. Chelsea, you must know how I feel about you. How I *burn* for you."

Perspiration gathered between her shoulder blades. She edged to the back of the sofa. "Please, release me."

His eyes hardened. "I've waited a long time for you, Chelsea, but I've done with waiting."

He shoved her down onto the cushions and hurled himself on top of her. Trapped between the sofa and his sprawling weight, panic paralyzed her. For a terrifying moment, she thought she would suffocate.

"Stop!" In vain, she pushed at his solid mass. "You were Father's friend. This isn't right."

"Not right?" His eyes narrowed. "Not *right*? 'Twas I who taught you the steps to the country dances so you'd not shame yourself at your first assembly. To ride astride even though your mama forbade it. 'Tis only right that I be the one to teach you . . . *this*."

His mouth sought hers. She turned her head, and his slathering kiss fell on her cheek. Bile rose in her throat.

He covered her ear with his mouth, his tongue filling the canal. "No one need ever know. It would be our secret. You used to like secrets when you were little. Do you remember how you used to reach into my pockets to fish for sweet-meats? Reach inside now and feel what I have for you."

He dragged her hand down to his trouser front and pressed her palm against the hard bulge. Shaking, she tried to yank free, but he held her. Helpless, she searched his face. Froth filmed his upper lip, and a stream of perspiration edged its way from forehead to temple. Obviously he was too much a prisoner of lust to respond to reason. *Reason*.

Cogito, ergo sum.

From the back of her brain, her father's voice urged her to chart a different course.

"Very well, then." She grabbed the vulnerable flesh through the breeches and squeezed. *Hard.*

He howled. Chelsea sprang off the sofa and ran to the door. The knob slipped in her damp grasp.

"Fancy it rough, do you?"

He caught her from behind and slammed her against the paneling. Her forehead hit with a heavy thud. Black, spidery shapes darted before her eyes. She screamed.

"Let me go!"

He wrenched her arms behind her and clasped a hand about her joined wrists.

"You'll not be sorry, my girl, I promise you. Five hundred pounds is a pittance compared to all that shall be yours. Fine gowns, jewels, you shall have them all." His grip slackened, and he shaped her buttocks with his free hand. "Now turn around and kiss me."

"No!" She whirled to face him. *God help me, not even to save Robert.*

She lifted her knee and drove it between his thighs.

Dumfreys's legs buckled, and he sank to the floor. Cupping his groin, he rocked back and forth.

He looked up at her, his face contorted. "Bitch!"

Wrenching open the door, Chelsea fled down the corridor, through the foyer, and out the columned entrance. Dulcinea was tethered to a post in the front yard. Gasping, Chelsea untied her mare's reins and scrambled into the saddle.

The squire limped onto the portico.

"You'll pay, Chelsea!" He shook a clenched fist. "I'll have you yet, and the next time I'll not be so gentle."

Chelsea had no intention of giving him a chance to make good on his chilling promise. She urged Dulcinea into a full gallop and flew through the hedgerow-bordered lanes. Her loosened hair lashed at her face, but she didn't slow her pace until she passed through her own entrance gate and Oatland's red brick facade came into view.

Riding into the stable, she dismounted on wobbly legs. Marcus, the stable boy, emerged from the tack room.

"Gooday, miss."

Not trusting her voice, Chelsea responded with a nod. Limbs weak, she handed over the reins and stepped away from the horse.

He stroked the side of Dulcinea's lathered neck. "Ye've ridden 'er 'ard, I see. Cain't say as I blame ye. 'Tis a glorious day for it."

Can it be that I don't look any different? "Yes, well . . . please see that she gets water, a walk, and a rub down before you feed her."

Chelsea caught the boy's puzzled stare and flushed. Ordinarily she cared for Dulcinea herself, but today was no ordinary day. Feeling as transparent as glass, she hurried from the stable. Outside birds sang and sunshine warmed her face, but all she wanted was to be inside where it was silent and cool. And safe.

She ran across the lawn to the path. Tall grass and weeds had overtaken the stones, and she hiked her skirts to keep from tripping. Ahead lay the house. With its fanlight-surmounted doorway, ionic columns, and fleet of symmetrically arranged sash windows, Oatlands had been the envy of the neighborhood when her great-grandfather had built it fewer than a hundred years before. It was as one drew near that the signs of neglect—cracked stone facings, a broken windowpane stuffed with a cloth, a column missing its capital—became apparent. But it was still home. Her home. The one place where she felt truly safe.

She gained the portico, turned the brass doorknob, and stepped inside. Teeth gritted against the yawning creak, she gently released the handle. The front hall was deserted, as she'd hoped it would be. She tiptoed toward the back of the house, the heels of her half-boots nearly soundless on the threadbare carpet.

The library had been her father's sanctuary. Now it was hers. Crossing its threshold, the scent of sandalwood—her father's scent—enveloped her like an embrace. Throat knotted, she closed the oak door and moved to the mahogany desk. She could almost see her father seated behind it, head bent, spectacles slipping toward the tip of his nose, big hands cradling one of his precious books. Tears misting her eyes, she touched the back of the cracked leather chair. It looked so big, so *empty*.

Papa, what shall I do? Her gaze fell on the brandy decanter. Denuded of its silver tray and crystal goblets, it sat at one lonely corner of the desk along with a single chipped glass. Hands shaking, she lifted the stopper and poured out three fingers' worth of brandy. Her father had permitted her the occasional "nip," reasoning that, in these modern times, a young woman should learn to hold her drink in case some young man attempted to ply her with it. "But 'tis our little secret," he'd say with a wink and a significant look toward the closed door, a reminder that what Mama didn't know wouldn't hurt her. Papa had been full of such delightfully liberal notions, including disengaging Chelsea's governess—a tight-lipped scold whom she'd detested—and taking over her education himself.

To the best of fathers. Facing his empty chair, Chelsea raised her glass and downed the drink. Eyes watering—this time from the brandy, she told herself—she set the glass aside, stepped behind the desk, and settled into the sheltering depths of the chair. Leaning back, she felt the knot in her stomach start to unfurl. Later she'd take a bath—a scalding one—to wash away Dumfreys's cologne and ease the achiness creeping into her upper arms and wrists. For the present, all she wanted was to pretend that the afternoon—the nightmare—had never happened. Closing her eyes and tucking her feet beneath her, she could almost believe.

She must have slept. The hallway clock struck a second chord, then a third. She sat up and stretched. The inside of her mouth felt fuzzy from the brandy and her head still ached, yet she felt better. More in control. A bath would be perfect.

She started up, but the brisk knock stayed her. Her heart caromed. The squire? No, it must be Jack, punctilious as ever, with her tea. Chelsea sucked in her breath, marshaled her calm, and gave the call to enter.

The butler shambled in. Gaze fixed on her face, he set the tray in front of her.

"Why, Miss Chelsea, ye look a fright."

Stooped with rheumatism, Jack sported only one working eye, but anyone could see he'd been a splendid Goliath in his day. When Chelsea was a child, he'd regaled her with tales of his bygone days as the notorious highwayman, One-Eyed Jack.

She suspected his exploits were greatly exaggerated, but

Jack had indeed been an outlaw. Fortunately her father was the magistrate when Jack was apprehended. The penalty for highway robbery was hanging, but Sir Richard argued that since Jack had never killed anyone, leniency was warranted. He presented the highwayman with a choice—he could either go into service in the Bellamy household or to prison. Jack submitted to gainful employment as the lesser of two evils. Under his watchful eye, not so much as a spoon had gone missing in well nigh thirty years.

Until, that is, Chelsea pawned the family silver to make ends meet. Her mother's tea service was the last to go. She'd sold it to Mrs. Pettigrew the month before for a fraction of its value.

Desperate times call for desperate measures.

Her father had placed his faith—and the last of the family money—in one of the hundred private banks that failed in 1810. That left only the estate, which was entailed. The adjacent properties had been parceled off one by one over the years to settle debts, and the few farms that remained were heavily mortgaged. Her eyes swept over the library. Other than the frayed furnishings and the dusty tomes lining the bookshelves, there was nothing left to sell. Nothing that would fetch anywhere near the sum she needed.

A loan from Dumfreys had been her last—her only—hope.

Oh, God, what am I to do?

Chelsea lifted the earthenware pot and poured tea through the strainer. Without warning, a year's worth of pent-up tears broke free. Suddenly she was seeing the tray of chipped and mismatched crockery through a veil of water. Her cup overflowed, splashing tea onto the saucer.

Jack took the teapot from her and set it down. "Blue devils got ye, lass?"

Blast, I'm crying. Head bowed, Chelsea nodded.

"I'll 'ave Cook make ye one o' her possets. Ye'll be right as rain in no time."

Weary, she picked up a napkin and wiped her eyes. "I'm afraid even Mrs. Potter's expertise with herbs will not remedy this."

She pulled the ransom letter from her pocket and held it

out to him. Then she remembered that Jack couldn't read. Unfolding the hated missive, she read the message aloud.

When she looked up from the paper, Jack wore a mask of bulldog fury.

"The filthy, yaller-bellied dog. To snaffle young Master Robert for a measly five hundred quid."

"Really, Jack, the amount is hardly the issue." The blackmailer might as well have asked for the crown jewels for all the hope she had of raising the sum.

Expression softening, he laid a gnarled paw on her shoulder. "Now, now, don't 'e worry yer pretty head, Miss Chelsea. Ole Jack'll think o' something. As One-Eye, I come through worse fixes than this."

Cogito, ergo sum. Chelsea peered over Jack's broad, lopsided shoulders, an idea taking shape in her mind. But no, it was too fantastic, too desperate. She didn't dare set such a scheme into motion. Or did she?

Desperate times call for desperate measures.

Telling herself she was merely thinking aloud, she cleared her throat. "As it happens, a solution of sorts has just occurred to me."

Jack's bushy eyebrows bolted upright. He straightened and folded his arms across his barrel chest.

"I knowed ye since ye was born, Miss Chelsea." He wagged a thick finger. "I seen that look enough to know it spells mischief. What kind o' plan?"

Her gaze floated to the ceiling. *Can I really do this?* "I was just thinking that perhaps the time has come to resurrect One-Eyed Jack."

Jack's square jaw dropped. "Lord luv 'e, Miss Chelsea, 'tis the shock. It's addled your brain."

Nervous energy thrummed through her. She shot to her feet and rounded the desk. "Nonsense. With the proper clothing—and an eye patch—I think I might make for a passable One-Eyed Jack junior, don't you?" Shoving her hands into her pockets, she swaggered across the room.

"Now wait one blasted minute. I 'ope ye b'aint suggestin' what I think."

"And what if I am? Robert isn't much taller than I am. I

used to dress in his clothing when we were children. Remember?" Giddy from brandy and nerves, she pivoted, submitting all of her five feet seven inches to his inspection. "He left some clothes behind. I can borrow a pair of breeches and a coat. No one would ever guess it's me."

He shook his head. "Are ye sure ye won't be wantin' one o' Cook's brews?" He started toward the door.

Chelsea twirled once more. "I may have had a brief attack of nerves, but I assure you that all my faculties are intact." *More or less.* Dizzy, she ground to a halt in the center of the worn carpet. "It's not as though I'm proposing to make a career of it."

He pressed a palm to his forehead. "But, Miss Chelsea, if ye was to be caught . . . They might not hang 'e but, child, think o' yer reputation. Ye'd be a ruined woman."

She lifted her chin. "As if I give a fig for that."

It was not as though being branded an outcast would be a drastic departure from the ordinary. With Jack as her nursemaid, Chelsea had grown up more interested in picking locks than in playing with dolls, in riding her pony than in stitching her sampler, in climbing trees and fences with Robert and his friends than in practicing her pianoforte. A "strange, unnatural creature," she'd overheard the vicar's wife call her on more than one occasion. Not that she cared . . . much.

Jack folded his arms and glared. "Well, *I* care. I b'aint raised ye only to see ye die an ole maid."

She shrugged. "I might as well. There's no one in Upper Uckfield I care to marry."

That was only too true. Mired as she was in the country and with no money for a London Season, the only men she ever met were farmers' sons. Nice boys, most of them, but a far cry from the Sir Lancelots, Childe Harolds, and sundry Greek gods she encountered in the pages of books.

But no romantic hero was going to come to her rescue— or Robert's. It was all up to her.

She forged ahead. "I don't intend on getting caught. I'll lay One-Eyed Jack to rest the moment I've gotten the money I need for Robert's ransom. And," she reminded him, "you've boasted often enough that I can manage a horse as well as any man. Better than most."

"That b'aint the point." Jack raked a hand through his few remaining threads of gray hair. "Why not ask the squire for the blunt?"

The recent memory, vivid and ugly, flashed through her consciousness. She shuddered. "As it happens, I've just come from calling on him."

Tread warily. Jack is fiercely protective of me. If I tell him the whole truth, he may just take it into his head to thrash Dumfreys within an inch of his life. Assaulting a gentleman could mean prison—or worse.

"And?" he prompted, watching her.

Suddenly weak-kneed, she subsided into her chair. "I'm afraid I was unable to meet his er . . . terms for repayment," she answered, deciding that a half truth would serve her better than an outright lie.

He rubbed his good eye. "What about yer mum's sister?"

Her chin snapped up. "You know perfectly well Aunt Esther hasn't a farthing beyond her widow's portion. That only leaves . . ."

"The *magistrate*." He spat the words.

Chelsea folded her arms, knowing she had won. Jack had little respect for the law and even less for Minnington, who thirty years before had called her father a fool for entrusting his plate to a convicted felon.

Jack curled the crooked fingers of his right hand into a fist. "That lily-livered, no-good . . ."

She waited for his diatribe to end, then concluded, "So, you see, we really have no other alternative."

"*We?*"

She nodded briskly. "I shall look to you to instruct me on all the finer points of highway robbery. The quick getaway, for one. You've said often enough that you know the roads from here to London like the back of your hand."

Jack grudgingly conceded that he might have made such a statement once or twice.

Her head felt as though rocks were pounding it, but she summoned a smile. "Naturally, I shall also want your advice on how to go about fencing the stolen items. Do you think that it shall be possible to enlist the help of some of your former colleagues?"

His craggy features drooped. "You're bound and determined, b'aint ye?"

"Quite. You'll help me?"

Jack gave her a look as if to say, *Was there ever any doubt?*

Gazing into his loyal face, guilt surged. She really had no right to ask him to take such a risk on her behalf. People in Sussex had long memories. If they were caught, she would lose her property. Jack would lose his life.

The image of his big body dangling from a gibbet bolted through her mind. She rose and rushed to his side. "Oh Jack, I'll be careful. We won't get caught. I swear it." She threw her arms about his neck and hugged him hard.

"I wish I could promise the same."

She lifted her head from his shoulder. "Jack?"

He gently disengaged her clinging hands. "I don't know how much good I'll be to ye, lass. There's a world o' difference between a young buck and a codger o' sixty odd."

Doubts churned inside her. At a loss to resolve them, she touched his sleeve. "Nonsense. There will be no physical labor involved. I'll only need you to show me the ropes . . ." she hesitated, thought better of it, and added " . . . and perhaps to hold the pistol steady while I gather the booty, at least until I get the hang of it."

She gulped. *Ropes. Hang* of it. In light of what she and Jack were about to undertake, the misspoken words only fermented her fear.

Chapter Two

Anthony Grenville, *né* Antonius Ignatius de la Fontaine Grenville, seventh Viscount Montrose and scion of the house of Grenville, was bored. Thoroughly, utterly, inexorably bored, he admitted, concealing a yawn in the back of his glove.

Not that either of his two traveling companions would notice. Caught up in wedding fervor, Phoebe and her mother began planning the trousseau almost as soon as their slippered feet hit his carriage floor. Merely the bridegroom, he wasn't expected to listen, let alone to offer an opinion, a state of affairs that suited him admirably. Far better to simply push the window curtain aside and try to lose himself in the Sussex countryside rolling by.

Green. It was all so damned green. He leaned out and let the dampness brush his face. How he'd missed the hedgerows, the gentle sweep of the hills, the mists that rose every evening and stayed until well past dawn. He'd even missed the rain. Especially the rain. How long they'd seemed, those two years he'd sweltered beneath a scorching Spanish sun, fighting for God and king and country—someone else's country.

He turned back inside and stretched his long legs, taking special care with his stiff right one. It was sixteen months since his wounds had secured his passage home from the Iberian Peninsula. It had been a shock to learn of Uncle Ignatius's death. His heir, Anthony had become a rich man overnight, the envy of his friends and enemies alike, most of whom still lived on their expectations. Free of his own father and flush with Ignatius's money, he'd sampled nearly every sinful pleasure known to man—and no doubt invented a few novel ones. The irony was that nothing pleased. Nothing satisfied. And nothing, *nothing*, could chase away the demons that haunted his nights. Or fill the dark, numbing emptiness that marked his days.

Wretched excess might have been his undoing had he not parted from Claudette, the delectable French opera dancer who'd eased the tedium of his first few months of convalescence. Claudette wasn't the first mistress to whom Anthony had given her *congé*. The abundant tears, flying objects, and foul curses were all to be expected, especially when one's mistress was French. But when she'd snatched the letter opener and threatened to plunge it into her heart, Anthony had known he was dealing with genuine hysteria. He'd wrested the deadly object from her just in time. A diamond bracelet, the deed to a summer cottage in Brighton, and the promise of an introduction to a wealthy baron finally convinced her that life without him was still worth living. And convinced *him* that it was high time he settled down to do his duty.

Which meant marriage. He glanced across the carriage to the woman who, in one month, would be his bride. Golden-haired, alabaster-complexioned, and blue-eyed, Lady Phoebe Tremont was the living, breathing incarnation of everything revered about English womanhood throughout the ages. She'd been the crowning jewel of the London Season when he'd spotted her six months before on the opposite end of Lady Chizzilwick's ballroom, a chaste nymph draped in debutante white and flanked by admirers. Competition flavored the encounter with the verve of a quixotic quest, and Anthony had not hesitated to storm the castle walls. He'd hobbled across the packed floor to breach the human turret surrounding her. Ignoring the shocked gasps from the chaperones' corner, the full dance card dangling from Phoebe's wrist, and the furious faces of the gentlemen who had bespoken those dances, Anthony waltzed her onto the dance floor before anyone thought to stop him.

If only someone had. The tepid attraction he'd first felt ebbed the moment she accepted his marriage proposal. Now he acknowledged that it was the thrill of the chase, not the final prize, that held his interest during the months of obligatory courting.

But what was done was done. He closed his eyes and leaned back against the leather squab. If only he could close his ears to the two buzzing female voices—his future mother-in-law's especially.

"I've bespoken a lovely barège silk for the gown. And of course you shall have Brussels lace for the veil and train."

Phoebe examined the stitching of her gloves. "Oh, Mama, do you think? Libby swears Honiton is all the rage."

Lady Tremont's lips curved into a sneer. "Olivia Whitebridge is a tasteless cow, just like her mother. I wouldn't trust either one to dress a window, let alone a bride."

The corners of Anthony's mouth lifted. What would Lady Tremont say if she knew he was a habitual patron of Madame Valen's London dress shop? What he'd spent on Claudette's undergarments alone would keep a family of four for a year.

Her ladyship's pale brows lifted as though she were indeed privy to his sordid thoughts. "Lord Montrose, what *is* so amusing? You seem quite in a world of your own."

Anthony eyed his future mother-in-law with cold dislike. The moment the ring was on Phoebe's finger, he'd send the shrew packing. Until then . . .

He found his smile. "I was just thinking that Phoebe could come down the aisle wearing sack cloth and still be a beautiful bride."

Phoebe's bow-shaped lips curved into a shy smile that failed to stir him.

Lady Tremont sniffed. "Prettily spoken, milord, but we shall endeavor to do Phoebe—and yourself—greater credit than that."

"Indeed." He looked to Phoebe, her gaze once more fixed on her folded hands. If only she had something—*anything*—to say for herself.

But it was no use. Swallowing a sigh, he leaned back and pushed his hat forward over his closed eyes. Like the pastoral panorama outside his window, his future unfolded before him.

It was all very neat, very conventional, and very dull.

Anthony dozed. When he awoke, it was dark. Still slouched against the seat, he looked across to Phoebe and Lady Tremont. Heads pillowed on each other's shoulder, they appeared to be sleeping soundly.

He shut his eyes and willed himself to drift off. If only his fatigue, his omnipresent ennui, were the sort that slumber could sate. Still, sleep could be a beautiful escape. Sometimes.

Horses—two of them, he thought—thundered toward them. He bolted upright.

"Halt! Prepare to stand and deliver!"

The hoarse shout sent adrenaline coursing through his veins, galvanizing his every limb for action.

Seconds later, the coach shuddered to a standstill, pitching Phoebe and her mother forward. Anthony threw out an arm to keep them from falling onto the floor.

Lady Tremont shook him off. "Lord Montrose, whatever is going on? Why have we stopped?" She drew back the window curtain and squinted outside.

Anthony reached for his carriage pistol, feeling the familiar emotional detachment descend. Both blessing and curse, this ability to step outside one's body, yet function within it.

He unbuttoned his jacket and slipped his pistol into an inside pocket. "Ladies, I believe we are about to be robbed."

Two pairs of blue eyes widened at that declaration. Lady Tremont paled. Her eyelids fluttered, then closed. A moment later, she slumped against the seat. The ostrich feather atop her bonnet snapped in two. One end dangled over her nose and mouth.

"Oh, Mama!" Phoebe's frightened gaze flew to Anthony. "Milord—Anthony—what shall we do?"

He surveyed his future mother-in-law, her plume rising and falling with each breath. How peaceful she appeared, how . . . *silent*.

"Better not to wake her."

Phoebe's mouth trembled. "B-but—"

"Hush, Phoebe." He reached over and patted the top of her icy hand. "Follow my direction and all will be well."

The carriage door flung open. Seconds later, they were staring down the butt of a pistol.

A bald head and a set of massive, crooked shoulders filled the narrow doorway. A black patch covered the intruder's left eye. Phoebe cowered against the seat.

"Out ye go, if ye please. Me master, One-Eyed Jack, craves a word wi' ye," the aging cyclops informed them cheerfully, his index finger poised on the trigger of the cocked pistol.

Like the man, the weapon was an antiquated relic. Still, if fired at point-blank range, it could hardly miss. He would wait until they cleared the carriage, then make his move. His chances of overcoming the footpads would improve infinitely if Phoebe and her mother stayed behind.

"My fiancée has a delicate constitution." Anthony shot Phoebe a look, warning her to silence. "I will go with you, only permit her to remain here to look after her mother."

The hulk shook his head. "'Er too." He studied the unconscious Lady Tremont. "She can stay."

This fellow is more intelligent than he appears. Hovering between outrage and amusement, Anthony disembarked and helped a shaking Phoebe down the carriage steps.

Still, if this brute was only a lackey, Anthony was not looking forward to encountering his master. He was, however, encouraged by the footpad's stiff, arthritic gait as he nudged them over to a stand of trees. The moon slipped free of a bank of clouds, silhouetting a slight figure in a slouched hat holding Anthony's driver, Masters, at gunpoint. One-Eyed Jack? The second highwayman turned toward them, and Anthony saw that he also wore an eye patch.

Why, One-Eyed Jack was no more than a lad and not a very sturdy one at that. The boy's long legs were encased in snug breeches that might have been painted on. A dark swallow-tailed coat hugged a trim waist and slim hips. Under more congenial circumstances, Anthony might have found himself asking the young man for the name of his tailor.

One-Eye slipped the driver's weapon into his coat pocket.

Squaring his narrow shoulders, he sauntered toward them, his own pistol held awkwardly in his gloved hand. The studied confidence of his gait did not match the uncertainty reflected in the depths of his gaze.

Eyes wide, Phoebe turned to Anthony. "For pity's sake, don't let him ravish me."

One-Eyed Jack halted a few paces in front of them, and Phoebe swayed. Anthony grabbed her arm, hoping the boy would not mistake the quick movement as a threat.

"Courage, my dear. Now is not the time to succumb to a fit of the vapors," Anthony warned beneath his breath.

Lantern light showed the boy's cheeks to be as smooth as a newborn's. The fragile felon wasn't even old enough to shave. Anthony suppressed a chuckle, confident that Phoebe would survive the adventure with her well-guarded virginity intact.

"Good evening, milord, milady."

The boy tipped his hat in Phoebe's direction, and Anthony sighted a smattering of freckles sprinkling the bridge of a pert little nose. *A redhead*, he deduced, storing away that bit of information for later.

"I am One-Eyed Jack, first knight of these roads," the lad informed them in a low, husky voice.

"So I gathered," Anthony replied, amused by the display of adolescent braggadocio.

Beneath the shadowing brim of his hat, the boy's fair face flushed. He looked over Anthony's shoulder to the hulk, as if waiting to be cued. Anthony didn't turn, but he sensed that some signal passed between the two.

The aging Goliath unwedged the pistol from the small of Anthony's back and stepped in front of him, proffering a hat.

"Yer purse and be quick about it, guv."

"Certainly," Anthony answered pleasantly, wondering if the oddly matched pair might be father and son, with the elder initiating little Jack into the family business. He seemed inordinately protective of his protégé.

Careful to keep his pistol concealed inside his jacket, Anthony removed his purse. He dropped the small leather satchel into the hat. When the gunman grunted toward the gold pocket watch dangling from his waistcoat, Anthony obligingly parted with it as well.

One-Eyed Jack smiled at Phoebe. Two rows of even, white teeth flashed in the darkness. "Now your turn, milady."

"M-me? But I have no valuables."

Both footpads stared at the beaded reticule dangling from her wrist.

"Oh this?" Her voice trembled. "But this is just pin money."

"In that case, you should have no problem parting with it," the boy sneered.

Sniffling, Phoebe slipped the reticule off and tossed it into the crown of the hat.

The boy aimed a forefinger at her throat. "I'll have that necklace as well."

Phoebe touched the double rope of pearls, her lower lip quivering in a way that Anthony found highly annoying under the circumstances.

She turned pleading eyes on Anthony. "Great-grand-mama's pearls. I was to wear them at our wedding. All the Tremont brides do."

Anthony's gaze never left the boy's face. "I promise I shall retrieve them for you ere then, my dear. With any luck, you shall have them to wear to this lad's hanging."

He had the satisfaction of seeing the boy's pupil dilate, nearly filling the turquoise iris of his uncovered eye.

Anthony's satisfaction proved short-lived.

One-Eyed Jack stepped up to Anthony. He lowered the pistol barrel over Anthony's trouser front and cocked the hammer.

"Your lady's jewels in exchange for the family jewels. Seems a fair trade to me." He poked the pistol into Anthony's manhood.

Anthony swallowed hard. One-Eyed Jack was soft as new cheese, but he knew how to hit a fellow where it hurt. He'd underestimated the boy, a mistake he'd not make the next time they met.

"Phoebe, do as he says," Anthony ordered in a low, determined voice.

"But . . ."

"I'd suggest you get your lady bird in hand, milord." The

boy grinned. "Otherwise you'll be able to do her scant service in the future."

Anthony looked down at the weapon lodged between his legs and silently prayed that One-Eyed Jack didn't have an itchy trigger finger.

"For God's sake, Phoebe, I've had this a damned sight longer than you've had those blasted pearls," he snapped when she still hesitated.

Phoebe reached behind and unfastened the necklace's clasp. She dropped the pearls into One-Eyed Jack's open palm, tears striping her pale cheeks.

One-Eye removed the weapon and stuffed the pearls into his coat pocket. "If 'tis any consolation, milady, these baubles will be put to good use. And," he added with a wicked grin, "I have left your lord his to console you."

"To the carriage, the lot o' ye, and be quick about it." The elder highwayman gave Masters a shove toward the coach.

The driver's knees buckled.

"For the luv of . . ." The hulk turned to Anthony. "Don't just stand there. 'Elp 'im."

Anthony shrugged even as his brain calculated his odds of success. "Can't, I'm afraid. Bad back."

Cursing, the highwayman slung Masters's limp arm around his beefy neck and lugged him toward the coach.

Phoebe lost no time in responding to the directive. She picked up her skirts and fled.

One-Eyed Jack's gaze darted between Anthony and the coach.

"W-why are you still standing 'ere?" He gestured to the coach with his pistol. "Go . . . *now*."

Smiling, Anthony advanced a step. "But I've no wish to end this encounter . . . just yet."

Anthony lunged forward. Locking both arms around the boy's torso, he slammed him to the ground. He pinned One-Eye's slender wrists above his head and squeezed. The pistol slipped from the highwayman's grasp.

"Let go!"

Even for a stripling, the boy was delicate as a sparrow, not nearly sturdy enough for such rough pursuits. Easily securing the joined wrists with one hand, Anthony pocketed the pistol.

He smiled maliciously into the frightened face, just inches below his own. "Well, my fine lad, alone at last." He clamped his palm over the boy's mouth. "What, nothing to say?"

The taunt seemed to bring his captive to life. His fingers curled into fists, his arms straining to break Anthony's hold.

Laughing, Anthony remarked, "Well, One-Eyed Jack, for a fierce knight of the road, you certainly fight like a girl."

Like a girl.

Anthony stared down at his prisoner. With a critical eye he examined the small, flushed face beneath the hat. The features were as finely wrought as those of a Dresden china figurine, the uncovered eye lushly lashed and set beneath a delicately arched brow. Could it be that Jack was really a Jacqueline in disguise? The body beneath his felt soft in all the right places. He uncovered his captive's mouth in order to better examine the softly curving lips.

"Get off me this instant, y-you . . . you big bully!"

The high-pitched voice, nearly drowned by the din of shrieking horses, could belong to an adolescent boy . . . or to a woman.

Intrigued, Anthony replied, "All in good time, my little highwayman. But first, I think I'll have a closer look at you."

With his free hand, Anthony groped for the lantern. His fingers brushed the toe of a large boot instead.

"Set 'im free as ye value yer life."

Cursing, Anthony rolled off the boy and stood. Ignoring the pistol prodding him, he offered One-Eye a hand up.

"Bugger off." Staring at his hand as thought it were a snake, the boy scrambled to his feet and took off toward a chestnut mare tethered to a tree branch.

Anthony started to follow, but the hulk blocked him.

"I'd save me strength if I was you." He gave Anthony a hard shove toward the coach.

Anthony swung around. Raising the lantern, he saw that the traces hung empty. Only his lead horse had not shied away. It stood nearby, ears flattened and nostrils narrowed. *God only knows how long it will take to retrieve the others.*

Muttering obscenities, he studied the direction of hoofprints and crushed grass.

Young One-Eye, you shall rue this day. Anthony whirled in time to see the object of his wrath push a booted foot into the mare's stirrup and throw a shapely leg over. *You're getting away and there isn't a blasted thing I can do about it. At least not tonight.*

Phoebe poked her head out the coach window. "Oh Anthony, that horrid old man unhitched the team!"

"Yes, I can see that," he snapped, tramping toward her.

Mounted, the thieves galloped past him, kicking up clouds of dust. Anthony's eyes burned and grit lined the inside of his mouth. When his vision cleared, he found himself standing alone in the middle of the road.

Coughing, he brushed the soil from his shoulders. *We shall meet again, One-Eyed Jack—or Jacqueline. And when we do, you shall either dance to my tune or at the end of the hangman's rope.*

Despite the dirt clogging his throat, he smiled in contemplation of the reunion.

Following Jack's lead, Chelsea slapped Dulcinea's flanks and horse and rider plunged into the safety of the trees. After going two leagues with no sign of pursuit, they stopped at a small stream. Only then did she realize that she was shivering much like the leaves stirring in the late summer breeze.

So now I'm a thief. Lantern in hand, Chelsea stumbled toward the stream. She knelt at the bank and splashed water on her warm face, feeling as though the dark, angry sky might crash down on her at any moment.

Jack loped behind her. "You all right, lass?" The concern in his rough voice sliced through her stupor like a diamond cutting glass.

She managed a reassuring smile, although she was far from sure herself. Wiping her face on the back of her sleeve, she cobbled herself together and stood. *I may be a thief but at least I'm not a murderer.* The pistol she carried wasn't loaded; otherwise, she never would have had the nerve to brandish it so brazenly. Pulling back her shoulders, she admitted she'd rather enjoyed wielding it to wipe the cocksure smile off that arrogant popinjay's face.

And a handsome face it was. Laughing brown eyes; aristocratic features; a strong, slightly cleft chin; and full, sensuous lips made for smiling . . . and kissing. For a moment when he'd loomed over her, a lock of dark auburn hair brushing his brow, she'd half hoped he would unmask her. What might have happened? Might he have *kissed* her?

Prior to the squire's assault, she'd been kissed only once, on her eighteenth birthday. One of Robert's school chums, a year her junior, had followed her outside after dinner and coaxed a kiss from her behind the old oak tree. The boy no doubt had been nervous. His lips were dry as sawdust, his mouth respectfully closed as it brushed hers. Beyond a vague sense of disappointment, she hadn't felt much of anything.

But the mere thought of kissing that rogue sent a chill racing her spine. Imagining his mouth covering hers made her feel cold and hot—and strange. *It's only nerves getting the better of me.* She felt her way to the rock where she'd stowed her clothes. A clump of yew bushes provided a convenient dressing screen. Crouching behind them, she quickly changed into her wrinkled riding habit, then stuffed the disguise into the saddlebag. She pulled the pins from her hair, and the thick braid thudded against her back.

Anyone encountering them would see Miss Chelsea Bellamy, out for a late evening ride with her family's aging retainer. Odd behavior, to be sure, but by no means criminal.

Calmer now, she picked up the lamp and bundle and stepped into the open. Jack was sitting near the stream, resting against the smooth side of a large rock. Holding the light aloft, she saw that his good eye was closed.

Poor Jack. She had a tendency to forget that he was no longer the strapping playmate of her youth, who used to hoist both her and Robert onto his broad—and then straight—shoulders. Judging from his labored breathing and heightened color, their evening's adventure had taken its toll. She hoped they would not have to repeat the experience many more times before she amassed Robert's ransom.

She bent and gently touched his shoulder. "Jack, wake up."

Jack came awake with a chortle. His open eye widened—and so did his grin.

"What's so funny? Don't tell me that my nefarious deed has me sprouting horns already?"

He guffawed. "Not 'orns, exactly."

She frowned. Still edgy from her narrow escape, she was in no mood for games. "Really, Jack, pray share the jest."

Tapping a finger against his covered eye, he sputtered, "Ye might want to—"

"Oh, dear." Chelsea reached up and pulled off her patch. She stuffed it into her knapsack with the rest of her disguise.

Her shoulders—and her spirits—sagged. She'd blundered . . . again. The patch linked her to One-Eyed Jack. In the future, she must be more careful . . . for Jack's sake as well as her own.

They remounted and emerged onto the open road. Although Chelsea's pulse was racing, she held Dulcinea to a canter throughout the ride home.

Later that evening behind the locked library door, she and Jack took stock of the haul. Seated at the desk, Chelsea opened the reticule first, pouring its contents onto the desktop. Remembering the woman's solemn promise that the purse contained only pin money, Chelsea was shocked at the quantity of gold sovereigns that tumbled out.

Jack came up behind her chair as she counted out fifty pounds. Dumping the coins back into the reticule, she tried to imagine what it would be like to belong to a world in which fifty pounds was pin money.

Putting the purse aside, she held the necklace up to a branch of candles. The pearls were of the finest quality, the workmanship of the diamond clasp exquisite. Even so, she found herself wondering what kind of woman would value jewelry over her fiancé's life.

She gave Jack the necklace. "How much do you think it will bring?"

Jack studied the clasp between his thumb and forefinger, holding it close to the light. "Too easy to recognize," he concluded at length. "Whoever we fence it to will 'ave to sell the pearls separate. Still, it should fetch a pretty penny."

Chelsea was too weary to ask just how much a "pretty penny" might be. Yawning, she handed him the gold pocket watch.

"What about this?"

He carefully bit down on the case. "Solid gold." He wiped the timepiece on his sleeve. "Have to melt it down, o' course."

"Why?"

He pointed to the scrollwork "M" engraved on the back. A falcon intertwined with a serpent formed the delicately etched background.

" 'Tis the same marking as were on the side o' the coach. I'd wager me last farthing this belongs to Lord Montrose."

"Lord Montrose! *Viscount* Montrose." Her heart landed in her chest with a sickening thump. "Do you mean to say I just robbed a viscount?"

At Jack's solemn nod, a tremor shot through her. The estate Montrose had inherited from his uncle was only some twenty miles north, but Chelsea had never laid eyes on the viscount . . . until that night. The nobility kept to their own, rarely fraternizing with the local gentry at assemblies or church bazaars. And, like so many of his peers, Lord Montrose preferred London to the country.

But even absentee nobles wielded enormous power. No one would give much notice if the carriage of a local squire were waylaid, but robbing a peer of the realm at gunpoint was another matter.

Shivering, she swept the stolen articles into a drawer, locked it, and dropped the key into her pocket.

Jack laid a reassuring hand on her shoulder. "Lovey, ye've gone as pale as a ghost. Someone step on yer grave?"

Chelsea met Jack's concerned gaze with a tepid smile. "No, but I have a sinking feeling that Lord Montrose may help me to put one foot in it."

Chapter Three

O ver the next five days, Chelsea and Jack robbed four more carriages. Although she hated to admit it, the risk they were taking far outweighed the gain. When they stopped a widow whose only valuable was a gold locket with her husband's miniature enclosed, Chelsea hadn't the heart to take it from her. But when on the fifth night she sighted a rickety traveling coach conveying the vicar's wife, Abigail Pettigrew, and her two obnoxious daughters, Chelsea had delighted in relieving them of their purses. They would have recognized Jack instantly from their visits to Oatlands, so Chelsea had bidden him stay hidden while she approached. The booty had amounted to less than twenty-five pounds, but striking unholy terror into Mrs. Pettigrew and her odious offspring had been priceless.

The following morning, Chelsea arrived at the vicarage. An hour late, she swept into the small dining room where the quilting circle Mrs. Pettigrew presided over was underway.

Bowed heads looked up from flashing needles.

"Forgive my tardiness, ladies." Untying her bonnet strings, Chelsea glanced guiltily at the pile of colorful fabric squares in the center of the table. "I'm afraid I overslept."

Chelsea didn't need to inspect the dark crescents beneath her eyes to confirm that her late night escapades were taking their toll. Highway robbery was proving to be a good deal of hard work.

"Pray have a seat and catch your breath, Chelsea." A big-boned woman with florid features and a pudding-bag figure, Abigail Pettigrew frowned when Chelsea removed her bonnet. "I do believe your hair gets redder every time I see you."

Chelsea felt her face reddening to match, but she looked Mrs. Pettigrew square in the eye. "I believe 'tis always been this bright, ma'am."

I don't fit in anywhere. Not even now that I'm a grown woman. Especially not now. Smothering a sigh, she smoothed a hand over the wild disarray of copper curls tumbling about her shoulders. Eyeing the other women's tightly controlled coifs—all sensible shades of brown and black and ash blond—she wished she'd taken the time to put up her hair.

No point in crying over spilt milk, as Jack would say. She set down her sewing bag and slipped into the only unoccupied chair, which unfortunately was directly across from Mrs. Pettigrew. Swallowing a yawn, she took up a half-finished square and threaded her needle. Today's was another mindless but worthy project—a quilt to be auctioned at the upcoming church bazaar. She despised sewing but, as the daughter of one of the neighborhood's leading families, she wasn't in a position to refuse.

Mrs. Pettigrew turned to her eldest daughter. "Rosamund, dearest, please pour Miss Bellamy a cup of tea."

"Yes, Mama."

Rosamund, plump and awkward at sixteen, pushed away from the table and shuffled over to the sideboard where Chelsea's mother's tea service gleamed on its silver tray. Chelsea winced as the girl clanked the heavy teapot against a delicate porcelain cup. Not bothering to ask if Chelsea preferred lemon or cream, she handed her the cup, swimming in a saucer of spillage.

"Thank you, Rosamund."

Rosamund grunted an acknowledgment and slouched into the chair next to her younger sister, Josephine, who was busy transforming a ball of thread into a series of Gordian knots. Two years Rosamund's junior, Josephine was a prettier, slimmer version of her sibling. To the despair of those around them, both girls had inherited Mrs. Pettigrew's surly disposition.

Glimpsing Rosamund's smirk, Chelsea took a small, experimental sip of the bitter, unsugared tea and set her cup aside. Mrs. Pettigrew made no secret of her plan to give Rosamund a London Season, but Chelsea privately considered the effort a waste.

The magistrate's wife, Mabel Minnington, a small, nervous woman with a fringe of mouse brown curls, turned to Chelsea. "I suppose by now you've heard about poor Abigail's ordeal at the hands of that dreadful highwayman." She shuddered. "With outlaws roaming the countryside, 'tis a mercy we all haven't been murdered in our beds."

Chelsea lifted her eyes from her sewing, careful to inject a note of surprise into her tone. "No, I hadn't heard. What happened, Mrs. Pettigrew?"

"The girls and I were on our way back from visiting our Colbrand relations in Bath. Although Brighton is really more the thing and so much closer, Cousin Minerva is a stickler for spending the Season in Bath. She takes the waters for her gout, you know."

In the five-and-twenty years since Mrs. Pettigrew's arrival in Upper Uckfield as a bride, she had never permitted anyone, including her long-suffering husband, to forget her connection to the Colbrands. But that illustrious family had many boughs on its tree, and Mrs. Pettigrew was a sprig from only a cadet branch—a point never raised. Through Rosamund, Mrs. Pettigrew resolved to regain the social status she imagined she had lost. When she'd discovered that her Colbrand cousins, including several eligible young bachelors, were to be in Bath for the Season, she had hustled her daughters there with unseemly haste.

"Of course, Bath isn't what it was when I was a girl," Mrs. Pettigrew sighed. "But how could I refuse with dear Minnie absolutely insisting we stay with her?"

Behind her spectacles, Faith Pinkerton, the village schoolmistress, rolled her eyes. "The robbery, Abby. Tell Chelsea how the rogue forced your driver off the road."

"Oh, yes of course." The vicar's wife's plump hand flattened over her heart. "It was dreadful, simply dreadful. When that brute tore open our carriage door, I thought the end had come for the girls and me." She leaned forward and added in a confidential tone, "And with Rosamund blossoming into womanhood, I am sure you can all understand a mother's fears."

Around the table, heads bobbed.

"He didn't . . ." Mabel Minnington coughed discreetly ". . . that is to say, he didn't make any improper advances, I hope."

Mrs. Pettigrew glanced to Rosamund, who had wrested the ball of thread away from her sister and was refusing to give it back.

Apparently satisfied that her offspring were oblivious to the dark undertones of the conversation, she continued, "No, but he had his lecherous eye on her the whole time. I must confess, ladies, the way he looked at my innocent child sent chills up and down my spine." Mrs. Pettigrew's gelatinous bosom shivered in recall. "'Tis a mercy she wasn't ravished."

"The brute!"

"Praise be!"

Chelsea bent her head to hide a smile.

Josephine lifted wicked eyes and announced, "Rosie has developed a tendre for One-Eyed Jack. In fact, she thinks she may be in love."

A deep berry blush stained Rosamund's plump cheeks. Dropping the thread, she reached out and swatted at her sister. "Be quiet, you stupid chit. You know I said no such thing."

Giggling, Josephine dodged the blow. "You certainly did. Why just last night, you said you thought One-Eyed Jack was the handsomest—"

"Hush, both of you." Mrs. Pettigrew pressed a palm to her temple. "You are giving me the headache."

"Sorry, Mama," Josephine apologized, sticking her tongue out at her sister as soon as her mother's gaze shifted.

Chelsea's eyes watered and her sides ached with the effort

to hold in her laughter. So, the oafish Rosamund fancied One-Eyed Jack. If only the ridiculous child knew that the object of her adolescent affections was seated at her mother's dining room table.

Giving way to an evil impulse, Chelsea summoned her most innocent voice. "Is One-Eyed Jack a large man, Mrs. Pettigrew?"

"Gargantuan." Mrs. Pettigrew used her hands to sketch in midair a silhouette that could have belonged to the real Jack. Her broad shoulders quivered. "And if you could have seen his evil face . . . the one eye covered with a patch, the other black as pitch. Why, the very memory gives me the shivers."

If the magistrate relies on Mrs. Pettigrew, I'll never be caught, Chelsea chuckled to herself.

Faith Pinkerton bit off a piece of thread from her finished square. "The sooner that wicked felon is apprehended and brought to justice, the better it will be for all of us."

Mabel Minnington surveyed the group and confided, "I have it on good authority that justice will not be long in coming."

Around the table, six needles, including Chelsea's, stalled. All eyes were riveted on the magistrate's wife, all ears pricked for her next word.

"How so?" demanded Mrs. Pettigrew, face flushed.

Clearly relishing her new importance and wishing to prolong the moment, Mabel hedged, "Well, I really shouldn't say more. You see, I promised John—"

"What fustian," Mrs. Pettigrew interrupted. "Mabel Minnington, you know perfectly well you can trust us not to breathe a word to a living soul outside this room."

Faith Pinkerton urged, "Yes, Mabel dear, do tell."

"You can trust us, Mrs. Minnington," said Rosamund.

Heart pounding, Chelsea added her voice to the chorus. "Pray, do tell, Mrs. Minnington."

"If you all give your word that anything I say shall be kept in the strictest of confidence."

Heads nodded in solemn assent.

"Very well then." Mabel Minnington put down her

sewing. "My husband has devised a plan to trap One-Eyed Jack and put a stop to this highway robbery business once and for all."

"What kind of plan?" Mrs. Pettigrew demanded.

The magistrate's wife hesitated a moment more, then blurted out, "As of tonight, one of the local lads will dress up as a woman and parade himself on the road to London in Squire Dumfreys's coach. To anyone watching the roads, it will appear as though a wealthy woman were traveling alone, with only her driver. The bait will be irresistible. John is confident that sooner or later One-Eyed Jack will make his move. What the rogue won't know is that some of the best marksmen in the county will be hidden in the hedgerows along the roadside, not to mention my own John crouched on the carriage floor, armed. When the blackguard gives his call to 'Stand and Deliver,' the men will come out of hiding and *bang*. *Adieu* One-Eyed Jack."

A hush fell. Even Josephine and Rosamund stopped kicking each other under the table to absorb Mrs. Minnington's revelation.

Chelsea, who had kept her eyes fastened on the square she was furiously stitching, gasped.

"Oh, Mama!" Rosamund shrieked, pointing to Chelsea. "Look, she's *bleeding* all over the tablecloth."

"Why Chelsea, you've pricked yourself." Tone vexed, Mrs. Pettigrew rose to inspect the damage to her best Irish linen. "Do try to exercise more care."

"'Tis nothing, really," Chelsea replied quickly, sucking the tip of the offending finger.

"Nonsense. We shall tend to that immediately. Rosamund, Josephine, one of you run and fetch a bandage and some salve." She frowned down at the small scarlet stain. "And send the housekeeper in with a cloth and some water."

It took every ounce of Chelsea's self-discipline to remain at the vicarage for the rest of the afternoon. Every time she felt on the verge of catapulting out of her seat, she reminded herself that to leave abruptly would only arouse suspicion. So, she forced herself to sit still, sewing and making obligatory conversation, until the hall clock chimed the four blissful notes that signalled her release.

What a relief it was to unhitch the pony cart at last. Anxiety soon replaced relief when she reached home and began to take stock of her ill-gotten gains.

She closed the study door, then went to the desk. Unlocking the drawer, she removed the pouch and spilled the contents onto the desk. The brief inventory confirmed what she had known already—she hadn't anywhere near five hundred pounds. Aside from the money, the only articles of value were the pearl necklace and the pocket watch she'd taken from Montrose and his lady. En route to London, the viscount had lost no time in raising the hue and cry. The word that a dangerous highwayman was afoot had spread like fire. Thanks to Lord Montrose's swiftness in alerting the authorities, most travelers passing through Upper Uckfield now took the precaution of leaving their valuables behind.

Thanks to Lord Montrose.

Having played football with the neighborhood lads every Shrovetide until she turned sixteen, Chelsea was no stranger to being knocked down and pinned beneath a strong male body. Even so, lying beneath Lord Montrose she'd been bombarded by new and confusing sensations. Nearly a week later, she could still summon the surge of excitement she'd felt at being crushed beneath his broad chest, his large hands wrapped around her, his long, muscular legs tangling with hers. The mere memory filled her veins with liquid fire.

Was this . . . passion?

Passion. Romeo and Juliet, Troilus and Cressida, Lancelot and Guinevere . . . Grand passions were invariably mutual—and invariably doomed. Focusing on the mutuality aspect, she asked herself if it were possible that Montrose felt even a flicker of the flame that still seared her? For a fleeting moment when their gazes collided, Chelsea sensed that his lordship's hold on her was motivated by more than the desire to retrieve his valuables.

Foolish, stupid girl. You were disguised as a boy.

Recalling Montrose's exquisite blonde traveling companion, Chelsea doubted that he would have looked on her more favorably even if she'd been dressed as a woman. Banishing that depressing thought, she allowed herself the luxury of slipping into pure fantasy. Embellishing on what might have happened if he'd succeeded in unmasking her made for a pleasant diversion from the torturous thought of Robert in the hands of a ruthless kidnapper.

A knock on the door jarred her out of the reverie. She dropped the bag into the drawer, locked it, then gave the call to enter.

It was Jack, announcing dinner.

When she made no move to rise, he prodded, "I know that look, child. Somethin's amiss. Out wi' it."

Chelsea flagged him to a chair. "You should sit first."

Jack seated, Chelsea lost no time in telling him what she had learned at the vicarage.

He shook his head dolefully. "I knew it. I just knew it. 'Twas only a matter o' time."

Chelsea drummed impatient fingers on the desk. "Knowing the particulars, I'm certain we could elude their stupid trap. Even so, now that the word is out, it's unlikely that we shall be able to filch anything that even comes close to the value of that pearl necklace. Even if we did, where would we find a purchaser of purloined valuables in this backwater?" *But, in London . . .*

Jack discharged a heavy sigh. "Thank the good Lord, ye've finally come to yer senses."

"Indeed," Chelsea murmured even as a new plan began taking shape in her mind.

Whitehall—and the War Office—were in London as well. She'd not yet received a reply to the letter of inquiry she'd posted five days before. But, if she were to arrive in person, she'd not be so easy to dismiss.

And, secreted in a dark hollow of her mind, a far less noble motive rattled. Lord Montrose was in London. The possibility of bearding the lion in his own den held an undeniable appeal, not to mention that the man was rich as Croesus. His abode must be chock-full of riches. Why, in one night alone, she could probably nick five hundred pounds' worth—and then some.

"Wool-gathering, Miss Chelsea?"

"Hem?" She looked up to find Jack's one-eyed gaze boring through her. "Oh, I was just thinking that a change in plans might be in order."

A worried frown stitched his brow. "What kind o' change?"

Painting a mental portrait of Montrose's face when he stepped inside his spacious—and empty—London residence, she found herself smiling. "While I had hoped to stay long enough to supervise the planting, I see now that we must away from here post haste. Move our base of operations to somewhere where one more thief—or even two—won't raise an eyebrow."

Jack's weary gaze followed her as she rounded the desk. "And where might that be?" he asked, although she felt certain he'd surmised her answer.

Just the same, she wasn't eager to witness his stricken face. She dashed toward the dining room. "Why, London, of course."

London. Anthony lifted the curtain and stared out the carriage window to the Thames. Black, sluggish, and swathed in gray mist, the river might have been a metaphor for his soul.

He'd hoped that being back in London would rouse his spirits but, like the country, the city failed to move him. Doctor Samuel Johnson had said that a man who was tired of London was tired of life. Well, perhaps Johnson had a point. Anthony thought back to his first visit as a boy of twelve. The *tonnish* men and women with their rouged cheeks, ornamental patches, and powdered hair; the monumental buildings and expansive pleasure gardens; the equestrian acrobats at Astley's Amphitheater—all had seemed part of a dazzling fairyland. He sank back against the leather seat. What he wouldn't give to feel a modicum of that magic now.

Feelings, magical or otherwise, eluded him these days. He felt passionate about nothing and no one, least of all Phoebe. He'd just escorted her home from Drury Lane where a young actor named Edmund Kean had delivered a brilliant performance as Shakespeare's Romeo. Attendance of the premier was by invitation only; His Royal Highness, the Prince Regent, had headed the distinguished guest list. But neither the tragedy unfolding on stage nor the steady stream of glittering personages filing in and out of the royal box had held Anthony's attention. Craving solitude, he'd begged off the post-play reception in the theater's Green Room, much to Phoebe's chagrin.

Alone at last, his thoughts returned to the robbery the week before. He'd felt something then. Anger, of course, but also curiosity and the vague stirring of lust.

One-Eye, you'd better be a woman.

According to the local authorities, there had been no reports of a one-eyed highwayman—male or female—in nearly thirty years. The trail, such as it was, had gone cold.

Jack or Jacqueline, where are you? Once more he stared into the night, half-expecting the spritelike footpad to materialize at the foot of Westminster Bridge. Instead, in the hazy light of the street lamp, he saw two silhouettes—one tall and gangly, the other squat and broad—dragging a blond-haired man down the stone steps to the towpath. Not caring for the odds, Anthony tapped his cane on the roof, and Masters halted a yard or so from the bridge.

The smacking sound of flesh meeting flesh pierced the quiet. A desperate voice choked out, "*Please*, I haven't got it."

Pistol in hand, Anthony opened the door and leapt out, landing on his good leg.

"Milord?"

"Quiet." He motioned Masters back to the box and crept forward.

Hand braced on the iron rail, Anthony peered down. Moonlight glinted on metal.

"You might as well 'and it o'er." The lanky footpad waved the knife in front of the young man's frightened face. "We'll get it soon enough when your brain's turned to mash."

The handsome visage crumpled. "I'll get it. I swear I

will." He swiped at his swollen mouth. "Only I need more time."

"Time's run out, ducks." The thug turned to his bull-necked accomplice. "Go to, Luke. Just see you save me enough o' 'im to gut."

"Aye, enough to gut." The second man raised his bat.

With nowhere to run, the victim sank to his knees, arms raised to shield his head.

Anthony aimed his pistol skyward and fired. The two attackers froze.

The bat lowered. "Gorm! What was that?"

"A gunshot, you idiot," snarled the man with the knife. "Let's get out o' 'ere." He rushed the stairs.

Anthony ducked behind a post just as he gained the bridge.

"But I b'aint finished." The remaining ruffian turned back to the huddled figure and hefted the club.

Christ, it would have to be the large one who stayed behind. With no time to reload, Anthony tossed the pistol and ran down the stairs, heels skittering on the slimy stone. Reaching the path, he launched himself forward.

The bully gasped. Turning, he swung blindly at Anthony's head. Anthony darted to the side. The weapon swished past his left ear. Unbalanced, the big man careened forward. The bat thudded to the ground. Seizing his chance, Anthony smashed his knuckles into the flaccid belly. He took a bruising punch on his upper arm before landing a blow to his opponent's jaw. Blood and saliva sloshed from the footpad's slack mouth. He toppled backwards into the black water, raising a fountain. Anthony waited. A low gurgling sound and the sluggish movement of heavy arms confirmed that he was progressing toward the opposite bank.

Anthony hauled the young dandy to his feet.

"Christ, Reggie, can't you be trusted to steer clear of trouble for a fortnight?"

The Honorable Reginald Tremont, known as Reggie to his family, friends, and creditors, grinned through his bruises.

"G-guess I should have g-gone with you to Sussex after

all. Would have s-saved a perfectly good pair of t-trousers."
He cast a mournful glance downward to the muddied knees
of his silk striped pantaloons.

"Not to mention saving me from nearly having my head
bashed in."

Stale alcohol oozed from Reggie's pores much like the
blood oozing from his split lip. Bending, Anthony hooked
his future brother-in-law's arm over his neck and helped him
to the carriage.

Masters, face white, opened the door to the compartment.
"Milord, are you all right? And the young master . . . ?"

"We're both fine, Masters. Just lend me a hand, will you?
Tremont is drunk as David's sow."

"I'm not s-so very d-drunk." Reggie allowed himself to be
helped inside.

Anthony settled into the opposite seat and passed Reggie
his handkerchief. "In that case, I'll see you home."

"Home!" Reggie paused in wiping away the blood, alarm
cutting through his stupor. "If Mama were to see me like
this, she'd . . . Well, I'd rather not think about what she'd
do. Please, Anthony."

Deciding that young Reggie had suffered enough for one
night, Anthony relented.

Stripping off his torn glove, Anthony sucked his bloodied
knuckles. "Very well. I'll take you to White's, but only if
you promise to behave. One bout of fisticuffs an evening is
all I can manage."

"Your club?" Reggie brightened. "Capital plan!"

"On the way, you can explain what the devil that was
about, and spare me your lies. Those two were professional
bullies, and I gather they were hired by someone to whom
you owe money."

Reggie's sheepish expression made him look even
younger than his two-and-twenty years. The previous London Season had been his first, and he had delved into the
epicurean indulgences of wine, women—and gaming—with
the unbridled zest of a sheltered young man tasting freedom
for the first time.

"The proprietor of that new gaming hall in Jermyn Street," Reggie admitted after an awkward pause.

"I suspected as much." *How he reminds me of myself at his age.* It was a herculean effort, but Anthony managed to compose his features into a stern mask. "Confess. How much are you in for?"

This time Reggie had the grace to hang his head. "Two hundred pounds, give or take a few quid."

"Two hundred, hem. And I suppose you expect me to make you a loan?"

"Just until the next installment of my allowance." Reggie looked up, blue-gray eyes beseeching. "I swear, I've learned my lesson. No more gaming. This time—definitely the last."

Since assuming the role of reprobate guardian angel to Phoebe's rakehell older brother, Anthony had learned that Reggie's promises were well-intentioned but short-lived. Even so, saving the young rascal from himself provided Anthony with a welcome distraction from his own dark thoughts.

Looking into his young friend's earnest face, Anthony could no longer stifle his chuckle. "It had better be. Given my father's robust health, it looks as though I'll have to make do with one fortune for quite some time."

Chapter Four

"Now that the Season's over, London's no bloody fun," Reggie lamented an hour later. Ensconced in White's coveted bow window alcove, sprawled in a leather wing chair, he surveyed the sparsely populated club room. "Ever since Parliament adjourned, everyone's gone north for grouse season." Expression morose, he lifted his coffee cup. "And with you rusticating in the country to play the dutiful son-in-law, there's been no one to go about with."

Anthony sipped his port. "I believe your parents are decamping to Scotland after the wedding. Perhaps you should join them?"

Reggie scowled. "I'd sooner rot in hell than spend four bloody months listening to Papa complain about his gout."

Anthony reached for the bottle and refilled his glass. "There are worse fates."

Worse fates indeed.

He swished the liquid about the rim of the glass. Peter and Stephen had been like Reggie once—young and handsome and greedy for all that life offered. But then so had he. The trio had been inseparable ever since Eton, more like brothers than schoolmates. When Anthony, in defiance of his father's threats of disinheritance, had announced that he was joining up, his friends had purchased commissions in the same regiment. Sailing for Lisbon, salt spray stinging their freshly sunburnt faces, they'd hardly been able to wait for the glorious adventure to begin.

If only I'd known. He drained his glass. Alcohol blazed through his throat. How he wished the spirit might score his brain as well, burn away the painful memories. The guilt.

Reggie eyed the port bottle. "How was the journey from Sussex? With Mama along, I'll warrant it was bloody dull."

Grateful to return to the present, Anthony smiled. "Not as dull as you might expect."

Reggie pressed, and Anthony recounted the robbery. When he came to the part about the pistol lowered over his manhood, Reggie howled.

"So, if it weren't for my sister handing over her pearls, you'd be a bloody eunuch right now." Reggie's eyes glinted. "I'd say that you, not to mention half the whores in London, owe Phoebe a debt of gratitude."

Reminded of Phoebe's grudging compliance, Anthony scowled. "She took her sweet time about it."

"Perhaps she thought you might make a more devoted husband *sans* manhood," Reggie suggested gamely.

Anthony flagged a footman circulating with a box of cigars. "You may have a point."

Given Phoebe's passionless nature, she probably would be perfectly content if they never consummated their marriage. But she'd not get off that easily. Later, after she'd given him a son or two, he'd gladly slake his desires elsewhere.

Reggie leaned back and yawned. "Tell me more about this One-Eyed Jack fellow. Great big lug like the one tonight, I collect?"

"Hardly." Anthony dreaded having to admit that he'd been bested by a slip of a boy. *Or, worse still, by a girl.*

The footman standing tableside afforded him a reprieve. Anthony took his time in selecting his smoke, hoping that Reggie would forget his question.

No such luck.

"So what was he like?"

Anthony trimmed the end of his cigar. "Who?"

"Dammit, Anthony, you know very well who I mean. The highwayman."

"Yes, of course." Anthony leaned forward and touched the

tip of the cigar to the candle flame. "The fellow was not your typical footpad."

Reggie's pale brows drifted upward. "Meaning?"

Anthony sat back and inhaled. How could he articulate what he felt in his gut? "He was younger than one would expect . . . and delicate. I vow he scarcely weighed eight stone. When I pinned him, I was half afraid I might break him."

"When you pinned him?" Reggie fixed Anthony with a lopsided grin. "You've not gone to buggering boys, I hope."

Reggie's teasing hit too close to the truth. When Anthony had looked into the highwayman's turquoise eye, he'd definitely felt . . . *something*.

He glared at his friend over the burning embers of his cigar. "If you were anyone else, I'd call you out for even suggesting it. The truth is, I'm not at all convinced that One-Eyed Jack was male."

Reggie's brow beetled. "What makes you think that?"

"His mannerisms seemed studied. His walk, even his voice, belonged more to a woman pretending to be male."

"Are you quite certain?"

Exhaling, Anthony contemplated the curling smoke. "Not precisely and yet the more I think on it, the more convinced I become."

Reggie chewed on his cigar. "Tits?"

Trust Reggie to cut to the core of the matter. "Not that I noticed. But then, with the jacket and waistcoat, it would be hard to tell, particularly if the lady were not well endowed. Even if she were, I suppose she could have been wearing some sort of binding."

"You must have it wrong." Reggie shook his head. "Everybody knows that females don't go around robbing carriages. 'Twould be against . . . well, against nature." His tone held the absolute certainty of the very young.

Anthony smiled to himself. There had been a time when he, too, had faced the future with absolute certainty.

Reggie emptied the rest of the bottle of port into his coffee cup. He stamped out his half-smoked cigar, confirming Anthony's suspicion that he didn't really care for tobacco.

The port, however, he quaffed. "Let's be on our way.

There's a new house on Brydges Street that specializes in blondes. A good roll in the hay's just the thing to celebrate our salvation."

"Afraid you're on your own tonight." Anthony rose and collected his cane. "I'm for bed, preferably one that's unoccupied and has clean sheets."

Reggie grasped the table edge and rose. "I suppose you've decided to reform now that you're about to be leg-shackled?"

Cigar clenched in the corner of his mouth, Anthony clapped an arm around Reggie's shoulders and steered him toward the entrance hall. "Moderate perhaps, but reform, *never*."

Anthony's carriage was parked beneath the swirling light of one of the West End's new gas lamps. Watching Reggie climb awkwardly inside, Anthony surmised his young friend would not be in any condition to do the whores of Covent Garden much good that night. It was more than likely that poor Reg would end up paying the proprietress for the privilege of passing out on some strumpet's soiled bedsheets. To each his own.

Reggie thrust his tousled head out the carriage window. "Sure you won't change your mind? Whoring isn't half as much fun when you've no one to go with."

Anthony closed the carriage door, reminding himself that he couldn't be Phoebe's brother's keeper every night. "Quite."

Reaching down, he massaged the cramped muscle above his right knee. The trouncing on the towpath had done his bad leg little good. Without exercise, it would be stiff as a board by morning, reducing him to a cripple.

He lifted his gaze to Masters, seated on the box. "I'm afraid you're in for a long night."

"Don't fret about me, milord." Grinning, the driver lifted his cloak to reveal a pewter flask tucked into his pocket. "I've Mother Geneva to keep me company while I wait for the young master. Shall I take you home first?"

Anthony shook his head. "Walking's just the thing for the leg. Only see that you bring him back in one piece."

"I'll do my best, milord."

The townhouse Anthony had inherited from Ignatius was in Berkeley Square, one of London's most fashionable addresses. The walk took Anthony a good half hour, time enough to examine his motives for declining a foray into the Covent Garden fleshpots. The simple truth was that the painted smiles of whores and the quick physical relief they afforded no longer held any allure for him. The fog inside Anthony's soul had lifted only once since his return, and that had been during the robbery. Perhaps he should arrange to have himself fleeced every so often, just to break the monotony?

"You're a sorry son-of-a-bitch, Montrose." He tossed a self-mocking laugh into the inky darkness and ground his cigar stub beneath his heel.

By the time he ascended the marble steps to his townhouse's Palladian facade, his knee was throbbing like the devil. Even so, with half of a bottle of port warming his belly, he should have slept like the dead. But instead of the battle-maimed specters that usually greeted him as soon as he put his head on the pillow, One-Eyed Jack's delicate visage floated before his eyes. No man could possibly have eyelashes so like paintbrushes, such sensuously curved lips, nor such shapely legs. At least he hoped not.

It was nearing one o'clock in the morning when, tired of thrashing, Anthony gave up on sleep. He fumbled in the dark for the tinder box, struck flint against steel, and lit a taper. Remembering the supply of French cognac he'd laid in, he shrugged into a velvet dressing gown and headed downstairs. Tonight was as good a time as any to find out whether or not the smuggler had exaggerated its quality.

Inside the library, he lit the brace of Argand lamps flanking the mantel. The flames flickered in the balmy breeze stirring the window draperies. He put down the taper to rummage through desk drawers for the key to the liquor cabinet. *Ah, success at last.* He bent and fitted the key into the lock. Out of the corner of his eye, he glimpsed something shift in the shadows. *My insomnia is beginning to get the better of me.* He straightened, rubbing his eyes. Hairs pricked the back of his neck. *Get hold of yourself, man.*

Slowly, very slowly, Anthony turned. In the hazy light, he could just make out the sofa, a table, and several chairs. The sofa, he observed, appeared to have grown a fifth leg—a small, booted foot.

Anthony crossed the room in slow, measured steps. He braced a hand on the sofa's serpentine back and leaned over.

Two very wide, very frightened, and very familiar eyes peered up at him.

With a startled exclamation, the housebreaker catapulted to his feet, the crown of his head clipping Anthony's chin. The man's slouched hat fell to the carpet.

Red hair flying, the thief rounded the sofa and dashed across the room to the window, a large leather bag slung over one slender shoulder. Cupping his throbbing jaw, Anthony dove forward, catching the intruder by the shirt collar.

"I've got you now, One-Eye!"

One-Eyed Jack pivoted in Anthony's arms. Anthony felt two soft mounds press against his chest just before a metal-sheathed fist slammed into his solar plexus. He doubled over, bile rising in his throat. Clutching his stomach, he looked up to see his attacker reaching for the rope strung outside the casement.

Oh no, you don't!

Anthony cinched an arm around the girl's slim waist and hauled her inside, her shapely—and unmistakably female—buttocks molded to his groin. Sidestepping the open satchel spilling his housewares onto the carpet, he dragged her over to the lamplight.

"Have done!" Hands on her shoulders, he gave her a jarring shake.

She swung at him again but this time he was prepared. He grabbed her wrist.

"Yield, or I swear I'll break it."

"Never!"

"So be it."

Anthony torqued the trapped arm, knowing he was providing the maximum amount of pain while falling short of doing real injury. He knew from experience that the white-hot streak shooting from shoulder to elbow would persuade her to surrender more effectively than any words he could utter.

Predictably, she went stock still, the color ebbing from her small, heart-shaped face.

He glanced at the brass knuckles covering the top of her right hand. "If I release you, will you promise not to fight me?"

Jaw set, she nodded.

He let go, and she slumped against the mantel, breathing ragged. She didn't resist when he slipped the metal sheath over her gloved fingers and deposited the weapon in his pocket.

Hands braced against the mantelpiece, Anthony inspected the tall young woman pinned between his arms. Relief surged through him. She'd foregone a jacket, leaving no doubt that One-Eyed Jack was all woman. The outline of her breasts—small but shapely—was visible through her white cambric shirt. As he had surmised, the eye patch had been nothing more than a prop. Her left eye, no longer hidden, burned the same brilliant blue-green as its mate. He had been right about the hair color, too. The thick braid slung over her shoulder glowed like the flames of a roaring fire. Wisps of hair formed a radiant halo around her flushed face. The effect robbed him of his breath almost as effectively as her earlier blow had.

Regaining his composure, he said, "Highway robbery not proving profitable enough? Come to London to try your hand at housebreaking, I see."

"Why I am here is none of your affair." She glared at him, eyes blazing blue sparks of pure defiance.

"Forgive me," he replied. "I was under the impression that this was my house."

"Well, er . . . you have no right to keep me here against my will."

"Do I not?" Amused, he shoved away from the mantel. "Unless I am mistaken, I believe this belongs to me." He plucked a silver candlestick from the carpet. "In fact, I feel certain I saw it at dinner."

"I take no more than I need and only from those who can afford it." She trailed behind him. "And, although you may not believe me, my cause is just although my actions may seem—"

"Blatantly criminal?" He set the candlestick aside.

Hands on her hips, she asked, "Tell me, my lord, if you hadn't walked in just now, would you have missed those few pieces of plate or those candlesticks?"

"Whether or not I would miss them is beside the point. You'd not be the first thief who, when caught, justified his— or her—actions as stealing from the rich to give to the poor." He tilted his head. "Care to explain?"

The look she leveled him could have melted iron. "I don't owe you an explanation."

"Oh, no? That is where you are mistaken, my dear. In addition to an explanation, you owe me a hundred pounds, a gold watch, and my fiancée's pearls. The money and the watch you may keep, but the necklace was a family heirloom. I must insist on its return. For your sake, I hope you haven't already set about fencing it."

"And if I have?"

"Then I have every reason to summon the Watch." He smiled to himself at the flicker of fear in her eyes. "With you clapped in irons, it shouldn't take a Bow Street runner long to track down that great ox of an accomplice of yours."

Terror bolted across her face.

He gestured toward the sofa. "Or you can have a seat and talk to me. The choice is yours."

"You win." She plopped down into his favorite armchair. "I still have the necklace. What now?"

Folding his arms across his chest, Anthony leaned back against the edge of the desk. "Return it, and I shall consider the slate wiped clean."

One ginger brow arched. "How do I know you won't turn me in once you have it?"

"You don't." *Droll, really, to have one's word of honor questioned by a self-confessed thief.* "But you might ask yourself why I would go to the trouble to set an elaborate trap when I have you already."

"I suppose you have a point." One leg curled beneath her, she no longer appeared poised for flight. "Very well. I don't have the necklace with me, but I can get it."

"Then come tomorrow, at midnight. The household will be abed, and I shall make certain the front door is unlocked."

"How very considerate of you." She untucked her leg and rose. "But I prefer the window."

"Suit yourself."

She stretched and walked to the window, each purposeful step shaping the breeches to curves that were sleek and utterly feminine.

Mouth dry, he called after her, "Wait! At least tell me your name."

She answered with a snort.

He grinned. "I suppose I could go on calling you One-Eye, but it hardly suits."

After a moment's hesitation, she pivoted to face him. "Robin is my given name, if you must know."

He rolled his eyes. "And I suppose your family name happens to be Hood."

She grimaced. "My family name is none of your affair."

Anthony smiled affably. "Very well then, I shall call you Lady Robin." *Until I discover your real name.* "And you may call me Anthony."

She bent to retrieve her hat. "Quite an honor for me, I'm sure, but I have no wish to call you anything."

Anthony's gaze gravitated to the creamy triangle of flesh at the open collar of her man's shirt. "Whatever your real name, I think Robin suits you. With your red hair, you remind me very much of that plucky little bird."

Tucking the hat under her arm, she patted away a yawn. "May I go now? Unlike you, I live by my wits. 'Tis late and I am wanting my bed."

Curiosity crystallized into desire. Anthony strode across the room, halting a few paces from her. *By God, I want to bed this breeches-clad gamine.*

"In that case, permit me to offer you mine."

He reached out and stroked his knuckles across her blush-warmed cheek. Smooth as silk, just as he'd known it would be. The heat between his legs began to build.

"You're awfully certain of yourself, aren't you?" Voice uneven, she stepped back.

He closed the distance. "A lack of self-confidence has never been a problem from which I've suffered."

He brushed back her heavy hair and traced the contours of one delicate, shell-shaped ear with a single finger. His fingertip registered her body's shiver. Like the sea, her irises shifted in color, the green overpowering the blue. Looking into her eyes, intense as any roiling sea, Anthony felt a fresh wave of desire crash over him. He was prepared, without compunction, to take her then and there on the floor of his library. The image of her lying naked beneath him on the Oriental carpet, her red hair splayed over his arm, shot through his mind.

His hand slid to the nape of her neck. Downy soft hairs teased his palm. He guided her face up to his, tasting her honeyed breath. Her moist lips were parted slightly, expectantly. She wanted him too. He could feel it.

Anthony could wait no longer to taste those full, ripe lips. Cupping her shoulders in his palms, he drew her against him, angling his face to hers. Their mouths met, hers closed beneath his. The light caress inflamed him. He wanted more. Much more.

He slid his tongue along the seam of her lips, probing. She hesitated, then opened. Anthony glided inside the cinnamon-spiced cavern. Exploring, he found the treasure of her tongue and entwined it with his own. She sighed and sagged against him, weightless as air. So soft, so sweet, so *willing*.

Somewhere in the background a clock ticked, reminding him that the night was slipping by. He dragged his mouth away to sample her blood-warmed ear. He took the lobe between his teeth and gave it a gentle nip before moving on to trace the heated whorls with the tip of his tongue. His mouth fastened on the hollow of her throat, tasting her racing pulse. Their struggle had left her skin salt flavored—deliciously so.

Her head fell back, and she arched against him. Wear had rendered the fine lawn of her shirt as sheer as silk. He could just make out the outline of her chemisette, feel the firm points of her nipples against his chest. He slid his hand downward until one perfectly shaped breast nestled in his palm. His thumb moved in a slow circle, finally grazing the taut peak.

"Bastard!" She pushed against his chest.

"Robin?" His brain enveloped in haze, he reached for her.

The sudden sting across his jaw cleared his head of the remaining fog.

Face bathed scarlet, Robin dropped her hand. "I may be a robin, Lord Montrose, but I assure you that I am no canary." She wiped her damp mouth with the back of one trembling hand. "I shall hand over the pearls to you at midnight tomorrow as agreed, but nothing more."

Rubbing his jaw, Anthony frowned. "I have never forced myself on a woman, Lady Robin. I have no intention of doing so tomorrow night or any other."

"Hah!" She dropped to one knee and began shoving the scattered articles into the leather bag.

He laid a slippered foot on the leather strap. "This remains here."

She tried to jerk the strap free.

"I'm afraid I must insist."

She scowled up at him but, to her credit, she was not fool enough to argue. Ignoring his outstretched hand, she gained her feet. Walking to the window, she climbed onto the sill and took hold of the rope. One foot braced on the slate eave, she levered herself onto the roof.

"Until tomorrow night, Lady Robin."

A soft thud announced that she had landed safely below.

Turning back inside the room, Anthony was uncomfortably aware that his manhood had come to its full, aching arousal.

God, what a woman.

Grinning, he allowed he'd never get to sleep now. He considered dressing and joining Reggie in Covent Garden, then dismissed the notion. With only twenty-four hours to discover the identity of the captivating Lady Robin, he must use his time wisely.

Besides, the brothel where Reggie was spending the evening specialized in blondes. After tonight, Anthony was definitely thinking redhead.

Ballocks, Montrose. You were supposed to be at the theater.

Hands trembling, Chelsea took hold of the rope. Even as she edged down the slick, moss-covered stone, she asked herself how the night could have gone so wrong. In stalking her quarry, she'd been so careful, so *thorough*. She'd even scanned the society column of the *Morning Herald* to be certain of which evenings Lord Montrose would be away from home. That morning's column had announced that dashing Viscount M. would be escorting his lovely fiancée, Lady P., to the premier performance of Shakespeare's "Romeo and Juliet" at Drury Lane. The gala in the Green Room, to be presided over by H.R.H., known among his familiars as "Prinny," was expected to last into the wee hours. *How perfect*, Chelsea had thought. She'd kept watch outside Montrose's townhouse until seven that evening when, formally attired and handsome as sin, he'd left in his carriage. As soon as the dust from his lordship's carriage wheels had settled, she'd raced home to fetch Jack. They'd waited in the alley out back until the last window in the house darkened. Then Chelsea had made her move. Thinking she possessed hours, she'd crept at her leisure from room to room, ending in the library.

Where she'd been nabbed—and by "Viscount M." himself.

What manner of rake returned home before midnight? With a huff, she released the rope and dropped the remaining few feet to the garden. Her knees buckled, more from nerves than from fatigue, she suspected. Fortunately, there was no need to climb the stone wall, for the gate was unlocked. Mentally thanking the careless servant who had neglected to bolt it, she lifted the hasp and slipped into the alley.

The cobbled thoroughfare was lit only by the moon and the candles left burning in the windows of a few houses. Earlier that day, she'd reconnoitered the alley. Now she easily slipped into its blackness, gliding her hand along the perimeter of garden fences and rubbish bins she'd committed to memory. Aside from surprising a cat, who darted into her path with an angry hiss, she gained the end without incident.

Lantern light illuminated Jack's taut features. She girded herself, but his expression eased when she approached.

"What the devil took ye so long? 'Tis after one o'clock. I was just about to come after ye."

Guilt lashed at her. It was bad enough that she'd been

wrapped around Lord Montrose like so much ivy, but to think she'd behaved so brazenly when her own brother was being held captive. And she'd abandoned poor Jack as well, leaving him on his own to wait and worry.

By the looks of him, he'd worried a great deal. Knowing how skittish he was, she hadn't told him that it was Lord Montrose's house they were looting. Which meant that she couldn't admit that his lordship had discovered her.

"Sorry. I heard a noise," she whispered, "but it was only the butler seeing to the candles. I hid in the library until he finished. By then, it was too dark to see much of anything, so I left."

"There's naught to be gained by takin' foolhardy chances." Jack cast one last look down the darkened alley and beckoned her to follow. "There's always tomorrow night, Heaven 'elp us."

Tomorrow night.

Taking the lantern, she led the way down the maze of intersecting alleys, all the while asking herself how on earth she was going to slip out. Jack would never permit her to go without him. But she must. If Montrose set a trap after all, at least Jack wouldn't be caught as well. Buried in the recesses of her mind was a far less noble motive: she wanted to be alone with Lord Montrose one last time if only to prove that her wantonness was an aberration, the result of jangled nerves and little sleep.

They emerged in the mew behind Mount Street and crept past the row of stables and coach houses. The whinnies of horses and Jack's footfalls were the only sounds to stir the silence.

Jack reached over the gate and lifted the latch. As they walked up the narrow stone path to the back door, Chelsea congratulated herself on her choice. Mount Street was cloaked in shabby respectability, a mixture of shops, lodging houses, and small, unpretentious private homes. The parish workhouse was located on the south side; otherwise, the neighborhood was the sort where people led quiet, uneventful lives and were abed by nine. The gray clapboard townhouse she'd let was neat and nondescript—the perfect spot to hole up until the ransom delivery. And, with the social season at its end, the landlady had been prepared to be reasonable about the rent, especially when Chelsea had arrived at the rental office wearing widow's black and offering to pay in advance.

They stepped inside the kitchen, and an unexpected sneeze provided her with the excuse she'd been searching for.

"Gawd bless ye." Jack set the lantern on the pine table and dug into his pocket for a handkerchief. "Ye're coming down with the headcold, I reckon. 'Tis what comes of dashing about 'til all hours, not takin' proper care o' yerself."

"I suppose you're right," she replied meekly, dabbing the tip of her nose with the cloth. "I had planned to try my luck again tomorrow night, but perhaps I should rest instead."

Jack headed for the pantry. "'Tis the first sensible thing ye've said since we got 'ere."

His back turned, she grabbed the pepper mill from the table and sprinkled the granules into her palm.

Bracing herself, she brought her hand to her face and inhaled.

"Ahhhh chooo!"

Her sneeze rocked the rafters. Jack found her doubled over and clutching a chair back, eyes streaming.

"Poor lamb. We'd better get ye to bed."

Still choking, she headed for the hall stairs. "Yes, I think I'll go right up."

Inside her bedchamber, images of Lord Montrose assailed her. Lord Montrose leaning against the desk, arms folded across his broad chest, unconcerned that his robe gaped open. The triangle of dark brown hair had confirmed that he wasn't wearing a nightshirt beneath the black velvet. *But then a Corinthian of his rakish caliber probably slept in the buff*, Chelsea decided, shoving her practical cotton nightgown over her head.

She unlocked the drawer of the bedside table to assure herself that the pearls were safe. Unwrapping the square of velvet, she carried the necklace to the open window and looked out onto the moonlit garden. Late-blooming roses scented the breeze wafting inside, ruffling her loose hair and molding her nightgown between her legs.

She unfurled her fingers, the rope of pearls slipping through them in a silken stream. *What would it feel like to stand in front of that window, naked but for the pearls, waiting for my lover to come to me?*

Having never had a lover—nor even a serious beau—she relied on her imagination. Closing her eyes, she stroked pearl-wrapped knuckles over her cheek, recalling Lord Montrose's silken caress. When her imaginary lover assumed Lord Montrose's form—this time, *sans* robe—Chelsea crushed the necklace into her fist. Clearly a life of crime was having a dangerously disinhibiting effect on her morals.

And her concentration. Finding Robert was of paramount importance; she couldn't afford to become distracted. These ridiculous, impossible fantasies about Lord Montrose must stop. *Now.*

Sighing, she stowed the necklace, blew out the candle, and slipped beneath the covers. The sale of the pearls was to have brought the lion's share of the ransom money. After returning them tomorrow night, she must devote herself to stealing enough to redeem Robert.

Tomorrow night.

She sat up and plumped her pillow, telling herself she had no choice but to return the necklace. Lord Montrose was not the sort who made idle threats. No doubt he would hire Bow Street's finest to track Jack and her if she attempted to renege on her promise.

Throwing off the worn coverlet, she pressed the back of her hand against her damp forehead. Perhaps she really was coming down with a cold. She did feel feverish. Sleep was what she needed. She lay back down and closed her eyes, but instead of blank darkness, Lord Montrose's face drifted before her mind's eye. With his seductive brown eyes, mussed auburn hair, and the ghost of a beard shadowing his strong, sculpted jaw, he had looked every inch the irresistible lover.

But resist him I must, she reminded herself forcefully.

Lord Montrose was a roué—and the next thing to married.

Even if he were neither, the difference in their social stations would render impossible any respectable association. Viscounts did not marry the daughters of penniless country squires. Just as well. She thought of how blithely he'd offered her his bed—as though he'd expected her to fall into it—and her cheeks burned with outrage—and shame. To a man like Montrose, women were playthings, to be used and tossed aside with no more thought than he probably gave to disposing of a worn pair of gloves. That didn't alter the fact that she'd waited a lifetime for a man to kiss her like he had that night.

Until Dumfreys's assault, she'd fended off would-be suitors with ease. But Lord Montrose was no callow, country-bred boy. Judging from tonight's expert performance, he was an accomplished seducer, and yet she did not believe him to be entirely without scruples. When he'd given her his word that he would allow her to go free, she'd believed him. To his credit, he hadn't forced himself on her, although he could have easily ravished her, especially after her own appalling lack of self-control had landed her in his arms.

But the knowledge that Lord Montrose was no rapist was cold comfort. With looks like his, she was certain he'd never had to resort to force to get what he wanted from a woman. It should be a crime for a man to possess such a disarming smile. How many hearts had he used it to capture?

She punched her fist into the pillow. *Lord Montrose, you are the true thief.*

Chapter Five

Anthony emerged into the sunlight. Adjusting his eyes to the glare, he descended the granite steps from Murdock's Lending Library, a yellowed newspaper folded beneath one arm. It had taken him the better part of the morning and afternoon, but finally he'd found what he sought. He smiled in contemplation of his midnight engagement. If all went according to plan, by the end of the night he would have Phoebe's pearls in his pocket and Chelsea Bellamy warming his bed.

He had his Lady Robin in hand now. Victory would be all the sweeter for the trouble she had caused him.

To Chelsea, Lord Montrose's study was a typical male preserve of musty books, leather furnishings, and the faint, sweet scent of tobacco. With cravat loosened and shirtsleeves rolled to the elbow, his lordship looked the part of a gentleman at his leisure—and even more dangerously attractive than he had on the previous night.

Lord Montrose tilted his chair from the desk and studied her. "So, Lady Robin, it seems you are a woman of your word."

Facing him across the width of the desk, Chelsea unhooked the small leather pouch from her waist. Willing her hands to stop shaking, she handed it to him.

"Your fiancée's necklace, as promised." She shivered when their fingertips brushed.

After a brief inspection, he dropped the pearls inside a desk drawer and locked it.

"Truce?" Rounding the desk, he offered her his hand.

His long fingers curled around her palm, and Chelsea's heart fluttered. Carrying her hand to his lips, he brushed her fingertips. A shudder shot through her.

Standing before him, she caught a whiff of the cool, clean scent of his shaving soap. The urge to let her fingertips trace the hard line of his freshly shaven jaw was so strong that, to be safe, she jammed her free hand inside her trouser pocket.

"I really should be going." Her voice held remarkably steady for a woman whose insides were churning.

He released her with a show of reluctance. "I had hoped you might stay to join me in a light supper."

Shocked, she crammed the hand he'd just released into her other pocket. "I'm afraid that is out of the question."

"Don't tell me that you've already eaten?" His face registered disappointment.

She was about to answer "yes" when her stomach betrayed her with a loud rumble.

He grinned. "I think not." Hand on her elbow, he steered her toward the door. "But we can remedy that."

She halted. "Lord Montrose, I don't think dining with you would be wise."

"Why not?" he asked, expression bland.

Was he mocking her? Annoyed, she answered through pursed lips, "I should think that would be obvious. I came tonight only to return the necklace I—" she faltered "—stole from you. I am hardly an invited guest."

He opened the study door and held it. "That is for me to decide."

Chelsea hesitated. To accept his invitation would be to chart a perilous course. But over the past twenty-four hours, her body seemed to have developed a will of its own. She laid her fingers atop his, butterflies dancing in her stomach. He linked his long fingers through hers, and her hand disappeared in his warm grasp.

"You needn't fear discovery." His other hand on her back,

he guided her through the sconce-lit hallway. "I have dismissed the staff for the night, including Chambers."

Recalling the frail, black-clad old man she'd seen answering Anthony's front door the day before, she asked, "I gather Chambers is your butler?"

"My uncle's butler." He paused, then amended, "My butler now, I suppose. Fellow must be in his eighties. He's blind as a bat and creaks like carriage springs when he walks, but I haven't the heart to retire him."

A sliver of light showed beneath ornately carved double doors. Releasing her hand, Anthony opened them and led her inside a large dining room with cream-colored walls, emerald velvet drapes, and plush carpet patterned in hues of cream and jade. The faint smell of fresh paint hovered. The night before, she hadn't stopped to admire the chamber's beauty, but now she found her gaze straying. Roundels depicting scenes from classical mythology dotted the intricate plasterwork ceiling. Flames flickered in the wall sconces above a burl walnut sideboard laden with food.

Lord Montrose stood in the center of the room, the pride of possession shining from his brown eyes. "Do you like it? It's one of the few rooms in this mausoleum that comes close to being habitable."

Habitable, indeed. Chelsea thought of the shabbiness of Oatlands, Robert's legacy—assuming he survived—and her heart tugged. Rotting woodwork and a leaking roof—calamities a few weeks before—were now the very least of her worries.

Aware of her host watching her, expectant, she suppressed a sigh and answered, "It's splendid. The most beautiful room I've ever seen."

"I'm glad you approve." He led her to the end of the long table where two places had been set, a brace of candles between them. "Right now, the thing I like best about this room is that there's no one here but you and I." He pulled out a shield-back chair. "So, you see, you shall be quite safe."

Safe? Alone in a chamber veiled in candlelight and shadows with an unrepentant rake—and a brain brimming with foolish fantasies—Chelsea had never felt less safe in her life. Everything about the room, and the man standing in its center, radiated romance.

Wanting to clear the air before matters got out of hand, she said, "I should tell you that, if you're planning to seduce me, you're wasting your time."

He smiled his mesmerizing smile. "I appreciate your candor, Lady Robin. Now that you've broached the subject, I must confess that the thought had crossed my mind, but I assure you that I shall respect your wishes. I meant what I said last night, that it is not my custom to force my attentions where they are unwanted." He gestured toward the sideboard. "But it would be a pity for all this to go to waste, don't you agree?"

Disarmed, Chelsea found herself returning his smile. "The toast I had for breakfast does seem rather a long time ago."

His smile broadened. "Even fierce knights of the road have to eat. Besides," he added, his connoisseur's gaze sweeping over her, "you look like someone who could benefit from a good meal."

She surrendered with a grimace, slipping into the chair he held out. "After such a gracious invitation, how could I possibly refuse?"

She quickly laid her napkin on her lap to cover the smudges on her trousers, the legacy of nights spent climbing garden walls and prowling alleys. She might have no designs on Lord Montrose, romantic or otherwise, but she was woman enough to wish for something pretty to wear. And to think Robert had always cared for clothes far more than she had. How smart he'd looked in his uniform, the creases of his spotless white trousers ironed as sharp as knife blades. Imagining how bedraggled and filthy he must be by now—if, indeed, he still lived—she felt tears burn the backs of her eyes.

Fortunately Lord Montrose had moved to the sideboard, affording her a moment to compose herself.

"Sending the staff to bed does have one disadvantage,

namely, that we shall have to fend for ourselves. This is my first time waiting at table, so you'll have to bear with me."

A bottle of wine had been left to decant. Slinging a napkin over his arm, he carried it to the table.

"Reputedly a very fine red bordeaux. I hope 'tis to milady's liking."

He gave a servile bow before bending to pour, and Chelsea couldn't help but smile. How charming he was, how amusing.

He stepped back. Awaiting her verdict, his dark eyes glinted with mischief. His playfulness was contagious, and Chelsea found her mood lightening. Falling in with the game, she swirled the liquid around her glass before raising the rim to her lips.

"It is rather . . . wonderful."

Reminding herself that red wine always gave her the headache, she set down the goblet. She couldn't afford a muzzy head tomorrow just as she couldn't afford to become tipsy in his lordship's presence. He'd promised he wouldn't force himself on her, and she trusted him to keep his word. Herself she trusted far less.

"I am pleased you like it." He finished filling her glass, then reached for his own. "Wellington sent it along to cheer me while I was convalescing. I've been saving it for more than a year now, waiting to celebrate a special occasion."

Feeling as though she had stepped into a fairytale, she heard a bemused voice, her voice, ask, "What are we celebrating?"

"I haven't decided yet." He raised his glass, enigmatic smile fraught with possibilities. "To your health, Lady Robin."

To Robert's health. Chelsea touched her glass to Lord Montrose's, and the crystal met with a soft ting. Even before the sound died, she found herself wondering what supper, if any, Robert was having. Was he making do with bread and water at the same time she was about to indulge in—her guilty gaze swept the sideboard—a feast?

Lord Montrose sipped his wine, apparently oblivious to

the mental jousting going on between her epicurean self and her contrite conscience.

Lowering the glass, he exhaled. "Very fine indeed."

His tongue darted over his lower lip. Even battling her guilt, she couldn't help but recall the strange, heady sensation of that moist member intertwining her own. The temperature in the room spiked. She tugged her collar.

"But I am forgetting my manners." Setting down his glass, he reached for her plate. "Allow me." He carried it to the sideboard.

"Lord Montrose, you must not wait on me."

With a household staff reduced to two—Jack and the cook—she was accustomed to labor, and to serving herself. Never in her most outlandish fantasies had she imagined being attended to by a dashing viscount. It was almost too much—certainly something to tell her grandchildren about. On second thought, perhaps not.

"Anthony," he corrected. She caught a flash of white teeth before he turned to lift the lid off a large silver serving platter. "I hope you like salmon in shrimp sauce." He lifted the lids off two other dishes. "If not, there is also roasted chicken or, if you prefer, florentine rabbits."

There was enough food to feed a multitude. Thinking once more of Robert, she bit her bottom lip. "Lord Montrose, are you certain that I am your only *guest*?"

He grinned at her over his shoulder. His very broad shoulder. "I didn't know what you would like, so I had my chef prepare several dishes."

Telling herself that she must keep up her strength, for Robert's sake as well as for her own, she swallowed her guilt. "In that case, perhaps I should have some of everything . . . except for the rabbit," she amended, in deference to her childhood pet, Mr. Wiggles.

His shirt strained across his back as he carved the bird. Fascinated, Chelsea watched the ripple of muscles beneath the fabric. Her gaze dropped lower. His buff-colored breeches accentuated every curve of his slender hips, firm buttocks, and muscled thighs. Obviously his self-indulgent lifestyle did not extend to gluttony.

"Jacket potatoes?"

"Yes, please."

"Gingered carrots?"

"A few."

He lifted the lid off a porcelain tureen. Bending over it, he sniffed the steam, then pulled a face.

Chelsea giggled. "What is it?"

"Creamed spinach, I believe." Turning to her, his expression registered skepticism. "Care for some?"

She hesitated, then confessed, "I've never been overly fond of spinach, creamed or otherwise."

"Personally, I detest the stuff. And, because I find myself wanting to please you in all things, I shall remove this offending vegetable from our presence forthwith."

He carried the tureen over to the open window. Brushing aside the sheer curtain, he called, "Look out below." His head and shoulders disappeared outside.

He turned back inside with the emptied dish, a schoolboy smile lighting his face.

Chelsea burst out laughing. "Do you always act so . . . impulsively?"

"No, not always, although I am a great believer in following one's instincts. Whenever I've ignored mine, I've usually ended up with the Devil to pay."

His smile faded like a summer sun slipping behind a bank of clouds. He set her full plate before her, then turned to serve himself. Studying the rigid set of his shoulders, Chelsea wondered what memory had triggered the sudden change.

When he took his seat next to her, at the head of the table, his scoundrel's smile was securely in place.

"*Bon appetit.*" He handed her the basket of rolls.

Chelsea barely tasted the succulent dishes that passed her lips. Instead, her hungry gaze devoured every facet of Lord Montrose's face—the way his auburn hair fell over his high forehead, the sculpted planes of his nose and jaw, the way the tanned flesh at the corners of his eyes crinkled when he smiled. The knowledge that, after tonight, she would never see him again imbued the intimate meal with a bittersweet poignancy.

He speared a carrot on his fork. "I like your hair that way."

Hoping that she hadn't been caught staring at him like a slack-jawed schoolgirl, she fumbled with the white satin ribbon that moored her waist-length hair. "My hair has always been the bane of my existence."

"I think your hair is beautiful," he said with conviction.

Her eyes fell to her plate. She shook her head. "Having red hair is a nuisance. As a child, I could never get away with the slightest prank, chiefly because I could be sighted a mile down the road. I was the only one in the neighborhood with hair this color. Not even my brother . . ."

What am I doing? Agitated, she tugged at a loose curl.

"Permit me."

He reached over and tucked the renegade strand behind her ear. The memory of the previous night was still achingly fresh, and his light touch turned her insides to pudding.

"There, now you are perfect." His dark eyes rested on her face. "And, I should add, very beautiful."

Chelsea didn't know what to say. She'd aroused her fair share of male admiration, but she'd never felt beautiful before. Until now. The frank appreciation in Lord Montrose's bold gaze made her feel like a fairy princess.

And damnably self-conscious. She took refuge in humor. "Never say you dress hair as well? Perhaps you should consider becoming a lady's maid."

He threw back his head and guffawed. "The prospect certainly presents some interesting possibilities, but I think for now I'll keep to table service. Which reminds me." He picked up the wine bottle and refilled her glass.

Sipping the wine, she felt a languid contentment roll over her like the gentle lapping of the sea against the shoreline. Her problems would be waiting for her in the morning, as overwhelming as ever. But for one night—the next hour at least—where was the harm in pretending they were solved? Or in taking pleasure in the company of a handsome, attentive . . . rogue?

Reckless, she put down the piece of roll she was buttering and asked, "If not to seduce me, then why have you gone to all this trouble?"

If Lord Montrose was taken aback by her frankness, he gave no indication of it. "From my experience, the intimacy of sharing a meal is usually one of the better ways to go about getting to know a person."

"Why would you care to know *me*?" *Especially when you're about to marry an exquisite, blonde enchantress, the very personification of everything I'm not.*

He put down his goblet and stared at her. "Because you are an enigma, Lady Robin, and I've always found enigmas to be utterly fascinating. The very idea of a beautiful, intelligent young woman taking up a life of crime piques my curiosity." His expression sobered. "I've been told that I'm a good listener. If you'd care to unburden yourself, I'd try to hear you out with an open mind. Perhaps I could even help?"

Her heart caught in her throat. The dangerous urge to accept his offer, to lean on his male strength, almost overwhelmed her.

Almost but not quite. For all his polished manners and handsome looks, Lord Montrose was a stranger. A stranger who, just the night before, had threatened to turn her over to the authorities.

"My reasons are my own." Seeking to steer the conversation into safer waters, she added, "At any rate, I believe it is you who are the true enigma, my lord. You're not at all what I would expect of . . ."

"Of a spoiled, debauched aristocrat?"

She nearly choked on the bite of salmon she'd just taken. "I might have worded it somewhat more diplomatically but, yes, basically that was the idea."

He chewed thoughtfully. "What about me surprises you?"

Regretting having gone down this path, she seized on the first innocuous thought that came to mind. "Your complexion for one thing. You're very sunburnt."

His smile stiffened. Fine lines bracketed the corners of his mouth. She'd judged him to be around thirty, but he suddenly seemed much older.

"Baking in Wellington's Peninsular oven has a way of banishing the Englishman's lily white. And then, again, I have always enjoyed outdoor pursuits. It was a great trial when my leg forced me to refrain."

So that explained the limp. Wondering whether he might be making a bid for her sympathy, she asked lightly, "Were you wounded in the war or shot by a jealous husband?"

"The former." His mouth softened into a smile. "I make it my policy never to seduce married women—" he winked "—at least not ones with jealous husbands."

What an ass I am. Flushing, she said, "I'm sorry. I shouldn't have made a joke of it. How long did you serve?"

"The better part of two years. I purchased my commission in July of 1809, just after Wellington beat the Frogs to a pulp at Talavera. Like my friends, I hadn't a clue as to what war was really about, but saving Europe from Boney's Butchers seemed gloriously noble." Tone shaded with bitterness, he added, "My luck held until Albuera."

"You were at Albuera!"

He nodded. "I was a captain in the Fourth Division under Cole."

Chelsea well remembered reading about the battle in *The Times* and the *St. James Chronicle*, beneath headlines that read, "Wellington's Costliest Victory," and "Peace with a Price." The grizzly accounts of the survivors and the long columns listing the dead and wounded had chilled her. When Robert had announced his intention to purchase a commission, it was the name of Albuera that Chelsea had invoked in a vain attempt to dissuade him.

"I read about it in the papers. It sounded . . ." She stopped, afraid any words she chose might trivialize what he'd endured.

Gaze focused somewhere over her shoulder, he said, "We lost almost six thousand men that day, some of them little more than boys."

They ate in silence, but his pain was palpable. It rippled between them, setting off waves of tension.

"Forgive me," she said at length, regretting her tactlessness. "I shouldn't have pried."

His gaze met hers. "No need to apologize. I'm flattered to be the object of your interest." He smiled, but his eyes were sad. "At the time, I assumed I would lose the leg, or at least the better part of it. The field surgeons were a harried lot. There was only one doctor to a battalion, and in the bigger battles there might be two hundred or even three hundred wounded, but that day the casualties were legion. The usual practice was to amputate rather than spend precious time digging out a bullet."

A tableau of Lord Montrose, bloody and writhing on a makeshift gurney, flashed before Chelsea. She'd always had a soft heart when it came to a fellow creature in distress, but the raw fervor of the feelings welling inside her transcended compassion. Lord Montrose might be a virtual stranger but, Dear Lord, she *ached* for him.

She reached out to touch him. "It must have been awful for you."

He glanced at her hand, resting atop his. "I was one of the lucky ones. General Beresford sent his personal surgeon to attend me. As a result, I kept the leg."

Self-conscious, she withdrew under the pretense of reaching for her wine. "Is there pain still?"

He lifted his glass and stared into its ruby depths. "Oh, I suspect that my knee will always tell me when it's about to rain, but otherwise I have no complaints." Voice flat, he added, "Most of the lads who fought under me were not so fortunate."

He drank deeply, then set his glass aside. "Now tell me, what else about me do you find not quite up to snuff for a peer of the realm?" She was about to demur when he reminded her, "You did indicate that my complexion was one of others."

She smiled, shaking her head in surrender. The man had a mind like a steel trap. Just when she'd lowered her guard, told herself he was no longer a threat, he'd ensnared her with her own words. She'd been a fool to forget that Lord

Montrose was not the sort of man for whom she could afford to feel compassion. Or anything else.

"Pray forgive me. I spoke rashly. I'm afraid I've not had much experience of society outside of Upper Uck—"

"Upper Uckfield," he finished for her, smiling like the cat that swallowed the canary.

She inhaled sharply. Her heart dropped. "Y-you . . ."

"Yes, I know it. Lovely little parish in central Sussex. Not far from Heathfield Park, if I'm not mistaken." Pouring more wine into her glass, he continued blithely, "Having a bit of trouble with the roads of late. Pity really."

What a dupe I am. "You tricked me!"

He flashed her a beatific smile. "On the contrary, Lady Robin. You volunteered the information." His grin widened. "I am, of course, honored to be the recipient of your confidences."

Not trusting herself with a knife in her present mood, she speared a potato on the end of her fork and bit into it savagely.

"If 'tis any consolation, the information you divulged doesn't amount to much of a revelation. Upper Uckfield is, after all, the nearest hamlet to the road I was traveling when you intercepted my coach. That it is also your home is hardly surprising."

Chelsea relaxed a fraction, although she inwardly cursed herself for her carelessness. The wine, not to mention the intoxication of flirting with a dashing viscount, had gone to her head. Out in the hallway, a clock struck one. It was time she left.

She set her utensils on the edge of her plate. "Supper was delicious. Thank you." Even now, after she'd made a bloody fool of herself—and risked Robert's life, to boot—her heart felt leaden with regret.

He pushed his plate aside. "My cook makes a marvelous blanc mange. I hope you saved room?"

"I'm afraid not." Laying her napkin aside, she pushed her chair away from the table. "I know it must seem churlish of me to leave in the middle of a meal, but I really must."

Tossing aside his napkin, he shot to his feet. "Don't go."

His big hands cupped her shoulders, the heat from his palms searing. Her resolve, like her knees, buckled.

"I don't want you to go." He wrapped one sinewy arm around her shoulders and pulled her against him. "I can't let you go."

Fear of the tingling heat building inside her kicked her heartbeat from a canter to a full gallop.

"But I've kept my promise. I've returned the necklace. What more can you want of me?"

His brown eyes probed hers. "Don't you know, Robin?"

"N-no." The liquid warmth of his gaze made it hard to find her tongue.

He traced her bottom lip with his thumb. "I only want one thing, but I want it very badly."

Her throat was as dry as sawdust, the space between her thighs treacherously moist.

She ran her tongue over her parched lower lip. "W-what is that?"

"*You.*"

Chapter Six

Anthony claimed Chelsea with a searing kiss. Her world stopped, spun, then stopped again with each velvet sweep of his tongue. Time—seconds, minutes, hours—held no meaning. For Chelsea, reality became Anthony's hot mouth, his teasing tongue, his nipping teeth. And his hands . . .

He broke away and cleared the table with the edge of his arm. Breathless, weak, bemused, she held onto the back of her chair and watched a fortune in china and crystal fly over the sides. A wine glass overturned, spreading scarlet across the white tablecloth. The next thing she knew, Anthony's hands were about her waist, lifting her.

He set her gently down on the table's edge. "I want you, Robin." His rich mahogany gaze melded with hers. "And, unless I am woefully mistaken, you want me too. Am I wrong?"

Logic and desire warred inside Chelsea. Logic urged her to deny the fierce yearning, to leave while her trembling limbs were still capable of conveying her safely away. Desire reminded her that she had been waiting a lifetime for a man like this. What could be the harm in one more kiss?

Desire won. Closing her eyes, she coiled her arms around his neck and crushed her mouth against his. Wanting to drink in the essence of him, she parted her lips, her tongue seeking.

A low rumble, part groan, part chuckle, rose from Anthony's throat. "Ah, Robin, you are indeed an enigma."

His deft fingers made short work of her cravat. Tossing aside the length of linen, he began to unbutton her shirt. Chelsea's eyes flew open. She had intended on yielding to his kisses, but the look in Anthony's eyes promised more.

Much more.

I must stop.

Dragging her mouth away, she flattened a palm against his chest and gave a weak push.

"Lord Montrose, I really don't think we should—"

"Don't think." He lifted her hand from his chest and pressed a kiss into her palm. "Only feel."

She started to answer, but his lips claimed hers, scrambling her few remaining wits. His tongue initiated a mating dance of advance and retreat that both tormented and tantalized . . . and left her swelling breasts screaming to be touched.

This has to end.

Against his lips, she pleaded, "Anthony . . . *please.*"

"That is exactly what I am trying to do, my sweet."

Nibbling on her lower lip, he slid the shirt off her shoulders. A damp draft wafted through the open window over her burning skin.

"God, you are beyond beautiful."

Chelsea followed his hungry gaze downward to her chemisette and blushed. She had outgrown the feminine article some time ago. The cream-colored silk stretched tautly across her bosom, concealing nothing.

He fitted his mouth over the point of one aching breast. Wetting the fabric to transparency, his tongue traced the outline of the dusky pink areola. Shiver after exquisite shiver rippled through her. She rocked back, clutching his shoulders to steady herself and draw him closer. As though reading her thoughts, he took the taut bud between his teeth and gently bit down. The warm, tingling sensation was immediate —it shot to the secret place between her legs, triggering a strange throbbing. Wanting more, she threw back her head, arching herself against him. He complied, his tongue snaking salaciously over her other nipple, bathing it, too, in sweet heat.

"God, I can't remember ever wanting a woman as I want you." His voice was a ragged whisper against her breast.

Caught in the maelstrom, Chelsea scarcely noticed when he gripped her knees, parted them, and stepped boldly between. The proof of his passion, hard and hot through his breeches, pressed against her inner thigh.

Anthony undid the buttons at her trouser front. The panel fell obligingly open, and a slow smile spread across his face.

"Definitely a true redhead."

He slipped a hand inside, his thumb massaging the mound of springy, russet hair.

The tingling heat building between Chelsea's thighs was rapidly becoming a bonfire, the throbbing keeping pace with each frenzied palpitation of her heart. Dizzy, she tightened her hold on his shoulders and anchored her legs to his hips.

His hand wandered lower. Parting her inner lips, he slid one finger inside. Chelsea's breath ended in a gasp.

Now. I have to end this . . . now.

He must have sensed her retreat, for when he entered her again, his finger imitated the teasing of his kisses. Slow, undulating movements promised to reduce her to a puddle on the table, with no more will or substance than the spilled wine.

And suddenly she no longer cared.

Each deft stroke skittered a delicate shudder down her spine and stoked the fire in her belly. Her nails bit into his broad shoulders, leaving crescent-shaped marks on the damp linen. Somewhere in the recesses of her mind, a warning bell sounded, telling her that this act was only a prelude to a more intimate possession, but she was too far gone to heed it.

He withdrew. His finger spun sticky, spiderweb patterns on the inside of her thigh. "You want me as much as I want you. The honey on my fingers tells me so, but I want to hear you say it."

Pride, like her shirt, lay crumpled about her. Even so, an obstinate voice urged her to deny his lordship this one satisfaction.

His demand was a husky whisper against her throat. "Say it."

She was a novice in love play but she knew that, if she denied him this, he would stop and send her away. Exactly what she should want and yet . . .

He lifted his face to hers, his dark eyes daring her to dissemble. She no longer wanted to. No, what she wanted was to draw Anthony inside her and hold him there forever. She wanted to give herself to him, whatever the cost. She wanted . . . God, she wanted . . . *him.*

She reached for his wrist. Beyond shame, she pressed his palm against her open trousers. "Y-yes. I want you."

His laugh was no less triumphant for its softness. "Then, milady, we are of a mind."

He parted her once more, the whorls on his thumb grazing her sensitized flesh. She moaned and rolled her hips, seeking some deeper satisfaction. He sought out the small, hidden bud of desire and flicked over it once, twice . . .

The tight knot of tension building inside Chelsea uncoiled. She cried out. Wave after wave of molten pleasure crashed over her until she thought she would shatter into a million pieces like the china scattered at their feet.

Finally the last tremor quivered through her, leaving euphoria in its wake. In the grip of a delicious languor, she dropped lead-weighted legs from Anthony's waist and sagged against him. She was beyond modesty or pretended indifference; there would be time aplenty for self-recrimination once her brain resumed functioning. For now, she was content to savor the moment. Eyes closed, she laid her cheek against the corded muscles of his neck, reveling in the sandpaper roughness of his budding beard and the wicked sensation of her breasts flattened against his hard chest.

Anthony was the first to break their embrace.

"I'll not last long this time 'round, my sweet, but I promise there'll be plenty more times ere morning." His hand went to the front of his trousers.

Startled, Chelsea opened her eyes. Her breath caught in her throat. Although life on a farm had given her a general idea of what happened between men and women, nothing had prepared her for the sight of Lord Montrose's swollen shaft surging out.

He took her hand and laid it intimately along the length of him. "Take me inside you, Lady Robin. I will be an inmate of Bedlam unless I can bury myself in your sweet heat."

Chelsea's fingers curved gently around him. The taut flesh was silken smooth and resonant with warmth. Curious, she slid her hand up and down.

Anthony groaned and thrust against her hand. A small bead of moisture dampened her palm. Fearing he was bleeding, she slackened her hold. "Are you hurt?"

He gave her a weak smile. "No, but I am in the grip of a very sweet torment. At this rate, I definitely will not last much longer."

Uncertain of his meaning, Chelsea wondered if he might be feeling as helpless as she had a moment ago. Experimentally, she flicked her thumb over the engorged tip.

Face spasming, Anthony reared back. "Oh, God, *Chelsea!*"

Anthony looked down in horror. Chelsea jerked her hand away as though she'd laid it atop a bed of hot coals. A good thing really, for he'd almost spilled his seed. Even so . . .

This can't be happening. Not to me.

"Why you filthy, lying cur!" Bracing both palms on his chest, she pushed, this time with determination. "How long have you known?"

Senses reeling, Anthony backed away just in time to avoid the vicious upward jab of her knee.

She stared down at her chemisette, transparent where he'd suckled. "Oh, God!"

Her shirt dangled from her waist. She yanked it up, sprang off the table, and headed for a shadowed corner.

Thoughts racing, he demanded, "Known what?"

Watching her struggle to right her clothing, he willed his head to clear. He hadn't experienced such an overwhelming sense of disorientation since the age of eighteen when he'd smoked his first—and last—opium pipe at the urging of his school chums.

She gave him her back. "My name." She glared at him over one shoulder. "Have you known all along?"

The fog lifted. "Damnation."

He raked a hand through his hair, cursing himself for a blundering idiot. *What the devil's come over me*. He tucked his throbbing sex inside his trousers. Earlier he'd bared his soul to her and now . . . this. Even in the throes of passion, he always maintained mastery over his reason—and his *erection*. Until tonight.

"I found out only this afternoon," he admitted. He'd intended on confronting her with his discovery eventually, but not yet. Not like this.

Shirt buttoned and eyes flashing, Chelsea faced him. "I suppose you set one of your servants to spy on me?"

Anthony shook his head, willing the desire to ebb from his still-hard body. "You are not the only one capable of stealth. A trip to Murdock's and a bit of research into the annals of Upper Uckfield revealed that there was indeed a One-Eyed Jack who worked the road to London . . . more than thirty years ago."

Fear filled her eyes. The last time he'd looked into wide, frightened eyes, he had . . . Perspiration broke out on his forehead. *Forget the war, Anthony*. He clawed his way back to the present. With patience and cunning, his plans for the evening might yet be salvaged.

"I venture to say that great hulking specimen accompanying you the day you waylaid my carriage was the original?" At her miserable nod, he continued, "The local gazette reported that One-Eyed Jack was apprehended but had the good fortune to escape hanging. Instead he was released into the custody of the parish magistrate, a reform-minded squire named Bellamy. Your father, I collect?"

She inclined her head. "With a bit of patience and training, Jack made a truly splendid if somewhat unconventional butler." Her gaze narrowed. "That still doesn't explain how you discovered me."

He shrugged. "From there on, it was easy enough to put two and two together. I came upon your father's obituary. A certain ginger-haired daughter named Chelsea was mentioned as a survivor, along with a son, Robert. The brief description hardly did you justice."

His gaze skimmed her. Even wearing men's clothes and bristling like an angry cat, she was exquisite. And vibrant. Just looking at her, he felt the cold place inside his chest begin to thaw.

"Flame-haired vixen suits you far better."

A rosebud blush climbed her delicate cheekbones. "But I was dressed as a man. It could just as easily been my *b-brother* playing the part."

A pained look crossed her face, and he wondered what, if anything, her stammer signified. Tomorrow morning, when she awoke in his bed, he would remember to ask her, but at present, there was a pressing matter to resolve.

His need still upon him, he replied, "You have the redhead's fair complexion, and the charming blushes that go with it."

His eyes fell to her open trousers. Chelsea's cheeks flamed. She ducked her head and began struggling with the fastenings. The knowledge that she was just as shaken as he enabled him to regain a measure of mastery over his own roiling senses.

"Here, allow me."

He crossed the room and stepped in front of her. Encouraged when she didn't shrink away, he went down on his good knee. He fastened the first trouser button, his knuckles deliberately brushing the damp curls.

His intimate touch mobilized her.

"How dare you," she hissed. Hands flying to his shoulders, she shoved him. *Hard*.

Desire weighing uncomfortably between his legs, he considered pretending to lose his balance and falling backwards, taking her down on top of him. Looking up into her ferocious face, he decided the ploy held too great a risk. In her present mood, she might very well kick him in the face. Or lower.

Gaining his feet, he asked, "As I have a vested interest in knowing, pray tell me, do you always attack your lovers after mating, like some sort of avenging black widow or praying mantis?"

She backed into the wall. "We were not . . . mating," she sputtered. "Besides, if I'd really wanted to hurt you, I wouldn't have missed when I kneed you."

"I shall bear that in mind for the future." He was so hot that he was sure the blood must be melting his veins.

"There shall be no future for us, Lord Montrose, so you needn't put yourself to the effort." Hands trembling, she struggled to retie the crumpled ribbon dangling from the tip of one silken curl. "You are never to come near me again, do you understand?"

For the span of a heart beat, anger surged through Anthony. Mastering it, he answered in a calm voice, "Perfectly, although I could point out that it is you who are in my home."

"Not for long." With a huff, she turned and marched toward the door.

"Very well, but there's no point in risking lung fever." He glanced to the open window where droplets of rainwater now dotted the sill. "At least permit me to escort you home."

He would instruct Masters to take the long route to wherever it was that she lived. Once her anger cooled, they'd finish what they'd begun in the swaying depths of his carriage. After the first fast, frenzied coupling, he'd bring her back here. Atop satin sheets, he'd make love to her slowly. Gently. Thoroughly.

"Not bloody likely." She turned the knob, opened the door, and stalked out into the hallway.

Thwarted desire gnawed at the edges of his patience. "Don't be stupid. The London streets at night are no place for a woman alone. Any number of mishaps could befall you, all of which you would find exceedingly unpleasant."

"I'll take my chances." She threw open the study door.

She collected her hat from a chair seat, then started for the window. Anthony came up behind her.

"Chelsea, be reasonable." He laid a restraining hand on her shoulder. "This is madness. If you won't allow me to see you home, then at least stay the night. This house has seven

bedchambers. You may have your pick of any one of them."
Including mine. "You can go in the morning."

"Lord Montrose." Her voice could have frozen fire. "You
promised that you would allow me to leave after I returned
the pearls. I have honored my promise." She stared at his
hand, still gripping her shoulder. "I only ask that you honor
yours."

Honor. She had him, and they both knew it. He had sworn
not to detain her.

"As you wish." Soldiering had taught him to recognize
when a strategic retreat was in order. He dropped his hand
and backed away. "At least leave by the front door."

"No, thank you." She strode to the window and reached
for the moored rope. Refusing to look at him, she took hold
of the swinging hemp and climbed outside, clearing the
ledge.

He raced to the window. Palms resting on the sill, he
leaned out, rain dampening his face. Watching her disappear
into the swirling mist felt like the hardest thing he'd ever
done.

The gentle shower was a steady downpour by the time
Chelsea gained the alleyway. Straining to see through the
peculiar yellow fog that had settled over the city, she held
her hands in front of her and hurried through the maze of alleys, praying she wouldn't lose her way. The rain that had
been collecting in the brim of her hat suddenly overflowed,
dumping its contents down her shirt collar. Cursing, she removed the useless article and threw it onto the cobbles,
grinding her heel into the crown.

"Damn you, Anthony Grenville! Damn you to hell." The
crack of thunder overhead nearly swallowed her choked cry.

What had she been thinking, accepting Lord Montrose's invitation to dine? No wonder he'd assumed she was no better
than she should be. Nor had her behavior proven otherwise.
She'd come close to submitting to him completely—and on
his dining room table, of all places! Her mother's spirit must
indeed be watching over her. If he hadn't called out her real
name, she would be ruined by now.

It was tempting to blame her wanton conduct on the wine, but, in her heart, she knew that her host's potent charm had been the true intoxicant. Well-traveled, intelligent, and witty, Lord Montrose was one of the few men she'd known other than her father whose conversation extended beyond fox hunting and the latest agricultural methods.

But she was attracted to more than his mind. Handsome, strong, and passionate, Lord Montrose—Anthony—embodied every knight in shining armor her romantic heart had ever conjured. He was Lancelot, Troilus, and Romeo all rolled into one. And, after a year of being solely responsible for managing a ramshackle estate, and an unruly younger sibling, it had been heaven to surrender her self-control. To let Anthony kiss and caress and tease her until she was incapable of forming a cogent thought.

But her life was far too complicated to admit anyone else into it. Particularly a devastatingly handsome rake with avowedly dishonorable intentions—and a fiancée. Tonight must be the last of their tête-à-têtes.

A crash sounded behind her, followed by what might have been a muffled groan. Heart pounding, Chelsea swung around, expecting to find a nightwatchman. Instead a large rat scurried from the overturned rubbish bin.

Shaken, she forged ahead, not stopping until she'd gained the alleyway to her house. There she braced her back against the fence and lifted her face to the starless night. Eyes closed, she let the rain wash over her, but not even the icy drapery of her drenched clothing could quench the fire burning inside her. Her previous two carnal encounters had been with a nervous boy and a lecherous man more than thirty years her senior. She'd begun to doubt that passion—true passion—existed outside of romantic novels. But, having experienced the wonder of Anthony's kisses, the magic of his hands, Chelsea was once more a believer. The mere memory of his hot mouth and long, sensitive fingers was enough to rekindle the pulsing heat between her legs. The last time she'd felt such fire, she'd been ten years old and in the grip of a raging fever. Then she had very nearly lost her life. In Anthony's arms, she'd very nearly lost her soul.

Perhaps she *had* lost it, along with her mind. Brutal honesty was the best—the only—antidote for what ailed her. And the disgraceful truth was that, during those magical moments in Anthony's arms, she hadn't simply set her problems aside. She'd forgotten them—forgotten Robert—completely. It was bad enough that she'd acted the harlot, shaming not only herself but her parents' memory. But to behave thus when her baby brother—the brother she was charged to love and protect—was kidnapped, perhaps even dead, was beyond shame. Beyond forgiveness. If—when—Robert was returned to her, she'd spend the rest of her life making it up to him. In the meantime . . .

What's happening to me? I used to be so responsible. So . . . controlled.

She hugged herself, fingernails gouging her numb upper arms. One thing was certain: she could, under no circumstances, risk seeing Anthony again. Thank God he had no idea where she lived.

Why was she standing out in the rain?

Anthony gripped the fence post, using his free hand to massage his smarting shin. Rainwater mingled with the sweat gathering between his shoulder blades. Chelsea was nothing if not fleet of foot, and she'd gotten a good head start by the time he'd surrendered to the impulse to go after her. Fortunately, he was well-acquainted with London. His hunch that she would avoid the main streets had proven correct, and it hadn't taken him long to catch up. Colliding with the rubbish bin that some idiot had placed in the center of the alley had been cursed ill-luck, but at least he'd managed to dive into the shadows before Chelsea had turned around. He also had managed to wrench his bad knee in the process.

At the other end of the alley, a gate opened. Anthony backed against the fence, keeping to the shadows. Pricking his ears above a distant peal of thunder, he could just make out the scraping sound of a hasp being lifted.

Chelsea's trim shadow finally disappeared inside the walled garden of a gray frame house. Anthony waited until he heard the gate screech closed before heading back. Not only had he seen her safely home, but he'd discovered exactly where home was. Tomorrow morning he would put that knowledge to good use, assuming he was reasonably ambulatory. Shifting his weight to his good leg, he hobbled toward the circle of yellow lamplight at the end of the alley. Racing over cobbled streets did not constitute an exercise regimen of which his doctors would approve. He knew from experience that there would be the Devil to pay tomorrow, but the lady was worth it.

Well worth it, he acknowledged, running a hand across his damp forehead. The musky scent of Chelsea's arousal fitted his fingers like a glove; the heat radiating from her had been scalding. Yet, when he'd unfastened his trousers, she'd stared down at him as though she'd never seen a naked man before. *Impossible*, he assured himself a moment later, recalling how her silken, courtesan's caress had brought him to the brink of his climax. Her confident carriage, her delightfully direct remarks, her boldness in dressing in trousers and becoming a thief—these were not the hallmarks of a shrinking virgin. He'd stake his uncle's fortune that Miss Chelsea Bellamy, despite her youth and erstwhile respectability, had amassed a fair share of worldly experience along with the baubles she'd purloined.

Did she have a ruined reputation waiting for her back in Sussex, along with her family's shambles of an estate? Was that why she'd left? It didn't take much imagination to see why the bold beauty would want to break free from a backwater like Upper Uckfield. By now she must be sick to death of assemblies, church bazaars, and the fumbling courtship of the local swains. What he couldn't fathom was why she seemed hellbent on seeing London through prison bars.

Thinking of the other men who'd had her set his blood to boiling. How many had succeeded where so far he had failed? One or two? Five? Ten? More than ten? Limping along Mount Street, he vowed he'd make her forget each and every one of them. He'd kiss and touch and taste her until the only man's name she could recall would be his.

The throbbing in his groin rivaled that of his injured leg, making him welcome the icy rain pelting his back. No other woman had ever affected him this way. Remembering the sensation of Chelsea's firm nipple beneath his tongue, he regretted that he hadn't taken the time to unfasten the tapes of her chemisette to discover how far the charming blush extended. Nor had he gotten around to removing her trousers to find out if her slim legs were as beautiful as the snug-fitting garment suggested.

But there was a great deal more to Chelsea Bellamy than a pretty face and long legs. The compassion in her eyes—and touch—when she'd asked him about Albuera had been genuine. Until that night, he had not spoken of the battle to anyone, relegating the painful memories to the dark recesses of his mind, where they served as ghoulish fodder for his nightmares. Fear, not stoicism, was behind his silence. To speak was to risk drowning his scarred soul in the deluge of anguish. But, looking into the turquoise pools of Chelsea's eyes, he'd felt his grief blunt to a manageable sadness.

Although he'd yet to bed her, he knew instinctively that the feelings Chelsea aroused in him were a world apart from the uncomplicated lust he was accustomed to sating. For the first time in his life, he wanted more from a woman than a casual coupling.

And, for the first time in years, he dared to hope that the peace he craved might be within his grasp.

Chapter Seven

Driving his curricle through Mayfair the next morning, Anthony allowed that his mind was anywhere but on the road. Fortunately even those who were unfashionable enough to remain in town after the Season rarely emerged from their residences before noon. At this hour, pedestrian traffic was limited to the milk maids, street vendors, and muffin men, all of whom were accustomed to darting clear of carriage wheels and horses' hooves.

He turned onto Mount Street, and a sudden sneeze sent him in search of his handkerchief. Bouquets of lilies, daffodils, poppies and, of course, roses, draped the carriage bench and floor. He'd even bought a bunch of blue forget-me-nots after deciding that the color reminded him of Chelsea's eyes. The flower seller had been speechless when he'd asked how much she wanted for the lot. Recovering, she'd haggled with cockney guile. Anthony had overpaid, not that he'd cared. What were a few more coins compared with the prospect of making love to Chelsea in a room filled with the heady scent of spring? The thought alone made him harden.

He drew the team of blacks to a halt beneath the shade of an elm tree. Bunches of flowers tucked beneath both arms, he headed for the gray house, his stride purposeful despite the limp. Eager, it didn't take long for his first polite knock to transform into a vigorous pounding.

Patience at an end, he dropped the flowers on the stoop

and clanged the heavy brass knocker. "Chelsea, I know you're in there. Open this door at once."

The hairs at the back of his neck prickled. Sensing he was being watched, he turned and glimpsed a capped head pop up from the other side of the stone wall. The boy hoisted himself to the top and swung his skinny legs over the side.

"Missus Bellamy b'aint at 'ome, guv."

Mrs. Bellamy. Anthony felt the force of those words like a fist slamming into his stomach. It had never occurred to him that Chelsea might be married. He contemplated the possibility that the rheumy-eyed goliath was her husband, and jealousy jolted him. No, it couldn't be. The brute was her butler and old enough to be her father. On the other hand, she did seem uncommonly devoted to him. He'd heard of husbands who sold their young wives into prostitution. Perhaps Jack was using Chelsea to do his thieving for him? The image of those gnarled paws groping Chelsea's lovely body brought Anthony's blood to the boiling point.

"How do you know this?" Anthony barked.

The lad pointed to the street. "I saw the big bloke flag down a hack and then they both got inside."

"How long ago was that?"

"'Bout an hour."

"I don't suppose you know when *Mrs.* Bellamy is expected back?"

"'Fraid not, sir."

No matter. She and the hulk would return sooner or later. Shielding his eyes with the edge of his hand, he looked up through the haze to the yellow ball of sun. Hopefully it would be sooner, before he dissolved, although he'd wait until Doomsday if need be. Damn, but he couldn't. He'd promised Phoebe a ride in Hyde Park later that afternoon.

He looked at the boy, still perched on the wall's edge.

"How old are you?"

"Twelve, sir."

Although small for his age, the child appeared intelligent and articulate. Anthony reached into his pocket and pulled out a half-crown.

Holding it out, he asked, "Tell me, do you fancy a chance to earn this?"

"Oh, yes, sir." He scooted off the wall's edge, landing at Anthony's feet. "What 'xactly do I have to do fer it?"

"Only to deliver a message. Do you know Grosvenor Square?"

The boy gave a brisk nod. "Me mum's cousin Jane works as a lady's maid in one o' the big houses there. Mum's taken me to visit 'er a couple o' times."

"You're hired." Anthony reached inside his breast pocket and pulled out one of his calling cards. "Go to number nine. Give this to the butler and say that Lord Montrose is detained and sends his regrets. Mind you say no more, no less."

The boy repeated the message, and Anthony handed over the card along with the coin.

"There'll be another one waiting for you if I'm still here when you get back."

His promise had the intended effect. The boy pocketed the money and sped away.

Anthony adjusted his coattails and sat on the crumbling stoop, heedless of the flowers. He wasn't accustomed to cooling his heels on anyone's doorstep, but there were some things in life worth waiting for. Last night he'd decided that Chelsea Bellamy was one of them.

Men!

Chelsea craned her neck out the carriage window and confirmed that they were still at it.

Jack shook his fist at the hackney driver, still seated on the box. "Five shillin's and not a ha'penny more."

The driver, red face working, scrambled down. "Five shillin's! Why that's bleedin' highway robbery. 'Tis ten or I calls the constable."

Oh dear. This is going to take a while.

Perspiration gathering beneath the sleeves of her black bombazine, Chelsea unpeeled her damp back from the tattered leather seat and scooted to the edge. Given the beastly heat, five shillings more made no difference to her. To a cockney, however, bargaining was a matter of honor. That point had been driven home earlier when she and Jack had visited Goldsmith's Row in Cheapside. A certain goldsmith, Tobbitt, was known to purchase valuables with no questions asked.

Before they set out, Jack had counseled her to leave the pearls behind. Depending on how they fared that day, they would either take the necklace back to Tobbitt or to another fence. Chelsea didn't know what she would say when the time came for her to produce it.

But, when she entered the goldsmith's musty shop, a more pressing concern supplanted that worry. Beetle-browed and bandy-legged, Tobbit had ushered them past dusty glass-topped counters to the storage area at the back. Drawing the curtain, he'd motioned for Chelsea to unwrap the scarf containing the jewelry. Without the pearls, the most valuable item was Anthony's gold timepiece. Even though he'd said she might keep it, she'd never felt more the thief than when she'd handed it over to the seedy little man.

"Can you sell it or not?" she'd finally demanded, hard-pressed not to snatch it back.

Still squinting over the engraving at the back of the case, he'd smiled, his teeth as yellow as the gold he dealt in. "Oh, not to worry, milady. Everything in London has a price—and a purchaser."

Even so, at first he'd offered them only fifty pounds for the lot. He'd finally doubled that offer, worn down by Jack's haggling and Chelsea's promise of more to come.

Just as baking inside this oven was beginning to wear down her patience. Like children, widows were expected to be seen—albeit rarely—and not heard. Were it otherwise, she'd pop outside and tell both Jack and the driver what to do with their five shillings. She slipped two fingers beneath her high collar and vowed that, if Jack didn't come for her within two minutes, she'd do just that.

At last he opened the carriage door and offered his hand.

Chelsea stepped out. Taking one look at his grinning face, she said, "I collect you settled the fare in our favor?"

He pulled a crown from his pocket. "Pretty, ain't she?"

"Really, Jack. You're incorrigible." Feeling less out of sorts, she settled the netted veil over her face, hiding her smile.

Looking out onto the world through webbing was an odd experience. Vibrant colors appeared ashen, objects were obscured. Crossing the street, she squinted at the large mound planted on her doorstep.

Judging by the dejected slant of the shoulders, it must be one of the urchins from the parish workhouse. Sometimes the older boys camped on her doorstep to beg for money or food. It was impossible not to pity their hollow eyes and gaunt, pale faces. Money was too precious to part with, but she always found something for them in the larder. No wonder they kept coming back.

At her approach, the mound straightened. This was no workhouse waif. She would know that cocksure smile and those broad shoulders anywhere.

Oh, God, no. It couldn't be him.

But it was.

Rising, Anthony leaned heavily on his walking stick. In his other hand he clutched a bouquet of bedraggled red roses. Literally hundreds more flowers wilted in the sunshine on her doorstep. Her heart lurched. No man had ever brought her flowers before.

"So, Miss Bellamy, we meet again." He shoved the flowers into her hand. "These are for you." He followed her downward gaze to the brown-edged blossoms hanging limply atop their sagging stems. "I assure you they were quite fresh when I purchased them."

Reminding herself that every inch of her, including her hair, was concealed beneath the black yardage, she did her best to imitate the cockney accent she'd heard all morning.

"I b'aint Miss Bellamy. 'Fraid you've made a mistake, guv."

"Oh, I don't think so." Before she could step away, Anthony snatched her veil and pulled it back. "Although perhaps you would prefer I address you as *Mrs.* Bellamy." He glanced to the key in her hand. "Aren't you going to invite me in?"

Defiant, she snapped, "As a matter of fact, I'm not. I don't want you anywhere near me or my house. Is that clear?"

Dark brows lifted. "My dear, felonious *Miss* Bellamy, must I remind you that you are hardly in a position to be selective about the company you keep."

"Hush!" She cast a nervous glance over her shoulder. Fortunately no one appeared to be about. "Someone might overhear."

He grinned, expression evil. "Indeed."

Jack appeared behind her, a cloth bag filled with the fruits of their marketing dangling from each wrist. He took a menacing step forward. "Stand aside and let the lady pass."

Anthony stood his ground. "Not until I've said what I came to say."

The two men eyed each other. Both stubborn as bulldogs, in another moment they would be brawling. A public spectacle on her doorstep could ruin everything. Chelsea stepped between them.

"Lord Montrose, I assure you that we have nothing left to say to each other."

He didn't budge. "Then you did yourself considerably more credit than I. Last night I did not have the wits about me to say even half of what I intended."

Jack's sudden, sharp inhalation filled the silence. Damn, the game was up. Chelsea's eyes dropped like stones to the flora blanketing her stoop.

"So, are you going to invite me inside or would you prefer that I remain out here to shout my message to the rooftops?"

"Oh very well, come in, but pray be quick about it." Hoping he wouldn't notice her trembling hand, she fitted the key to the lock.

A smile of victory plastered across his face, Anthony followed her inside, his limp more pronounced than she remembered. She wondered if she'd hurt him when she'd tried to knee him the night before. Suppressing the pang of guilt, she reminded herself that last night he'd displayed the cunning of a fox and the scruples of a street cur. And the charm of a snake. A dangerous combination.

Turning her back on him, she led the way to the parlor.

Standing in the humble little room, Anthony appeared even more imposing than he had in his own grand surroundings. And even more handsome. Despite the fact that he'd spent the better part of the morning baking on her doorstep, he managed to look very dapper in an amber coat and buff breeches. If she bent forward, she was certain that she would be able to see her reflection in his highly polished top boots. His only concession to the unseasonable heat had been to loosen his neck cloth and unbutton the top button of his shirt. A dark brown curl peaked out at the base of his throat. God, what an absolutely beautiful man. What a pity he was also an absolute cad.

"May I inquire where you've been all morning?" he asked.

"No, you may not." She jammed the rose stems into a chipped vase and untied her bonnet.

After leaving the goldsmith's, she and Jack had stopped at St. Mary-le-Bow. To get the "lay o' the land," Jack had said. The church was deserted when they entered, heels clanging on the stone flagging. Chelsea selected a back pew and knelt to pray. The sanctuary was pleasantly cool, the air scented with incense and cedar. But, as soon as she closed her eyes, images crowded her head. Robert, head bowed, confessing that he'd bought into the Army. Herself, marching across the library, demanding to know how anyone, even someone who'd gotten himself thrown out of Oxford, could be so foolish as to pay—actually *pay*—for the privilege of getting shot at. Robert on that final day, handsome in his officer's red coat and white breeches, waving one last time before he turned his horse and rode off. She'd refused to come outside, but he must have known she couldn't resist watching him from the window. But then Robert could always read her.

And so, it seemed, could Anthony. Heart-meltingly handsome in the candlelight, he'd known just how to kiss and fondle and coax until she gave in. Until she wanted to do things she hadn't names for. Until she came a hair's breadth from becoming the kind of woman respectable women shunned.

The torturous thoughts twisted about her brain like a tourniquet. She couldn't form a cogent prayer, let alone a cogent thought. Communicating with the Divine required peace, and she hadn't a shred left. She would have bashed her forehead against the pew in front of her if she'd thought it might help.

Now that Anthony was here, she'd much rather bash him. Or better yet, toss him out on his ear. She swung around, only to find him making himself at home in a bedraggled armchair.

"I suppose next you'll be expecting to stay for tea," she said with deliberate sarcasm.

He flashed her a brilliant smile. "Tea. What a delightful suggestion. I'll stay, of course."

A traitorous trill of excitement sliced through her anger. Only cold reserve would save her. Summoning her frostiest voice, she said, "Of course," and handed the vase to Jack. "Put these in water, please."

Scowling, he snatched it from her. "I don't knows as I should leave ye alone wi'—" he shifted to glare at Anthony "—*him*."

"I'll be quite all right until you return. Lord Montrose did not come here to ravish me, did you milord?"

"I believe I shall be able to hold myself in check this once."

Jack backed into the hallway. "If the blighter tries anything, scream."

As soon as Jack was out of earshot, she whirled on Anthony. "You followed me last night, didn't you?"

His eyes, unrepentant, met hers. "I did."

"At one point I fancied I heard someone in the alley, but I thought it was only a large rat. Now I see that I was right." Her eyes narrowed. "I don't care for being spied on."

"And I don't care for being burgled and lied to, so I suppose we're even."

Since there was no defense against the former charge, Chelsea concentrated on defending herself against the latter. "How dare you accuse me of lying."

Anthony stood and hobbled over to the mantel. "I suppose Jack really is your butler then?"

What was he getting at? "Jack is more than a servant. He's family really."

"Family?" He stared at her. "Care to elaborate?"

"Why are you looking at me like that?"

"The lad next door called you *Mrs*. Bellamy. I thought that perhaps . . ."

"That Jack was my husband?" She started to laugh but stopped when he didn't join her. Could he be serious? A look at his stiff expression told her he was. "Jack practically raised me. He's been like a second father to me, particularly since . . ." she paused, struggling to push the words over the lump in her throat. "Since my own father passed on." Grief descended on her chest like a lead weight.

All at once, his features relaxed. "I see."

A squeal outside provided her with the opportunity to turn away from him. Blinking back surreptitious tears, she crossed to the window and peered out. A cluster of ragged boys congregated around a polished crimson curricle. One lad, older and bolder than the rest, climbed up onto the velvet seat. Another followed suit, pulling on the fringed canopy.

Over her shoulder, she asked, "I suppose that perfectly vulgar vehicle is yours?"

"One of them." He came up behind her and laid a light hand on her shoulder. Even through the stiff twill of her gown, she could feel the heat radiating from his fingertips.

She faced him. "I really should chase them off before they do any damage."

"To the devil with the carriage. I've been up most of the night thinking about you . . . about *us*."

"Us?"

He braced a hand on the window sill and leaned into her. "You're all I can think about. All I want to think about." His other hand cupped her cheek, his thumb moving in small, slow circles. "I hoped you might feel the same."

A quiver of desire shot through her, settling in her belly. Her nipples tightened beneath the heavy fabric. A moment more of him touching her like this and she would melt in his arms like butter left out in summertime.

Annoyed by her body's treachery, she lashed out. "Think about you? Why should I want to? So far, in our blessedly brief acquaintance, you've shown yourself to be insufferable, conceited, deceitful . . ." She groped for fresh insults.

"Don't forget rakish." He grinned. "You see, I own my faults freely. As Wellington once said, 'better the devil you know.' "

Only Anthony could manage to be so infuriatingly charming while she insulted him. And so blasted attractive.

"You're . . . impossible." To her chagrin, she was smiling.

His hand moved to the nape of her neck, his fingers kneading away the stiffness.

"And you're beautiful, particularly when you're angry."

She looked at him askance. "Really, Lord Montrose, given your reputation, I was expecting more originality."

A roguish smile that might have belonged to the Devil himself stole about the corners of his mouth. "Give me time, Miss Bellamy, and I shall endeavor to produce something more worthy of you."

Time. The word jarred her. Only nineteen days to raise Robert's ransom. Now was the worst possible time to dally with a dangerously attractive viscount, one who seemed to have no other avocation than to follow her like her proverbial shadow.

Her smile dimmed. "You came here because you have something to say. I'm listening."

He took a deep breath. "Last night, when I said I've never wanted another woman as I want you, I meant every word."

Heat crept into her cheeks. And between her legs.

She shook her head fiercely. "Last night was a mistake. A terrible mistake."

He grasped her shoulders. "I don't believe that and neither do you. Last night can be the beginning of something wonderful for us both."

His fingers flexed on her shoulders. She looked up into his face, the eyes dark and earnest. *The beginning of something wonderful.* What did he mean?

It was impossible to think with him touching her. She tried to lift his hands. "What are you saying?"

"That I think I could make you happy. That I'd like to try." His hands went around her waist, drawing her against him.

Her stomach fluttered. This, him . . . It was all so perfect. Exactly how she'd envisioned her future husband proposing. But they were virtual strangers. Could it be that the night before had meant something to him beyond physical gratification?

He cupped her buttocks, crushing her into the cradle of his thighs. Even through layers of clothing, she could feel his arousal. "Last night convinced me that you and I will deal well together."

Deal well together? The words ripped the fabric of her romantic reverie.

She tried to step back. "What did you say?"

"That we will deal well together." He rubbed against her, his hardness probing her belly. "*Extremely* well, I should say."

And then understanding dawned. And with it, hurt, anger—and disappointment so bitter it nearly choked her. "Are you offering me . . . can it be that you want me to be your *mistress*?"

Smile lines bracketed bright, brown eyes. "You will find me a generous protector. I will keep you in style such as you've only dreamt existed. Gowns, jewels, a townhouse in London. Of course you must have your own carriage and driver as well. Do you fancy a box at the theater? Then you shall have it, provided it sits across from mine. I'll want to be able to look out and see you gazing back at me."

"Lord Montrose!"

He held up a hand. "No more titles and formality. From now on, you are to call me Anthony."

"Anthony, I'm—"

"Speechless, yes of course you are." He beamed at her. "After the ramshackle life you've been leading, it must seem too good to be true, but I assure you 'tis not." He brushed his lips against hers. "But first, you are to have done with mourning. No more black. I want to see my lady in bright colors from now on . . . or nothing at all." His fingers went to the jet buttons at the front of her gown. "Let me help you out of this hideous thing . . . now."

"Stop." She batted his hands and backed away, bumping against the window seat.

He was little better than Squire Dumfreys with his talk of gowns and jewels. Worse, because Anthony had made her want him. The night before he'd changed her from a child into a woman. He'd used gentleness and pleasure to destroy her defenses with the single, calculated aim of making her his whore. Didn't he understand how deeply he'd hurt her, how complete was her humiliation? She searched his face. Obviously not. But he would. He would.

"Lord Montrose, I am not your lady and you, most certainly, will never be my protector."

Anthony frowned. "What are you saying?"

"What I have been trying to tell you since you arrived. I will never consent to be your mistress."

His frown deepened. "Do you realize what you're giving up? Most women in your position would not take it amiss to be offered *carte blanche* by a viscount."

Such conceit. Such arrogance. What a snob he was, expecting her to be impressed by his title. "Then I suggest you offer it to one of them and leave me in peace."

He shook his head. "I thought you would be pleased."

"*Pleased!*" Needing to put some distance between them, she brushed passed him and crossed to the fireplace. "I assure you, Lord Montrose, I find nothing remotely pleasing in your revolting suggestion."

Hypocrite. Even with his true colors blazing, she wasn't sure what she wanted most—to slap him or to kiss him. Summoning all of her willpower, she did neither.

Facing the chimney, she dug her fingernails into the plasterwork mantel and added, "Why, you are practically a married man."

"That did not seem to bother you overmuch last night," he reminded her, an edge to his voice.

The taunt amounted to salting a very large, very open

wound. Emotions raw, Chelsea pivoted to face him. "Last night, I had drunk too much wine. Today I am perfectly sober, and I tell you that I find your offer loathsome, just as I find you!" *Liar.*

He advanced on her. "Loathsome, am I?" He stopped, so close that she could see the angry muscle working in his jaw. "You did not appear to find me so very loathsome when you were clawing at my back and arching against me."

"Kindly lower your voice." She peered over his shoulder to the open door. Fortunately Jack was nowhere in sight. Teeth set, she whispered, "Just because I forgot myself for a moment or two last night does not mean that I will agree to be made into a plaything to gratify your beastly lust."

"Lust went both ways," he roared, ignoring her shushing. "Or have you forgotten that you were the better part of naked and writhing in my arms. The way you moaned and begged for my kisses gave me the distinct impression you rather enjoyed them . . . among other things."

"Eh hem."

They both looked to the doorway.

"Yer tea's ready." Expression murderous, Jack plunked the tray down with a bang that set the contents rattling. "I'll bide in the kitchen." Over his shoulder, he cast Anthony a menacing scowl. "Meat cleaver wants sharpenin'." With that, he shuffled into the hallway.

Chelsea turned on Anthony, still lounging by the mantel. In his eyes Jack was only a servant and a rough-hewn one at that. But Chelsea had not exaggerated when she'd said Jack was like a second father. Jack's good opinion had always mattered to her. Never more so than now when, thanks to Anthony, it seemed she'd lost it.

"Now see what you've done!" She stabbed a forefinger toward the door. "Leave, *now*! I never want to see your face again."

"I'll leave, if that is your wish, but not until you've told me why you've just turned down my offer in favor of a life of crime." His dark gaze narrowed. "This may come as a shock since you find me so *loathsome*, but it has been my experience that most women would choose to satisfy my *beastly lust* over going to the gallows any day."

His steady gaze unnerved her. She looked away. "I prefer my independence."

He shook his head. "I know this much. You are no common thief. As I discovered the day you overtook my carriage, you're not even terribly good at it."

That was going too far. "Why is it that men always think they are the only ones who can *do* anything?" Chelsea raised a fist and punched the air. "I had everything under control . . . at least until you grabbed me and I dropped the pistol, a mistake I was careful not to repeat."

"Oh really. I suppose then that you were aware that I had my Manton tucked into my jacket pocket the entire time? Had I not been traveling with my fiancée and her mother, I would not have submitted so tamely to your demands."

Chelsea felt the blood leave her face.

His dark eyes blazed. "You little fool, you could have easily found yourself shot or . . . worse. You've not an inkling of the damage a bullet can do at close range. I've seen men, whole one minute, reduced to pulp the next."

She thought of Robert. What deprivations, what *tortures*, he'd endured by now, God alone knew. "Enough!" She covered her hands over her ears. "I shan't listen to another word."

"Oh yes, you shall!" Following her, he tugged her hands downward, clasping them in his.

If his intention was to break her, he'd succeeded. Chelsea pulled away and folded into the nearest chair. Elbows on her knees, she hid her face in her hands.

Stiffly, he went down on one knee beside her. "The day you robbed me, you weren't out simply for a lark, were you?" Gently, very gently, he drew her hands away. "Look at me."

She obeyed. How could he be so cruel one minute and so compassionate the next? She felt herself weakening. She wanted to trust someone. She wanted—needed—to trust *him.*

Misery weighed on her. It was hard to breathe but she managed to answer, "A life is hanging in the balance. My brother's life. Now please, *please*, don't ask me anything more."

"If your brother is ill, I shall be glad to pay for a physician to . . . ?"

A traitorous tear rolled down her cheek. She swiped at it. "No, you don't understand."

Gripping the chair arm, he got to his feet. "Then help me understand."

His kindness mastered her in a way that his anger couldn't. She rose and retrieved the ransom note from the writing desk.

He took it from her and quickly perused it. He looked up, eyes dark. "I knew you must be in some sort of trouble, but I never suspected anything like this."

She slipped the well-worn paper into her pocket. "Well, now you know. Robert has been kidnapped and I have fewer than three weeks to raise the rest of his ransom."

His eyes widened. "So you plan to continue burgling houses until you get it?"

She stiffened. That was precisely her plan, if one could call it that. Being confronted with the obvious truth that it didn't amount to much rankled. "Perhaps to you, Lord Montrose, with a title and fortune at your disposal, my actions do seem laughably absurd, but we humble folk must live by our wits."

He spread his hands. "Why didn't you just bring this before your magistrate?"

She couldn't resist a soft snort. "He and my father were political rivals, polite enemies if you will. I doubt he'd go out of his way to help me and, even if he did, he's . . . well, he's an idiot."

"I see. If you are determined to pay the ransom, why not take out a bank loan? Or are such conventional means of acquiring funds too lackluster for your tastes?"

He might be only trying to understand, to help, but his clipped tone and disdainful attitude grated.

"A loan. How clever of you," she flung back. "As a matter of fact, the possibility did occur to me, but the tiresome requirement to guarantee it caused me to abandon the notion."

Expression skeptical, he said, "But your family owns a sizeable portion of prime farm land."

"*Owned.* What isn't tied up in entail is mortgaged to the hilt."

"Surely you have some relations who could advance you the sum?"

She'd hoped for advice, perhaps even sympathy. Instead she'd received skepticism and reproach. And this pointless, tiresome interrogation.

She tapped a foot. "Only an aunt, in Kent. I can't imagine her widow's portion would come close to the three hundred pounds that remains to be raised. Even if it did, I couldn't ask. It's all she has to live on."

"A neighbor, then?"

Dumfreys. The despicable memories pushed to the forefront of her mind. She shivered.

"There was a neighbor, one of the local squires, who was willing to make me a loan, but I found his terms for repayment . . . unacceptable." She glared at him, daring him to press her.

He didn't. "I see." His features relaxed. "Then you'll just have to take the money from me." She tried to gainsay him, but he held up a hand. "To a spoiled, debauched aristocrat like myself, a few hundred pounds is a pittance. I won't miss it."

She was sure he wouldn't. But, if she accepted, she'd miss so many things—independence, self-respect, the ability to meet her own eyes in a mirror. No, she'd strip the houses of the *ton* bare before she'd let Lord Montrose take those priceless commodities from her.

"I love my brother dearly, Lord Montrose. He's all I have left." She squared her shoulders. "I may have turned thief to save him, but I'll not turn whore as well."

His mouth thinned into a grim line. "Your gratitude is touching to behold, but I assure you that my assistance is not contingent on your becoming my mistress."

Flustered, she sputtered, "Naturally, I thought that since you had only just . . . well, what I mean to say is that . . ."

His face registered disappointment and something else. Hurt, perhaps?

" 'Tis settled." He dismissed her attempts at apology. "But you should know that delivering the ransom provides no guarantee that your brother will be returned. You must prepare yourself for the possibility that he may already be dead."

She'd acknowledged that horrifying prospect but, to maintain her sanity, she'd swept it to the recesses of her mind. Now the effort to hold back her tears was making the back of her throat burn. Robert was the only family she had left unless one counted an aunt whom she'd met only twice.

"Are you certain you don't want to take this to the authorities? The Bow Street magistrate is a friend of my late uncle. He might be prevailed upon to—"

Her vigorous nod cut him off. She fitted a hand over her pounding brow. "Other than the letter, I have no proof that Robert has been kidnapped. For all intents and purposes, he is fighting under General Campbell on the Peninsula. I went to the War Office the day I arrived, but the clerk told me it would take at least a month to verify his location. By then it will be too late."

"I have a friend at Whitehall. Let me see what I can do to hurry things along. In the interim, if I cannot dissuade you from ransoming your brother, at least accept the money from me and allow me to deliver it when the time comes."

She shook her head in despair and frustration. Didn't he understand that there was no other way? "You read the kidnapper's instructions. If anyone other than me makes the delivery, he will kill Robert."

"Not if we find him first."

She started. "We?" Shock rolled over her.

He nodded. "Keeping your secret is one thing, allowing you to continue risking your life is quite another. You are bound to get caught sooner or later." She was about to protest when he added, "You can hardly deliver the ransom from behind prison bars, now can you?"

Perhaps he had a point. Fear and misery had banished passion, leaving her capable of rational thought. Even with her desire in check, his strength, his *maleness*, drew her. After a year of caring for everything and everyone, it would be heaven to step aside and let someone else—Anthony—wrestle her problems.

But she still didn't trust him. "I've told you that I won't be your mistress. What do you stand to gain from helping me?"

He shrugged. "A chance to redeem my reprobate past by doing a good deed."

She smiled. "Do you think one will suffice?"

"Probably not," he admitted, "but we all have to start somewhere." He collected his walking stick from the corner. "I shall call on you tomorrow morning at nine. By then I will have devised a plan for tracking down our kidnapper. In the interim, try to stay out of trouble."

He limped into the hallway.

She followed. "You barely know me. Why would you take such a risk?"

"Frankly, I'm bored."

"*Bored*." She gasped the word. "Do you mean that resolving my troubles means nothing more to you than a temporary refuge from boredom?" If it was true, she'd been a fool to think him kind.

He nodded. "I am to be married shortly. Until then, I have nothing to occupy my days—or nights, for that matter. A happy coincidence for you, Miss Bellamy, because I fully intend on locating your kidnapper and liberating your brother." He retrieved his hat from the console table. "As for your more *personal* concerns, you have my word as a gentleman that I shall make no romantic overtures until I receive your express invitation to do so."

She crossed her arms and glowered. "What exactly are you implying?" she demanded, although she suspected she already knew.

"Implying—nothing." He smiled. "Put simply, Miss Bellamy, I shall bide my time until you beg me to make love to you."

Chapter Eight

The acrid odor of death dragged Anthony back from the blackness. He opened his eyes. Twilight. The rain had ceased, but dampness enveloped the battlefield like a funeral shroud. Gunpowder, a fine mist, hung in the heavy air, burning his eyes.

Somewhere in the distance, an English voice called out, "Frogs've turned tail. It's cost us dear, but Beresford's held the field. We've won, lads! Victory is ours!"

Victory? His gravelly vision began to clear. At first, just shadowy shapes silhouetted in silvery light. Then . . . *Oh God.* Headless trunks, severed limbs, discarded weaponry. Above him the flap of wings, dark shapes circling. Bats? He craned his neck, looking skyward. Then he saw the crows, understood their hideous cawing. More on the ground, picking their way through the carnage. Feasting.

By God, they'll have to wait a while yet for me.

To live, he needed water and soon. His canteen was shot through but, a few paces away, the French cavalryman who'd tried to trample him lay silent and still next to his downed horse. He spotted his friend Peter's sword lodged in the beast's neck. But where was Peter? Surely Peter hadn't left him for dead? Unless . . . Squinting, he glimpsed a pair of familiar, low-heeled boots peaking out from beneath the horse's flanks.

Peter—what was left of him—was trapped beneath. The

beast's massive body sprawled across his torso and upper legs. And everywhere there was blood.

Anthony's stomach churned, then came up. Sourness scored his throat. Gagging, he turned his head to the side, chest heaving. He ran his tongue over his cracked lips, tasting gunpowder and vomit.

And guilt. To save him, Peter must have rushed the charging Frenchman. On foot, he'd managed to sever the horse's jugular, unseating the *cuirassier*. Judging by the unnatural angle of the Frenchman's head, the fall had broken his neck. But not before his dying horse had crushed Peter.

If God had any mercy, Peter was long dead. Levering himself on his forearm, Anthony inched toward his fallen friend. The least he could do was to keep Peter from falling prey to the scavengers, both the crows and the human looters who would surely follow. Eyes streaming and throat constricted, he shoved at the horse's carcass. When it wouldn't budge, he grabbed hold of Peter's arm and tried pulling him out. Twice thwarted, he ended by pummelling the ground, his smacking fists the only outlet for his grief and frustration.

Life, which had seemed so precious, now struck him as worthless; survival as the cruelest of punishments. If he lived, he'd not only lose his leg but his mind as well. It wasn't to be born.

His own rifle was long gone, but Peter kept a small pistol tucked inside his coat. Resolved, Anthony dragged himself to the other side of the horse. Panting, he shoved his hand into his friend's pocket. His sleeve caught the brim of Peter's rifleman's hat, knocking it off.

Chelsea!

He looked down. Confusion bubbled to the surface of his befuddled brain. What was Chelsea doing at Albuera, wearing Peter's blood-stained uniform?

Her lovely face was caked with gunpowder and dirt and her hair clung to her head in wet ropes. When she opened her eyes and stared up at him, apparently unharmed, he thought he'd die of gladness.

"Anthony?" Her face crumpled. "Save me, Anthony, before it's too late. Save me!"

"Chelsea!"

Anthony bolted upright, the echo of his scream still ringing in his ears. Sweat slithered down his naked body and, for a terrifying moment, he thought he was bleeding. Then he realized he was in his bedchamber, not Albuera, and that the wetness was only perspiration.

Shivering, he reached for the tinder box on the bedside table. Fingers clumsy, it took him several attempts before the wood splinter flared and he could light the candle. Amber sliced through the darkness, and he exhaled with foolish relief.

It had been more than a week since his last nightmare, quite an achievement. At one time, the terrifying dreams had been a nightly occurrence. Of late he'd been too preoccupied with a certain flame-haired felon to spare much thought, waking or sleeping, for demons. Until the day before when Chelsea told him in no uncertain terms that she wanted none of him. That she *loathed* him. Her scathing refusal had been humiliating enough. Now it seemed she must invade his nightmares.

He rose and put on his dressing gown, then carried the candlestick to his armchair by the window to await the sunrise. To attempt sleep would be not only pointless but dangerous, for he often returned to the beginning of the dream. Better to use the hour or so until dawn to mull over what he'd learned so far.

The previous afternoon he'd called on Reggie, who had a civilian post at Whitehall and owed him more favors than either of them could count. By evening, Reg had sent a courier with a message confirming that Ensign Bellamy had never reported to the Horse Guards. His corps had set sail for Lisbon without him.

So, it would seem that the boy had been abducted, but by whom and to what end? Five hundred pounds was modest recompense for saddling oneself with a hostage for a month. He massaged his throbbing temples. Could it be that the kidnapper was driven by a more insidious motive than simple greed? Revenge, perhaps?

Chelsea's father had served two consecutive terms as magistrate. Perhaps it was some convicted felon, now free,

who sought to wreak vengeance on the magistrate's only son
and heir? Timing the kidnapping would be child's play;
hamlets like Upper Uckfield were hotbeds of gossip. For the
price of a few pints purchased at the local pub, anyone could
have discovered the date of Robert Bellamy's departure. But
why move the ransom delivery to London? And why insist
that Chelsea deliver it in person?

Could Chelsea be the kidnapper's target? The more he examined the possibility, the more sense it made. He had no
evidence beyond his gut intuition, and yet he hadn't felt so
certain of anything since he'd urged Cole to mount the counterattack that had saved the day at Albuera. Robert Bellamy's abduction was nothing more than a ploy to lure
Chelsea to London where she would be alone and friendless.

Not entirely friendless. The kidnapper hadn't counted
on . . . him.

He must come up with some excuse to keep her close, to
guard her, without her suspecting. He combed his fingers
through his damp hair. She was the most intelligent woman
he'd ever known—and the most stubborn. It wasn't going to
be easy.

He'd have to hold himself in check. Another seduction attempt might send her fleeing from him—and into danger. He
would, he *must* control the hot flashes of desire that surged
through him every time she was near. How much easier restraint would be if their tongues had never mated, if he'd no
notion of how perfectly her lithe body fitted his or of how
generously the honey flowed from that hot, damp fortress
between her thighs.

If nothing else, hunting down the kidnapper would provide him with an outlet for his frustration. If he succeeded,
there would be no need to go through with the ransom delivery. To be required to do so would be highly inconve-
nient, for the thirtieth was also his wedding day. He had
declined to volunteer that small detail to Chelsea. Some
things were better left unsaid.

Less than three weeks to ferret out a felon, rescue a
hostage, and convince an independent hoyden that she

couldn't live without him. A tall order and not much time. Not much time at all.

He would be a candidate for Bedlam by then.

The cuckoo clock chirped its ninth and final note. Chelsea looked up from the shirred egg she'd been pushing about her plate. Where was he?

She went into the parlor, bypassing Jack on her way to the window. Wearing a calico apron and wielding a feather duster, he launched an all-out assault on the scarred surface of an ancient court cupboard. The cleaning rampage had begun the previous afternoon after Anthony had revealed her deception.

For the fourth time that morning, she peered outside, searching for a crimson curricle. But the street was deserted except for a tethered draft horse.

Jack came up behind her. "'E'll be here. Mark me words. Now eat your breakfast before ye turn into a scarecrow."

Slinking back to the table, she fingered a square of cold toast. Her nervous stomach churned, but eating would give her an occupation other than pacing. And, if her mouth were full, perhaps Jack wouldn't ply her with questions.

No such luck. He stomped into the dining room. She tore off a morsel of bread and crammed it into her mouth.

Fists planted on his hips, he demanded, "Perhaps ye'd be good enough to explain where ye got to two nights ago when ye was supposed to be upstairs nursing a chill?"

The years fell away. She was ten years old, and Jack had caught her pilfering the gingerbread that Cook had set out to cool.

Chewing, she answered, "It's something of a long story."

"I've plenty o' time."

She swallowed, the toasted bread sticking to the back of her throat like glue. "Very well. Do you recall that townhouse we hit in Berkeley Square?"

Jack bobbed an impatient nod. "Aye."

"It's Lord Montrose's."

"The viscount!" Jack stormed, dashing the duster to the ground. "But we robbed 'im a'ready."

She released a heavy sigh. "I know, I know. But, with the

Season at an end, his is one of the few houses that isn't cleared out and shut up. I'd thought to take just enough to make the rest of the ransom, then retire One-Eyed Jack, Junior for good. Unfortunately he came upon me in his study."

"I thought 'twas the butler who found ye?"

"That was a fib I told to spare you worry."

"Another fib." He snorted. "Very considerate o' ye. Go on."

"I made a run for the window, but my hat fell off and he saw that I was . . . that is to say, that I am, female." She blushed, recalling just how far Anthony had gone in exploring her femininity.

"And then?"

The remainder of the toast turned to crumbs in her nervous fingers. "He swore he'd turn me over to the Watch and then hunt you unless I returned the pearl necklace. I didn't have it with me, naturally—"

"Naturally."

"So I had to go back the next night." *Then stay for supper and, very nearly, breakfast.* "I never expected to see him again—" *That part was true enough.* "—but he must have followed me home. I was just as surprised as you when he showed up yesterday."

"Wi' flowers enough to fill a field," he reminded her.

"Well, yes, er . . . I suppose he wished to thank me for the necklace." Spicing the lie with a dash of authenticity, she admitted, "I did take my leave in rather a hurry."

Jack's gray brow rose. "Queer that he'd go outta 'is way to thank 'e for a bauble ye nicked in the first place." He shook his head. "He wants somethin', and it b'aint no pearls."

She picked up her fork and poked at her eggs. "I'm sure I can't imagine what you're insinuating."

Retrieving the duster, Jack shook it at her, emitting a small cloud of down. "I may 'ave but one peeper, but I b'aint blind. 'Tis plain the toff fancies ye. I saw the way he was sniffin' about your skirts like ye was a bitch in h—"

"That will do, Jack." She felt the telltale warmth creep into her cheeks. "I think you're forgetting that Lord Montrose is the next thing to a married man."

His look was all-knowing. "I didn't say he'd come to pop the question, now did I?"

No, but there was a moment yesterday when I was foolish enough to believe so.

Face warm, she replied, "As I told you yesterday—" *And last night, and twice this morning.* "—he's offered to help us find Robert."

He scowled. "Why should the likes o' him want to 'elp us?"

She pushed away from the table. "How should I know? He said something about being bored. I, for one, am not going to look a gift horse in the mouth."

The door knocker clanged, signaling the arrival of the *gift horse.*

"I suppose ye want *me* to answer that?"

She shot to her feet and raced into the parlor. "Yes, Jack, and do hurry."

Snatching a book, she curled up on the window seat, striking a casual pose. The door opened. Nose buried in the open pages, she strained to make out the low murmur of voices— Jack's hostile, Anthony's only slightly less so. Then Jack's heavy footfalls and Anthony's lighter ones were coming toward her.

Without looking up, she knew the exact moment that Anthony materialized in the doorway. A shiver of awareness shot down her spine, curling her toes.

He cleared his throat. "Good morning, Miss Bellamy."

She closed the book and looked up, patting away a feigned yawn. "Lord Montrose." Edging off the cushion, she struggled to smooth the nervous trill from her voice. "Can it be nine already? Faith, I lost all track of the time."

Behind Anthony, Jack rolled his eye.

Anthony removed his hat and stepped forward into a shaft of sunlight. His face was gaunt and there were bluish smudges beneath his eyes. His red-rimmed eyes. He looked as though he'd been up half the night and then some and it didn't take much imagination to guess what he'd been about. *Had it taken one woman or two?* she wondered, feeling ill. And stupid. What a fool she'd been to lie awake until dawn, her treacherous body aching with regret even as she'd assured herself that she'd made the right choice, the moral choice. The *lonely* choice.

Smile cool, he came to the point. "I trust you are ready to begin our venture?"

"As ready as I shall ever be," she answered with false brightness, vowing he'd never know how close she'd come to reconsidering—and accepting—his offer. Or what it had cost her to refuse. Remembering her manners, she added, "Pray take a seat."

Even reaping the wages of his debauchery, he was handsome as sin, the personification of her every fantasy. She bit her bottom lip. What right had she to passion—to fantasies even—when her only brother was likely to be enduring any number of unspeakable torments.

He sat on the sofa. "I have some news."

Chelsea's heart stopped. "What kind of news?"

Jack scowled from the doorway. "Ye'll want to be alone then."

"On the contrary," Anthony replied equably. "Pray join us. I want you to hear this too."

"Aye?" Jack loped into the room.

Anthony divided his gaze between them. "I checked with my source at Whitehall. Robert never reported for duty." He paused. "I'm sorry, Chelsea."

She sank down on the cushion beside him, shaking her head. "I thought as much and yet I suppose a part of me continued to hope that the ransom note was someone's idea of a cruel joke. At least now I know the truth." She managed a tremulous smile. "For that, I thank you."

"Don't thank me yet. There's a great deal of work to be done if we're to track down the kidnapper and rescue your brother before the month's end. Did Robert have any enemies that you know of? Perhaps someone he'd met at university?"

She shook her head. "Like any young man, he'd gotten into his share of scrapes, but 'twas mostly high spirits." She smiled in wistful recall of the misdemeanor that, a few short weeks before, had seemed a heinous crime. "He and some of his friends put a goat in an instructor's bed. Robert was sent down for his part in the prank, so I doubt the victim would have bothered with kidnapping him."

"A goat, you say?" Anthony threw back his head and laughed. The flesh around his eyes crinkled and, despite everything, Chelsea's heart fluttered. "Your brother sounds a fellow after my own heart. Anything else? Perhaps the father or brother of a girl he'd compromised . . ."

The fluttering stilled, replaced by indignation. Really, the rogue must think all men were cut from the same cloth as his lecherous self.

"My brother may have gotten into the occasional mischief, but he is a gentleman. I assure you, he would never compromise an innocent."

"Forgive me. I do not know him as you do," he replied, although she fancied there was skepticism in his voice.

Piqued, she crossed her arms over her chest. "Perhaps you'd better tell us your plan."

"One has only to examine the penmanship, the quality of the foolscap to know that the author of the ransom letter is no common criminal but a person of education—and means. Such a person would not devote a whole month to guarding a prisoner when, for a pittance, he could hire henchmen to carry out the deed."

From the corner, Jack gave a grudging nod. "Aye, 'tis the right o' it."

Anthony continued, "If we locate the lackey, chances are that, in time, he will lead us to your brother."

Almost afraid to hope, she said, "But London must be full of cutpurses and other villains." The sudden sparkle in Anthony's gaze brought home the hypocrisy of that statement. She blushed. "Where do we look for him or—them?"

"London taverns and gin shops have traditionally been fonts of gossip. I propose we start in Cheapside. We'll begin with those closest to the church where the ransom is to be delivered, then gradually expand our search."

" 'Tisn't a half bad plan," Jack conceded, eyeing Anthony with what looked suspiciously like respect.

Recalling the myriad alleys and narrow, snaking lanes with their profusion of tradesmen's shops, public houses, and tenements, Chelsea was skeptical. "Won't it be like searching for the proverbial needle in a haystack?"

Ignoring her, Anthony started toward Jack. "The East End is an alien world to me. If I am to infiltrate it, I shall require tuition." He held out his hand. "Will you give it?"

Jack regarded the proffered hand for a long moment, then clasped it. "For the young master, I'd make a pact wi' Satan hisself."

Anthony grinned. "I'll accept that as a yes."

Chelsea looked between the two men. A moment before they'd nearly come to blows and now they were behaving like two happy co-conspirators. It was all well and good that they were getting on, but she was beginning to feel shut out. Time to take charge.

She summoned her most rallying voice and said, "Now that we're all agreed, we'd better get started."

Both men turned on her. "*No,*" they said, in unison.

Anthony gained his feet. "Jack will accompany me. You, young lady, are going to stay put."

Indignant, she shot to her feet. "Don't be ridiculous. Robert is my brother. Of course I'm going."

"No, you are not."

To her shock, Jack agreed. "This is men's work. For once in yer life, yer goin' to 'ave to accept that you're a girl."

A *girl*. Chelsea felt as though she'd just been slapped.

"But Jack—"

"No buts. I've gone along wi' yer schemes in the past, but this time I'm puttin' me foot down." Jack stomped his large foot, and the floorboards beneath shivered. "His lordship and meself, we knows what we're about."

"But Jack, you and I, we're . . . partners." She searched his face for signs of softening.

"Now, lovey . . ."

He's calling me lovey. That's always a good sign.

"Ye've already shouldered more than any woman aught. There's naught more fer ye ta do. Is there, milord?"

Deflated, furious, she glared at Lord Montrose. Damn him, this was all his doing.

"Not a thing," he seconded, victory blazing from his brown eyes.

Chelsea felt her cheeks heat with anger. How dare Lord Montrose turn her own servant, her Jack, against her. "But—"

Jack cut her off. "We'll tell ye as soon as we knows somethin'."

"The very second," Anthony agreed, and it took all of her self-control not to slap the complacent smile from his face.

Jack laid a hand on Anthony's shoulder. "The first thing to be done is to get ye out o' them clothes. I've a cousin who owns a rag-and-bone shop by the docks. 'E'll see to it you're rigged out proper."

Anthony's hand flew to his starched cravat. "What's wrong with my clothes?"

Jack cocked his head and regarded Anthony. "Nuffin, if ye wants to be pegged as a member o' the Fancy as soon as ye crosses the threshold. 'Tis to the ale 'ouses we're 'eaded, not the bloody palace."

"Hm, you may have a point."

"And for Gawd's sake, mind your *h*'s, man." Stripping off his apron, Jack started toward the door.

Anthony tossed Chelsea a parting smile. "Have a pleasant day," he had the audacity to say before following Jack out.

A pleasant day, indeed. Chelsea's gaze stabbed his retreating back. For a former military man, Lord Montrose was woefully ignorant of one timeless truth—losing the battle was not nearly the same thing as losing the war.

Robert pulled himself up onto his elbows and stretched his legs. The chains connecting his manacled wrists to the wall rattled.

How long have I been in this dank prison? His last memory was of crouching down to examine a fellow traveler's horse that had thrown a shoe. A moment later, his head had exploded.

He awakened here, wherever *here* was. There were only two of them, the "traveler" and his accomplice, a brawny half-wit called Luke. They'd kept him blindfolded at first, and drugged. Eventually they'd removed the cloth, even allowed him a candle. Not that there was much to see—the straw pallet he now occupied, a chamber pot, and the pine table where he took his meals, such as they were. Of late, his repasts had dwindled to watered-down ale and barley bread. His once skin-tight inexpressibles hung loosely from his shrinking waist; with each day, he could feel his strength ebb. Perhaps it was his debilitated state that caused them to grow careless, for they often spoke in his presence. "Only a fortnight to go." "Why cain't we finish 'im now?" "Don't be a bleedin' idiot, Luke."

The door opened, and the "traveler," Stenton, swaggered in. He set a trencher of something foul-smelling and a mug on the table.

"Supper's served, me boy. 'Tis a bit late, but I'd business to attend. Better eat up while it's 'ot."

Propped against the slimy stone wall, Robert steeled himself to ignore the hunger gnawing at his belly. "I wouldn't feed that rubbish to my dogs."

Stenton snarled. "If I had me way, I'd feed *ye* to the dogs. After yer sister delivers the blunt, I may do just that."

Robert gave a bitter laugh. "If you believe that, you're a bigger fool than you look. My sister hasn't a farthing to her name." *Thanks to me*.

"Ye're lying!"

"Am I?" Defiance roiled through him. He glanced behind him to his red officer's coat, rolled up and serving as a pillow. "I used the last of our money to purchase my commission."

"*Liar!*" Stenton swept the edge of his arm over the table. The heavy pewter plate and tankard thudded to the packed dirt floor. He stepped over the muddy pool and advanced on the pallet. Robert braced himself.

Stenton lifted his boot and kicked.

Robert fell sideways into the filth, clutching his ribs. Pain, knife-sharp, spasmed through him. Knees drawn to his chest, he bit his lip to keep from crying out.

Stenton loomed over him. "For yer sake, ye'd bloody well better 'ope yer wrong. *Dead* wrong."

Chapter Nine

Transformed by a tattered frock coat, checkered trousers, and several blacked-out teeth, Anthony had spent the better part of the morning, afternoon—and now evening—with Jack, trolling the seedy taverns fronting Cheapside's crooked, cobbled lanes. The *pièce de résistance* of his disguise was a wooden crutch like those used by the Cripplegate beggars. Given the quantity of gin he'd imbibed, he was feeling the need to lean on it in earnest. The tattoo in his temples had begun beating a half hour before, as they were leaving pub number nine. Or was it number eight?

It was dusk when they closed in on the entrance to yet another timber-framed tavern. The lamplighter had yet to make his rounds. Anthony could just discern the faded black lettering on the wooden sign swinging from the jettied overhang.

"The Rutting Bull." Beneath the name, a benign bovine countenance, paint peeling, regarded them. "Looks more like an old milch cow to me." Glancing back at Jack, he asked, "Are you sure this is the same place the kidnapper mentioned in his letter?"

"Aye, I'm sure. The Bull's been around since I were a lad. Longer, most like." He pulled open the knotted pine door. "'Tis one o' a kind."

Over the past eight hours, Anthony had identified three immutable characteristics of East End drinking establishments—all the men were villains, all the women were fat, and all the liquor—rotgut. Despite Jack's optimism, he doubted the Rutting Bull would provide much in the way of novelty.

Following Jack inside, Anthony ducked, narrowly avoiding smashing his forehead into the low lintel. Straightening, he surveyed his surroundings through the hazy glow of the tallow candles lit throughout. With its low, timber-framed ceiling, wooden booths, and profusion of tapped ale kegs, the tavern looked much like the others they'd visited.

They pushed through the press of unwashed bodies and settled into a corner booth. Various metal objects, all with different and intricate configurations, hung on pegs from the plaster walls. Anthony leaned his crutch against the wall and reached up to pull one off.

"What the devil is this?" He held it up. "Looks like an instrument of torture."

Jack snorted. "'Aven't ye ever seen a tavern puzzle before?" He snatched it from Anthony's grasp. "This one's called Satan's Stirrup."

Anthony frowned at the tangle of metal. "What has Satan to do with it?"

Jack shrugged. "How should I know?" He deftly disconnected the interlocking pieces. Expression triumphant, he looked to Anthony. "Now that I've done the 'ard work, think ye can put it back together?"

"Of course," Anthony snapped. It was bad enough that Jack had matched him drink for drink and somehow managed to stay sober. He'd be damned if he was going to give way over a blasted toy. "I've maneuvered a company of a hundred strong through Spain and Portugal. I think I can manage a puzzle."

Jack crossed his beefy arms and leaned back. "'Ave at it, then."

Struggling to recall the original configuration, Anthony picked up one of the metal pieces and began searching for its mate.

"Give up?" Jack's good eye gleamed.

"Of course not." Anthony frowned at the pieces scattered across the table, willing his muzzy head to clear.

Jack singled out two seemingly unrelated sections and fitted them together.

Anthony looked up from his attempt to shove the curved ends of the horseshoe through a narrow band. "Beginner's luck."

Jack snorted. "There's only one beginner 'ere, and I b'aint him."

Ears burning, Anthony watched him shift the orientation of the pieces until the open end of the horseshoe slid easily through the narrow oval.

"Why do I have the impression you've done this before?" he asked after Jack handed him the completed configuration.

Jack winked. "Compared wi' pickin' locks, this is child's play."

He was about to ask if Jack would consider going for two out of three when a flaxen-haired barmaid sidled up to them.

She peered over Anthony's shoulder to the novelty. "Good show, luv. That's one o' the 'arder ones."

Jack guffawed, and Anthony's ears grew hotter.

"Welcome to the Ruttin' Bull. Me name's Bess." She fixed her smile on Anthony. "Name yer pleasure."

Anthony lifted his gaze and found himself staring into two enormous breasts, the brown areolas visible through the thin muslin blouse. Looking at the barmaid's big, soft body, he couldn't help remembering how perfectly Chelsea's small, shapely breasts had fitted his palm.

"Brandy," he said, throat dry.

Bess slapped her well-padded thigh. "Brandy indeed! You'm mortal funny."

Blundering fool! First the blasted puzzle and now this. "Make that two gins."

"Ye've got 'em . . . and anything else ye wants."

Laughing, she turned and headed for the bar, wide hips swaying. Waiting for the tavern keeper to pour the drinks, she struck up a conversation with a gaunt, dark-haired man leaning over the rail.

Anthony nudged Jack. "Look over there. See the man talking with Bess?"

Jack glanced over his shoulder. Turning back, he asked, "The gallows-faced chap wi' the scar across 'is brow?"

Anthony nodded. "He's been watching us ever since we arrived. I've the oddest feeling I've seen him somewhere before, but I can't think where."

The man inclined his shaggy head, his dark, beetle's gaze locking with Anthony's. Anthony reciprocated the salute just as Bess returned with their drinks. She served Anthony first, the side of her breast grazing his cheek when she set down his glass.

"Is there nothin' else I can offer ye?" she purred. She nodded toward a flight of crooked wooden stairs. "I've a room upstairs. 'Tis a steep climb, I'll grant 'e, but ye'd not be sorry."

Summoning a raffish smile, Anthony said, "Pretty Bess, ye tempt me sorely, but we're 'ere on business. As a matter o' fact, we was wonderin' who yer mate might be?"

She batted her sandy lashes. "Jealous already, ducks?"

"Mebbe. Mebbe a tad curious, too? I've some business that wants conductin', and he seems a—"

"Sharp shaver," Jack supplied.

Brow furrowed, she fingered a flaxen curl. "Name's Stenton. Bob Stenton. But his be a bad business. Take a piece o' free advice from her that knows and steer clear o' 'im."

"Why is that?" Anthony rubbed his jaw, wondering if the barmaid knew in just how "bad a business" Stenton engaged. If so, she might prove a useful ally.

Lips pursed, she shook her head. "Cain't say as I know." She was lying, Anthony was certain of it. Her next words confirmed it. "Besides, I b'aint no snitch."

"Best see that ye keep it that way."

Following her frozen gaze, Anthony looked up into Stenton's gold-toothed grin.

Eyes downcast, she fiddled with her apron. "Blimey, you knows me better than that, Bob."

Stenton grabbed her chin and pulled her to him, ignoring her yelp. "See you keep it that way. T'would be 'ard t'earn a livin' wi' that pretty nose o' yers slit."

Anthony leapt up beside her. "'Ave done, mate. Bess and me was just 'avin at a bit o' slap an' tickle."

"Oh well then, 'tis no 'arm done." Stenton released the girl, who was shaking visibly. "There's plenty o' Bessie to go about, ain't that right me girl?"

The barmaid's voice quavered. "Right o', Bob."

"O' course I is. Ain't I always." Cackling, Stenton slapped her buttocks. "Now fetch us a round and be sharp about it." He gestured to a bull-necked man sitting at a table in the corner, shoulders hunched. "Come o'er 'ere, Luke. There's gentlemen I wants ye to meet."

Luke. Why did that name ring familiar?

He couldn't recall. But, if Luke were anything like his mate, he likely wouldn't think twice before slitting his own mother's throat and selling his sister if the price were right. Thank God he'd insisted Chelsea stay behind. Sliding his hand toward the tavern puzzle, his fingers closed around the horseshoe. Forged of solid iron, if brought up hard between the eyes, it would render a man unconscious.

"Me name's Bob. Bob Stenton." Helping himself to a seat, Stenton held out his hand, the nails jagged and dirt-rimmed.

"Pleased to meet ye, Bob." Anthony released the puzzle piece and clasped the proffered hand. "Me Christian name's Tony, though these days me mates call me Toeless. The big bloke is me mate, Jack."

Stenton's gaze shifted between Anthony's crutch and Jack's patched eye. Looking back at Anthony, his thin lips cracked into a smile, revealing a gold front tooth.

"You looks like two blokes who've tangled wi' Boney an' come back the worse fer it."

Stenton's conclusion was a logical one. These days former soldiers from the enlisted ranks flocked to British cities, swelling the already substantial beggar population. Maimed, ill of body—and often of mind—pensionless, they seemed to Anthony a constant reminder that he ought to try harder to count his blessings.

"Aye," Anthony replied, tone sober. "Lost the better part o' me foot at Albuera. Jack here lost his eye."

"Albuera, was it? A bloody business that."

Anthony's scowl needed no coaxing. "And a good deal bloodier than it need 'ave been."

"'Ow so?"

Anthony was about to launch into his carefully crafted tirade when Stenton's associate loped over. The ruffian took the seat opposite him, and Anthony immediately recognized the sloping brow, flat nose, and slack mouth. His every muscle tensed. Luke was undoubtedly the same man Anthony had fought on Westminster Bridge a few nights before. The gaze, meeting Anthony's from across the table, was blank.

For now. Who knew when Luke's recollection of that night might surface. If Anthony were found out, Robert Bellamy would be a dead man. And he doubted either he or Jack would stay healthy much longer.

Jack's elbow, crashing into his side, returned him to the task at hand. Taking a deep breath, he continued, "Jack and me served in the Fourth under Cole. Safe and dry we was wi' orders from the top t'old back. But no, this infantry captain, Grenville were the bloody bastard's name, decides to play the 'ero and talks Cole into advancin'. I was one o' the first to go, sent out wi' a patrol of skirmishers. 'Twas less than an hour later that I felt the kiss o' the cannon." He paused for effect. "The ball landed square on me foot."

Stenton shot a wad of spittle onto the dusty floor. "Bloody lousy luck."

"Luck be hanged." Warming to his story, Anthony smashed a fist onto the table. "'Twas the work o' that devil, Grenville. 'E got off wi' barely a scratch and shipped 'ome to lick 'is wounds. Came into his uncle's blunt and lands, too, while blokes like me an' Jack must beg our bread or starve."

"Calm yerself lad." Reaching across the table, Jack slapped Anthony's shoulder. Catching Stenton's eye, he shook his head. "Poor blighter. Can't seem to forget that, 'twere it not for Grenville, 'e'd be a whole man. I'm afeared 'e'll do 'imself an injury one o' these days."

Stenton scratched his stubbled chin. "Ye sound like a man wi' an axe to grind, Toeless."

"That I am. Fortunate for me, I've me nest egg tucked

aside, though I'd wager the lot for the chance to dish up 'is lordship's just deserts."

"I might be able to 'elp ye settle the score if ye're interested. How bad d'you want this Grenville bloke?"

Anthony and Jack exchanged glances.

A moment later, Anthony replied, "Bad enough as I can taste it."

"Dependin' on how big your *nest egg* is, Luke and me might be able to arrange fer the good captain t'ave a l'il accident."

A subdued Bess returned, served their drinks, and hurried away. Luke cupped his glass in both hands and lapped, gin and saliva trickling down the side of his round face. Still no sign of recognition.

Encouraged, Anthony went on, "Accident, pshaw. Where'd be the gain in that? Way I see it, the bastard owes me a pension, and I aim to collect."

Stenton rubbed the gold tooth with the edge of his thumb. "'Ave you a plan?"

"Aye, that I 'ave. Grenville's family is even richer than he is. What do you reckon they'd do if 'e was to disappear sudden like, the night afore his wedding, no less?" He paused. Seeing Stenton's blank look, he supplied, "Why, I think they'd dig deep into their pockets to get 'im back, that's what."

"A kidnapping!" Stenton's eyes glowed. "What'd you say to me and Luke lendin' a hand, for a share o' the take?"

Now was not the time to appear overly eager. Anthony curbed his impatience. "That depends. Ever done this sort o' work before?"

Stenton flushed. His heightened color emphasized the milky whiteness of the scar slicing through his brow. The next thing Anthony knew, the tip of a knife was pricking his Adam's apple.

"Ask anyone hereabouts and ye'll find there's not a finer cutpurse than Bob Stenton nor a grander bully than L'il Luke."

Eyeing the proximity of the tavern puzzle, Anthony held up his hands. "Peace, friend. I meant no 'arm."

Stenton's anger died as quickly as it flared. Tucking the blade back inside his boot, he confided, "Me and Luke pulled off a like job a'most a fortnight ago."

"Ye don't say?"

"Aye." He picked up his glass and dragged the gin noisily through his front teeth. "Me *employer* wanted a boy kept outta the way for a month. The lad were passing through the Downs on 'is way to London, so 'twas a bit tricky. Luke hid in the bushes and I stood by the roadside and pretended me horse 'ad throwed a shoe. The lad, bein' green as a leek and a proper soldier boy, stopped to 'elp. Luke came at 'im from behind wi' a rock." He smiled. "I reckon ye can fill in the rest."

"He's not . . . ?" Anthony held his breath.

Stenton smoothed his greasy hair over his ears. "Naw, no reward for a dead man. He were out cold, so we trussed 'im up, stuffed a sack o'er him, and slung 'im in the cart. Since then I've been tempted more'n once to finish 'im off, but me employer wants 'im kept alive until the sister delivers the blunt. After that it's . . ." He drew a forefinger across his throat and made a low, gurgling noise.

Careful to keep his tone conversational, Anthony asked, "How much longer 'ave you to keep 'im?"

Stenton's thin lip curled. "'Til the thirtieth. I b'aint ne'er worked so 'ard in me life. Me employer gave us some powder to put in his food to make 'im sleep. At first it did the trick but he must be gettin' used to it now because he's a proper handful."

"A month is a long time to hold a man," Anthony commiserated. "Where d'you keep 'im?"

Stenton's eyes narrowed, receding further into their cavernous sockets. "What's it to ye?"

Anthony shrugged. "Just curious is all."

"'E's safe and snug nearby, 'ave no fear. If ye're willing to make it worth our while, there's room for one more."

Anthony pretended to prevaricate. "All right," he said at length.

Stenton raised his glass. "To partners."

To my luck holding. Anthony took a bracing swallow of his drink.

Stenton polished off the rest of his gin, then swiped his mouth on his coat sleeve. "How much d'ye reckon Grenville's kin'll part with?"

Anthony traced the rim of his glass, recalling his latest bank draft. "Two thousand, easy."

Stenton's eyes bulged. He leaned back and folded his arms across his chest. "We split it fifty-fifty."

Anthony knew that the thief expected him to haggle. To keep up appearances, he countered, "Sixty-forty, my favor o' course."

Stenton didn't hesitate. "Agreed. Now tell us, what's the plan?"

"Grenville roosts at Number Twelve Berkeley Square. 'Is bedchamber's on the second floor, third one from the right."

"How do we get in?"

Fortunately Anthony had anticipated the question. "I've a friend who works in the kitchens. I'll make sure she leaves the back door unlocked. Wait 'til the 'ouse's dark, then make your move."

"What if he b'aint there?"

"He'll be there. War's turned 'im timid. Won't go out after dark. And I 'ave it on good authority 'e takes a drop o' laudanum before bed."

Stenton drained his glass and wiped his mouth with the back of his hand. "When do we make our move?"

"The twenty-ninth."

"Luke and me's got expenses. We'll need a few quid to tide us o'er."

Luke paused from making a thorough excavation of his left nostril. "Aye, to tide us o'er."

Counting on Stenton's greed, Anthony had come prepared. He reached into his pocket just as a drunken shout rang out.

"Look, we've got a girl 'ere, and she's a beaut!"

Anthony stared in horror across the room.

Chelsea, face flushed and shirt torn, struggled to free herself from brawny arms. Her cap lay crushed on the floor and hairpins hung loosely from the braid shimmering over her shoulder.

"Let go of me, you big oaf!"

The seaman dipped a hairy hand inside her shirt. "Not so fast, luv. First I'll see if yer other pap be as soft and sweet as this 'un."

Murderous rage thundered through Anthony. He shot to his feet, grabbed his crutch, and shoved through the jeering crowd.

"Let go of her . . . *now*."

The sailor's gaze fixed on Anthony's crutch. He sneered. "And if I don't, who's goin' to make me?"

Anthony squared his shoulders. "I am, as a matter of fact."

The seaman's thick lips twisted. Shoving Chelsea to his companion, he raised his fists. "Go to, then."

"Very well." Anthony tossed his crutch to Bess in the gathering crowd and raised his fists.

Shouts of "A ring! a ring!" went up as the spectators moved back to make room. Anthony's opponent was more than twice his size and, Anthony felt sure, would have no qualms about enlisting the aid of his mates if he began to lose. When the night was over, all he asked was to be left one good arm to apply to Chelsea's backside and a knee to throw her over.

Jack stepped between the sailor and Anthony.

"If ye want the lass, ye'll 'ave to deal wi' me as well."

The seaman's fists dropped like anchors. "Peace, friend. I didn't mean no 'arm."

Freed, Chelsea darted to Anthony's side. He looped an arm around her and steered her toward their table.

He shoved her down onto the bench between him and Jack. "If we get out of this alive, I'm going to throttle you."

From across the table, Stenton's brooding gaze rested on the front of Chelsea's torn shirt. "A bit flat upstairs, but a pretty piece all the same. Lemme guess—your doxy?"

Chelsea's mouth fell open but, catching Anthony's glare, she clamped it closed. Turning back to Stenton, Anthony nodded.

Stenton's slow smile raised the hairs on the back of Anthony's neck. "Fact is, in these parts we believes in sharin'. Sort o' like a fambly, right Luke?" Stenton jabbed the brawny man in the ribs.

Snorting, Luke repeated, "Aye, like fambly."

"An' like a fambly, we shares all the little necessities o' life. Everything a body needs—food, drink . . . wenches." Stenton's grin widened, baring long, yellowed canines. "Take me meaning?"

Fear trickled through Anthony. He remembered the Spanish peasant girl he'd found after Barrosa, huddled in a ditch, clothing torn, eyes . . . *blank*. Part of the English victory celebration, she'd been passed from one drunken soldier to the next until she'd finally fainted.

He swallowed. "Aye, that I do." He slipped a hand inside his breast pocket and pulled out his knife, yet another item he'd purchased for the occasion.

Chelsea gasped. Two stragglers congregating nearby scrambled away, but Stenton didn't budge.

Hoping he'd not have to produce the pistol in his pocket, Anthony clenched the knife hilt. Lowering his voice to a hiss, he said, "Now take my meaning—anyone who lays a hand on the girl answers to me and—" He plunged the point into the table. "—*this*."

Out of the corner of his eye, he glimpsed Chelsea flinch. Jack tucked an arm about her.

Stenton faced him over the quivering blade. "I wouldn't 'ave pegged you as the type to fling your life away for a wench." He turned to Luke and snickered. "Faith, it must be luv."

That last remark acted on Anthony like a bullet striking bone. Beneath the table his free hand fisted, and he itched to plant it in Stenton's leering face. And Chelsea? He'd never gone to such lengths for a woman—let alone a woman he hadn't bedded. He didn't know what he wanted most—to pulverize Stenton or to carry Chelsea upstairs to Bess's bed.

But, before he did either, he had to save her. He forced his features into a bland mask. "I admit I've grown fond o' the trollop, despite 'er snorin' and fartin'."

Jack chuckled, and Chelsea's cheeks flamed.

Stenton studied her. "Talented is she?"

Anthony feigned a yawn. "Oh, she's not wi'out a trick or two, I'll give 'er that, but she'd be poor sport for a lusty bloke like yourself. Besides, soon you'll be able to hire all the whores in Covent Garden, if you've a mind." He looked between the two henchmen, then at Chelsea, who was gnawing on her bottom lip. "Are you and your mate prepared to walk away from the chance o' a lifetime fer one *flat-chested* girl?"

"'Tis a lot o' blunt." Stenton's gaze sharpened. "On the other hand, like they says, a bird in the hand's worth two in the bush."

"Which reminds me . . ." Anthony reached inside his coat pocket for the worn leather purse. He tossed it to Stenton, who caught it. Coins jingled.

Stenton weighed the purse in his palm. Loosening the string, he fished out a sovereign and bit down on the edge. Satisfied that the coin was solid gold, he stuffed the purse in his pocket.

"Very well. The blunt goes wi' me, and the slut wi' you." He wagged a finger at Chelsea. "But, if she darkens the door o' the Rutting Bull again, she's fair game. Agreed?"

Concealing his relief, Anthony stood. "Agreed."

Chelsea rose from the bench. Stenton's gaze slid over her. "Tall for a woman," he muttered. "A bloke I know is always babblin' about a tall, ginger-pated wench."

Anthony felt himself grow cold inside, but he mustered a cheeky grin. "I feel sorry for him, then. This one's more trouble than she's worth."

He grabbed Chelsea and slung her over his shoulder like a sack of meal. There was a whoosh as the breath rushed from her lungs.

"Come along, Ginger," he said in a carrying voice. "'Tis a sound beatin' for you, then to bed."

Ignoring her shrieks, he bore her toward the door to wild shouts of approval and a bevy of bawdy advice.

"'Ave at 'er, Toeless!" The seaman, apparently bearing no lasting ill-will, lifted his tankard in a salute.

"Always wanted to play bitch and 'ound wi' a redhead."

"Ne'er bedded a Long Meg, meself. Get a leg o'er for me too, lad."

It was working. They were halfway to the door. Playing to the crowd, Anthony squeezed Chelsea's buttocks. Another round of cheers went up—and a pathway to the exit cleared.

She responded with a kick and a string of colorful curses. "Why you friggin', bloody . . ."

He shifted her to his other shoulder. "Hem, your vocabulary is definitely . . . *comprehensive*. Shall I consider that last remark a request?"

In answer, she pummeled his back. Weathering the blows, Anthony reached the door and stepped outside, Jack bringing up the rear.

Chelsea yelled, "Jack, make him set me down."

Jack cast an apologetic look at his mistress's upturned head. "If I was ye, Miss Chelsea, I'd be glad 'is 'ands was full."

Out of earshot from the tavern, he set Chelsea none too gently on her feet. Glaring, she grasped the lamppost to steady herself.

Face flushed, braid unraveling, she jammed a finger in the vicinity of his chest. "Was that . . . that humiliating display *really* necessary?"

Now that she was safe, Anthony's fear exploded into full-blown rage. He couldn't recall when he'd been this angry at a woman. Never, he decided.

"You dare to question *my* actions. Why, that's rich." He took a menacing step toward her until her back was pressed against the post, and she had no choice but to withdraw her wagging finger. "Idiot! Willful, impertinent baggage."

The lamp's mellow glow pooled over her, illuminating the stark fear in her wide eyes. The sight kindled in him a dark, savage pleasure.

She licked her bottom lip. "Anthony, I didn't mean to cause trouble. I just—"

He sunk cruel fingers into her shoulders and shook her. "Trouble was the day you were born, lady." Several ragged, wraithlike shapes floated by in the fog, but Anthony ignored their stares. He shook her again. Hard. "What the hell were you thinking to follow us here?"

Gasping, she sputtered, "I d-didn't t-think—"

"You've got that much right. Can it be that you're too pea-witted to realize what nearly happened back there?"

"I only w-wanted to help—"

"Me to my grave, more than likely. Didn't I tell you to stay put, that it would be *dangerous* for you to come?"

"Yes, but—"

"No buts." He steeled himself to ignore her trembling lower lip and his need, which was rapidly rising. "I've a mind to teach you a lesson you're not likely to forget."

"That's enough." Jack laid a restraining hand on Anthony's arm. "She was ever an easy bruiser."

But the storm was over. All Anthony really wanted was to take her in his arms, gently this time, until her trembling ceased. Until *his* trembling ceased.

He'd stopped shaking her, but her teeth still chattered. From fear, he realized. Fear of him.

Sickened, he released her. She flung herself at Jack, burying her head against his chest. Anthony would have given the world to change places with the giant.

Chest heaving, Anthony turned away. His trembling hands, no longer instruments of threat, hung at his sides. "If I leave bruises, 'tis no more than she deserves and a great deal less than Stenton would have done."

"Oh, I b'aint such a bad sort." Stenton stepped out of the shadows and into the yellow circle of lamplight. The hazy glow glinted on smooth metal.

Anthony glanced over his shoulder and saw Jack shove Chelsea behind him. Satisfied, he turned back to Stenton. "Don't tell me you missed us already?"

Smiling, Stenton handed Anthony the knife. "Ye forgot this."

Anthony's fingers curved about the handle. "'Twas meant for you to keep. A gift." *A reminder.*

Stenton's gold tooth was the only visible feature of his shadowed face. "Thank ye, but I've no shortage o' me own."

Scraping the side of his boot against a sharp-edged cobble, he added, "Yer a man o' secrets, b'aint ye, Toeless?"

Sweat gathering between his shoulder blades, Anthony fingered the knife. A sword would serve him far better but no doubt he could hold Stenton off long enough for Jack to get Chelsea safely away. "All men have secrets."

"Secrets is all well and good . . . to a point." Stenton's smile broadened. "Then they can get downright . . . *dangerous*."

Anthony returned the smile. "Is that a threat?

The henchman shrugged. "A friendly warning, is all. The last bloke who played me false wound up in the Thames as fish food. I'd 'ate for that t'appen to you. Bess'd ne'er forgive me."

Chapter Ten

Nine Days Later

Anthony refolded the newspaper that, for the past hour, he'd pretended to read. Rolling onto his side, he pulled himself up on one elbow and looked over at Chelsea. Dressed in his amber and brown footman's livery, her spectacular hair concealed beneath a powdered periwig, she lay on her stomach in the center of the Oriental carpet in his study. As usual, she had her nose buried in a book. Today it was a novel by Fanny Burney. She was too engrossed in it to notice his open stare.

The only thing that engrossed him these days was Chelsea.

After leaving Stenton standing on the street corner nine days before, Anthony, Chelsea, and Jack returned to Anthony's house.

Seated behind his uncle's polished mahogany desk, Anthony had confessed, "Stenton and Luke assaulted a friend of mine a few nights ago. Stenton fled, but I tangled with Luke on Westminster Bridge. He didn't appear to recognize me tonight, but we may not be so lucky the next time. Jack, can I count on you to lead the watch?"

Ensconced in Anthony's favorite armchair, Jack had snorted. "I were up to 'ook and snivey when ye was still 'avin' yer arse wiped."

Anthony grinned. He was beginning to understand where

Chelsea acquired her sometimes colorful vocabulary. "Good. I'll take the midnight to dawn shift when they'll be least likely to spot me. We'll need a third person as well, someone they haven't met yet, who can mingle freely at the Bull without arousing susipicion."

Jack scratched his jaw. "Like who, milord?"

Anthony girded himself, unsure of how Jack would react to joining forces with the law. "I'll go to the Bow Street justice first thing in the morning. There's a runner, Mugglestone, whom my late uncle used on occasion. I'll request him to assist us. Between the three of us, we should be able to shadow Stenton and Luke's every move."

Chelsea had been subdued during the ride home but now her brow crinkled in a frown. "The three of us? You mean four, of course."

Anthony regarded her over the tips of his steepled fingers. She was determined but then so was he. And he had a plan. "I have a special role in mind for you."

She softened her scowl. "What kind of role?"

He drew a deep breath. "Strategist."

"Strategist?" Jack echoed.

Chelsea was studying him with suspicious eyes. "What exactly do you have in mind?"

"You know your brother better than anyone. You're certain to be the best judge of how he's likely to react when we barge in. You're also the only one who would know any special words or phrases that would convey an underlying meaning to him and yet remain undetected by Stenton."

"I see," she said, but her voice was skeptical.

Now came the sticky part. "The next few weeks are critical. We must be prepared to strike at any time—day or night. You'll move in here, of course."

"The 'ell she will." Jack's ham-sized fist crashed down onto the top tier of a delicate pie-crust table, nearly knocking it over. "I'd sooner give 'er o'er to the Devil than see her turned into a fancy woman by the lecherous likes o' ye."

"Don't be ridiculous," Anthony snapped, secretly annoyed by Jack's acumen. Chelsea would indeed become his "fancy woman," but not yet. Not until her brother was safe, and she too was out of danger. "I'm going to pass her off as my footman."

"Footman!" She sprang from the sofa. "What has fetching your slippers and lighting your cigars to do with rescuing Robert?"

"Footman be 'anged," Jack thundered. "Come along, Miss Chelsea. We're done for 'ere." He stomped toward the study door, grabbed the knob, and turned it.

The door wouldn't budge.

Jack swung around. Face contorted and fists dangling at his sides, he growled, "Unlock the bleedin' door."

Anthony slipped the key into his coat pocket and rounded the desk as Jack advanced toward him. "Not until we are in agreement."

He looked beyond Jack to Chelsea. Face drained of color, she stood by the locked door, worrying her hands.

He turned back to Jack. "She'll be far safer in a house full of servants than she would be on her own."

"Aye. Safe from everybody but ye."

"Don't be ridiculous. Everyone will think she's a boy. Were I to be seen anywhere near her, my servants would swear I'd turned pederast. Hardly the reputation a man wants bandied about London." In a whisper, he added, "After the caper she pulled tonight, do you really trust her not to follow us again?"

That final argument won Jack over.

Chelsea came around eventually, although he suspected she'd agreed to the ruse mainly to keep he and Jack from killing each other.

The first day they were awkward with each other, tiptoeing around the scattered shards of their fractured trust. Then the discoveries began. He preferred dogs, the bigger and sloppier the better, while she was a confirmed cat lover. They were both passionate about horses. Purple was her favorite color, but she'd never dared to wear it. Riding to hounds wasn't just a bore; it was cruel, she maintained. He admitted he'd never thought beyond the sport, but he'd wager she'd look splendid in purple. Like him, she preferred sitting on the floor to the furniture. And, of course, they both hated spinach.

Chelsea, he was learning, was inordinately easy to be with. She didn't care about the usual things—social position, money, clothes that seemed to obsess the other women he knew. When he was with her, he felt under no pressure to impress, to charm, nor even to control. He had only to be himself. After years of wandering, he felt as though he finally were coming to some understanding of who that person might be. Chelsea, however, remained very much a mystery.

"Tell me about your life before you came to London," he asked suddenly. "Your home, your family."

A pained look stole over her face, and he immediately regretted his tactlessness. Her parents were dead; her brother kidnapped. Of course she wouldn't want to dredge up childhood memories.

"You don't have to answer. Forget I asked. We'll talk of something else."

He reached for her, then remembered himself and pulled back. By tacit agreement, they never touched, although he consumed countless hours making love to her in his mind.

"No, that's all right. I don't mind." She marked her place, then set the book aside. "What do you want to know?"

He shrugged. "Nothing in particular. Whatever you'd care to share." *Everything. Absolutely everything.* "What were you like as a little girl?"

She laughed, and the soft trill reminded him of the tinging sound that crystal wine goblets made when they met. "A holy terror. Next question."

He decided to avoid mentioning her brother. "Your parents, were you close to them?"

She nodded, expression once more sober. "Very. To Papa especially."

He'd guessed as much. It was absurd but he felt almost . . . jealous. "What was he like?"

Tracing the carpet pattern with her forefinger, she replied, "Scholarly, kind, impractical sometimes but always loving. The best of fathers."

"And your mother?"

Her thoughtful gaze met his. "She was kind, too, but in a different way. Serene, I suppose. And beautiful. I always wanted to grow up to be like her but then I suppose I never tried terribly hard. Father adored her but then we all did, Robert especially."

Her eyes clouded. Suddenly he wanted to be the one to banish those clouds, to lead her back into the sunshine. More than he could remember wanting anything. Or anyone.

"I don't know," he said, summoning a lazy smile. "You strike me as kind." His gaze drank in the purity of her pro-filed features, the elegant column of her throat, the grace of her slender hands folded beneath her chin. "Beautiful, certainly."

She looked away but not before he glimpsed the pink creeping into her cheeks. "Isn't it a bit early in the evening for blandishments, milord?"

He smiled. "I'm relieving Mugglestone at midnight, so this is my only chance."

Already the runner had proven his worth. On his first day of employment, he'd tracked Stenton and Luke back to Newton Street in St. Giles. It seemed the two felons were holed up somewhere in the Rookery, a labyrinth of crumbling tenements, decayed mansion houses, and makeshift shanties. Stenton and Luke could be holding Robert in any one of a hundred or so nooks and crannies. Equipped with a wad of banknotes that Anthony replenished daily, Mugglestone was busy cultivating spies from amongst the dwellings' numerous occupants. Soon, Anthony was convinced, he would locate their hiding place, and they would move in to rescue Robert.

In the interim, Chelsea would remain in Anthony's house. The constant contact was pushing his fragile self-control to its limit. He'd never spent an evening, let alone nine of them, closeted with a beautiful woman and not made love to her. He was certain to be shoring up all kinds of character and fortitude but it was hard, bloody hard, when she was so appealing, so *near*. Yet the friendship they were forging was a precious gift, the trust they'd rebuilt too fragile to test. Yet.

He smiled at his beautiful tormenter. Toying with the braiding on her jacket, she looked completely guileless. Completely adorable.

"That was as honest a compliment as they come," he continued, vowing never to let her know—at least not entirely—what a potent effect she had on him. "And, to prove I'm an evenhanded fellow, I'll ask you where you inherited that temper of yours."

She looked at a loss. "I honestly don't know," she finally admitted, and they both laughed. "What about you?"

"I come by my temper honestly." He winked. "Mother's half French."

"Tell me about *your* family."

He shrugged, feeling his spine stiffen. "There's not much to tell. Father's a typical English gentleman. Staid, conventional." *Disapproving, mainly of me.* "A bit bellicose when he's taken too much port but otherwise not a bad sort, I suppose."

"Have you any brothers or sisters?"

"I have . . . *had* two brothers. They . . . uh, died years ago."

"Oh, Anthony, I'm so sorry."

Her lovely face registered the same sympathy—the same empathy—he'd seen when she'd coaxed him into talking about Albuera. Once again he found himself melting. And confiding.

"Alex was a puny fellow but the sweetest three-year-old imaginable. Ethelred—that's our elder brother—"

She screwed up her face. "Ethelred?"

"Named after Father. He died the year I went to Eton. Smallpox epidemic."

"It must have been hard, being away from home and not having the chance to say good-bye?"

She was far too perceptive. Even he hadn't fully realized how much it hurt to talk about his brothers, even after all these years.

He shifted his shoulders, trying in vain to loosen the tautness. "I have a sister, Hortense. She's older than I am—six-

and-thirty. Lives in Horsham with her husband and their brood of five."

"It must be nice for you, having family so close?"

"I see them once a year, at Christmas. We correspond occasionally. Infrequently, really. Otherwise . . ." He stopped, shocked to hear the bitterness in his voice.

"Oh, I see."

She couldn't possibly, but he let it go. How could someone reared in a nurturant cocoon such as the Bellamy household comprehend the glacial politeness that, in his family, substituted for true affection?

But who was he to criticize? Wasn't he about to continue the family tradition of practical, loveless marriages? With one exception. His children would know that he loved them. He swore it. Until then, the only constant in his life was the warm, vibrant woman at his side.

The hallway clock struck five, and Chelsea got to her knees. "I'd better go."

"Must you?" He knew she was only going belowstairs and yet he felt oddly . . . bereft.

She stood. "I'm to help in the kitchen and, later tonight, to help Chambers serve. It seems our *lord and master* has invited some very important guests to dine."

Alarm bells sounded. Inside his head, a familiar voice hissed: *Tell her, idiot. She's likely to find out in a matter of hours anyway.*

"My parents, as a matter of fact," he admitted, talking over the voice that was cursing him for a coward. "What happened to the footman who usually serves?"

"Geoffrey?"

He nodded although, apart from his valet and butler, he'd never bothered with learning his servants' names.

She drifted to his desk. He sat cross-legged on the floor, watching her. Was it his imagination or was she as reluctant to leave as he was to let her?

"He's abed with the gout. You really should think about hiring more servants." The corners of her mouth turned up in the impish smile that he'd come to love. "*Real* ones, starting with a secretary." She gestured to the piles covering his desktop. "What is all this anyway?"

Inside him a storm was raging but he only shrugged. "Investment reports, old newspapers, account ledgers. No doubt a few stray invitations on the upper stratum."

"Hem." She walked to the door. "I'll see you at dinner, then."

"Chelsea?" He gained his feet and was beside her in an instant. "Don't wait at table tonight."

Her brows lifted. "Why ever not?"

"It's a small party—" He caught himself, and added, "—just family. Chambers can manage. Make some excuse, say you have the headcold."

"Don't be silly." She pushed open the door and his heart plummeted. "Tonight is my first dinner party as your footman. I wouldn't miss it for the world."

The dinner bell clanged. Chambers, Anthony's ancient butler, limped toward the parlor to announce that dinner was served. Alone for the first time in hours, Chelsea looked about the chandelier-lit dining room. The last time she'd been in this room, she'd ended the evening by nearly surrendering her virtue—and her heart. She took a deep breath. Just thinking about that night made her knees tremble and her heart skip.

She forced her thoughts to the present. The sideboard was crowded with covered dishes as was the linen-draped table. No simple family meal, but a feast. Did the Grenvilles always dine so lavishly or was tonight a special occasion?

The rustle of skirts and a girlish giggle interrupted Chelsea's thoughts. Anthony's mother? Surely not? Chelsea folded her hands behind her and waited for the door to the adjoining parlor to open.

Anthony, restored to his customary elegance in starched white neckwear, russet jacket, and nankeen breeches, stepped inside. Even though they'd been living in each other's pockets for more than a week, she still couldn't control the tiny thrill that tripped down her spine every time he entered a room. For a few precious seconds their gazes met.

He looked quickly away. Then she noticed the pale, elegant blonde on his arm. And the pearl necklace hanging from the girl's slender, white throat.

The fiancée. Chelsea's heart slammed into her stomach. *Just family*, Anthony had said. Seething, Chelsea watched the girl's high forehead for the telltale flicker of recognition.

There was none, and she relaxed fractionally. Telling herself that no one would recognize her—as One-Eyed Jack *or* Chelsea Bellamy—in her livery and wig, she studied her rival.

Lady Phoebe's porcelain complexion was tinted with pink, not ashen as it had been when Chelsea had sighted her down the barrel of a pistol. Almond-shaped slate blue eyes, a delicately molded nose, and small rosebud mouth testified to centuries of breeding. And beauty.

She's everything you're not, heckled the voice inside Chelsea's head.

"Oh, my lord, you are wickedly droll," the girl drawled, slipping into the chair that Anthony held out.

Chelsea suppressed the urge to retch. She turned her attention to the two middle-aged couples completing the party. A fortyish, fair-haired woman disengaged her arm from that of a stout, balding gentleman and slipped into her seat. She might have been Anthony's fiancée twenty years hence, so close was the resemblance. The second pair was a petite woman with Anthony's brown eyes and aquiline nose and a florid-featured man in an ill-fitting frock coat.

When they were all seated, Chambers plucked an uncorked champagne bottle from a bucket of shaved ice and began making the rounds.

The stout gentleman—Lady Phoebe's father?—grinned and lifted his glass. "To the betrotheds. May this blasted wedding business be over with as quickly as possible so that you two can get on with the business of married life."

"Huzzah. Well-spoken, Tremont."

Around the table, glasses clinked. Chelsea's heart sank. *They're celebrating Anthony's wedding*. No wonder he'd tried to discourage her from serving. She'd known he was to marry, but somehow she'd relegated that event to the shadowy—and distant—future. Tonight's celebration brought home that it was not only inevitable but imminent. Numb, Chelsea couldn't seem to move. She stood, stiff and still, as though the soles of her buckled leather shoes were rooted to the floor.

"Serve the vichyssoise," Chambers hissed, nudging her toward an unwieldy china tureen.

She hefted the tray and started toward the table. Hovering, she dipped the silver ladle. The tureen was full and soup splashed over the sides. Fortunately the guests were too absorbed in their conversation to take notice.

"I say, did you know that Lord Ambrose returned from his expedition to Greece last week?" ventured the florid-featured man—Lord Grenville? "He and Elgin brought back enough artifacts to fill the British Museum's coffers and make themselves richer than Croesus into the bargain."

Around a mouthful of champagne, Lord Tremont replied, "Yes, and word has it he's keeping a king's ransom in Greek and Roman coins in his house."

Ransom. Chelsea's ears pricked, and she held her breath. A moment later she released it, reminding herself that she no longer needed to steal. Anthony would pay Robert's ransom——as well as deliver it—should their rescue attempt fail.

"He's hosting a supper party at Vauxhall to celebrate his success," Lady Phoebe's mother trilled. Tapping her spoon against the side of her bowl, she seemed oblivious to Chelsea laboring to fill it. "I assume you've all received invitations?"

"He's let one of the pavilions." Lady Phoebe's voice was animated. "He's even promising to have *fireworks*!"

Tracing the gold rim of his champagne flute, Anthony said, "Delightful to be sure, but I've no plans to attend."

"Oh, Anthony." Lady Phoebe's tone skirted a whine, and Chelsea had the unkind urge to slap her pretty, pale face. "Everyone who is still in town shall be there."

Anthony's smile thinned. "In that case, I shan't be missed."

"Really, Anthony, how can you be so churlish?" This time

the reproach came from his mother. "To deny Phoebe this small pleasure."

Anthony's voice hardened. "I deny her nothing. She is free to go. I am sure Reggie can be prevailed upon to escort her."

Chelsea dunked the ladle into the thick broth once more. *He doesn't love her. She . . . bores him.* For the first time since supper commenced, Chelsea's spirits lifted.

Phoebe's voice trembled. "Go with my *brother*!" She turned to her mother. "I would be a laughingstock."

"Hush, dearest," Lady Tremont soothed. Her steely gaze locked on Anthony. "What fustian, Montrose. You simply must attend. If Phoebe were to be seen without you, the *on dit* would be you'd jilted her. The gossips would have a field day."

"They usually do." Anthony's laugh was tinged with bitterness. "And yet they will look mightily foolish after we are wed."

An awkward silence descended. Chelsea finished serving and stepped back.

"'Tis such a pity that hateful Bonaparte is still at large; otherwise, you might honeymoon in Milan as Tremont and I did," Lady Tremont lamented at length.

Lady Grenville's slow smile was reminiscent of her son's. "Indeed Beatrice, and yet an autumn honeymoon in the English countryside can be charming as well."

Lady Tremont sniffed. "I suppose. I trust the arrangements are all made?"

Lord Tremont lifted his empty glass. "Egads, they had better be with the thirtieth just over a fortnight away."

The thirtieth.

Chelsea felt an invisible fist plow into her abdomen. On her way to set down the tray, she halted mid-step. The thirtieth was the day Robert's ransom was due. Anthony had promised to deliver it should they fail to foil the kidnapping. How could he possibly plan to keep that midnight appointment when the thirtieth was his *wedding night*!

The answer was simple. He couldn't. Chelsea looked to Anthony, silently beseeching him to say something. Anything. But he only stared straight ahead, a bland smile pasted onto his face. His stranger's face.

He won't even look at me. Tears burned the back of her eyes, clogged her throat, weighted her chest until she could barely breathe. And then the room began to reel. And the tureen began to slip.

Phoebe shrieked. "My gown.. . . you've ruined it!"

For a second, Chelsea just stared at the shards of pottery, potatoes, and cream covering the Aubusson carpet. Then, cheeks flaming, she fell to her knees and began scooping.

Phoebe pulled at her puffed sleeve, globby with soup. "Bother the carpet. Someone get this off me."

Chelsea jumped to her feet, then stood helplessly, her hands full of the muck.

Lady Tremont's eyes snapped. "Don't just stand there. *Do* something."

"Bloody good fortune she wasn't scalded," Lord Tremont remarked, delving into his soup, "though never did quite grasp the point of serving the stuff cold."

His wife glared. "Really, Tremont, you do make the most irrelevant observations."

Chambers' wrinkled face flushed, hurried forward with a wet cloth.

"My apologies, milady." He turned anguished eyes to Anthony. "In my sixty years of service, nothing like this has ever happened." To Chelsea, he barked, "You, get to the kitchen. Fetch water and a brush and don't dawdle."

Chelsea didn't have to be asked a second time. She turned and fled.

Lady Tremont finished blotting Phoebe's sleeve and resumed her seat. "Where is that footman?"

"I have a feeling he may not return," Anthony replied, picking up his champagne flute.

Sipping his smuggled champagne, presiding over his plentiful table, gazing at his beautiful—if somewhat soppy—fiancée, he told himself that he had everything a man could possibly want. So why did he feel as though his entire world had just caved in?

He'd meant to tell Chelsea about the wedding date, of course, but in his own time and in his own way.

*Who do you think you're fooling? You didn't want her to
find out at all.*

Puffed with pride, he'd all but convinced himself there
would be no need to make good on his promise to deliver the
ransom. Surely the savior of Albuera could manage to rescue one hostage, guarded only by a two-bit felon and his
half-wit accomplice?

It was obvious that Chelsea didn't believe so. The memory of her look of shocked betrayal would stay with him for
some time.

Still flushed, Chambers started to clear away their bowls
to make room for the next course.

Taking advantage of the bustle, Lady Grenville laid a
hand on Anthony's arm. "Why not offer Phoebe your escort?" she whispered. "It would mean so much to her."

"It is but one night from your life," Lady Tremont chimed
in. "Surely at your young age you can spare it."

Around a mouthful of roll, Lord Tremont said, "Take the
advice of a man with twenty-odd years of marriage under his
belt and give way now. They'll only pester you 'til you do."

This time Anthony made no attempt to smile. "No offense, sir, but I don't intend on spending my married life
under the cat's paw."

Lord Tremont guffawed. "No man does, my boy. No man
ever does."

Knees weak, Chelsea made it down the back stairs to the
kitchen where the rest of the servants were still at dinner.

A pie-faced scullery maid popped up from her place at the
end of the long pine table. "Can I 'elp ye?"

"Sit ye, Lettie." The cook, a pig-faced matron, tugged the
girl back down. "By the looks o' 'is trousers, I'd say 'e's already helped hisself."

Raucous laughter rose. Face aflame, Chelsea followed the
sea of sly gazes to her breeches. A large dollop of cream
crowned the crotch. Wishing she might join the pile of ashes
in the fireplace grate, she hurried to the sink.

God, what a bloody fool I am. She grabbed an empty
bucket and started cranking. She who had always prided

herself on her level head had been deceived by a handsome face, a lying tongue, and a practiced pair of hands.

She dipped a cloth in the water and began furiously scrubbing herself. Touring East End taverns, staking out the kidnappers' lodging, arranging Robert's rescue—to Anthony, all were nothing more than components of an elaborate game. Hadn't he said as much himself? "Frankly, I'm bored," he'd answered when she'd pressed to know why he would help her after she'd insulted and refused him.

Emotions—anger, humiliation, confusion—rushed her. She threw the balled cloth into the bucket, and water sloshed over the sides. Anthony was toying with her. He'd used her tragedy, her growing dependence on him, as a means to seduce her. What a dolt she was not to have seen through him before now. The man was a self-confessed rake. Preying on trusting women was what rakes did, after all. The past nine days, he'd worked hard to charm her, to win her trust. God help her, he'd nearly succeeded.

Nearly? Earlier in his study she'd very nearly bared her soul to him. Now she had to face the hard truth: she was perilously close to falling in love with the cad.

She thought of how he'd avoided her gaze after his future father-in-law blurted out the wedding date, and fresh anger bubbled. He wasn't just a liar; he was a coward, too.

She might be a dupe—Anthony's dupe—but she was no coward.

Her chin snapped up. She must forget Anthony. Only then could she focus all her energy, all her *intellect*, on saving Robert. Somehow she had to raise the rest of the ransom money. Her time—and Robert's—was rapidly running out. A plan, a solid one this time, was what she needed. Not only must it be solid but fool-proof.

Her thoughts flitted to the dinner conversation she'd just overheard. *A king's ransom in Greek and Roman coins . . .* What was it the goldsmith, Tobbit, had said? *Everything in London has a price—and a purchaser.*

Anthony was adamant about not attending the Vauxhall affair. Even so, he was invited. No doubt his invitation was lying about somewhere. Perhaps it was on his desk in the study?

She left the bucket in the sink and headed back upstairs, ignoring the curious stares that followed her.

The dining room doors were ajar, an artifact of her hasty escape. Tiptoeing past, she caught the scraping of cutlery and muted conversation. Consuming all that food would take hours more. Plenty of time.

Unlike the servants' area, the upper floors were well-lit, and she easily found her way to the study. She cracked open the door and peaked in. Empty.

Slipping inside, she closed the door behind her and went to the desk. The invitation must be somewhere amidst the clutter. Drawing the lamp closer, she began sifting through. Like excavated ruins, the most recent papers were closest to the top. At last she came across a likely candidate. The gold-embossed foolscap looked expensive and the scrollwork "A" could easily stand for Ambrose. *Eureka.* She broke the seal.

Montel, Fifth Marquis of Ambrose, requests the pleasure of your company at . . .

She'd present the invitation and slip inside with the other guests. Somehow she'd find out where the coins were, filch one, then leave. In a day or so, she'd take it to Tobbit. It would be difficult—and dangerous—for him to fence, but then such a treasure was likely to be worth thousands. She'd seen the gleam of greed in his eyes. He was certain to take it from her, especially when all she required were a few hundred pounds to complete the ransom.

It was a bold plan, a desperate plan, but what choice had she? After tonight's revelation, she'd be a fool to place her brother's life in his lordship's fickle hands.

She stuffed the note into her pocket and stepped into the hallway. Resisting the urge to look into the dining room one last time, she headed for the foyer. Her hand was on the brass doorknob when the tears started.

Anthony Grenville, you can take all your fine promises and go straight to the devil.

Chapter Eleven

Dressed in Anthony's livery, Chelsea turned the corner from Bond to Oxford Street. After one-and-twenty years spent in the country, she found London's fashionable shopping district, with its beveled glass shop fronts, paved streets, and elegantly appareled patrons, as exotic as any foreign city. It virtually throbbed with vitality and untried pleasures.

Robert would love this.

The familiar dull stabbing pain landed in her chest. While she was free to roam, even to enjoy herself, her brother was still a captive. And Anthony, the man to whom she'd entrusted Robert's rescue—his very *life*—had betrayed them both.

After decamping from Anthony's house the night before, she'd returned to Mount Street. Thankfully Jack was snoring on his cot in the pantry; otherwise he would have taken one look at her tear-streaked face and dragged the truth from her. By the time she'd quit the house that morning, he'd already left to relieve Anthony at the Rookery.

Dear Jack. There was one man whose good intentions were beyond suspicion. But Robert was her brother. Saving him was her responsibility.

She'd strolled the Mayfair streets for more than two hours, Anthony's invitation tucked in her pocket. *Can I really do this?* she'd asked herself, followed by *How can I not?*

By noon, she was resolved. She turned away from a bookseller's that beckoned and instead headed for a cluster of clothing shops at the end of the street.

Five well-dressed young women, bags and boxes stacked at their feet, congregated beneath a painted wooden sign that read "Maison Valen." More purchases were heaped on the seat of a wrought iron bench. Two brawny footmen, foreheads gleaming, ferried packages back and forth between the sidewalk and a gilded carriage parked across the street.

Behind them in the shop window, several examples of the modiste's skill hung on dressmaker's forms. Chelsea peered through the glass, drawn to a simple green silk gown. The high waist and clean, classical lines suited her, and the rich color glittered like crushed emeralds. In the days before she'd worn mourning, she'd favored green. Studying the gown, she couldn't help but overhear the lively conversation going on around her.

"A new gown, shawl, bonnet, *and* gloves. Fess up Olivia. You've received an invitation to Montrose's wedding and you've been keeping it from us."

The green gown forgotten, Chelsea snapped around.

Olivia, waxily pretty, frowned beneath the brim of her leghorn bonnet. "And what if I have? I knew you'd only be jealous, so I thought it best to keep it to myself."

"You can't really mean to go?" Her friend stared at her aghast. "Not after the shameful way Montrose treated you last Season."

"Really, Caro, it's mean of you to taunt her so," chided a sloe-eyed brunette. "I'm certain everyone has quite forgotten the way his lordship raised poor Libby's hopes . . ."

Chelsea edged closer.

"And then dropped her like a hot potato when Phoebe crooked her little finger," put in another, her mouth curving in a nasty smile.

A gangling, freckle-faced girl leaned forward and confided, "They say he's positively mad for her, and who can blame him. She's spectacular." She sighed. "Looks just like a fairy princess with that blonde hair and those blue eyes."

"And the intelligence of a sheep." Olivia's mouth quirked.

She fiddled with her bonnet strings. "She's not even *that* pretty."

"Now look who's jealous."

Me, Chelsea thought, catching her own sad-eyed reflection in the shop window. She turned away and leaned against the glass.

Giggles and more sly comments followed, and Chelsea reminded herself that they weren't directed at her. The recipient was Olivia, who ducked her head and examined the toes of her slippers.

The brunette's expression turned dreamy. "If you ask me, 'tis his lordship who's the spectacular one." One gloved hand stole to her bosom, heaving beneath her high-necked calico gown. "Faith, he's the handsomest man I've ever laid eyes on."

The pronouncement prompted a collective sigh.

Chelsea had heard enough. No more weepy sentiment and school girl crushes, she resolved. From now on, only action. She squared her shoulders and opened the shop door.

Inside, the shop hummed with competing female voices. Women thronged the marble-topped counter; others draped themselves over divans and damask-covered chairs, sipping tea, gossiping, and offering advice to friends emerging from the velvet-curtained dressing rooms. Still others stood atop carpeted pedestals. Frowning into pier glasses, they beckoned imperiously to the harried seamstresses working the parquet tiled floor.

And then all activity, all conversation, suddenly ceased. Everyone in the shop went as still as mannequins. Following their frozen stares, Chelsea glanced behind her to the closed door.

She turned back to confront a sea of bulging eyes and outraged faces. Good lord, she was the only male—or so everyone thought—in the room.

Courage, Chelsea. No turning back now.

If they thought her a boy, she'd better act like one. Hooking her thumbs into her waistcoat, she sauntered to the front of a snaking queue of shoppers.

She bowed to the tall, elegant woman behind the counter. "Madame Valen, I presume?"

"*Oui, c'est moi.*" The modiste eyed Chelsea over the bump of her Gallic nose and frowned. "You come on behalf of your *maîtresse*? *C'est trés irregulaire.* Still, you must wait your turn." She motioned Chelsea to the back of the line.

Confident that her breasts were securely bound, Chelsea puffed out her chest. "For me master, truth be told. Lord Montrose."

The modiste's scowl dissolved into a smile. "*Le vicomte*! But of course." She waved a hand to indicate Chelsea's livery. "*Tu portes ses couleurs.*" She smoothed a hand over the chignon at her nape. "Such *un gentilhomme*, le vicomte. *Si beau, si charmant, si . . .*"

Riche, Chelsea added to herself. An inveterate womanizer with a bottomless purse, Anthony would be a dressmaker's dream come true. Her hunch that he would be one of the shop's best customers had proven founded. And, judging by Madame's animated face as she rounded the counter, a personal favorite.

"How may I be of service to *le vicomte*?"

How, indeed? Chelsea forced down her rising jealousy. "He bade me fetch a ballgown he bespoke for a lady." She winked. "A very special lady, if you take me meaning."

"A ballgown?" Madame's high forehead furrowed. A moment later, she wrung her hands. "I know nothing of a ballgown."

She beckoned to a dark-haired shop girl across the floor. "Nicole, *vite vite. C'est le garçon de* Montrose."

Around a mouthful of pins, the girl squealed, "*Le vicomte*! He is here?" She dropped the bolt of fabric she'd been carrying and hurried forward, dark eyes bright and face flushed.

Chelsea gritted her teeth. "No, he sent *me*."

Really, the silly women were behaving as though Anthony were the only man alive and making royal fools of themselves into the bargain. He must have half the women in London eating out of his hand . . . and the other half waiting in line for the privilege. Including . . . *her*.

Madame Valen sobered. "Nicole, do you know of a ball-gown bespoken by Lord Montrose?"

The girl shook her head. "We have received no commissions from his lordship in these many months, Madame."

Eyes pleading, the modiste turned to Chelsea. "There must be some mistake? Perhaps another shop?"

Chelsea folded her arms across her chest. "All I knows is what 'e told me. 'You goes to Madame Valen's,' he says, 'and bring me back that frock straightaway.' If I goes back empty handed, 'e'll flay me backside, 'e will."

"Lord Montrose?" The two women's faces registered shock, a refreshing change from the moon-calf expressions they'd worn only moments before. "He beats you?" they asked in unison.

"Black and blue." Chelsea leaned closer and whispered, "Last time, they had to call for a surgeon."

"*Vraiment!*"

"Aye, 'is lordship can be a proper brute when 'e feels 'e's been ill-served. Quick to anger, slow to forgive, that's me master. What 'e'll do to you when I tells 'im you've lost his ladybird's frock is anyone's guess."

The modiste pressed a fist to her mouth. "*Mon Dieu*, I'll be ruined. *Ruined!*"

"Maybe, maybe not." Chelsea crooked a finger, beckoning them closer. "Maybe we could 'elp each other?"

"Heh?"

"I'll warrant 'is lordship don't even remember what he ordered." She almost added, "You know how men are," but stopped herself in time. Instead she pointed to the window platform. "That green 'un'll do."

"Oh no, not that one. That is for *une autre cliente*."

But Chelsea had set her heart on the green gown. For once, *this* once, she wasn't going to settle.

She dug in her heels. "Then why is it still 'ere?"

The modiste lifted her thin shoulders in an utterly Gallic shrug. Lowering her voice, she confided, "Wealthy women. They love to shop, but they do not always have the money to pay. I promise I keep for her another week, until she receives her next allowance. We have many beautiful gowns. Can you not choose another?"

Chelsea shook her head. "Unless the gown—that gown— is delivered this evenin', I doubt 'e'll darken your doorstep again. And once 'e puts the word out to his fancy friends, they're certain to do the same."

The modiste paled. She hesitated as though weighing Anthony's wrath against that of her other patron. She looked so distraught that Chelsea almost took pity on her. Almost.

Madame's shoulders sagged in defeat. "Do you perhaps know the lady's measurements?"

Chelsea smiled. "As a matter o' fact, I knows 'em like they was me very own."

Chelsea's final triumph was to have the gown, slippers, and sundry matching accoutrements charged to Anthony's account. The lot would be delivered to her Mount Street townhouse early that evening, in plenty of time for her to change and find her way to Vauxhall.

Well-pleased with herself, Chelsea walked out of the shop. As soon as she cleared the door, her pent-up laughter erupted. Further efforts to contain it only brought the tears streaming. Hugging her sides, she started across the street.

And walked straight into a pudding bag form.

"Oh, excuse me," she apologized, stepping back from the sagging bosom.

"Mind where you're going, you stupid oaf."

That voice. Chelsea slowly looked up. Hard, angry eyes glared down at her from a familiar fleshy face.

Abigail Pettigrew.

For a second, Chelsea and the vicar's wife stared at each other. Shock, then fear entwined Chelsea in a paralyzing grip.

Mrs. Pettigrew was the first to recover. "It is . . . *you.*"

Denial was probably pointless, but Chelsea shook her head anyway. She backed up, Mrs. Pettigrew advancing on her. Rosamund, standing behind her mother, came into view.

She set down her shopping bag and pointed. "Oh, Mama. You're right. 'Tis him."

Mrs. Pettigrew grabbed the sleeve of a passerby. "It's him!" she shrieked to the startled gentleman.

He tried to shake her off as though she were an annoying insect that had landed on him. "Unhand me, Madame."

"But it's him. The blackguard who robbed me!"

"Robbed you!" He frowned at Chelsea from beneath shaggy gray brows. "By God, we can't have that."

For an agonizing second, Chelsea stood still as though the soles of her shoes were nailed to the ground. Then the blood pumping from her frantic heart galvanized her leaden limbs. She turned and ran.

"Stop! Thief!"

Mrs. Pettigrew repeated the shrill exclamation. Chelsea stole a glance over her shoulder. The gentleman was running after her, trailed by a red-faced Mrs. Pettigrew and Rosamund.

Holding onto her wig, Chelsea fled toward Bond Street. She found herself pitted against the pedestrian stream, which seemed to be uniformly flowing in the opposite direction.

A stout, bearded man with a tray of italian ices strapped to his chest stepped in her path. They collided, the tray upturning. Cursing in Italian, he stared down at the rainbow spread across the front of his white shirt. Chelsea sputtered an apology and kept running, dimly aware when he tore off the tray and started after her.

None of her pursuers were particularly nimble, but having to weave through the strolling shoppers was slowing her down as well. She needed to find a way off the main street and fast. She sighted a side alley. Perfect. She could hide there, then sneak back out after Mrs. Pettigrew and the others tired of the chase.

She darted across the street.

"Hey, lookout you!"

The horse reared. Chelsea screamed as front hooves bore down on her. She jumped back, and the horse bucked again, dumping its rider into a rubbish bin. Groaning, the young dandy climbed out and brushed garbage from his pants seat.

Chelsea handed him his crushed top hat and sped away.

"Why you little . . . I just bought this."

The alley would never do now, for he'd seen where she was headed and was sure to tell the others. Another shout of "Stop thief!" had her looking back over her shoulder. Dear Lord, there were five of them now and the horseman, despite his limp, was gaining on her.

She didn't see the tree root buckling the sidewalk until it was too late. Feet slipping in her oversized shoes, she tripped and fell.

"Uh!"

A fruit seller's stand broke her fall. Arms flailing, she grabbed at the mounds of neatly stacked fruit. Oranges and apples scattered to the four winds.

"Sorry," she shouted over her shoulder, grapes squashing beneath the soles of her shoes.

"Sorry my arse." The costermonger tore off his apron and scrambled after her. "You're payin' for this."

She ran on. Her lungs burned, a stitch scored her side, and her knees throbbed as though someone had struck them with a hammer. But still she ran, one thought racing through her mind.

Anthony, where are you?

Anthony glanced at the small gold wedding band, closed the box, and slipped it inside his pocket. "And the other commission. I trust it is ready as well?"

"Of course, milord." The jeweler, Gray, bent to unlock a drawer beneath the glass counter. Straightening, he presented Anthony with a long velvet case. He opened it and laid the contents on a swatch of midnight blue velvet.

The triple rope of pearls was striking in its simplicity, except for the clasp, an intricate confection of diamonds and emeralds. An "A" and "C" were entwined in the delicate filigree.

Anthony lifted the necklace with reverent care. "May I?"

"Of course, milord." Gray handed him the loupe.

Peering through the magnifier, Anthony examined each pearl. They were flawless, nearly as smooth and creamy as Chelsea's skin. He couldn't wait to see her wearing the necklace—and nothing else. But first he had to persuade her to speak to him again.

She'd obviously left his house while his dinner party was still in session. None of the servants he'd questioned the night before remembered seeing her—him—past nine o' clock. He'd been tempted to rush to Mount Street—where else would she go?—to plead his case. But he was due to take over the watch at midnight. Which, he'd decided, was for the good. If womanizing had taught him anything, it was that an irate female should be given at least a night to cool her temper.

Chelsea might be the least materialistic woman he'd ever known, but she was still a woman. Surely such a costly gift—accompanied by his most charming apology—would quell any doubts she still harbored about the genuineness of his promise to rescue Robert.

Smiling, he put down the loupe and handed back the necklace. "You've outdone yourself, Gray."

Gray bowed his head. "Your sketch of the clasp was most explicit, milord." Replacing the necklace in its box, he added, "Even so, 'twas something of a feat to fashion a piece so intricate in little more than a week."

Anthony hid a smile at the less than subtle hint. Despite his gentlemanly affectations, the jeweler was a tradesman at heart and adept at haggling. No matter. He fully intended to reward Gray for his diligence.

Anthony reached inside his coat and withdrew his purse. "Add both pieces to my account. And Gray?"

"Yes, milord?"

Anthony pulled out five ten-pound notes. "I trust this will suffice as a token of my appreciation for a job admirably done?"

He dropped the stack of bills on the counter and picked up the necklace case.

"Very handsomely, milord."

Sweat sheaned the jeweler's brow as he pocketed the money. He hurried to the front of the counter to open the shop door for Anthony.

"Good day, milord."

"Good day, Gray."

Angry shouting—and one particularly piercing cry— drowned the soft tinkle of the shop's bell as the door closed softly behind him. Stepping out onto the sidewalk, Anthony frowned. Such raucous activity was to be expected in Billingsgate Market but not in Mayfair's exclusive shopping district. It made no sense, and yet he recognized the clamoring of a mob when he heard it.

And then a slim figure in brown and gold flashed by.

Good God, Chelsea! Her pursuers, nearly ten of them, represented a variety of social stations, but they were united in one thing—their livid faces, fixed on Chelsea's retreating back, radiated malice. Had Chelsea taken to picking pockets in broad daylight?

But now was not the time to contemplate that question. Anthony cut across the street, long strides devouring the distance separating him from Chelsea. Throwing himself dead center of her path, he caught her in his arms. The force rocked them both, knocking the breath from his lungs.

"A-An-thon-y."

She threw her arms about his neck and collapsed against him.

Across the street a lone man, dressed all in black, observed the spectacle from the outdoor table of a tea shop. The girl was her own worst enemy. Were it not for Montrose, it would be child's play to pluck her off the streets. As it was, she'd been holed up in his lordship's townhouse for more than a week. The chaos unfolding before him was his first chance to get close to her. Until Montrose, damn him to hell, interfered once again.

The man was becoming a problem.

Still, a notorious libertine like the viscount must soon tire of the game he'd been playing and relax his guard.

When he does, the girl will be mine for the taking.

Until then, he would wait. And watch. He could be patient when the situation warranted it. The thirtieth was but nine days away.

He raked a trembling hand through his hair. *I can wait. I must wait.*

For Chelsea Bellamy, he would wait for hell to freeze.

Chapter Twelve

Anthony untangled Chelsea's arms from his neck. She looked so small, so fragile, so frightened that he was afraid his heart would burst with the need to keep her safe. But to do so, he had to be strong.

He took a step back, holding her away from him. "Say nothing and follow my lead," he murmured.

Face flushed and eyes wide, she nodded.

Then all hell broke loose.

Anthony scanned the horde of angry, perspiring people spilling around them, voices raised in a cacophonous chorus. He sighted several raised fists and one riding crop but otherwise Chelsea's pursuers appeared devoid of weaponry. Thank God for small favors. He signalled for silence.

"Quiet, all of you!" He held up a palm. "This young man is in my employ. Whatever wrongs he has committed, I assume responsibility for ensuring that you are recompensed. Now, one at a time."

A young dandy hitched forward, his elaborately arranged neck cloth splashed with mud.

"This . . . rapscallion leapt out in front of me. Blasted fellow nearly lamed both me and my horse. And my hat, it will never be the same."

Anthony eyed the hat. Made of cheap felt, it was worth no more than ten pounds. To be safe, he would offer twenty. "Allow me to express my regret." He reached into his coat pocket for his purse.

Upper lip curled into a sneer, the dandy turned to address the gathering spectators. "Keep your money, sir," he said in a carrying voice. "Dare you suggest I would sully my honor by accepting payment from you? No, nothing shall satisfy me but your apology and seeing this lad publicly flogged." Turning back, he eyed Anthony's walking stick, the knob made of solid gold, and added beneath his breath, "Of course, if you were to *loan* me that stick of yours so that I might make my way back to my horse . . ."

Anthony pressed the cane into his hand. "Apology made."

"In that case, I accept." He grabbed the cane and skulked away, his hobble more pronounced than when he arrived.

"Madonna, what of me?" A bearded street vendor gestured to the array of colors staining his once white smock. "My finest shirt. She's ruined. And, *Dio*, my ices. The entire tray, *finito*."

Ten pounds sent the Italian on his way, a smile cracking beneath his waxed mustachio. Listening to the litany of Chelsea's other offenses, Anthony quickly determined that only a handful of her pursuers had a genuine grievance; the majority appeared to have joined the chase for sport.

He was paying off a fruit seller when a stout, ruddy-faced matron pushed her way through the dispersing crowd. Organdy flounces swayed about her thick ankles.

"I am Mrs. Josiah Pettigrew of Upper Uckfield." She lifted a hand, the fleshy wrist weighted with packages, and pointed to Chelsea. "And I demand you turn that felon over to the authorities at once."

Righteous indignation mingled with the sweat streaming down her porcine countenance. *Damn*. The termagant was no disgruntled tradesman but one of One-Eyed Jack's— Chelsea's—robbery victims. And a neighbor!

Anthony summoned the look of aristocratic hauteur he reserved for such occasions. "Felon, madam?"

She nodded briskly. "Indeed, 'tis the highwayman who waylaid my carriage a fortnight ago. The villain stole my purse and terrorized my poor daughters out of their wits."

Out of the corner of his eye, he saw Chelsea stiffen. "I can assure you, madam, Robin here is no highwayman. Obviously you've mistaken him for another."

Square jaws set, she turned to the flushed, pie-faced girl who had just joined them. "My daughter will bear me out. She, of all people, is qualified to identify the rogue. Rosamund, is this not the same vile creature who called himself One-Eyed Jack?"

The girl hung back, fingering a rosy pimple blossoming on her square chin.

Her mother jabbed her with her elbow. "Speak up!"

"Tell me, miss, does this pitiful stripling really resemble the brute who terrorized you?" Anthony asked gently.

The girl—Rosamund—glanced at Chelsea, then back at him. "I can't be certain, sir. I did think it looked like him at first, but now I'm not so sure."

Relief surged through him. "Well I can vouch that he is not your highwayman. Robin has been in my service for well nigh a year. He's a hard worker and strong for his size." *And badly in need of being taught a lesson.* "But, in truth, he's a bit thick in the pate."

He nudged Chelsea. Glaring at him, she hunched her shoulders and adopted a slack-jawed expression.

"But he so resembles this One-Eyed Jack fellow," the harridan persisted. Stepping closer, she raised her lorgnette and examined Chelsea's flushed face through the glass. "Perhaps if I could hear him speak?" She poked Chelsea's stomach with the tip of her closed parasol. "What, have you nothing to say in your defense?"

Despite Chelsea's fiery cheeks and glinting eyes, Anthony knew she'd hold onto her temper, at least until Mrs. Pettigrew and Rosamund were out of earshot. But, if pressed to speak, could she summon a passable male voice, one sufficiently dissimilar from the squeaky rasp she'd affected as One-Eyed Jack?

Not about to find out, Anthony spoke up, "Robin cannot speak, in his own defense or otherwise. You see, he's mute."

The shrew's brows lifted. "Really?"

"Oh, he makes a few guttural sounds now and again, but at heart he's a primitive. Mostly he uses hand gestures to communicate his basic wants." He slid Chelsea a sideways glance. Brows crossed and jaw set, she looked as though she were biting her tongue—literally. "And his facial expressions are quite eloquent."

Frowning, Mrs. Pettigrew circled Chelsea, examining her as though she were a museum exhibit. "Still, something about him seems disturbingly . . . familiar."

"I suppose Robin just has one of those faces. I apologize if his offends." He shrugged, turning from Chelsea to Rosamund.

Spoony-eyed, the girl was more than ready to believe anything he said. Her mother, however, would require a bit more persuasion.

Anthony turned his smile on the elder Pettigrew. "It might interest you to know that my own carriage was overtaken by the very same rogue. Robin here was quaking in his boots the whole time. I fear One-Eyed Jack may have frightened him out of what few wits he possessed. Poor lad, he's not been the same since."

The matron's mouth flew open. "Never say you were robbed too?" At Anthony's nod, she demanded, "I'll have your name, sir."

"Of course. Montrose, at your service." Anthony tipped his hat and swept his most courtly bow.

"Lord Montrose? Viscount Montrose!"

He inclined his head.

"Why, we are practically neighbors! My husband is the vicar. Allow me to present our eldest, Rosamund."

The girl remained immobile, her worshipful gaze still riveted on him.

"Don't tell me you've gone mute, too," her mother snapped.

As if emerging from a trance, Rosamund mumbled a greeting and careened into a curtsey. Anthony caught her and carried her gloved hand to his lips.

Looking down at the pudgy hand he'd just released, she sighed, "You are too kind, sir."

"An impossibility when one finds himself in such amiable company," he countered, suspecting she'd refrain from laundering that glove for some time. "May I be so bold as to ask what brings you two lovely ladies to town?"

Frowning at her daughter, Mrs. Pettigrew replied, "Rosamund is to make her bow next Season, and we are on a shopping expedition to see that she is rigged out in style." She paused. "She turns seventeen next month. I myself was barely out of the schoolroom when Mr. Pettigrew snatched me from the bosom of my family."

Looking between the two, Anthony thumbed the cleft in his chin. "That explains it, then."

"Milord?"

"Why at first I thought you two ladies were sisters."

"Oh, Lord Montrose, really!" Mrs. Pettigrew twittered.

Anthony glanced at Rosamund, who had resumed picking her chin, and wondered whether or not Mrs. Pettigrew might be sufficiently desperate to arrange for Robert Bellamy's abduction. Five hundred pounds would go a long way in ensuring a lavish Season for her daughter. Or perhaps the ransom might be intended to supplement the chit's dowry. Poor thing, she would require a sizeable one to attract a husband. "Only do show compassion for the other young ladies, Miss Rosamund, and try not to win away all their beaux."

A pink blotch dotted each of Rosamund's apple cheeks. She raised a hand to her mouth, muffling a giggle. He caught Chelsea rolling her eyes heavenward and shot her a scowl.

Turning back to Mrs. Pettigrew, he inquired, "May I inquire how long you will be staying in town?"

"Less than a fortnight, I'm afraid. Had we met you earlier, we might have altered our plans."

"Less than a fortnight, you say?" What an improbable coincidence it was that the Pettigrews' London excursion should coincide with Chelsea's brother being held hostage. Although Mrs. Pettigrew didn't appear clever enough to execute a kidnapping, he shouldn't rule out the possibility until he'd questioned her at length. "I know that you will think me forward for asking but—"

"Oh, fie, your lordship." Mrs. Pettigrew waived a dismissive hand. "Ask away."

"The Claridge Hotel is not far, and its tea room is London's finest. Dare I hope to persuade you and your daughter to join me for refreshments?"

Mrs. Pettigrew's piggy eyes glowed with triumph. "We did have a prior engagement, but nothing that cannot be broken."

"Then 'tis settled." He took their packages and handed them to Chelsea. "Here, boy, see to these."

She lifted her face to his, and they exchanged silent glances. *Must I really?* her eyes implored him. *Yes, I'm afraid you must,* came his mum reply.

With a grimace, she reached out and snatched the parcels from him. Arms full and eyes snapping, she stomped toward the back of the conveyance. Anthony released the breath he'd been holding.

"Good heavens," Mrs. Pettigrew exclaimed as he handed her up onto the bench. "You really must take a firmer hand, milord."

Out of the corner of his eye, he watched Chelsea deposit the packages in the boot, then climb onto the footmen's rest. "I couldn't agree with you more, madam. I couldn't agree more."

Stiff-kneed, Chelsea climbed down from the carriage, ignoring Anthony's outstretched hand. Of all the humiliations she'd suffered since coming to London, being forced to dance attendance on Mrs. Pettigrew and Rosamund was by far the worst. And the hardest to forgive.

She turned and started limping down the street.

"Where are you going?" Anthony asked, keeping pace beside her.

"Home." She was too proud to look at him, but she sensed he was smiling.

"It's a long walk. Why not join me in the study for a drink? Afterwards, I'll drive you."

"Die," she hissed.

"Eventually but first we have to talk." He clasped a hand about her upper arm and commandeered her toward the townhouse steps.

Inside the foyer he let her go. Marching behind him to the

back of the house, one hand supporting her aching back, she thought about making a run for the door. *I'd probably fall on my face.* Besides, why turn her back on this golden opportunity to give his lordship his comeuppance?

She slammed the study door and swung around to face him. "Not overly bright, am I? A bit thick in the pate."

Anthony lifted the stopper from a crystal brandy decanter. "Had they thought you a genius, you might very well be cooling your heels in Newgate now. Would you have preferred prison to one uncomfortable hour on the back of my carriage?"

He was right, of course. Playing the lackey for an afternoon was a small price to pay for escaping the hangman's noose. That didn't mean she had to like it. Then or now. Especially not *now* when a cocksure smile curved his lips.

Hands on her hips, she mimicked, " 'Oh, Lord Montrose, you are too kind.' 'Your carriage is divine, your lordship. I've never ridden in one so well sprung.' O-ooh, I'd like to do some springing." She pulled off her wig and slung it to the ground. A cloud of powder rose to her ankles. Stepping through it, she advanced on the desk. "It was all I could do to keep from retching."

He looked up from the drinks he was pouring, laughter glinting in his eyes. "In that case, having you ride outside was even a wiser decision than I'd credited."

Furious, she combed fingers through her itching scalp, spraying pins. "I rather think you enjoyed having those two ridiculous females fawn all over you. When I think on the blandishments you lavished on that chubby child, I wonder if you have any shame at all."

His gaze widened. Then he grinned. "Don't tell me you're jealous of the attention I paid Miss Pettigrew?"

She took the glass from him. Swirling the amber liquid about the rim, she replied, "Don't be absurd. Only know that her mother has set her cap for you as a future son-in-law. Don't blame me when you find yourself pestered to death."

His smile fell. "You forget, I'm already spoken for."

She swallowed against the lump constricting the back of her throat. "I forget . . . nothing." The pain of his betrayal washed over her anew. "Last night I didn't have the chance to wish you happy." She lifted her glass, and her gaze, to him. "Allow me to do so now."

"Chelsea, I should have . . ." His voice faltered, but his gaze never left hers.

"Told me you were to marry Lady Phoebe on the thirtieth. Yes, you should have."

He drank his brandy in a single swallow. "I'm sorry." He set the empty glass aside. "I meant to but every time I tried . . ."

"Tried, milord?"

He exhaled. "I suppose I wanted more time to get to know you."

"Before you admitted you'd lied?"

His brown eyes snapped. "Lied! I never—"

"Do you honestly expect me to believe that you mean to leave your wife on your wedding night to deliver my brother's ransom?"

"Yes . . . I mean no. Chelsea." He swiped a hand through his hair. "I never meant for it to come to that. With any luck, Jack and I will have Robert safely away before the thirtieth arrives."

"With any luck!" Her outrage surged. She slammed her glass on the desk. Brandy lopped onto the polished wood. "This isn't a game. My brother's life is at stake. His *life*. Do you even understand what that means?"

He slammed a fist onto the desktop. "Yes. God, yes, I do."

She started. Then she glimpsed the haunted look in his eyes and her traitorous heart began to melt. She'd not seen him thus since the night he'd spoken of Albuera. But this time she mustn't soften.

He turned away. "If you believe nothing else I've said, believe this: I will do everything in my power to save your brother."

How I want to believe you. But Robert's life was on the line. She must be absolutely certain of Anthony's commitment.

Regarding his taut profile, she asked, "Even if it means postponing your wedding?"

He hesitated, and her heart sank. "In for a penny, in for a pound," she quoted in a brittle voice. Even he wasn't certain of himself; how on earth could she be?

"If it comes to that, yes, I suppose so," he said after a lengthy pause.

"You *suppose* so?" Despair washed over her. "I believe you've just answered my question."

Was this what the dying felt like when they finally realized there was no more hope? She eyed the door, wondering if she could reach it before the tears started.

Intercepting her gaze, he swung around and gripped her shoulders. His flexing fingers sent shock waves rippling through her. "Very well—yes. Yes, I will cry off, if that's what it takes."

But the longed-for words came too late. She couldn't trust him. Not with Robert's life. And not with her heart.

I'm on my own. There would be no more prevaricating. She would forge ahead with her scheme to steal the coins and ransom Robert.

She glared down at his hands, still holding onto her, and he dropped them to his sides.

"Don't go. Not like this," he said, but his eyes told her he didn't really expect her to stay.

She backed away from him to the door. To safety. "We've nothing more to say."

Reaching behind her, she found the doorknob. Now all she needed was the courage to rotate it. And leave.

Turn your back on him and go. Now!

It wasn't her inner voice or her father's, but Robert's that called to her. Pleaded with her to save him. And herself.

The brass knob slipped in her damp grasp, but this time she found the willpower to turn it. Behind her, the door fell open. Cool air brushed her back.

Someone must be stepping on my grave. That was how the expression went, wasn't it? Appropriate to this occasion, too, for didn't she feel as though she were dying inside?

"Chelsea, don't . . ." His voice trailed off, as thin and broken as the childish dreams she'd harbored about him.

Across the room, he stood as still as any graveyard statue,

his face a mirror of her own misery. She didn't want to be
moved by him but, God help her, she was. If only she
weren't so weak where he was concerned. If only she could
manage to hate him just a little. If only . . .

Good-bye Anthony. Swallowing against the lump at the
back of her throat, she stepped into the hallway and pulled
the door closed.

I'm too bleedin' old for this.

Crouched in the alley across from the Rookery, Jack
hugged his coat tighter. The wind was picking up, and he
could feel the autumn chill seeping into his bones. His knees
and shoulders ached, and he had hours yet before his shift
ended. A few doors down, the corner gin shop announced
"Drunk for a penny, dead drunk for two pence, clean straw
for nothing." Inside it would be warm; it might even smell
better than the alley. He glanced at his companion, a large
white rat foraging through a rubbish heap a few paces away.
There had been times, in his youth, when he'd eaten rats to
stave off the hunger gnawing his belly.

Jack, lad, ye've gone soft.

What if he had? At his age, he was entitled to a few comforts. What would one drink, or even two, hurt? He started
up. It was then that he sighted a figure in black moving
down the other side of the street.

The man was one of them—a gentleman. Swathed in a
caped greatcoat and with his face hidden by a scarf and sloping hat brim, he headed up the cracked limestone steps of
one of the Rookery's crumbling tenements. Jack shrank further into the shadows. The heel of his boot smashed into
something soft.

The rat squealed, then skittered away. Across the street,
the man in black stopped, turned back, and scanned the
street. Back flattened against the brick, Jack held his breath.
It was dusk, but the lamplighter had yet to arrive. Dark but
not quite dark enough for hiding someone his size.

Jack's heart pounded out the passing seconds. Finally the
man turned back and opened the door, then disappeared inside the dark entrance.

Jack exhaled. His drink would have to wait. Ignoring the stiffness in his knees, he rose and bounded across the street.

The gentleman in black ventured one last, precautionary look into the dark, deserted hallway. Satisfied, he stepped into the low-ceilinged chamber. As soon as he closed the door, the stench of human waste and rotting food hit him in the face like a fist. His stomach heaved, causing him to regret having stuffed himself earlier with sherry and biscuits. But, had he not stopped at the tea shop, he never would have seen *her*.

Slumped over a table littered with dirty dishes, Stenton came awake with a loud start. Recovering, he said, "Well, well. If it b'aint hisself." He turned his empty ale mug upside-down and pulled a sad face. "I'd offer ye a drink, but the well's gone dry."

The newcomer eyed the uncovered chamber pot that commandeered the far corner. *The poor are no better than animals*, he mused, pulling a cologne-scented handkerchief from his pocket.

He held the linen to his nose. "You should know that I don't care for being summoned. Were I to be seen here—"

Stenton's eyes narrowed. "And I don't care for bein' cheated."

The gentleman frowned. "What are you talking about?"

Stenton's bony fist crashed onto the table. "The lad says his sister don't 'ave the blunt."

Oh, was that all. He'd prepared himself for worse news than that. "And you believed him?" He made a *tsk tsking* sound. "What our young friend doesn't know is that his sister has been a very enterprising young lady since she received my ransom *request*."

"What's that supposed to mean?"

"That what money she hasn't stolen on her own, no doubt her wealthy lover will provide. Anthony Grenville is one of England's richest peers."

As well as an accomplished seducer. An image of Grenville's too handsome face flitted before him, and his right eye skittered. He concentrated on relaxing the tick.

"Anthony Grenville! The same Grenville that's about to get hisself hitched?"

He raised his brows. "Don't tell me you've been reading the society column?"

Stenton rubbed his gold front tooth with the back of his thumb. "Let's just say I 'ave me sources."

The felon's sudden smile made him anxious, exacerbating the twitch. The rogue was hiding something, but what? If his nerves weren't already unraveling, he might stay long enough to find out. As it was, a dose of laudanum and a nap were in order.

"Fair enough." Eager to be gone, he walked to the door. On afterthought, he asked, "How fares our young charge?"

"Still ornery as all get out, but me an Luke is workin' to beat the devil out o' 'im."

"Just see that he stays alive . . . until the thirtieth."

"O' course." Grinning, Stenton pushed away from the table. "And after?"

He shrugged. "Do with him what you like, but make certain you bring the girl to me. Unharmed and . . . *untouched*."

Stenton followed him to the door. "Ye still owes us two hundred pounds, and me and Luke's got expenses. What say ye come up wi' a hundred pounds o' it now?"

He felt his jaw tighten. Really, did the man think he was an idiot? "You'll get the rest of your money when I get the girl."

"But—"

He adjusted the scarf over his face and reached for the door handle. "Unharmed and untouched, Stenton."

Jack ducked into the abandoned wardrobe at the end of the hall. He'd just pulled the door closed when the man in black emerged. Squinting through a knothole in the wood, he saw Stenton leaning in the open doorway. The other man's back was to the wardrobe. The two men exchanged more words.

Jack pricked his ears, but it was no use. Even standing outside Stenton's door with his good ear pressed to the wood, he hadn't been able to make out much of the conversation going on inside. Still, the few odd phrases he'd pieced together—*the thirtieth, beat the Devil out o' 'im*—threatened to turn his bowels to water. The bloke in black was involved somehow with Master Robert's kidnapping. Mayhap he was even the villain who'd commissioned it? The voice sounded familiar but, muffled, he hadn't been able to place it.

Before he could ponder that possibility, Stenton's door slammed. The visitor started down the hall, his footfalls keeping pace with Jack's thudding heart. He reached Jack's hiding place and stopped.

"Quite a fine piece," he murmured, his hand on the wardrobe door.

Oh God, I'm done for.

Sweat broke out on Jack's forehead and palms. The ticking of the battered timepiece in his pocket suddenly seemed as loud as the pealing of the Bow Bells.

The man moved on. The creaking stairs confirmed his departure.

Weak with relief, Jack slumped against the back of the cabinet. Now that the immediate danger was past, the sick feeling in his gut intensified. In his sixty-odd years, his gut had never lied to him. Now it was telling him that Stenton wasn't about to wait until the thirtieth to make his move. He must go to Lord Montrose at once. He was certain his lordship would see that their safest course was to call in Mugglestone and begin preparations to rescue Master Robert—mayhap that very night.

Jack waited a minute more, then opened the wardrobe. Gritting his teeth against the squeak, he stepped out. Behind a closed door, a baby started to cry. Taking advantage of the loud wailing, he thudded across the bare floorboards to the stairs.

Outside, he headed for the alley where he'd left his horse. The lazy beast wasn't much for galloping, but Jack dug in his heels and the horse bolted.

But when he reached Lord Montrose's townhouse, the butler informed him that his master had left for the evening.

Muttering curses, Jack stepped off the stoop. That was the

Fancy for you. Always out and about, rushin' to this or that. Not a one of them had the sense to stay home of an evening.

No sense in cryin' o'er spilt milk. He'd just have to find Miss Chelsea and tell her everything. She'd know what to do.

But when he returned to the house on Mount Street, he found it empty.

Chapter Thirteen

He should never have come.

Why had he? Anthony asked himself as he strolled down Vauxhall's Grand Walk with Phoebe on his arm.

Foolish question. Guilt, of course.

That afternoon, standing in his study with Chelsea in his arms, he'd been tempted to jettison everything—his father's earldom, his marriage, his future—and beg her to run away with him. Even if his father disinherited him—God knew the old man had been looking for an excuse to do so for years—Ignatius's money and lands would enable them to live in comfort. But would it be enough for them to live down the scandal, silence the wagging tongues that would brand Chelsea as a title-seeking adventuress, buy respectability for their children? No, they'd have to go away, leave England. But go where? With Napoleon cutting a blazing swath through Europe, the Continent was out of the question. And, across the Atlantic, another war waged between Britain and America, so there could be no thought of starting afresh in Virginia. No, for the time being, they would have to hole up in Sussex, for they would never be able to show their faces in polite society after they were wed.

After they were wed.

The outrageous thought had raced through his head ever since that afternoon. He stifled it now. He must think clearly, rationally. He had an ancestral home, a noble legacy—a seat in the House of Lords, no less. His future was here, now, his fate inextricably linked to the pale blonde keeping pace beside him.

So he'd sent Phoebe the message, late in the afternoon, that he'd escort her to the supper ball after all. And then, deuce take it, he hadn't been able to find his blasted invitation. He'd sworn he'd laid it on his desk, but when he'd gone to look for it, it hadn't been there. Or anywhere, for that matter. Fortunately Phoebe had kept hers.

"Oh Anthony, I simply adore Vauxhall." Eyes sparkling and face flushed, Phoebe pointed to a miniature minaret. "Why, look at that adorable little tower. That dome behind it is shaped just like an onion."

What a child she is, he thought, forcing a smile. "It's called a minaret. In Turkey, the *muezzin* stands on the balcony to call the people to prayer."

"Humph." She screwed up her face. "Why don't they just ring the church bell?"

Anthony was asking himself whether he should expend the energy to form a reply when, thankfully, the Roman Pavilion came into view.

True to its name, the pavilion's interior was decorated to give the illusion of a classical temple. Waiters wearing togas and laurel wreaths—no fig leaves, thank God—ferried silver trays of champagne and iced lemonade through the bejeweled assembly of London's elite. At one end of the tent was a buffet table in the form of a sarcophagus; smaller tables fashioned from cornices lined the wooden dance floor. A musician playing panpipes circulated the crowd while, behind a crumbling stone altar, the orchestra tuned their instruments.

Seated, Phoebe lost no time in taking stock of the assembly.

"Oh look, Anthony, there's Libby." She waved at her friend, who waved back and started toward them.

Anthony stifled a groan. Olivia—Libby—Whitebridge was an inveterate gossip and about as silly and spoiled as women came. To make matters worse, she seemed to have formed a *tendre* for him, although he could recall having danced with her only once.

Watching her friend advance, Phoebe pulled a face. "I

know that white is all the rage, but I wish someone would tell her that she looks like death in it."

God, but it was going to be a long night. Anthony fell back against a columned post and flagged a waiter. Seconds later, he handed Phoebe a glass of lemonade and took one of champagne for himself.

She indicated a pale-faced young man with sad eyes. "Anthony, isn't that Junius St. John?"

"I believe so."

She hesitated. "Is it true what they say—that he staked the deed to his estate on a single game of hazard and lost?"

"I have no idea," he lied, not inclined to whet Phoebe's appetite for gossip by confirming the rumor.

He imagined that Phoebe and he would share a lifetime of such meaningless, empty evenings. He tilted back his flute and swallowed the rest of the champagne.

"Anthony."

"Hem?"

"The redhead in that gaudy green gown. I've not seen her before. Do you know who she is?"

"Phoebe, half the women here have red hair." This time he didn't bother to hide his annoyance.

"In the *green* gown." She pointed her closed fan to the dais at the far end of the pavilion. "The one flirting with Lord Ambrose."

Knowing he would have no peace until he complied, he looked to where his nemesis loomed over an alluring figure in green, her back to the crowd. Whoever Ambrose's mystery lady was, Anthony pitied her. No woman, be she lady or whore, deserved what Ambrose would visit on her.

The woman turned to look below. Anthony caught his breath.

No, it couldn't be, he assured himself, even as his own eyes provided the irrefutable proof.

But it was.

Chelsea.

At least he thought it was she.

The Chelsea he knew swaggered about in breeches, scaled

roof tops, and didn't shrink from performing the most menial chores. She didn't have a coy bone in her lovely body.

This Chelsea moved with the seductive grace of the most expensive courtesan. Stunned, he watched her slowly draw her closed fan across her rouged lips in a blatant invitation to be kissed. As though her appearance weren't invitation enough. Her red curls were dressed *à la grecque* and topped with a glittering tiara; the upswept style only emphasized the graceful column of her throat and the elegant set of her milky shoulders. But it was her gown that caught and held his eye. The emerald silk clung to every delicious curve, and what wasn't outlined in shameless detail was left bare. His regard riveted itself on the high slopes of her breasts. The rake in him yearned to take her somewhere secluded—the Gardens' infamous Dark Walk came to mind—and tug the silk down to her waist; his more sober self wanted to snatch some matron's shawl and wrap it around her torso.

Ambrose pointed to something below, and she leaned forward. Anthony held his breath, certain that she would overflow the flimsy silk barrier. Predictably, Ambrose's gaze dropped. Rage boiled the blood in Anthony's veins.

The master of ceremonies emerged from the orchestra to announce that supper was being served. Almost immediately, guests thronged the center aisle leading to the buffet tables.

This might be my only chance. Anthony shoved away from the post. "I'll bring you a plate."

Phoebe shook her head. "Thank you, but I'm far too excited. Perhaps I'll have something later."

Sweat pricked his palms. "What nonsense, you must eat."

Her pale brows crossed. "I'm really not the slightest bit hungry."

"You know how prone you are to fainting. And," he added, "you wouldn't want to miss the fireworks, now would you?" He held his breath.

She hesitated. "Well, perhaps just a bite."

He exhaled. "That's the spirit."

He made his way toward the front of the pavilion. Several acquaintances approached him to offer their congratulations on his coming nuptials, but he only nodded and kept on. At the canopied entrance, he turned and glanced back. Phoebe had been joined by her friend, and the two were immersed in an animated and, he felt certain, inane conversation. Which, this once, was a stroke of luck for him.

He darted outside and skirted the pavilion, praying his luck would hold.

"It was so good of you to invite me to your table, Lord Ambrose," Chelsea simpered.

Batting her eyelashes, she asked herself just what it was about her host that she found so repellant. He wasn't as tall as Anthony, nor as muscular, nor as young. Even so, she supposed he cut a pleasing enough figure in his dark evening clothes. Yet there was *something* about him that disturbed her.

Beneath his neatly trimmed ginger mustache, the corners of his mouth lifted. Dark teeth marred an otherwise brilliant smile. "Tut, tut, Mrs. Brighton. You are to call me Monty."

"You're the only person I know in London—" she paused, then added "—Monty. When I received your invitation, I nearly burst into tears." She glanced downward. "In truth, I never would have expected you to remember me."

"Not remember *you*! Perish the thought."

Liar. She shot him a coquettish smile from over the top of her open fan. He was so easy to read. She could almost hear the wheels of his mind turning as he struggled to place her.

"But we met so very briefly and 'twas so long ago," she said. "Not everyone is so keen to rekindle a former acquaintance . . . especially with a widow who finds herself alone and friendless."

He lifted her hand and patted the top. Eyes on her breasts, he asked, "Do you truly find yourself all alone since your husband's death?"

Chelsea admitted the barest hint of regret into her voice. "I did have a protector for a time, but he had to give me up when his father-in-law threatened to cut off his allowance."

"Spineless cad. But now you are once again . . . alone?" His feral gaze belied the sympathy in his voice.

She shivered, feeling like prey. "I'm afraid so."

"In that case, perhaps you will do me the honor of joining

me after the fireworks. My chef is preparing a buffet breakfast back at my house. Nothing elaborate, mind you. Just an
intimate gathering for a few *close* friends." His fingers
skimmed her bare shoulder.

Swallowing her revulsion, she smiled up at him. "Why,
that sounds delightful. I would so love to see your home."

Especially your coin collection. Earlier she'd trekked to
Murdock's Lending Library where, she'd rightly reasoned,
Anthony would hold a subscription. She'd searched out several volumes on rare and ancient coins from the musty
stacks. A Roman *aureus*, in reasonable condition, could
fetch several thousand pounds. Her plan: locate the coins,
filch one of the lesser ones, then plead illness and leave.
Even a voluptuary like Ambrose would not welcome a
retching woman into his bed.

"Then 'tis settled."

Their backs were against the curtain. He slipped a hand
over her buttocks and squeezed.

Chelsea jumped. He laughed, and she forced an insipid
giggle. If she was going to play the harlot, she could hardly
complain when a man like Ambrose felt at liberty to paw her
in public, no matter how much she yearned to slap him.

Suddenly the curtains parted, and Anthony burst inside,
an evening cape slung over one broad shoulder. Chelsea's
heart fluttered, then dropped. Surely Anthony wouldn't ex-
pose her? Or would he?

"Good evening." Anthony glared at Ambrose's hand, still
cupping her bottom.

Heart pounding, she moved away from Ambrose. "Why
Lord Montrose, I didn't expect to see you here."

"I am sure you did not," Anthony murmured, eyes glittering.

Ambrose looked from Chelsea to Anthony. "You two
know each other?"

Eyes hard, Anthony smiled. "We're old friends."

Chelsea sent Anthony a beseeching look. "What Lord
Montrose means is that his *sister* and I are old friends."

"Indeed." He gave Ambrose his back and reached for her.

His powerful fingers closed around her upper arm just below the puffed sleeve. "A word with you, if I may."

Ambrose stepped forward. "Now see here, Montrose. Mrs. Brighton is my guest."

"Then you won't want to monopolize her." Anthony lifted the tent flap. "After you, *Mrs. Brighton*." He dragged her through the opening and down the back steps.

"You're hurting me." Squirming, she tried in vain to break his bruising grip.

"Too bad."

He steered her off the torch-lit path into a small, hedge-trimmed garden. In the center, a fountain splashed. Lights winked from the boughs of a spruce tree; otherwise the garden was cloaked in twilight shadows.

He maneuvered her toward a marble bench. "Sit."

"No."

"Suit yourself."

Still holding onto her, he buried his free hand in the elaborate arrangement of curls gathered at her nape. Fingers on her scalp, he steered her toward him until she was inhaling his peppermint spiced breath.

Outrage, fear, and . . . desire struck her at once. Her chest heaved, her pulse raced, her head spun. She felt warm everywhere except for her hands, which had frozen to blocks of ice. And between her thighs, a slow staccato had begun to beat.

Outrage was by far the least threatening emotion. She sought sanctuary in it now.

"Just what do you think you're doing?" she demanded, twisting in his arms.

"Saving you from yourself."

"I don't need saving."

"Maybe I do."

He bent and claimed her with a savage kiss.

Chelsea gasped. Anthony devoured the small, choked protest—fear, anger, and passion all rolled into one—and backed her against the tree. He pressed into her until they fitted together from shoulder to thigh, so tight that he couldn't be sure where his body ended and hers began. She struggled, the futile movements chafing his lower body until his rock hard erection smashed against her stomach.

And it was then that she surrendered. Her body softened and her mouth opened, not in submission but in invitation. He accepted and plunged deep inside. She moaned. He slipped an arm behind to cushion her against the bark. At least that was his intention. But she felt so good, so right, in his arms, the silk the nearest thing to having her naked. His hand slid down her spine, his fingers slipping between the lobes of her rounded buttocks. She trembled, and he felt a matching shudder charge through him.

"Oh Chelsea. What have you done to me?"

He rubbed against her, his manhood chafing her softness.

And suddenly he was the one in danger of losing control, of being taken prisoner.

He broke off the kiss.

In the dim light, Chelsea's angry eyes glittered like crushed emeralds. "I d-don't need s-saving," she repeated between heavy breaths.

Her mouth, swollen from his assault, no longer owed its rosy hue to paint; her cheeks, burned bright, were scoured of rouge.

He reached for her. "You have no notion of the type of man you're dealing with."

"At the moment, I would say a rather brutish one." She cast a pointed look at his fingers still wound about her upper arm.

Anthony followed her gaze and scowled. He hadn't meant to hurt her. "I'm sorry. I don't know what came over me." He shook his head, hoping to clear it. "But God, Chelsea, how you try me. Rifling through my personal papers. I'd thought we'd moved beyond that."

She bit her bottom lip. "I don't know what you're talking about."

"Don't you? Am I to believe my invitation to tonight's fete sprouted legs and walked off my desk?"

"Oh, that. I found it lying atop a pile of papers. You said

you weren't coming, so I didn't think there would be any harm in my borrowing it."

"And that gown. Did you borrow it as well?"

She opened her mouth, then closed it. Finally she admitted, "Actually I purchased it, or rather you did."

Had she worn it for him, he would have gladly bought her a closet full. But she hadn't. She hadn't even expected him to be here. Jealousy surged through him, dissipating desire.

"I see. It's very daring," he sneered, deliberately fixing his gaze on her breasts.

Face flushed, she said, "I'd hardly make a convincing courtesan buttoned to my chin."

"So that's your game, is it? Lucky Ambrose." His tone dripped with bitterness, but he was too wounded to care. "Given the shameless way you've been behaving, I collect you mean to lift your skirts for him here, or will you wait until he takes you to his bed?"

She looked as though he'd struck her. "That is the cruelest thing anyone's ever said to me."

He ached to recall the scathing accusation, but it was too late. And why should he when she had as good as admitted that she planned to sleep with his enemy?

"Do you deny that he's invited you back to his house? He has, hasn't he?"

"That is none of your affair."

"Meaning I'm right. Tell me, Chelsea, have you decided that having a wealthy protector may not be so *loathsome* after all?"

She regarded him, lips pursed, eyes snapping. "I suppose that would depend on the protector."

"And you fancy Ambrose?"

She shrugged, which did interesting things to the cleavage edging out of her bodice. "He is not unattractive."

She was the worst liar he'd ever known. "Were I to hazard a guess, I would say that a certain rare coin collection is behind this sudden attraction."

Silence.

"I thought so. And is your plan to give yourself to him and then claim a priceless coin as your reward?"

"Don't be insulting. I plan to steal it, of course, and then leave."

It was a harebrained scheme, fated to fail, and yet the realization that she didn't intend to turn whore was an inestimable relief.

"This may surprise you, my dear, but not every man is prepared to show my . . . restraint. Some men, when they have been brought to a certain—how shall I say this—level of excitement, will not honor a woman's last minute change of heart."

Even in the encroaching darkness, there was no mistaking the berry blush branding her cheeks.

Encouraged, he continued, "Ambrose is not some country swain whose hand you can slap if he steps out of line. The man is totally amoral, the lowest of rogues."

She rolled her eyes. "Surely you must realize how absurd that sounds coming from you."

Anthony's jaw tightened. "At least I make no pretense of being other than what I am. And, unlike your good friend Lord Ambrose, *I* have never forced a woman."

Her mouth formed a shocked circle. "Just what are you saying?"

"He forced himself on the sister of a friend of mine. Brutalized her, actually. One night Fanny showed up on my doorstep a bloody mess and with rope burns on her wrists." He exhaled. "To make matters worse, there were . . . *consequences*."

"Consequences?"

"A child, a little boy, whom even now Ambrose refuses to recognize."

"What happened to him?"

He smiled when he thought of his godson. "Little Anthony just turned four. In spite of the circumstances of his birth, he is strong and healthy and very much loved."

Her brows lifted. "Little Anthony?"

He looked away, torn between friendship and the desperate need to keep Chelsea safe. "At first Fanny didn't want her family to know. Her brother, Peter, was one of my two best friends, and I felt closer to their parents than to my own.

But the decision wasn't mine to make. I kept her secret and helped her as best I could until after Anthony was born and she struck up the nerve to go home. Naming the child after me was her way of thanking me, I suppose."

Unfortunately it had also fueled the rumor, instigated by Ambrose, that Anthony had gotten Fanny *enceinte* and then deserted her. Small wonder that buying colors and joining the fight against Napoleon had seemed so appealing.

"I'm sorry for what happened to your friend, truly I am. But I am not she. I can take care of myself . . . and my brother."

She turned to go, but he caught her arm. "Don't do this, Chelsea. Don't go back to him. My carriage is just outside the front gate. I'll have Masters drive you home . . . or anywhere you like." *Anywhere but here.* He was pleading now, no longer in control.

She shook her head. "The fireworks will be starting soon. I have to go back," she said, mouth trembling.

It was no use. He let her go. Turning on her heel, she fled.

As soon as she disappeared, he knew he'd made a terrible mistake. *Go after her, you fool*, his instinct urged.

But, even if he caught her, what good would it do? She'd never listen to him. Knowing Ambrose, if Anthony tried to force her to leave, he would be the one to be escorted to the gate.

Heading back up the path, Anthony told himself that Chelsea Bellamy wasn't his problem. He'd warned her, even violated a friend's confidence to do so, and still she rebuffed him. Temper mounting, he told himself that she deserved what she got.

He didn't believe it for an instant.

The crowd inside the pavilion had thinned by the time he returned. He found Phoebe where he'd left her, alone now and looking miserable. Guilt pricked him, particularly when he recalled how close he'd come that afternoon to abandoning her. Since coming to London, he'd been too besotted by a certain flame-haired felon to give his fiancée much thought. Perhaps he should spend more time with her, get to know her. Perhaps, if he gave her a chance . . .

"Anthony, you've been gone an eternity. Nearly everyone's left for the fireworks." She stared at his empty hands.

He flushed, recalling that he'd excused himself under the pretense of fetching food. He offered her his arm. "Then let's find a good spot to view them, shall we?"

Once outside the tent, he led her toward the South Walk at the outskirts of the park.

He pointed to a knoll overlooking the Thames. "We'll have the best view from over there."

Panting, Phoebe lifted her skirts. "Must we go so far?"

"Just a few more paces," Anthony encouraged, taking her hand.

They crested the hill and settled on a carved stone bench beside a folly of a Grecian temple. Strains of Handel's "Music for the Royal Fireworks" reached them from the orchestra pit in the Grove.

Facing him, she tilted her face upward and closed her eyes, his cue to claim the one chaste kiss it was her custom to permit at an evening's end. In the course of their courtship, he'd come to find the childlike gesture inordinately annoying, but never more so than now.

"The fireworks will be starting any minute," he said harshly.

Her eyes flashed open. Her face registered hurt, perhaps even disappointment. Might Phoebe enjoy his kisses more than she let on? That night was as good a time as any to launch a small experiment.

He draped an arm about her thin shoulders and drew her closer. "You look very pretty tonight."

Encouraged when she didn't move away, he brushed her mouth lightly with his. Nothing. He felt nothing. At that moment, he would have traded his good leg for the ability to rid himself of the heated memory of copper hair and emerald eyes searing his brain.

Dammit, he was not going to allow his life to be turned topsy turvy by any woman, particularly not a sharp-tongued shrew who'd made it abundantly clear that she didn't want his protection. Didn't want *him*.

He forced his attention back to the woman sitting stiff as

a board in his arms, her mouth motionless beneath his own. Defiant, he swept his tongue along the seam of her closed lips.

Phoebe's eyes shot open. She scooted away.

"Really, milord!" A patch of pink stained each cheek. "I have never known you to be so . . . *familiar*."

So much for the hope that he might be able to stir to life a feeble flame of passion between them. But then how could he when he himself had felt *nothing*.

"Forgive me, Phoebe. I didn't mean to alarm you. But we are to be married in less than a fortnight. You must know that, on our wedding night, we will become very familiar indeed?"

Terror and something else—revulsion perhaps—filled her eyes.

He tried again. "Surely your mother has explained . . ."

She pressed the back of her hand to her mouth. Tears filled her eyes. "Must we talk about this now? I was so looking forward to the fireworks, and now you're r-ruining everything."

He exhaled heavily and handed her his handkerchief. "No, of course not."

A trumpet blared, the signal that the fireworks were about to commence. Dread settled into the pit of his stomach. Fireworks, how he hated them. At least, if he lost control, there would be only Phoebe to witness his humiliation.

The first rocket fired. Anthony girded himself. The next moment, the black sky was ablaze.

Her upset forgotten, Phoebe clapped her hands. "Oh, how marvelous! It has a tail like a dragon." She rattled his arm. "Don't you think it looks just like a dragon?"

He gripped the edge of the seat with both hands to keep from covering his ears. "The very image."

Perspiration filmed his body. His evening clothes clung. Fear shrieked through him, urging him to flee or at least to take cover beneath the bench. Instead he concentrated on sitting very still, gaze focused on his feet.

Next a girandole—fuscias, ambers, greens, and brilliant

orange—erupted over their heads, drumming a sick tattoo through his temples. He started to tremble.

Get hold of yourself, man. It's only fireworks.

But it was so much more. Every spectacular combustion brought back the roar of the cannon, the crack of artillery; every crimson explosion sparked memories of fields and friends awash in blood. Even breathing the acrid air made his stomach tighten and his lungs burn.

Oblivious, Phoebe's gaze was fixed heavenward. Every now and again she would pluck at his sleeve and remark on some particularly impressive specimen, but Anthony never looked up, and she never noticed. Never noticed that his limbs were trembling, that his breathing came in shallow gulps, nor that damp hair clung to his sweating forehead.

Never noticed the battle he was waging inside his head.

And then, silence. Like the eerie quiet that descended before a battle, this interlude was but the precursor to the greatest explosion of them all. Breath held, jaw clenched, fresh perspiration breaking out on his face, Anthony waited. And then, suddenly, a deafening salvo. The grand finale. A hush fell as the exploding missiles formed the British flag. The orchestra struck up "God Save the King," and the crowd began to sing as the magnificent display dissolved into ash.

Anthony reached for his handkerchief and scoured his forehead. His heartbeat was still erratic, but he'd managed to get through the exhibition with Phoebe none the wiser.

Chelsea would not have been so easy to fool. She would have taken one look at his face and known that something was wrong. Chelsea would have . . .

God, he had to find her. He'd been a fool to let passion and pride get in the way of saving her. This time, he'd carry her out kicking and screaming if need be.

Resolved, he stuffed the damp linen square back into his pocket and rose. "We should go back now."

Even now, Chelsea might be struggling to free herself from Ambrose's lecherous embrace.

He helped Phoebe up and they started down the hill. Despite the limp, he increased his pace until Phoebe was tripping over her feet to keep up.

The strains of a waltz flitted through the night as they gained the pavilion. Anthony scanned the packed dance floor. There was no sign of Chelsea or Ambrose among the twirling couples. His gaze slid over the rest of the enclosure, already knowing he would not find her there.

An invisible fist smashed into his abdomen.

Chelsea had vanished.

He sighted Reggie by the dessert table, helping himself to a slice of the centerpiece cake, an elaborate rendering of the Parthenon. He hauled Phoebe toward her brother.

"I must get back immediately," he said without preamble. "I need you to take Phoebe home."

Around a mouthful of cake, Reggie said, "All right."

Anthony slapped his friend's back. "Thank you." To Phoebe, he said, "Forgive me, my dear, but this cannot wait."

Mouth trembling, she said, "But the dancing is only just beginning."

"I'm sorry to disappoint you, but I'm afraid I must." He chucked her chin, then dashed away.

"Milord!" Phoebe called after him, her voice shrill. "At least tell me where you are going?"

Anthony wasn't about to waste precious seconds fabricating a reply. Already hundreds of people packed the main paths. He could take his carriage or hire a boatman to row him across the river; either way it might take an hour or more to cross to the other bank. Plunging into the milling crowd, he shouldered his way to the entrance. In the torch light, he sighted his carriage among the other vehicles parked outside the wrought iron gate.

Masters broke away from the group of congregating drivers and started to lower the carriage steps.

Anthony shook his head. "There isn't time. I have to get to Mayfair immediately. Help me unhitch the lead horse, then hand me that blanket from the seat."

"But, milord, there is no saddle."

"It won't be the first time I've ridden bareback. Now, do as I say!"

Chapter Fourteen

The intimate gathering at Lord Ambrose's townhouse proved to be very intimate indeed. As soon as Chelsea stepped inside the empty marble foyer, she understood that they would be breakfasting *à deux*, if at all. Except for the stone-faced butler who lit them to the parlor, the only signs of life came from her own clamoring heart.

The simple truth was that Ambrose frightened her. True, he'd kept his distance on the drive home, although he could have easily pounced on her in his carriage. And yet the way he'd looked at her, his tongue rolling over his bottom lip, she'd been hard-pressed not to abandon her plan and call for his driver to stop.

But thoughts of Robert kept her in her seat. What right had she to cling to safety when her brother was somewhere in the city—helpless, alone, and afraid? His very life depended on her discovering the coins.

And so she was here, in the parlor of Ambrose's tomblike townhouse, searching.

"Where are your other guests?" she asked, curious as to what lie he would tell.

Lounging on a Grecian couch, he shrugged. "Still quaffing my champagne, I would imagine."

Eyeing the carved chimneypiece, she wondered if one of the Egyptian figures might conceal a hiding place for valuables.

Deciding it was unlikely given the heat from the fire, she

roamed the room, exclaiming over Oriental vases, statuary, and ancient artifacts, all the while searching.

"What interesting decor. Such unusual wallpaper." She knocked her knuckles against the wall, searching for a hollow compartment. To cover the sound, she asked, "These dancing figures—are they symbols from some ancient script?"

He put down his drink and rose. "Indeed, the oldest language known to man." Coming up beside her, he laid a proprietary hand on her shoulder. "Take a closer look."

She did and heat suffused her cheeks. The black cutouts weren't dancing. They were *copulating*. Their two-dimensional bodies contorted into positions she'd never even imagined.

"Do you like it?" he asked, watching her face.

A chill raced her spine, bringing with it the urge to flee. *Calm, Chelsea. Stay calm.* "It's ehm . . . certainly original."

"Yes, isn't it." His pale eyes danced. "The ancients were far less inhibited than our own drab culture. It was common for Greek females as young as twelve to participate in the festival of Aphrodisia where there would be feasting, dancing, and . . . flagellation." He sighed. "So few women today truly appreciate the close association between pleasure and pain."

Her heart kicked against her chest, and the beginning of a sick headache drummed her temples. And, inside her head, Anthony's voice rang out: *He forced himself on the sister of a friend of mine.*

If only she could find those blasted coins.

"Have you anything to eat?" she asked suddenly. Nerves pitched her stomach but, with all the servants abed, perhaps he'd leave her alone to go forage through the pantry? "You did promise me breakfast," she added with what she hoped was a sultry smile.

His gaze slid over her. "You're a little thing to have such a voracious appetite, but I like that in a woman." His arms went about her, drawing her against him. "I'm a man of strong appetites myself."

She started to pull away, but he buried his face in the curve of her neck and nuzzled. His nipping teeth hurt, and fear churned her stomach. Oh God, she'd played out a similar scenario once before, with the squire. Only this time there was no fast horse waiting for her. In fact, no one even knew where she was.

She'd finally gone too far.

"Time for my midnight snack." He licked her cheek, raising fresh waves of nausea.

And fear.

Events were spinning out of control. Perhaps she should just ask him to show her his collection?

"But I haven't seen the coins yet."

He stepped back, eyes narrowed. "They will be on exhibit at the British Museum at the end of the month. Why not wait and see them displayed properly?"

Was that suspicion in his voice? She forced her lips into a pout. "Oh, but I'd so much rather you show them to me now. 'Twould be so much more *intimate* than a stuffy old museum."

His lips stretched into a smile. "Very well. The coins are in a case in the trophy room."

"Oh, they're not in here?"

Thank God she'd asked him outright; otherwise she could have searched the rest of the night. Given the way Ambrose was looking at her, she doubted he'd grant her that much time.

"Because of their value I keep them under lock and key."

He picked up a taper and lit their way to the grand staircase. Chelsea paused at the bottom and glanced back at the main door, grappling with indecision. Freedom and safety lay only a few feet away.

Ahead of her, Ambrose called out, "You do want to see them, don't you?"

The urge to flee was strong, but the lure of the coins—of securing Robert's release—was stronger. Gulping back her fear, Chelsea nodded and ascended. At the top, Ambrose opened a door to their right.

He stepped back for her to enter. Heart trouncing, Chelsea

stepped over the threshold and into the blackness. She heard Ambrose's footfalls behind her, felt his breath on the back of her neck. Gooseflesh pricked her bare arms.

"Like it?" He held the candle aloft.

A redheaded woman, eyes wide and face ghostly pale, stared back at her. She gasped, then realized she was facing herself in one of the room's many mirrors. Yet another mirror, a gilded monstrosity, hung from the ceiling above the bed. Candlelight glanced off the chains moored to the wall behind.

Chelsea swung around, her cry mingling with the soft squeal of the closing door.

"I thought you said the coins were in the trophy room?"

In the dim light, she could just discern his wolfish smile.

"My dear, this *is* the trophy room."

Anthony reined in his sweating horse across from Ambrose's house. Light shone from an upstairs window, otherwise the house was dark. He dismounted and quickly tied the reins to a nearby post, unable to shake off the dread weighing like bricks on his chest.

Dear God, please let her be all right.

But she wasn't all right, and he could feel it. Her fear trembled through every sinew of his own body; every palpitation of her heart hammered in his own breast. Just when this psychic connection, this spiritual joining, had come about he hadn't a clue nor did he have the time to ponder it.

Blood drumming his ears, he crossed the newly paved street, vaulted up the front steps, and tried the door. *Locked.* He lifted the brass knocker and struck it. Twice. Thrice. Still no response.

"Open, damn you. I know you're in there."

He pounded the black lacquered wood with both fists, determined to break through, if need be.

The door finally opened, and he looked up into a craggy visage, topped by a tasseled nightcap.

"I must see Lord Ambrose at once."

The butler tugged together the lapels of his striped night robe. "I'm afraid his lordship is not at home."

"Then I'll wait."

Anthony shoved past the old man and stepped inside the foyer. Something fluttered in his periphery, and he swung around. Chelsea's shawl waved at him from a hook inside the vestibule. A man's top hat hung beside it and a walking stick was propped in the corner. He snatched the shawl and pressed it to his cheek. Chelsea's scent wafted to his nostrils. He could almost swear he felt the heat of her body trapped in the cashmere fibers.

She *was* here. And so was Ambrose!

Remembering the upstairs light he'd seen, he grabbed the butler by the lapels of his robe. "Give me that candle and your keys."

Hands trembling, the butler reached inside his robe pocket and produced a brass ring from which at least twenty keys hung.

Anthony wrenched it away. "The key to the master bedroom? Which one is it?"

"The t-third o-one from the r-right."

"You'd better be telling the truth, old man."

Anthony took the stairs two at a time. He stepped off the landing just as Ambrose's angry voice rang out, "That vase was Yüan Dynasty! You'll pay for it in flesh, you little slut! Now get on the bed."

The smack of a blow and a woman's shriek froze the marrow in Anthony's bones. Heart pounding, he turned the key in the lock, tore open the door, and burst inside.

Ambrose stood in the center of the room, one hand flicking a riding crop against his calf. Chelsea lay in a crumpled heap at his feet, her face hidden by her loosened hair.

"Well, well, Montrose, this is a surprise." Ambrose swiped the back of his hand across the ugly cut on his forehead. "Care to join in or have you come simply to watch? Even a rake like you might learn something."

Shoulders quivering, Chelsea pulled herself onto her knees. "Anthony?" She brushed her hair out of her eyes, and candlelight played on the livid bruise mottling her cheek.

Cannon fired inside Anthony's skull. "*Bastard!*"

He rushed Ambrose, just as the other man raised the crop.

Anthony darted to the side, and the leather strap hissed over his shoulder. He grabbed Ambrose's wrist, squeezing until he felt the snapping of bones. Ambrose groaned and dropped the whip. Anthony kicked it aside, then smashed his fist into the center of his foe's face. Bone and cartilage crunched beneath his knuckles, filling him with primitive satisfaction.

Ambrose staggered backwards, blood spurting. He cupped his nose. "Christ, I think you've broken it."

Panting, Anthony backed against the bedpost. "Then it'll match the rest of you when I've done."

"You're battle-crazed, Montrose. The war rotted your brain and now you belong in Bedlam, caged with the other lunatics."

Anthony lifted one of the bejeweled manacles from the velvet counterpane. Chains rattled.

"I'm not the one whose sanity is in question, but you're right on one score—I've killed men for less." He threw down the cuff and stalked toward Ambrose.

Ambrose flew to the door, but Anthony tackled him. They rolled across the floor, shards of the broken vase crunching beneath them. Anthony grabbed Ambrose's collar and stood, bringing the other man with him.

"This is for Fanny." Anthony raised his fist and plowed into Ambrose's jaw. Blood and saliva sprayed from the slack mouth. "All the rest are for tonight."

Drunk with rage, he fisted Ambrose in the gut again and again. His last blow sent Ambrose hurtling across the chamber into one of the mirrors. He fell forward, shards of glass raining down on him.

Sweat streaming his brow, Anthony picked up the riding crop and stalked toward the fallen man.

I've killed men for less.

He raised the whip.

"Stop it, Anthony!"

Chelsea pulled on his arm. She hadn't the strength to stay him but, when he looked into her pleading eyes, he felt the madness recede. He tossed the weapon aside.

She stared at the blood streaking the broken mirror. "Oh, Anthony, you don't think he's . . . ?"

He dropped to his good knee beside Ambrose and pressed two fingers against the side of his enemy's neck. A steady pulse beat beneath the pads of his fingers, proving that the Devil did indeed protect his own.

He stood. "He'll awaken with the very devil of a headache, but he's alive."

She exhaled. "Thank God."

She turned away and began fumbling with her bodice but not before he noticed that the top of her gown was rent, revealing her undergarments and a generous swell of cleavage.

His eyes flew to the bed. It wasn't mussed but, knowing Ambrose, that didn't prove anything. If Ambrose had violated her, neither Chelsea's pleas nor the certainty that he'd hang for murder would keep Anthony from finishing what he'd begun.

"Chelsea. He didn't r—?" He couldn't bring himself to say the word.

She managed a wan smile. "No, he didn't."

Relief flooded him. He'd thought the war, the death of his two best friends, had drained him of tears, but he'd been wrong. So bloody wrong. Choking down the lump in his throat, he stripped off his cape and brushed it free of debris.

He draped it over Chelsea's shoulders. "Let's get you home."

They descended the stairs. In the front hallway, Anthony tossed the keys to the butler, who cowered in a corner.

He took Chelsea's hand, and they stepped outside into the cool night. "My mount is across the street. Can you ride?"

"I think so."

He untied the reins and mounted, then lifted her. Setting her in front, he tenderly tucked his cape around her.

"Ready?"

She nodded, and he dug in his spurs.

After a few blocks, he slowed the horse to a walk, then reined in beneath a street lamp.

She pushed away from his chest. "Why are we stopping?"

"Because we need to talk and this is likely to be one of the only places we can be assured of privacy."

Light touched her bruised face and weary eyes. "You were right, I was wrong . . . again. What more is there to say?"

"A great deal." He touched her swollen cheek, his fingertips tingling from the light contact. "I want us to come to an understanding. Surely, after what nearly happened to you back there, you must realize that there are worse fates than becoming my mistress?"

Her gaze fell from his face and settled on his chest. At least she wasn't spurning him. Hope spiraled inside him.

"Darling, you've been through so much." He ran his thumb along her lower lip. "Let me take care of you. Let me . . . love you."

She lifted her eyes to his face. A steely expression stole over her features. "I can't."

"Can't or won't?" Desperation stabbed him like a knife in the gut.

"They're one and the same." She turned away, and the knife plunged deeper.

"Are they?" He pulled her back into his embrace. "Even if I vowed to care for you, to cherish you, all the days of my life?"

"Those are wedding vows, milord. You had best save them for your bride."

Her voice was cold, but a fierce yearning fired her eyes. She cared for him. He knew it. And he wasn't going to let her walk out of his life. Not without a fight.

"Damn it, Chelsea, Phoebe means nothing to me. I scarcely know her. Our marriage is a contract between two families, not two people."

She jerked away from him. "Anthony, I don't want to hear—"

He laid a finger over the juncture of her soft, open lips. "But you're going to." He drew a shuddering breath, steeling himself. If spilling his soul was what it took to convince her, then so be it. "I understand what it means to lose people you care about. I lost my two best friends in the war. Stephen took sick just after Barrosa. In the end, 'twas the malaria, not the French, that got him." His fingers clenched the reins. What he was about to admit was tantamount to

pulling the stitches from a barely healed wound. "And later
at Albuera, after I'd been hit, my other friend, Peter . . .
Well, the bloody fool unseated the French cavalryman who
was charging me . . . and got himself trampled into the bargain."

Her eyes softened. "Oh, Anthony." She brushed his cheek
with the back of her hand. "You mustn't torture yourself.
You would have done the same had you been in his place."

He gave a hollow laugh. "Would I? I'm not so sure. Even
now I can't help wondering . . . if I hadn't pushed Cole to
advance . . . hell, if I hadn't persuaded Peter and Stephen to
join up in the first place. Why should I be the one to survive
when better men . . . ?" His voice cracked, but he'd come
too far now to turn back. He bit back the shame and forged
on. "And then I met you. For the first time in more than two
years—no, in my whole life—I felt . . ." He hesitated,
searching. ". . . whole. As if my surviving—Peter's sacrifice—might be to some purpose after all." He lifted her
slight hand and pressed the palm to his mouth, heedless of
the tear trailing his cheek. "Now that I've found you, I can't
bear to lose you. I *won't* lose you." He rested his forehead
against hers. "Be my lover, Chelsea. I'll steal away as often
as possible to be with you and, in those stolen moments,
we'll know greater happiness than most lawfully wedded
couples find together in a lifetime."

"Oh, Anthony." The clip-clop of approaching horses'
hooves striking the cobbles nearly drowned Chelsea's
choked sob. "If I've learned anything from tonight, it's that
nothing good ever comes of stealing."

They passed a strolling lamplighter, torch in hand, but otherwise Mount Street was as dark and desolate as Anthony's
soul. But he wasn't ready to concede defeat. Not hardly.

They dismounted. When he turned to tether the horse,
Chelsea flew across the street.

He caught up with her at the townhouse entrance. Vault-
ing to the top step, he said, "I only want to see you safely inside."

"I'd rather you didn't." A lantern hung beside her door.

Standing inside the feeble pool of light, she rifled through her reticule for the door key.

Metal rang against the flagging, then glanced off the step.

"Blast." She fell to her knees.

Anthony came down beside her. "Allow me." Feeling in the dark, he found the key in the bushes. "*Voila.*" Brushing soil from his hands, he got to his feet and helped her up.

"Thank you." She held out her palm.

He hesitated. *You really are a rogue, Montrose.* He wasn't proud, but he was resolved.

He pocketed the key. "The price is one kiss."

One kiss. What he was about to do was wrong, but he closed his mind to the niggling self-reproach. Chelsea Bellamy might not yet realize it, but she needed him almost as much as he needed her. And he was willing to call on every dirty trick in his rake's repertoire to prove it to her.

"Oh, Anthony, for pity's sake." A tear splashed her cheek.

He reached out and brushed it away with his thumb just as another took its place. Seeing her like this tore at his heart, but he told himself he must be ruthless for both their sakes.

He lifted her chin on the edge of his hand. "One kiss, then I'll leave."

He kissed her forehead, her closed eyes, each of her satiny cheeks. When he moved over her soft mouth, his lips butterfly light, she turned her face away.

"I must go inside," she said, one hand balanced lightly on his chest. "Jack will be waiting up."

Anthony glanced beyond her to the darkened windows. "I rather think he's still at the Rookery." *Where I'm supposed to relieve him, inside of an hour. God, if only I had more time.* "I'll go in with you. We'll wait for him together."

She moved away. "*No.*" This time she sounded as though she meant it. "You've seen me to the door, you've had your one kiss, you've . . ." She threw her hands in the air. "This *is* goodnight."

Anthony hesitated. A second later, inspiration struck. He lifted his right hand to the light. The torn evening glove revealed busted knuckles and an impressive smattering of dried blood. At least he hoped she was impressed. Most of the blood was Ambrose's but, if she assumed it was his, who was he to gainsay her?

"May I come inside long enough to wash my hand?" he asked mildly.

Her jaw dropped and her eyes softened. "Of course," she said and quickly unlocked the door. "But then you're leaving."

"Of course," he replied.

Following her inside, he reminded himself that he was doing this for them both. She cared for him, he knew it. It was only her provincial morality—and her pride—that stood in the way of their mutual happiness. Once he breached her defenses, she would probably thank him.

She paused in the hall to light a candle, then led the way through the house to the kitchen.

"Sit," she commanded, nearly shoving him into a spindle-back chair set at one end of the pine table.

The very sturdy table. He thought of that evening less than a fortnight before when he'd nearly succeeded in having her on his dining room table. His desire, which he'd managed to keep dormant on the ride home, leapt to life.

Still swathed in his cape, she went to a cupboard, pulled down a heavy white bowl, then moved to the sink to fill it. His offers of help brought more stern orders to sit still.

"At home we always used rainwater for washing," she said, her voice rising above the sound of the crank. "But here, the air is so filthy . . ."

She was doing her damndest to behave normally, but by now he knew her too well to miss the nervous trill in her voice or the way she caught at her bottom lip with her teeth. She was unraveling before his very eyes, which signified . . .

I'm winning. In another few minutes he'd have his cape off her and then the gown. Or perhaps, in the interest of time, he'd leave the gown on. Either way, this time they'd finish what they'd begun.

But his certain victory rang hollow. Certainly he wasn't the first lover to use trickery to woo his lady. But what he was doing—about to do—was far worse. He was using Chelsea's own fine qualities, her caring, sympathetic nature, as a weapon against her. And he felt profoundly, deeply ashamed. Good God, could it be that Anthony Grenville, one of London's most notorious libertines, had grown a conscience?

He was still pondering the possibility when she returned to set the bowl of water, a clean cloth, and a dusty bottle of some spirit—whiskey?—on the table.

He picked up the bottle. "Hm, scotch. Dare I hope you've changed your mind and are planning on having your wicked way with me after all?"

"No, you dare not."

Cheeks flushed, she pulled out a chair beside him and sat. Careful to avoid his gaze, she reached for his hand. Through the remnants of his glove, he felt her fingers, cold as ice. And suddenly he knew that, as much as he wanted her, he didn't want her this way.

"This isn't necessary. I'm fine." He gripped the chair arm, starting up.

She braced a hand against his chest. "You're not going anywhere until I clean those cuts."

Several shirt buttons had gone missing in the fight with Ambrose, and springy dark hair teased her palm. When she pulled away, her hand was shaking.

He brushed her bruised cheek with gentle fingers. "If anyone needs tending, it's you."

She winced. His touch was light, but the contusion had begun to throb.

And her cheek wasn't the only place she throbbed. Liquid warmth pooled in her lower belly, trickling downward to the feminine core that Anthony once had manipulated so skillfully.

Now that the danger was past, she realized that she wanted him to touch her there again . . . and everywhere else.

Powerful, conflicting emotions wrenched her but somehow she found herself smiling. "We're quite a pair, aren't we?"

He grinned back. "Quite."

By now she knew that their easy comradery was deceptive; at any moment, passion could flare between them like flint striking steel. Determined to avoid being singed by the flame, she concentrated on easing off his glove.

"Ouch!"

"Sorry."

He hadn't exaggerated; his right hand really was a mess. The cloth was embedded in the broken flesh and, when she finally tugged the glove free, a generous measure of skinned knuckles went with it. She bent to dip the cloth into the water, and his breath fanned the side of her face. Resisting the urge to press the cloth to her burning cheeks, she gently sponged the fibers from his torn flesh.

Sitting alone with him in her dark, silent house, nursing him in her rustic kitchen, she felt almost . . . *wifely*. Domestic intimacy was proving to be a powerful aphrodisiac, more erotic even than the elegant supper of a fortnight before. She found herself deliberately drawing out the process of washing his wounds—any excuse to keep touching him. At the same time, guilt pricked her. Every moment she lingered felt like a betrayal of Robert, a mockery of every fine principle her parents had instilled. Yet when she caught his hungry stare fixed on her bosom, she couldn't seem to muster the will—or the decency—to move away.

She pulled the cape closed and tried to cover her self-consciousness with a light laugh. "I believe you'll live." Time to send him on his way. She reached for the scotch bottle.

He pulled back, eyeing her as she dribbled whiskey onto the cloth. "What do you intend to do with that?"

She reached for his hand. "I'm going to put some of this on to prevent infection."

Her fingers closed around his wrist. Beneath her thumb, his pulse raced. Panic over being stung? She doubted it.

Even so, she teased, "What an infant you are." Leaning forward, she dabbed the cuts, blowing on them to ease the smarting. "There, all done." Laying the cloth on the tray, she wiped her damp palm on her ruined gown. "I could bandage it, but it would be better to let the cuts air overnight."

Overnight.

He glanced down at his hand, and Chelsea realized she still held it.

Release his hand and move away. Ignore the sensual promise in his dark eyes, and the way the light plays on the indentation cleaving his square chin. Resist the urge to explore the crisp curls peaking out from his open shirt collar. Give him back his cape and show him to the door . . . now.

Despite the haranguing of her better self, Chelsea couldn't bring herself to move. Or to let go. When exactly had Anthony managed to insinuate himself into her soul, becoming her touchstone in a life that grew more precarious with each passing day? When had simple physical desire become this all-consuming longing, this conviction that she would never feel this way about any other man?

In a sennight, he would be someone else's husband, but he wasn't a husband yet. They had no future together, but the present suddenly bloomed, a precious gift.

Perhaps it was time to adopt a new motto. *Carpe diem.* Seize the day. Or, in her case, the night.

She lifted his hand and gently brushed the battered flesh with her lips.

Anthony's eyes flew open. He sucked in his breath.

"You could murder a man with your gentleness, do you know that?" His voice, several decibels below its usual timbre, cracked.

She rubbed her cheek across the back of his hand. "I don't want to murder you, milord. I want to make love with you."

There, she'd said it. She hadn't begged as he'd once told her she must, but surely she'd come close enough? She searched his face—the furrowed forehead, the eyes stark with need, the tightly drawn mouth, the muscle jumping in the square jaw.

Finally he asked, "Are you certain? In the morning, this night and all its horrors will be only a memory. You may have regrets."

Regrets. Relief washed over her. Yes, there would be regrets, she was sure of it. But there would also be glorious memories of love and laughter to warm the cold, lonely nights ahead.

Her trembling lips formed a smile. "In that case, we had better make a memory to last a lifetime."

Joy, desire, relief lit Anthony's face. His arms went around her and he leapt up, bringing her with him.

Cradling her head between his hands, he murmured, "We shan't need memories when we have a lifetime of days and nights ahead of us."

Chapter Fifteen

Behind the closed door of her bedchamber, Chelsea stepped out of the last of her clothing. Anthony's mouth went dry. Naked except for her stockings, she was all moon pale skin and wide, wary eyes—and more enticing than the most expensive of courtesans.

He swallowed hard. "You're beautiful, Lady Robin."

A mortified blush spread from her face to the tops of her apple-shaped breasts. She crossed one arm over them; the other hand shielded the russet triangle between her milk-white thighs.

"Please don't do that." He drew her hands down to her sides. "I want to look at you. I *need* to look at you."

He brushed back the loose copper curls cascading over her front. Rose-tipped breasts pricked his palm. She shivered and so did he.

She raised shy eyes to his. "Shall I at least take off my stockings?"

"Definitely not." His gaze riveted on her garters—black bands of lace tied above her dimpled knees. "You have beautiful legs, even longer and more shapely than I'd imagined . . . and I have a very good imagination." Indeed, the thought of them wrapped around his torso stoked the fire in his belly.

She worried her hands, looking anything but pleased by the compliment. Given their other passionate interludes, he was unprepared for this maidenly modesty, this reticence.

She seemed almost . . . virginal. Enchanted, he found himself grappling with feelings that were fundamentally at odds. He wanted to ravish her and protect her all at once.

"Shouldn't we blow out the candle?"

He chuckled. "I'm not an owl, milady."

She hesitated, then laughed. The tinkling sound was a siren's call to sea. Cast adrift in the depths of her turquoise gaze, Anthony cupped her face between his palms and prepared to drown. She winced.

"Sorry." He brushed her bruised cheek with his knuckles. Not thinking of the angry mark, he said, "I'd never hurt you, Chelsea."

She looked down. "Perhaps we shouldn't make promises we can't keep."

His gaze fell to the faint bruise budding on her upper arm, the one *he'd* made when he'd gripped her to keep her from going back to Ambrose. After everything that had happened, he'd nearly forgotten the episode. Obviously she remembered it only too well.

"Earlier tonight, in the garden, I didn't mean to hurt you." He lifted her chin on the edge of his hand. "I'm not really such a brute."

Silence.

"I don't want you to be afraid of me. You aren't, are you?"

She shook her head. "No . . . and yes. But not because of tonight. Even then, when you were angrier than I've ever seen you, I trusted that you wouldn't really hurt me."

"Do you trust me now?" He inhaled, waiting.

"Y-yes."

He lifted her chin on the edge of his hand and smiled at her. "Good, because my fingers are itching to untie those fetching but rather fragile looking ribbons. May I?"

Her smile was tentative. She nodded. "If you like."

Stiffly, he lowered himself onto his good knee and untied the right garter. He kissed the side of her knee, her calf, and finally her ankle, slowly rolling the silk down, then off. At the second garter, he deliberately brushed the inside of her thigh with the back of his hand. Musk teased his nostrils. He leaned forward and angled his face upward.

"That's enough." Breathing hard, Chelsea backed into the bedpost. "Fair is fair. Now I want to see you."

Drunk with desire, he stumbled to his feet. He glanced down to the bulge at his trouser front and grinned.

"This is all I have to offer you. I hope you weren't expecting more."

She swatted his shoulder. "You know perfectly well what I mean. Your shirt . . . I've never seen you without it."

"That's easily remedied." His fingers went to the top button of his waistcoat.

She slid one hand inside his open shirt front and shook her head. "My turn."

Wondering who was seducing who, he reined in his desire and stood motionless, suffering her to remove first his waistcoat, then his shirt. Both garments joined the mounting pile at their feet.

"You're the one who is beautiful," she intoned with a sigh, soft fingers skimming his chest.

He followed her gaze. From the elbow down, his arms were tanned a Spaniard's bronze, but his upper arms and chest were lily white, his pectorals and abdomen covered with dark auburn hair.

And scars.

A saber wound, ugly and jagged, slashed across his left shoulder. That same arm bore the hole from the bullet that had passed through his bicep. He tensed, watching her face for signs of revulsion.

Instead she pressed her lips to the milk white ridge. She looked up, tears gathering in her eyes. "Oh, Anthony. Albuera?"

"And before." He laid a finger over her trembling mouth. "There'll be plenty of time for you to explore the ruins later."

His restraint, like his heart, was fast melting. Blood pumping to his loins, he swept her into his arms and carried her to the narrow bed. Carefully, reverently, he laid her in the center, then turned to undress. By the time he shed his boots and trousers, she'd slipped beneath the covers, the faded quilt tucked demurely beneath her chin.

"You won't be needing that. I promise to keep you warm." He yanked the covers down and climbed in beside her.

Propped up on one elbow, he glided a hand down the front of her, weighing her breasts in his palm, trailing his fingers over her ribs and flat abdomen. She was drawn as taut as a bowstring, her eyes round and watchful.

He bent to sip one rosy nipple. It budded beneath his tongue. "You're nervous, aren't you?"

She hesitated. "A little."

"'Tis only natural." He flicked his thumb over her other nipple.

"It is?"

He nodded. "What you've been through tonight would be more than enough to blunt any woman's desires, even one as passionate as I know you to be. Fortunately I know a way to persuade your body to relax."

"H-how?"

"If I told, it wouldn't be a secret." At her blank look, he added, "Surely you can guess?"

She shook her head.

His palm settled over the plump mound between her silken thighs. "No?"

Could it be that Chelsea's previous lovers had taken their pleasure without ensuring hers? His chest swelled at the prospect of being able to claim first, to brand her as his in this intimate act of lovemaking.

There had been countless—and occasionally nameless—women over the years. He'd always taken pains to ensure that he returned satisfaction, be his bedmate a lady or a whore. But this powerful yearning to please Chelsea, to have her writhe in his arms, transcended manly pride. This time was different from any other. This time it was for love.

The realization rocked him to the core of his being, shattering all prior precepts and nullifying vows. He hadn't believed in love before, not really. Not until . . . now.

He looked down at Chelsea, a fierce tenderness sweeping over him.

I'll never hurt you, Chelsea. And I'll never let you go.

"Trust me." He threaded his fingers through the thatch of dark copper curls, smiling at her sudden, sharp exclamation. He palmed her with light, circular strokes, coaxing her legs apart. Then he did what he'd dreamt about doing ever since that night in his dining room. He lay on his stomach and slid down until his head was between her raised thighs.

She lifted herself on her elbows, blinking owlishly. "Anthony, where are you going?"

Smiling, he brushed his stubbled cheek against her inner thigh, lightly grazing the tender flesh. "I've captured you at last, my little thief, and I'm determined to see, feel, and taste every luscious bit of you before this night is over."

Her pupils dilated. "You can't mean to . . . that is to say, you're not going to kiss me *there*?"

She tried to lock her knees, but his shoulders were in the way. Instead, her legs ended up wrapped around his torso, pulling him even closer.

He eased her apart, and his tongue slid inside the slick cleft. She gasped, her fingers tangling in his hair.

"Anthony!"

Hands balled into fists at her sides, she fell back against the pillow.

The pink flesh was hot as a brazier and juicy as a ripe plum. His own flesh felt on fire, the shaft between his legs erect and blazing with desire.

Moaning, she lifted herself to meet each liquid sweep. He paused, and her frustrated whimper was like music to his soul. He'd been right—clearly none of his predecessors had introduced her to this. Her sea-green eyes were dark and dazed with desire and her glorious hair fanned across the pillow, the damp tendrils forming a halo about her flushed face. Her pink tongue darted out to moisten her full bottom lip and the throbbing in his groin intensified.

He bent his head once more and fitted his mouth over her quivering flesh. Hips churning and fingernails clawing the covers, she perched on the precipice of her release. And she was fighting it.

"Anthony . . . please. No more. I can't b-bear it."

"Yes, you can. Surrender to it, darling." *Surrender to me.*

Her head tossed on the pillow. "I can't . . . Someone . . . Jack . . . If he's back, he'll hear me."

"He won't, I promise. I won't let him. Trust me."

He sought out the small nubbin amidst the slippery folds and gently suckled the swollen flesh.

"Oh, *Anthony!*"

He slid up the length of her and covered his mouth over hers, drinking in her keening cry. Gathering up her shuddering body, he absorbed each convulsive wave rippling through her until she stilled beneath him.

She looked up at him, moisture spangling her bottom lashes. "I never imagined that it could be like this."

But Anthony was in no state to bask in her afterglow. The need to be inside her was eclipsing all reason. Straddling her splayed hips, he lifted himself.

Her eyes shot open. "Anthony, what are you doing?"

Desire weighed heavily between his legs, and the dull, fisted ache demanded immediate attention.

He gave a ragged laugh. "Chelsea, love, this is no time to play the virgin."

He thrust into her.

Chelsea's sob ricocheted inside his head, breaking the sensual spell.

Anthony froze. He looked down at her pale, stricken face and knew that his worst nightmare had come to pass.

He had just debauched a virgin.

Anthony braced a palm on either side of her and slowly withdrew. Judging by his harsh, frozen features and the bunched muscles of his neck and shoulders, the retreat had siphoned every smidgen of his self-control.

"Why didn't you tell me?" he demanded, voice sharp as honed steel.

Chelsea gnawed her bottom lip. "I'd rather hoped you wouldn't notice."

He leaned back against the headboard and raked a hand through his sweat-slick hair. "Not notice. Christ, Chelsea, blood doesn't lie."

He hadn't bothered to cover himself. Following his downward gaze, Chelsea saw the scarlet flecks on his penis.

And the anger in his eyes.

She swallowed against the thickness strangling her. When the moment of truth arrived, she'd promised herself that she'd be sophisticated, stoic even. Instead she'd made a complete hash of things, and Anthony was glaring at her as though he despised her. And, to make matters worse, she was about to cry in front of him.

Hoping to spare herself that humiliation, she turned onto her side and gave him her back. "You seemed so sure I wasn't. I didn't want to disappoint you."

The bed creaked. He must have gotten up.

"I just assumed . . . Christ, Chelsea, what was I supposed to think?"

Footfalls on the floorboards announced his passage across the room. Clearly he intended on dressing—and leaving—immediately.

Humiliated, she hugged the pillow tight and buried her face in its comforting white lumpiness. "There's no need to explain. It was a perfectly logical assumption under the circumstances. I suppose any woman who becomes a highwayman, then a housebreaker—all within a fortnight—would be considered fair game by most men."

From across the room, he growled, "I'm not most men. And stop being so damned reasonable."

"I'm sorry," she mumbled, not quite certain why she was apologizing. Not that it mattered. She might as well apologize for her whole miserable life.

She heard the swish of water lopping into a basin. He must be at the washstand. Of course, he would want to expunge all traces of her before he left. Misery engulfed her. She lay listening for the chamber door—the first creak to open, the second to close. Why didn't he just leave so she could vent the sobs welling inside her?

She started when she felt his hand on her shoulder.

"You're crying." It wasn't a question.

"No I'm not." Using a corner of the pillow case, she dabbed her wet cheeks.

"I beg to differ." The mattress groaned as he sat down beside her. "Chelsea, turn over and look at me."

She sniffed. "No."

"Please."

She rolled onto her back, holding the sheet up with both hands. Earlier he'd made her feel beautiful, desirable; now she felt ugly and ashamed.

Still, she forced herself to look at him. He was barechested, but he'd put on his trousers. The lightweight fabric outlined the hard ridge of his sex.

"I'm sorry I hurt you. Believe me when I say, I had no idea you were a virgin."

She twisted a corner of the sheet in her hand. "If you'd known, would it have made a difference?"

"Yes . . . I mean, no." He drew a heavy breath. "I would have gone slowly, taken care not to hurt you . . . at least, not nearly so much." He pressed the heel of his hand to his temple. "Christ, I wouldn't have breached you like some rutting animal."

And suddenly she understood. He wasn't angry with her but with himself. Self-loathing gave way to relief, then to a rush of tenderness.

She reached up and touched his hard cheek. "It's not your fault. You mustn't blame yourself." She summoned a cheerful smile. "At least it was over quickly."

He scowled. "That, my dear, was just the beginning."

Her mouth dropped open. "How much longer could it last?"

He cocked a brow as though asking himself if anyone could possibly be that innocent. "That depends on a number of factors, not the least of which are the stamina and control of one's partner. But I was—*am*—very excited. I wouldn't have lasted very long this round."

This round! "You mean you intended for us to do this—" She swallowed. "—more than once?"

He smiled. "Indeed, I had thought we would do this several more times ere morning."

She was so shocked that she didn't notice him unfurling

her fingers from the sheet until it was too late. He tugged it down to her toes in one swift motion.

Pulling herself up on her elbow, she grabbed for the quilt.

He sat next to her, his thigh brushing hers. "It's a bit late for modesty, don't you think?"

She looked nervously at the basin on the bedside table. "That depends. W-what are you planning to do with *that*?"

He dipped a cloth inside and wrung it out. "I only want to make you more comfortable."

He eased her back against the pillows, and his hand slipped between her knees. When she felt the cool cloth on the sticky inside of her thigh, she thought she would die of shame.

"Really, this isn't necessary," she sputtered, cheeks flaming. "I'm fine. 'Tis nothing that a soak in a hot bath will not remedy."

"If only that were so," he muttered, wiping her with brisk, efficient strokes.

He spread her legs wider and began sponging the tender folds. Mortified, she tried to grab the cloth from him, but he only urged her to lie back. She surrendered, focusing her gaze on the ceiling shadows cast by the guttering candle. He began to hum softly—some odd but vaguely familiar melody—and almost against her will she began to relax.

He tossed the cloth in the water, covered her, and sat back down. "You should know that tonight was a first for me as well."

She snorted. "Really, milord. I may be a virgin—well, an almost-virgin—but that doesn't make me a fool."

He frowned. "I meant that I've never lain with an innocent before." His eyes glinted with the familiar mischief. "Of course, I've never lain with a highwayman either. Sex with the person who once held a pistol to my manhood lends a certain novelty to the encounter as well."

Tears still veiled her eyes, but a smile tugged the corners of her mouth. "You may have a point." She searched his face, levity fading. "I'm sorry for keeping the truth from you . . . and for being so woefully inept."

He smoothed the hair from her forehead. "Virgin yes,

inept, hardly." He bent and kissed the tip of her nose. "I was just surprised. And, while we're on the subject, terribly honored."

"Truly?"

He nodded. "As for experience, you have a standing invitation to sharpen your womanly wiles on me anytime and anywhere you like."

A sick emptiness drifted to the center of her chest. What good could come of confessing that there would never be another night? If she did, he would only spend what was left of this one remonstrating with her, alternately begging and bullying her to change her mind.

He glanced at the door. "I should leave you now."

"Leave? Why?" She fretted her bottom lip, scouring her bemused brain for the words that would coax him to stay. "The damage is done, you may as well finish the business."

Those obviously weren't the words. He looked as though she'd struck him.

Blast, Chelsea, what an idiot you are. "I'm sorry. That's not what I meant. What I meant to say, to ask is . . . Do you want to go?"

"Honestly, no. But I also know that, if I stay, I can't promise that I won't try to *finish the business*, as you so charmingly put it. And, after the way I bore into you, you're bound to be sore."

"I don't feel that sore."

Expression grim, he rose. "Just wait until tomorrow."

Tomorrow. Forcing nonchalance into her voice, she replied, "Why not let tomorrow take care of itself?" *Especially when tomorrow's physical pain will be a welcome distraction from a far greater grief.*

"Get some sleep." He kissed her forehead and left her to scrounge for the rest of his clothes.

She bolted upright, too alarmed to care that the sheet fell to her waist. "Anthony, don't go." It was almost a whisper.

His fingers paused on his shirt. "What did you say?"

She screwed up her courage and blurted out, "I said, don't go. I want you to stay. Please stay."

"Even if it means—"

"Especially if it means . . . *that*." She took a deep breath. "I want to try again. This time I promise I won't make a sound."

That made him smile. "In that case—"

He tore off his clothing, sending buttons popping. He swooped down beside her, pulled her against him, and feathered kisses over her brow, her eyelids, her throat.

"This time I'll make it good for you, I swear it."

He wooed her with whispered endearments; soft, coaxing kisses; and gentle, questing caresses. He was all lean muscle and corded sinew, strong where she was weak, hard where she was soft. He rubbed his pelvis against her lower belly, and a frantic anticipation gripped her. She arched against him, hot, tingling heat pooling inside her.

He pulled back. "Christ, Chelsea, I've wanted you, this, for so very long." His breathing was labored as though he'd been running. "But if I go any farther, I won't be able to stop."

She looked up into his strained face, the dark eyes almost feral, and vowed that this time there would be no retreating, no crying off. Whether or not there would be pain, she no longer cared. She wanted Anthony inside of her.

"I don't want you to stop. Only show me . . . how to . . . where to touch you."

He took her hand and placed it along the length of him. Her fingers curled around him. He was granite hard and velvet smooth, and he throbbed against her palm. She dipped her thumb in the moisture glistening at the tip of his shaft. Tracing a slow circle, she marveled that the small, innocent droplet carried his seed. The seed that could result in a child. *Their child.* The prospect both terrified and thrilled her.

He shuddered. "This time, we do it together." His hands slipped beneath her knees, lifting them. "Take me inside you," he whispered, positioning himself between her parted thighs.

She still held him. His fingers encircled her wrist, guiding her hand downward until he pressed against her soft woman's flesh.

Despite all her fine resolutions, Chelsea tensed when he

entered her. The pressure began to build, and she gritted her teeth, waiting for the rending pain.

He reached down and stroked her breasts, his fingertips fluttering over the tips. "Try to relax."

He eased the rest of the way inside her, then stilled.

He looked down on her, gaze intense. "All right?"

Dumb with awe, she managed a small nod. All right didn't begin to capture the sensation of being stretched and filled beyond her wildest imaginings. And, this time, her body mounted no resistance. A tingling awareness had replaced the pain.

He began to move back and forth, slowly at first, his eyes intent on her face. Gradually he increased the pace, slipping in a slickness that owed nothing to blood or pain. Long, languid strokes interspersed with short, intense ripostes stoked the heat between her thighs to a raging firestorm.

And then she was nipping his neck, clawing his back, matching him stroke for stroke, and begging him to do things that would have shocked her only hours before.

"That's it," he whispered, slipping a hand beneath her buttocks. "Meet me halfway, darling. That's all I ask."

Chelsea felt her breasts flatten against the hard, unyielding plane of his chest, felt herself crushed into the cradle of his thighs as he buried himself to the hilt.

Withdrawing, he rasped, "Chelsea, I've waited so long, wanted you for so long. I don't think I can wait any longer."

Hands slipping in the sweat rolling down his back, she pressed a kiss to his taut jaw and arched against him. "No, don't wait."

His mouth closed over hers in a bruising assault that murdered reason. At the same time, he reached down between them and tweaked her hidden nubbin with his thumb.

And then the world exploded with pleasure so intense it skirted pain. Chelsea squeezed her eyes closed and clutched Anthony as wave after wave of molten lava poured over her. Her toes curled, perspiration filmed the backs of her knees, and even her fingertips tingled.

"Oh, God, Chelsea."

Chelsea opened her eyes to Anthony's spasming face

looming above her. He pumped into her, his hoarse shout of satisfaction filling her with feminine triumph as old as Eve. She wrapped her arms about him and closed her eyes, filled with reverence. For this night, this moment, this magnificent man belonged to her and she to him.

Love, completion, wholeness teemed through her.

Everything but peace.

Chapter Sixteen

Anthony rolled onto his side. He wrapped an arm around Chelsea's waist and drew her against him until her back and hips fitted to his chest and groin. Like two stacked spoons, they were a perfect fit just as this was a perfect moment. Almost perfect.

He lifted his head from the pillow and kissed the top of her satiny shoulder. Screwing up his courage, he whispered, "I love you, Chelsea."

He waited, heart thumping. *Please, God, let her say she loves me too. Let her say . . . something.*

But a soft snuffle was her only response.

"Chelsea?" Wondering if she were crying, he pulled up on one elbow and peered over her.

She wasn't crying. She was sleeping.

Long lashes fanned velvet shadows across the contours of her high cheekbones. Her lips, bright pink from his kisses, parted softly. Above the white sheet, the high tops of her breasts rose and fell with each heavy breath.

Anthony flopped onto his back, releasing a soft laugh in deference to life's little ironies. Women had been throwing themselves in his path, protesting their love for him, since he was fourteen. And yet, now that he had finally declared *himself*, the object of his affection could only . . . snore.

How utterly humbling.

He lay, fists clenched at his sides, battling the selfish urge to nudge her, to jiggle the mattress just a little. As soon as she awoke, he would say the words again, make love to her again, hopefully hear her say that she loved him too.

But waking her would be brutish. Her head weighed like an anchor on the pillow and her heavy breathing bespoke of an exhaustion that was only partly physical. Now was not the time to press her for a declaration of her feelings. He could be patient when the situation warranted it. He'd willingly wait a lifetime to hear Chelsea say those four magical words: *I love you, Anthony.*

A lifetime. His lifetime.

Reality crashed down on him, burying bliss beneath the rubble of responsibility. He lay still, lungs tight and chest burning.

Lost in the wonder of the woman lying beside him, he'd managed to forget that, in eight short days, he would take Phoebe Tremont—not Chelsea Bellamy—to wife. Having received the full measure of Chelsea's generous passion, marriage to Phoebe seemed more sacrilege than sacrament, more ending than beginning.

Sitting up, he combed his damp hair from his face. He must do his duty, go through with the marriage, even though the thought of bedding his future wife shot ice water through his veins. The banns had been read. It was too late to cry off. Surely Chelsea would see that he had no choice. Surely she'd not walk out of his life now, not when her virgin's blood stained the sheet on which they lay?

But this was Chelsea. The independent, willful, *wonderful* woman he'd fallen in love with. As much as he'd like to believe that last night signified her capitulation, he couldn't. He may have breached her maidenhead but her will was another matter. It would further his cause enormously if he could manage to get her pregnant over the next week. Then she'd be in no position to refuse his protection. She might stubbornly deny herself even the most basic creature comforts, but surely she'd not deprive an innocent child?

He stopped himself, sickened by the machiavellian workings of his mind. Christ, what was he thinking? Chelsea deserved better than a life lived in the shadows. She deserved better than . . . *him.*

As if sensing his inner tumult, Chelsea stirred and turned to face him. One shapely bare calf kicked free of the covers and flung itself possessively over his lower body. Anthony stifled a groan as his desire rose again.

Think pure thoughts, his nobler self counseled, willing the passion to ebb. It was damn difficult to do when she was exquisitely naked and wound around him like a skein.

Not difficult. Impossible.

He should leave, for his mind and body were too active for sleep. And a predawn departure would spare Chelsea the embarrassment of having to explain his presence to Jack.

Jack. Damn, he'd been due to relieve him hours ago. He'd return to his house, quickly don his Toeless Tony garb, then ride to St. Giles. On the way, he'd think up some excuse for why he'd been detained. Anything would be preferable to, "Jack, old sod, so sorry to be late. I've just come from deflowering your mistress, and it took longer than I'd anticipated."

But placating Jack was the least of his problems, he acknowledged, swinging his legs over the side of the bed. He wouldn't—he couldn't—lose Chelsea, he told himself, gathering his scattered clothing. Somehow he'd find a way for them to be together, although *how* was a conundrum that set his head—and heart—aching.

He finished dressing, then stood at the foot of the bed, gazing up at Chelsea's contented face, the tension smoothed away for the moment. She looked so young, so innocent, so adorably disheveled that he couldn't resist coming up beside her to press a chaste kiss on her forehead.

Chelsea sighed and nuzzled the pillow. A fresh spate of love welled inside him. She was the best thing that had ever happened to him. If only she had happened sooner.

But pondering *what ifs* was a fool's pastime. Somehow, somewhere, he'd hit upon a solution they could both live with. He refused to contemplate the alternative.

"I've got you now, my little thief, and I'll not let you go. Not now, not ever."

• • •

Thirty minutes later, Anthony stepped over his own threshold. Chaos greeted him. His entire household staff, from scullery maid to butler, milled about the entrance hall. With the exception of Chambers, who was fully dressed, they all wore their night clothes. Capped heads bobbed and nervous hands fidgeted with rope belts. And everyone—*everyone*—was shouting.

Anthony called several times for silence, but his bellow barely dented the din. Finally he puckered up and whistled.

A hush fell. All eyes turned to him.

"Attention! Full kitty . . . *now*."

Backs straightened, shoulders pulled back, and chests puffed. A moment later, they scrambled into the military-style formation he'd taught them.

"No shoving," he ordered, quelling his impatience.

He waited until they'd assembled into a reasonably straight line, then gave the call to "At ease." Turning to Chambers, he demanded, "What the bloody hell is going on?"

Chambers hobbled forward. "Milord, 'tis my sad duty to report that last night two ruffians broke in." He paused, voice quaking. "And you should also know that 'tis all my fault."

"Your fault, Chambers? How so?"

"I heard the front door rattle. I was so sure 'twas you, milord, that I opened it without ever asking who was there." He shook his grizzled head. "I tried to close it again, but they forced their way inside before I could reach the bolt."

"They?" Anthony massaged his pounding temple. He'd been burgled. What next?

"There were two of them, milord. A gallows-faced chap with a scar and a gold front tooth. The other was a bull-necked fellow, built like a prize fighter."

"I see."

And, by God, he did see. Stenton and Luke must have tired of waiting and abandoned his—Toeless's—kidnapping scheme in favor of burglary. Anthony only hoped they didn't experience a similar impatience to dispense Chelsea's brother. To be safe, he'd alert Mugglestone and Jack. The three of them would mount the rescue that night even if they had to raze the Rookery to do so.

"Was anyone harmed?" He kneaded the tightness at the back of his neck. To think that, but a few weeks before, his life had seemed so neat, so conventional, so dull. How he would welcome a spot of dullness now.

"Master Reginald received a black eye and there are rope burns on his wrists from where he was bound but otherwise he is unharmed. He's lying on the sofa in your study."

"Good. Have you sent for the magistrate?"

"Only just now, milord." Anthony frowned and Chambers hastened to add, "I was tied alongside Master Reginald. One of the scullery maids found us this morning when she came in to sweep out the grate."

"I see. When the magistrate arrives, show him into the study." His gaze slid over yawning faces. "Unless someone else has something meaningful to contribute, you are all dismissed."

Anthony brushed past the dispersing line. He was anxious to hear Reggie's version of the break-in before the magistrate arrived.

"Wait, milord, there is more."

Anthony turned on his heel to face his butler. "A full accounting of the stolen articles can wait until later."

"Yes, milord but . . ."

"But what?" Fatigue lent a sharp edge to his voice.

"Master Reginald didn't come alone last night."

Damn Reggie. As if Anthony didn't have enough to cope with, it seemed he'd have to discreetly remove one of Reggie's paramours from his house—preferably *before* the magistrate arrived.

Anthony blew out a breath. "Where is she?"

"I don't know, milord."

"What do you mean you don't know?" The way his luck was running, he'd probably find the trollop ensconced in his own bed.

The butler's voice broke. Tears pooled in his rheumy eyes. "I tried to stop them but the gold-toothed one held a . . . a k-knife to my t-throat while the big one carried her outside, kicking and screaming."

Alarm bells sounded in Anthony's head. "Carried *who* outside?"

"Lady Phoebe, milord. Your bride has been kidnapped!"

Anthony stared down at the ransom note he held. One line— *we got yer woman*—scrawled across the greasy page.

Incredulous, he turned to Reggie, who rose from the sofa, a raw beef steak covering the left side of his face.

"You brought Phoebe *here*?" Didn't the young Corinthian have a grain of sense or propriety?

Reggie adjusted the steak to a more comfortable position. "There was no help for it. She made me."

"Made you? And just how did she . . ."

Anthony stopped himself. The past few weeks of trailing after Chelsea had taught him just how formidable one slight woman could be.

Reggie groaned. "You should know that Phoebe can be almost as stubborn as Mama once she sets her mind. Last night, after you left, she flew into a temper. She said you'd been behaving oddly ever since the robbery and demanded I bring her here so that she could get to the bottom of why."

Anthony had thought he'd easily pulled the wool over Phoebe's naive eyes, but it appeared the chit was sharper than he'd credited. And that he wasn't nearly as smooth as he thought. Yet another lesson in humility.

"Oddly? Did she say anything more?"

Reggie lifted the slab of flesh from his face, revealing a truly magnificent shiner. Anthony curbed his impatience while his fastidious friend set the steak on the plate and wiped his hands on the napkin.

"Only that you'd been canceling rendezvous at the last minute, changing your mind about whether or not to accept invitations. Running out on her at Vauxhall was the last straw. When you weren't at home, she dug in her heels. Said she'd wait until dawn if that's what it took to get a straight answer about why you'd left so suddenly. By the way, why did you?"

"I had business to attend."

Reggie grinned through his bruises. "Indeed, and I'll wager it had red hair and was wearing a green gown."

Anthony remained silent. His behavior must have been obvious indeed for Reggie to have seen through him.

Reggie's grin dissolved. "Now see here, Anthony. You know I'm the last person who'd ever expect you to reform, but . . ."

"But?" Anthony folded his arms across his chest, knowing where this was leading.

Reggie sucked in his breath. "But when you're out with your wife, or fiancée as the case may be—my sister—it doesn't seem very decorous to go chasing after some light skirt."

Rage blazed through what remained of Anthony's patience. He pinned Reggie beneath his stare, wondering how the young scoundrel would look with a second black eye to match.

"Number one: the lady in question is no *light skirt*. Number two: unless we locate your sister and rescue her, she isn't going to be my wife—or anyone else's." He advanced a step, and Reggie backed up an equal distance. "Which brings me to number three."

Reggie gulped. "Number three?"

"Leaving *you* to explain to your mother how *you* brought Phoebe here—to my wicked bachelor's abode—after midnight without a proper chaperon, risking her reputation and, it seems, her very life."

As if on cue, the study door crashed open and Lord Tremont stormed inside. A ferocious scowl replaced his usually placid expression.

"Where's my little girl?" he roared. His bulbous gaze settled on his son and heir. "I know you have a hand in this, Reginald, so don't bother denying it. I saw your rig outside."

"Papa, I can explain."

"Later." The tubby lord swung around and aimed his forefinger at Anthony. "And, you, Montrose. Fiancé or not, how dare you practice your rakehell ways on my innocent child! Good God, man, you'd only a week more to wait. Couldn't you cool your heels with some whore 'til the wedding night?" He shoved past Anthony. "Phoebe, girl, 'tis Papa. Come out, my angel. I'm going to take you home."

Tremont stalked the study as though he expected Phoebe to slide down the chimney flue or to pop out from behind one of the bookshelves. Watching the agitated lord, Anthony wondered how he would react to the far-worse truth.

Begin with the good news. "Calm yourself, sir. No one has ruined Phoebe."

God, how he hoped that were still true. He recalled the rapacious looks Stenton had given Chelsea and shuddered. Hopefully Phoebe's social station would afford her some protection.

"Then where is she?" Lord Tremont frowned at Reggie, who had drifted over to the liquor cabinet. "Well, I'm waiting." His lordship's bushy gray brows lifted. "How the devil did you come by that eye? On second thought, I don't want to know. Just answer my first question—Where the hell is your sister?"

"Papa, I er . . . Anthony has something he needs to tell you." Reggie slunk farther away.

Now, the bad news. Anthony squared his shoulders. "I'm afraid Phoebe was kidnapped last night."

"Kidnapped!" The color drained from Tremont's puffy cheeks. "I don't believe it."

"I'm afraid 'tis true, sir."

"Oh, God." He sunk into a chair and fitted a hand over his sweaty forehead. "Montrose, you must help me. My wife is still abed and, based on her habit, shall remain so for several more hours. Before I set out, I left the message that I'd taken Phoebe for an early ride in the Park. She'll find that odd— Phoebe rarely rises before noon—but 'twas the only excuse I could think of. If she should discover the truth . . ." He stuffed a fist in his mouth.

Anthony laid a hand on his future father-in-law's shoulder. "I'll do everything in my power to bring Phoebe safely home, sir." Reasoning that any man who'd remained married to Lady Tremont for five-and-twenty years must possess some metal, he added, "But I'm going to need your help."

Tremont looked up at Anthony, his faded blue eyes earnest. "I'll do anything to bring my daughter home." His voice cracked. "*Anything*."

Moved, Anthony nodded. "Very well. I believe Phoebe's kidnappers are the same two who abducted the brother of a friend of mine. I've set a Bow Street runner to watch them for two weeks now. We have reason to believe they're hiding the boy inside St. Giles's Rookery. My guess is that they've taken Phoebe there as well."

"Good Lord!" Lord Tremont's face puckered. "Do you mean to say that my Phoebe's been taken to a den of prostitutes and pickpockets!" Tears filled his eyes even as he fisted his hands. "They wouldn't dare harm her . . . would they?"

"I don't believe so," Anthony replied, hoping it were true. "But, if word leaked that she'd spent the night in such a place—"

"Her reputation would be ruined," Lord Tremont finished, shoulders drooping.

Anthony inclined his head. "Which is precisely why I want you and Reggie to stay here and keep the magistrate occupied for as long as possible. As soon as I've given my statement, I'll set out to search."

Tremont popped from his chair. "She may be your fiancée, but she's my daughter. I'm coming with you."

Anthony tried to imagine Lord Tremont trolling the Rookery. Or Reggie. He couldn't.

Adamant, he shook his head. "Unless you want to put Phoebe in even greater danger, you and Reggie will remain here." In a milder tone, he added, "All I ask is that you give me a few hours. If I haven't found her by noon, I'll send for the magistrate—" He looked from Lord Tremont to Reggie. "—and for you both."

"Very well." Tremont grabbed the drink from Reggie's hand and set it firmly down. "There's no time for that. We need to start rehearsing your story. And I strongly suggest you make it *good*." He shuddered. "If your mother ever finds out Phoebe went missing—and *overnight*—we'll both be taking rooms at the club."

The scraping of the key turning in the lock brought Robert sharply awake. Stiff and bruised, he sat up just as the door opened. Light, blessed light, sliced through the darkness.

Stenton sauntered inside, candlestick in hand. "I've brought ye company, lad."

Luke followed, a granary sack slung over one shoulder. Robert cleared the crust of sleep from the corners of his eyes and squinted to adjust his vision to the light. A kick in the ribs had not been his only punishment for taunting Stenton with the truth that he and Chelsea were poor as church mice. He'd been without a candle for more than a week, left to grope in the dark like the animal he was becoming. The day before he'd accidentally overturned the chamber pot. That had earned him another beating as well as a day without food—not even the miserable gruel they'd taken to feeding him.

Lack of food probably explained why the sack Luke was lugging appeared to end in two tiny, slippered feet. Female feet with delectably slim ankles.

"Set 'er down."

Luke obeyed. The sack weaved. Laughing, Stenton caught it in his arms. Imitating the sound of a drum roll, he stepped behind.

"Ta da." He pulled the cover up, then off.

Robert held his breath. In the center of the chamber stood an angel. A slightly disheveled one, with a dirt streak across one pale cheek, but an angel nonetheless. Silver-blond hair framed her fine-boned face, and her sylph's figure was clad in celestial blue.

I must be hallucinating. They must have started administering the sleeping draught again. Or maybe I've finally starved to death and this is heaven?

The angel stared back at him, pale eyes wide. He got to his feet, chains rattling. Her eyes darkened and her lips parted.

A piercing peal rang out. Then another and another.

Robert winced. He'd been wrong. The lovely newcomer was no angel but a demon sent to bleed his eardrums and freeze his blood.

Laughing, Stenton covered his ears. "Don't appear she fancies 'im, do it Luke?"

The giant's thick features twisted. "She's 'urtin' me ears. I'm gonna make her stop."

Large palm outstretched, he walked toward the woman. She shrank away, still screaming.

At the last minute, Stenton intervened. "Leave 'er be. Let's you and me get some supper while 'er and lover boy 'ere get acquainted. She'll pipe down soon enough."

The kidnappers left. The new arrival fortified herself with a fresh gulp of air, then opened her mouth.

Fully, *painfully* awake, Robert realized she was neither angel nor demon. Just a very frightened girl.

He held up a palm. "They're gone. You can stop now."

Miraculously she did. Looking about, her lower lip quivered. Then her face crumpled.

Splendid. She's stopped screaming only to start bawling.

He pulled a chair—the *only* chair—from the table and held it for her.

"Please, won't you sit?"

She hesitated, brushed the seat, then plunked down. And then the floodgates opened.

"Look, it's not *that* bad," he consoled. Dragging his chains behind him, he stood across from her, feeling helpless. "At least they've left us the candle."

Sniffling, she lifted her face and peered up at him. "Not so bad?"

The disdain in her watery eyes made him painfully aware that he hadn't bathed, shaved, or changed clothes in weeks. What a sight he must be with his greasy hair brushing the back of his collar and a matted beard blanketing the lower half of his face. He didn't even have a clean handkerchief to offer her.

"Not so bad!" she repeated, wiping her eyes. "I've been abducted, stuffed into a smelly sack, and brought here. And . . . and I don't even know where I am or who *you* are."

Her waspish words stung but at least she was neither screaming nor crying. Progress.

"I can't answer the where, only the who. Allow me to introduce myself." He took a step back and bowed as best he could. "Robert Bellamy, at your service." He straightened. "And you are?"

She hesitated as though weighing whether or not she should reveal her name. "Phoebe Tremont."

A final tear spilled from the corner of her eye. Fascinated, Robert watched it flow down her alabaster cheek, through the dark streak of dried mud, until it brushed the corner of her delicate mouth.

"Phoebe. What a beautiful name." *What a beautiful girl.*

She frowned. "You are impertinent, sir. If we must speak at all, you will address me as Lady Phoebe."

Robert's patience began to slip. He braced a palm against the table edge and regarded her. "Rather formal given our circumstances, don't you think? Especially as there is no one to overhear save these four walls."

"Mama says there is no excuse for bad manners, Mr. er . . . Bellamy." Expression decidedly *un*angelic, she added, "Your family must not be very important, for I've never heard of them."

Delicate mouth or not, Robert's ire rose. "I'll have you know that my father was the best magistrate Upper Uckfield ever had."

"Was?"

A lump blocked the back of his throat. "He died in a carriage accident last year, along with my mother."

"Oh, I'm . . . sorry. It must be terrible to be an orphan. Have you any brothers or sisters?"

He nodded, feeling the lump expand. "I have an older sister. Her name is Chelsea."

"And she lives with you, in Upper Uckfield?" She wrinkled her nose. "Such a funny name. Exactly where is that?"

"In East Sussex, six leagues or so from Maresfield. Why?"

"My fiancé, Lord Montrose, has an estate not far from there."

"You're engaged?" He felt an odd twinge in his upper chest. Disappointment, perhaps? No, that was ridiculous. She was a stranger and a hoity-toity one at that.

"Of course. Otherwise I couldn't have a fiancé, could I?" She lanced him a superior smile, and Robert had the sudden urge to crush her mouth beneath his. "When I marry I shall be a viscountess and someday a countess."

"You don't look old enough to be either."

She frowned. "I shall be nineteen next month. Mama wed when she was only seventeen."

"I see." He smiled. "By comparison, you are a woman of the world."

"You are making fun of me, aren't you?" Her pale eyes darkened. "When Lord Montrose comes to rescue me, I shall tell him of your insulting manner." Her expression turned smug. "Perhaps he will call you out."

Robert tossed back his head and guffawed. It was the first time he'd laughed since . . . well, better not to think about that now.

Wiping his eyes, he said, "If he does, he must be an excessively proud and pea-witted gentleman." *And a very fortunate one*.

Her face fell. "What is that supposed to mean?"

"That he would be more likely to direct his energies toward capturing our kidnappers than redressing *imagined* insults."

Her shoulders slumped. "In truth, I do not know him well enough to say."

Her sad admission piqued his curiosity. "And yet you are marrying him?"

Her chin snapped up. "I know everything that I need to know. He is handsome and amusing and very rich, although a good deal older than I. Thirty, I believe."

Thirty. It was none of his business whom she married and yet Robert couldn't help feeling indignant on her behalf. She was too proud, to be sure, but she was also young and comely. Too young and comely to be married off to some middle-aged lord, no matter how rich he might be.

"Do you love him?" he asked suddenly.

She opened her mouth, then closed it. She twisted her hands in her lap, and he began to suspect she'd never considered the question before.

"He is always courteous," she replied after a lengthy pause. "Our parents believe we shall suit. I . . . esteem him."

"You *esteem* him?" He started to laugh, then realized she was serious.

"What more is there?"

"A great deal more, I should hope. When I marry, it shall be for love and no other reason."

She shot from her chair and marched toward him. "How dare you criticize me! Had I desired your opinion, I should have asked for it."

She planted both palms on his chest and pushed. Weak as he was, he held his ground and pinned her wrists in his one hand.

"So, Miss Prim-and-Proper has a temper, does she?"

"Let me go." She pulled back, but he held her easily.

"If you said please—as well as my Christian name—I might consider it," he suggested gamely.

He felt stronger than he had in days and very much alive. Missish girls usually bored him, but something about this one intrigued him.

"You're hateful." Her pink nostrils flared. "And you smell horrid."

It was the truth and it hurt. He released her abruptly. "As would you had you not stirred from this chamber or been allowed to bathe for . . ."

He turned away and propped one shoulder against the wall. Struggling to hold back tears, he felt a light touch on his back.

In a soft voice, she asked, "How long *have* you been here?"

He ground his forehead against the rough stone. "I can't be certain. They drugged my food at first, and I slept most of the time. Weeks. Almost a month, I think."

Looking over his shoulder, he saw her stamp her tiny, slippered foot on the packed earth floor.

"My papa and Lord Montrose will not stand for this. They

will rescue me and, when they do, I shall insist they rescue you as well."

He turned. "You shall, shall you?" He folded his arms across his chest and regarded her, once more amused. Like a feisty kitten with claws sheathed and back raised, she was utterly adorable. Unable to resist teasing her, he added, "But perhaps they will not want to sully themselves by rescuing someone from such an *unimportant* family."

Two hot spots appeared on either cheek. "Then I shall insist."

"That's awfully decent of you. Thank you."

"You are welcome." She cleared her throat. "Er . . . how much longer will they keep us here?"

Suddenly drained, he slumped against the wall. "Would to God I had the answer to that."

Chapter Seventeen

Chelsea awoke to milkmaids, egg men, and saloop vendors shouting their wares below her window. She hiked the quilt over her head, closed her eyes, and concentrated on slipping back into the dream. She had dreamt of Anthony before but never had the fantasy been so vivid, so *real*. She could almost feel his big hands stroking her with shocking intimacy; hear his whispered endearments; smell his musky scent as he labored over her, pleasuring her until she exploded in a place that had no name. The same place that now throbbed with a dull rawness.

Her eyes flashed open. She lifted the covers and peaked beneath. Pale flesh—her flesh—greeted her. The night before was no dream.

What have I done?

Face hot, she edged the sheet below her chin. She and Anthony had made love. Twice, she now recalled, if she counted the first time when he had . . .

She had not merely allowed Anthony to make love to her but had brazenly invited him to do so. The circumstances leading to that momentous decision—their argument at Vauxhall, the confrontation with Ambrose, Jack's absence—trickled through her mind. As she grew accustomed to the idea, she discovered that she wasn't really sorry she'd lain with him. In fact, she was prepared to do so again.

"Anthony?" She rolled onto her side and reached for him, but her hand fell on empty space.

Loneliness, a far keener ache, stabbed her. She sat up and smoothed her palm over the imprint where he had lain. The mattress was cold. He must have left in the middle of the night.

She picked up the pillow that had briefly been his and buried her face in it, inhaling the faint, lingering scent of musky male. She shut her eyes, the better to recall every detail, every nuance—the rasping of his jawline against her cheek, the minty aroma of his shaving soap, the solid hardness of his chest rising and falling with each ragged breath, and the reassuring pressure of his palm cradling the small of her back. If she had any doubts about how deep her feelings ran, the bleak depression engulfing her dispelled them. She loved Anthony. Completely. Irrevocably. Forever. That realization would have been a cause for rejoicing were her beloved not bound to another. But he was. She would, she must, leave London as soon as they liberated Robert.

Robert. Last night, absorbed in the wonder of making love with Anthony, she'd all but forgotten about the brother she'd pledged to save. She *had* forgotten about him, for several hours. And she'd already wasted the morning in feeling sorry for herself. Shame washed over her. She was facing a life without Anthony, but Robert might not have any life at all if she didn't bestir herself.

A sharp rap on the front door sent her bolting out of bed, searching for her wrapper. Despite her resolution, her heart raced. It must be Anthony, for who else would call this early? Hoping to reach him before Jack awoke, she ran barefoot down the stairs. She unbolted the door, and her welcoming smile died.

"Good morn, missus." The milkmaid lifted the ladle from one of the two pails dangling from the yoke she shouldered and dragged it through the froth. "I seen the empty jug by the door and thought ye might be wantin' some o' this lovely fresh milk?"

Chelsea nodded, afraid to answer lest her voice crack. Anthony had left in the middle of the night without a word, not even a note. Doubtless there were any number of explanations for his abrupt departure, but only one kept lancing through her muddled mind—he didn't want her after all.

The milkmaid cast a skeptical glance at the stoneware vessel. Gnats swarmed the spout. "Shall I pour it into this 'un or . . . ?"

Chelsea barely noted the insects. "Yes, that's fine."

The woman shrugged. "Suit yerself." She eyed the jug. "That'll be sixpence for full or thruppence for half-full?"

He doesn't want me. I should be relieved. No, I am relieved.

Anthony's decision would save them—save her—the pain of a protracted farewell. In a few days he would be out of her life. That was what she wanted, wasn't it?

The milkmaid tapped an impatient foot. "Beggin' yer pardon, but I've me rounds to make. D'ye want that jug filled or not?"

With her future left hanging, full or half-full suddenly seemed too weighty a decision. "Whatever you think best," Chelsea murmured.

"Then full 'tis." The woman held out her palm and cleared her throat.

Thoughts tangled, it took Chelsea a moment to interpret the gesture. "Oh, the money. Of course."

She drifted into the parlor, found her purse, and returned, her movements as heavy and mechanical as a sleepwalker's.

The milkmaid dropped the coins into her apron pocket. "Oh, dearie me, I nearly forgot. A gentleman bade me give ye this."

The crinkle of paper cut through Chelsea's lethargy. A message—from Anthony? Of course, it must be from him. She knew no one else in London.

Impatience surged, and she nearly snatched the crisp square from the woman's outstretched hand. Then she saw the ebony border, and her heart dropped.

Dear God, no.

The note slipped through her fingers and fluttered to her feet. Everywhere she felt numb, frozen, except for her heart, which was pounding wildly.

The tradeswoman bent and picked it up. "Black-edging,"

she said, shaking her mob-capped head. She pressed the paper into Chelsea's palm. "I hope it ain't a close relation?"

Throat tight, Chelsea slipped the letter into her pocket. "My brother." She could barely coax her lips to form the necessary syllables.

"A brother, that 'tis a pity." Solemn-faced, the woman ladled milk through a funnel into the mouth of the jug with brisk efficiency. "I've lost two o' me own to the typhus. 'Tis terrible hard, losin' a brother."

"Yes, it is." Chelsea's frozen brain began to thaw. "You er . . . said a gentleman asked you to deliver it?"

The milkmaid removed the funnel from the jug, replaced the lid, and wiped her hands on her apron. "Aye. Handsome he were and so polite. Quite the gentleman," she sighed, coarse features softening. "Well, good day to ye."

Chelsea nodded and closed the door, leaving the milk to spoil outside. *Handsome and polite. Quite the gentleman.*

By now she had seen enough women react to Anthony to recognize the signs of adulation and lust. Other than Jack, Anthony was the only person to whom she had shown the black-edged ransom demand. And he had been well and truly angry with her for flouting him with Ambrose.

Grappling with this newest possibility, she hurried to the parlor window. An eastern exposure provided sufficient sunlight for reading, and she settled on the window seat. *Surely Anthony wouldn't stoop to playing such a cruel practical joke?* she told herself, her shaking hands struggling to break the wax seal.

She unfolded the note. Relief, fear—and guilt—crashed over her. The penmanship and cloying cologne were the same as before and undoubtedly the kidnapper's.

> *My Dearest Love:*
> *How could you deceive me so? Last night you allowed that vile rake to despoil what I would have deified. For that I must, I will punish you, my inconstant darling. I shall expect you at the Rutting Bull within the hour. Yes, I am that eager to begin your reformation, my fallen angel. Use the tradesmen's entrance, which*

will be unlocked, and come alone. If Montrose follows, Robert dies, as will your fine lover.

Your fine lover. These past weeks, she'd clung to the notion that the kidnapper was a stranger. How could she have been so blind, so unequivocally stupid? Only one man loved—and hated—her so absolutely.

Squire Dumfreys.

Why even the paper reeked of his cologne. That same cloying scent had clung to the original ransom note. And to her clothing after he'd assaulted her.

Painful as it was, she forced her thoughts back to that frightful day. Dumfreys hadn't seemed surprised to see her, nor taken aback by the money she'd requested. When she'd asked for the five hundred pounds, how quickly he'd concluded it must be for Robert. And then, of course, he'd tried to rape her. Determined to put the ugly memory behind her, she'd blinded herself to its connection to the kidnapping.

Like a jealous lover, he'd stalked her ever since. Clinging to the shadows, he'd bided his time. Waiting. Watching. As he might be doing even now.

Chills skittered her spine. She whirled to the window, scanning the awakening street. A housewife stood on her stoop, waving to her departing husband. An old man loaded produce into the back of a wagon. Two little girls played hopscotch while a spaniel dog looked on. A squat matron headed toward Shepherd's Market, a wicker basket over her arm. All commonplace sights, but Chelsea wasn't comforted. Somewhere, anywhere, *he* might be lurking, watching her even now.

The scenery spun. Chelsea turned away from the window and gripped the edge of the seat.

I am the ransom.

Had Anthony suspected as much weeks before when he'd insisted she move into his house? At the time she'd thought he was only out to seduce her; a part of her had agreed for the pure pleasure of thwarting him. But he hadn't tried to seduce her at all, only to protect her.

Now it was up to her to protect him. If he followed her to

the tavern, she had no doubt that Dumfreys would kill him. And, if she told him her intention—to take Robert's place as hostage—he would never let her back out the door. No, she would have to do this alone.

Heart pounding, she raced up the stairs, grateful that her bare feet were nearly soundless. Jack might be deaf as a doornail, but he had an uncanny knack for hearing what she didn't want him to. And, for his own good, he mustn't follow her either.

She quickly donned her men's attire and came back downstairs, Jack's pistol tucked inside her coat pocket. Praying for the courage to fire it—if not on Dumfreys, then on herself after she'd freed Robert—she tiptoed through the house. Inside the kitchen, she peered around the pantry corner to Jack's cot. It was empty. Odd that he'd risen so early when he must have been out half the night. But there was no telling when he might return. She snatched a sugar cone from the pantry shelf and hurried out the back door. Mist brushed her face as she crossed the small yard and let herself out the gate.

The horse Jack had let from the lending stable was in the mews across the alley. She entered the carriage house. Autumn poked her head over the stall door and whinnied.

"Good morning to you, too." Chelsea stepped back to avoid being *cleaned* and turned the horse's head away. "This probably constitutes spoiling but you'll earn it before this day is over."

She took the sugar from her pocket and offered it. A second later, the stable was filled with the sound of chomping.

The treat devoured, Chelsea wiped her wet palm on her trouser leg and headed into the tack room. She'd left the door to the carriage house open and enough light filtered inside for her to find the necessary gear. She returned and settled the blanket, then the saddle, across the mare's swayed back.

"Robert's been kidnapped." Speaking her thoughts aloud, she bent to tighten the cinch beneath the beast's belly. "I can't ask Anthony or Jack for help, so it's up to us to save him. Understand?"

Autumn snorted as if indignant on Chelsea's behalf. Ears pointed forward, she pawed the straw.

"I thought you'd see it my way." Chelsea tugged on the noseband, drawing the horse's head down. "A kiss for luck."

Standing on tiptoe, she pressed her lips to the white star between the wide-set eyes. Then she led the mare out of the stall, stepped onto the mounting block, and climbed up.

How precious—and precarious—life seemed as they cantered through the city streets, a brisk breeze stinging Chelsea's cheeks and teasing her hair loose from its braid. Scenes from her one-and-twenty years played before her mind's eye. So many times it was Anthony who took the lead—wrestling her to the ground after she robbed him; pouring her wine and spilling his soul; loving her with such exquisite gentleness that the memory melted her insides. She had known him less than a month and yet he dominated her thoughts, even now when she was about to throw herself on the mercy of a lust-crazed lunatic.

It was as though her life had begun the moment they met. The previous night, she'd felt her soul merge with his even as their bodies merged into one. She smiled. At once humbling and exalting, this experience of losing herself in another—in Anthony—was one she'd never forget. She had only one real regret.

She'd never told him she loved him.

Mr. Bellamy—Robert—was sleeping like the dead. That is, if the dead could snore. No matter where Phoebe moved—and she'd visited all four corners of the tiny chamber by now—the sonorous booms followed. Finally she gave up and claimed a corner of the straw pallet at his head. Stifling the wicked urge to pinch his nostrils—a sure cure for male snoring, according to her mother—she lifted the guttering candle. The dying light pooled over his profile, and she found herself wondering what he looked like beneath the beard. Handsome, she decided, her gaze settling on his mouth. Earlier, when he'd dared to flash that impudent grin at her, she'd noticed that his teeth were white and even. Now she saw that he had beautiful lips as well and, she suspected, a strong, square jaw.

Thrashing, he muttered something unintelligible and threw off his red military coat. Badly rumpled, it had been pressed into service as a blanket. Picking it up, she settled it back over him. She sighed. He wasn't a tall man, but she suspected he looked splendid in uniform.

Even so, if he snored like this every night, she pitied his future wife.

Really, Phoebe Elizabeth, Mr. Bellamy's nocturnal habits are none of your affair.

Her mother's voice, strident with disapproval, sent her edging away from him. At any rate, it was likely exhaustion that made him sound off so. Their confrontation had sapped what little strength he still possessed for afterward she'd had to help him to the pallet. She giggled. *What a fit Mama would have if she'd seen me with my arm around his waist— leading him back to bed, no less!* Her mirth faded when she recalled the sharpness of his protruding ribs and the way his trousers hung from his shrunken shanks.

The prospect of deteriorating to a similar state chilled her. Young as they both were—she'd pressed him, and he'd admitted to being not yet twenty—they might be in their graves ere long. Youth was no protection against starvation . . . or murder.

A key jiggled in the lock on the other side of the door. She thought of how the scar-faced man had leered at her and how fierce the big oaf had looked when she'd screamed, and her courage curdled.

The door handle turned, and she huddled closer to her fellow captive. A moment later the scar-faced man lurched inside, bringing with him a supper tray and the stench of stale spirits.

"My, ain't this cozy. Settled right in, I see."

Phoebe followed his gaze to her fellow inmate's sprawled form, and heat rushed her cheeks. She jumped up, spattering candle wax on her arm.

"He's been asleep the whole time," she whispered as

though explaining herself to one of the dowager patronesses of Almack's.

He cocked a black brow as though he didn't believe her. "Oh, 'as 'e now?"

He set the tray on the table and beckoned her forward. Phoebe put aside her misgivings and crept closer. She hadn't eaten since *nuncheon* the day before and hunger gnawed at her.

He dragged out the chair and held it for her. "Come 'ere and take a load off."

Knees shaking, she complied. Turning away from his insulting gaze, she surveyed the tray's contents—two trenchers of gray pottage, a round loaf of brown bread, and two tankards of ale.

Why, there isn't enough here to keep one person alive, let alone two. "Is this all there is?"

"Aye." His lips slid back from his yellow teeth. Gold flashed. "Cheer up, ducks. If he sleeps through, ye can 'ave 'is share."

The villain. As if she'd stoop to stealing food, let alone this vile stuff, from a starving man.

He backed toward the door. "Will there be anything else, Miss High-and-Mighty?"

Remembering her mother's injunction to be firm with inferiors, she forced back her fear. "Indeed, we shall require several items. A basin of warm water and a razor for Mr. Bellamy to shave—"

"*Warm* water?"

She nodded, searching for a spoon. "And we shall shortly require another candle."

There was no cutlery, so she tore off a slab of bread, dipped a corner in the broth, and nibbled. *Ugh.* Her stomach heaved. Not only was it stale but, she suspected, molded too.

Choking it down, she pushed her plate aside and turned her attention to the candle. The tallow had burned to a nub and the dangling wick, in need of trimming, dribbled wax everywhere.

"On second thought, perhaps you might bring two candles and a trimmer."

"Might I now?" He came forward and leaned over her, a hand resting on either chair arm. "I might be able to arrange that . . . if ye was nice to me, that is."

Accustomed to order rather than ask, she gritted her back teeth. "I'd like two more candles . . . *please*."

Bending low, his foul breath brushed her nape. "Mister Stenton."

Squeamish as she was, she'd savor the sight of him swinging from the gibbet. "Please . . . *Mister* Stenton."

He fingered a loose curl that brushed her shoulder, his long nails scraping her skin. "Oh, I'll wager ye can do even better than that."

Panic paralyzed her. The only part of her anatomy she seemed capable of moving was her mouth.

"If you hurt me, my papa will see that you hang."

He pulled the chair out from under her. It crashed to the floor. Instead of landing with it, she was bent face-first over the table, her gown and petticoats riding above her waist.

"Always 'ad a mind to see what kind o' drawers the Fancy wears," he cackled. "Silky," he rasped, palming her buttocks.

"Stop it!" she cried, tears stinging her eyes.

He forced a bony leg between her thighs. She tried to close them, to rise, but the hot muzziness was upon her, and her screams muted to whimpers.

Suddenly her tormentor's groping hands fell away. Limp with relief, she lifted herself and tugged her gown back down.

"How dare you lay hands on a lady."

She turned to find Mr. Bellamy standing behind Stenton, his chains wrapped about their jailer's scrawny neck.

Stenton was surely gasping his last when a large shadow fell from the doorway. The second man, the one with a pugilist's stocky strength, bounded inside. This time Phoebe had no difficulty screaming.

"Look out, Robert!"

He tore Robert from his confederate's throat and tossed him against the wall as though he were made of India rubber.

Except that Robert didn't bounce. Phoebe cringed as the back of his skull crashed against the hard, unrelenting stone.

One hand to his throat, Stenton rasped, "Hold 'im, Luke."

Obedient, the bully went to Robert and hoisted him to his feet. Limp as a rag doll, Robert mounted no resistance when Stenton came at him from the front, bony fists raised.

" 'Ere's some sauce for yer supper."

His first blow landed Robert in the pit of the stomach. He groaned and doubled over. He would have fallen, but Luke held him. Another punch and another fell until droplets of blood speckled the earthen floor.

"Stop it!" she screamed. "You'll kill him!"

Stenton's fists fell to his sides. "Why, what a bloody good idea. *Bloody* good." Laughing, he pulled a knife from inside his boot and ran the dull edge along Robert's throat. "If I had me way, I'd flay ye alive 'ere and now. Way matters stand, I won't have to wait much longer."

Robert lifted his bruised face. Defiance blazed in his hazel eyes, making Phoebe ashamed of her own cowardice. "Why not do it now and be done with me?"

Captor and captive eyed each other. Phoebe's heart thudded to a standstill.

Then Stenton replaced the knife in its sheath. "Eager ta go, b'aint he, Luke? Don't 'e worry, ye'll get your comeuppance sooner than ye reckon. Before tonight, as a matter o' fact." He gestured to Luke. "Let 'im go."

Luke complied, and Robert folded to his knees.

Phoebe started toward him, but Stenton cut her off. Hating herself, she shrank from him, but he only snatched the candle from her shaking hands.

" 'Ere, luv, ye won't be needin' this. Yon young friend looks a sight better in the dark," he snickered, heading for the door.

Luke followed, closing the door behind them. This time the sound of the lock clicking in place was a comfort.

Phoebe felt her way through the blackness. Refusing to think about what might be living on the filthy floor, she knelt beside Robert.

"You should lie down." She put a tentative hand on his arm.

He shook her off. "I don't need any help. Go away."

"I've nowhere to go. Besides, I want to help you. *Please?*"

This time he didn't resist when she braced an arm about his shoulders and helped him up. Together they stumbled toward the pallet.

She settled him onto his back. "There, isn't that better?" she asked, trying to sound cheerful.

"Just grand," he snapped, voice dripping with sarcasm. "I haven't had a decent meal or a bath in God knows how long. I'm drugged and, when I do wake, I'm beaten to a bloody pulp. Not to mention that my life is in the hands of a sadist with a knife and his idiot friend. What more could I hope for?"

Wetness trickled into the beard covering his chin. Saliva? She leaned closer. No, blood.

Blood. Woozy, she braced a hand against the wall. What had Anthony said during the robbery? *This isn't the time to succumb to a fit of the vapors.*

Telling herself that now, she drew a steadying breath and said, "Close your eyes."

"Why? It's already black as pitch in here."

"Because I asked you to."

With a huff, he complied. She lifted her gown and tore a strip of linen from the hem of her petticoat.

"You can open them now."

"Oh thank you, your ladyship."

More sarcasm. Good, he must be feeling better. "Be quiet and hold still."

Lifting his chin, she dabbed the blood. There was no help for it—her hand brushed his beard. She'd expected it to scratch, but instead it felt soft and not at all unpleasant. Tamed by a proper trimming, it might actually become him.

"There, all finished." She tossed the bloodied strip into the far corner.

He folded his arms over his chest and stared at the ceiling. The whites of his eyes were all she could see of him in the darkness.

Twice now she'd conquered a fainting spell *sans* smelling salts. Emboldened, she ventured into the silence. "I thought you were very brave."

"Scant good bravery does a man when he's trussed like a chicken. If I'd had my hands free, I'd have taught those two a lesson they'd not soon forget."

She hid a smile. "Even so, no one has ever fought for me before."

Nor nearly died for me. The image of the knife pressed against his jugular wiped away her smile. She covered her face with her hands.

"Phoebe, what is it, what's wrong?"

Too distraught to reprimand him for making free with her Christian name, she shook her head.

Chains clanked. He pushed himself up beside her. A moment later, his thin arm—surprisingly warm and reassuring—encircled her. She should move away. But leaning against him, resting her head on his shoulder, felt so natural, so *right*.

She started to cry, softly this time. "When that horrid man drew his knife, I was afraid he really might . . ."

"Oh, Phoebe." He buried his cheek in her hair and gently rocked her. "I'm safe and so are you . . . for a few more hours at least."

Safe. Chelsea reflected that she'd passed twenty of her one-and-twenty years in the bosom of her family, safe, protected, and loved. Even after her parents' death, with Robert back at school, she and Jack had formed a family of sorts. And then, of course, she'd met Anthony. She'd never felt warmer or safer than she had the previous night, enfolded in his arms. But she couldn't bear to think of that now when, in all likelihood, she was riding to her death . . . or worse.

I will punish you, Dumfreys had written. For the second time that morning, she thought back to the episode in his study. Shivers ran through her. This time would be far worse. She mustn't allow herself even to imagine it. If she did, what courage she had would flee—and so would she.

But she couldn't, she wouldn't, desert her brother. How

could she even think of it when everything he'd endured was because of her? Robert was an unwitting third in a minuet of twisted desire, nothing more than the means for Dumfreys to ensure that Chelsea danced to his tune. The final figure was approaching. It was up to her to take the lead.

She tethered Autumn, then ducked down the alley, praying no one would steal the gentle horse. Skirting the gutters, where the rubbish flowed ankle-deep, she emerged behind the tavern. The gate to the high stone wall was unlocked, the padlock hanging open. She passed through the arched portal and crossed the courtyard, wading through waist-deep weeds. Three stone steps led down to the tradesmen's entrance.

She descended, drew a deep breath, and pushed open the wide-planked door.

Clanging overhead sent her heart caroming. She fell back against a stack of barrels, feeling for her pistol and fighting for breath.

The din died. Composing herself, she looked back at the door. The cowbell hanging above was a rusted relic but, growing up in the country, she'd seen a bevy of similar ones.

Her inner voice *tut-tutted* even as she swept the back of her hand over her clammy forehead. She, who had taken so many foolhardy risks over the past weeks, finally knew what it meant to be afraid. Fear, the coward's poison, coursed through her.

Determined to conquer it, she pressed on, brushing aside the cobwebs that hung like Chinese lanterns from the low-beamed ceiling. She was in the storage cellar. The air was fetid with cedar and must, and casks of wine and hogsheads of beer and ale occupied most of the available space. In summertime it would be pleasantly cool down here but, now that autumn had arrived, it was an ice chest.

She left the main chamber and came to a narrow passageway. Moisture dripped from the low, vaulted ceiling onto her head. A yellow circle of light capped the far end. She drew the pistol from her coat pocket. She'd hated close spaces ever since she'd gotten herself locked in the attic as a child.

Now the stone walls, sheathed in mildew, seemed to cave in on her as she drove deeper into the bowels of the building.

Something dark fluttered ahead. A bat, perhaps? She girded herself to duck.

"You're late." The reproach hissed through the hollow tunnel. "If you don't make haste, that precious brother of yours is a dead man."

Not a bat but a tall, hooded figure, backlit, materialized at the opposite end of the tunnel. She couldn't see his face, but she no longer needed to.

She raised her weapon, cocked the hammer, and called out, "As you will be unless you tell me where he is."

I won't really be doing murder if a life is saved, she told herself, her index finger inching toward the trigger.

Behind, in the chamber she'd just quit, a bolt smacked home. She whirled. The pistol fell from her sweaty grasp just as the light ahead went out.

She was drowning in darkness, in fear, her lungs too tight to draw in air. Footfalls, slow and measured, thudded toward her. Frantic, she dropped to her hands and knees, feeling for the pistol. If she could only reach it, then . . .

Something hard and heavy slammed into her skull. Bright, hot spots blistered the backs of her eyes. She squeezed her lids closed until water streamed, but it was no use. Like lava, the searing pain spread around her, through her. There was no dousing it. Finally it swept her up and bore her away, leaving only her heavy head rolling about the floor.

Then blackness, blissfully cool, enveloped her.

Chapter Eighteen

"With any luck, I won't be long," Anthony told his stallion as he finished tying the reins to a post. *Or end the day clapped in irons*, he added to himself, starting down Newton Street.

Back at his house, the magistrate was interviewing Tremont and Reggie. Anthony's own statement had been truthful but terse. He'd admitted he'd spent the night elsewhere and returned shortly before dawn to find his household at sixes and sevens.

"Did you pass the night at your club?" the magistrate had pressed.

Lying outright to His Majesty's lawful representative carried grave consequences, even for a peer. However, if the man simply mistook his meaning . . .

"Why no," Anthony admitted with a deliberately sly smile. "With a lady. I'm not at liberty to reveal her name." He winked. "You understand, of course?"

Coloring, the magistrate mumbled, "Of course, of course." He assured Anthony that his word of honor would suffice. They were both gentlemen, after all.

Anthony had taken his leave and immediately set out for St. Giles. Unfortunately, given the magistrate's presence, he'd been unable to change into his disguise. He could only hope that his bleary eyes, unshaven jaw, and rumpled clothes would present a convincingly raffish image.

The Rookery still slept when he came upon the curved

portal of its ancient gatehouse. His thunderous pounding finally brought a gin-breathed slattern to answer. Cinching the sash of her tattered blue robe, she fixed her gaze on the brass buttons of Anthony's waistcoat.

Hatred mingled with the fear pooling in her red-rimmed regard. "You'm wi' the charleys, b'aint ye?" She swiped a grizzled lock of hair back from her eyes.

He wedged his foot and one shoulder inside the iron-studded portal before she could slam it in his face. Forcing a winsome smile, he drawled, "How now, Mistress, you couldn't be more wrong. 'Tis me mate, Ned, I've come to see. Ned Muggle," he added, recalling Mugglestone's abbreviated alias.

"You'm a mate o' Neddie's?" She stepped back to allow him entry. "Why didn't ye say so before?"

Why indeed, Anthony mused, following her through a close corridor rank with unwashed bodies and rotted fish. It ended in an oblong doorway that opened to the outside. They passed through and Anthony found himself in a cobbled courtyard, along with a goodly number of London's homeless, bedded down on mattresses or beneath makeshift tents or, in a few cases, the bare stones. Most still slept although a few curious eyes cracked open.

"'Tis 'ere ye'll find him . . . if 'e come 'ome last night," she amended with a wink. "'E's a randy one, our Ned."

Anthony looked about. There must be at least fifty people here. It could take an hour—or more—to find Mugglestone, assuming he were here. Precious time that might be better spent.

The landlady started for the door, but Anthony's carrying whisper called her back. "Might you know another o' me mates, Bob Stenton?"

Her mouth pulled down at the corners. "Aye, I knows 'im and that half-wit he goes about wi' too. Good riddance to the both of 'em."

Anthony was almost afraid to ask, but he had no choice. "Good riddance?"

"Aye. That no-good Stenton's a month behind on the rent.

He promised me just t'other day he'd deliver it *wi' interest*, but I ain't seen hide nor hair o' him since."

Cold fear gripped Anthony. "I've a mind to surprise ol' Bob. Where is it that he roosts?"

She poked a crooked finger to a decayed mansion festooned with crumbling gargoyles. "'Is flat's on the second floor, at the end o' the hall. Number nine." She pulled a ring of keys from her robe, fumbled through them, then tossed him one.

Anthony caught it, then flipped her a farthing in return.

She smiled broadly, revealing tobacco-stained teeth. "I knowed ye was a gentleman from the moment I clapped eyes on ye."

Anthony strode down one row of bare and booted feet to Stenton's building. He opened the door. The sounds of wailing infants and shouting couples followed him as he bounded up the two flights of stairs. He came to the door marked nine and tried it. Unlocked, it fell open. Silence greeted him.

Cold foreboding seeped inside his chest, but he shook it off and began searching. A full slop bucket, a chicken bone crawling with ants, and a discarded neck cloth were among the leavings, but there was nothing to hint at where Stenton might have taken young Bellamy and Phoebe. Perspiration streaming, he fell on his hands and knees before the hearth, clawing the ashes for a note or some other clue that Stenton might have tried to burn before leaving.

Even as he searched, he knew that he would find nothing. All these weeks he'd been so sure, so bloody sure, that Stenton and Luke were holding Chelsea's brother in their lodging. His strategy had been to watch, await the proper moment, then strike.

But the time had never seemed quite right. Or had it? Had he unconsciously prolonged Robert Bellamy's misery only to give himself that much longer to woo his sister?

No, that was ludicrous. Of course he'd worked in earnest to bring about the young man's release. The hero of Albuera wouldn't resort to such mean tactics to win a woman.

But Chelsea wasn't any woman.

And I'm no hero.

Nor was he any nearer to locating Robert than he'd been when Chelsea'd first entrusted him with the task. Three weeks before.

Footsteps sounded outside in the hall. Shooting to his feet, he pulled the pistol from his pocket and trained it on the door.

A lean man with sandy-colored hair and a scruffy beard of like shade rushed inside, his own pistol drawn.

Anthony took his finger from the trigger. "Mugglestone?"

"Lord Montrose." The runner pointed his weapon to the floor. "I thought 'twas you I glimpsed in the courtyard." A frown crumpled his high forehead. "I thought the plan was—"

"The plan has changed." Anthony pocketed his pistol. Brushing ashes from his blackened hands, he briefly relayed the events of Phoebe's abduction and Stenton's apparent flight. "You go along to the Bull and see what you can find out. I've a feeling that barmaid knows a great deal more than she lets on." Mugglestone nodded, and Anthony headed for the door. "I'm off to fetch Jack. We'll meet you back there within the hour."

And what of Chelsea? He had to tell her. As much as he dreaded doing so, she deserved the truth. When she learned how he'd bungled, would she despise him? Perhaps as much as he despised himself?

Half an hour later, Anthony stood on the steps of Chelsea's townhouse and steeled himself to knock. It took courage to stand against an advancing column of French foot soldiers and not fall back. He'd held his ground more times than he cared to remember. But battlefield heroics were paltry compared to what it took to face the woman you loved and admit you'd failed her. Miserably.

Eschewing the brass knocker, he fisted his swollen right hand and banged on the door. No response. He pounded harder, but still no one came. He was reminded of that other day when he'd camped on this stoop, waiting for Chelsea to answer so that he could make her his mistress. Unlike that day, he wasn't all that eager to be admitted.

Coward. Brimming with self-loathing, he smashed his knuckles into the solid oak, accepting the bruising pain as his due.

It was Jack who finally answered.

"Oh Lord Montrose, thank God ye've come."

He'd expected Jack to be furious with him for failing to relieve him the night before. Instead the giant's weathered face was twisted in anguish, the uncovered eye red-rimmed. There was only one thing that could reduce Jack to such a state.

Dread dropped anchor in Anthony's chest. *Chelsea.* "What's happened?"

Jack's mouth worked, but no words emerged. Anthony pushed past him. At the bottom of the stairs, he shouted, "Chelsea!" until his throat was raw, but she didn't materialize. The fist in his gut twisted, painful as a dull blade.

He swung around, nearly colliding with Jack. Chelsea's butler had aged at least a decade since the night before. Under other circumstances, Anthony might have felt compassion, even pity. Now he had no patience for anyone's anguish but his own.

"Where the hell is she?"

Jack's head fell forward. His large frame seemed to shrink before Anthony's eyes.

Desperate, he grabbed Jack's lopsided shoulders and shook him. "Get hold of yourself, man, and answer me."

"G-gone." Tears trickled down Jack's leathery cheeks.

His worst fear confirmed, Anthony dropped his hands. Questions jetted from his brain like water from a geyser but all he could do was repeat stupidly, "Gone?"

"Aye. I've been searchin' for her ever since yesterday evenin'. Just got back 'ere meself."

Since yesterday evening. Guilt-riddled, Anthony turned away. Confessing would be easier if he didn't have to meet Jack's earnest gaze.

"She was with me last night." *And this morning.* "I saw her home. I can vouch for her safety until . . . dawn."

There, he'd confessed. Jack would likely pulverize him now—a far more palpable punishment than the tongue-lashing Chelsea would mete out when she learned he'd betrayed their secret. But he'd willingly accept both penalties in exchange for finding her safe.

"So, that's the way o' it." Jack's eye narrowed and his hands twisted into fists at his sides.

"Yes." Anthony met the older man's gaze head-on. Seconds crawled by as they stared each other down, neither willing to be the first to look away. "You should know that I love her," he ground out through gritted back teeth.

"Humph." Jack looked unimpressed. "Then ye must mean to marry 'er, aye?"

Anthony's reply was his silence. Jack knew damn well he was betrothed.

Jack unballed his right hand and jabbed a thick forefinger in the vicinity of Anthony's face. "Look's like ye and me 'as a score to settle."

Anthony didn't flinch. "Absolutely. *After* we find her."

Jack lowered his hand, signalling the beginning of their temporary truce. They'd put aside their differences and work together to locate Chelsea. Only after she was safe would they kill each other.

After she was safe.

Heart pounding, Anthony stalked down the hallway to the parlor. Deliberately brisk, he asked, "I trust you've searched the usual places?"

Jack's heavy footsteps trailed him. "Aye. I even went to the church where the blunt were to be left, but 'twas no sign o' 'er there either." Jack hesitated. "Yesterday, while I were on guard duty, I seen a toff in black go into the Rookery. I were suspicious so I followed 'im inside and saw him meet wi' Stenton. I couldn't 'ear much o' what they said, but what I did catch I didn't much like."

Anthony swung around. Now it was his turn to rage. "And yet you didn't tell me!"

Jack scowled. "When I went to yer 'ouse, they said ye was out for the evenin'. And when I came back 'ere to find Miss Chelsea, she were gone, too. Now I know where."

Fresh guilt struck Anthony like a fist in the face. The previous night he'd been so busy conniving ways to get Chelsea into bed that he'd missed his golden opportunity to rescue her brother. He'd botched everything, and now Phoebe—and, judging by her disappearance, Chelsea too— were paying the price of his selfishness.

Deflated, he sank down on the window seat, Chelsea's preferred perch. Her faint fragrance—orange blossom, he thought—wafted from the worn needlepoint cushion. Elbows on his knees, he kneaded his pounding forehead. Not even in the thick of battle had he known such despair, such helplessness.

God Chelsea, where are you? Talk to me, darling. Send me some clue.

He shifted. Something crunched beneath his pants seat, and he snapped upright. Reaching beneath, he pulled out a crumpled sheet of paper. He saw the black-edging, and his chest tightened. He unfurled it, and his gaze swept over the contents, branding his brain with each word.

I shall expect you at the Rutting Bull within the hour.

Self-loathing assumed new, uncharted dimensions. He shot to his feet, balled the note into a fist, and slammed it into the wall. Once, twice . . . The third time, plaster cracked beneath his knuckles. Tomorrow his hand would probably be in a cast but for now the bruising pain felt right, even comforting.

"What a fool I am! What a goddamned, bloody fool."

Watching him, arms folded, Jack shook his head. "Tell me somethin' I don't know."

"Very well." Breathing hard, Anthony leaned his forearms and head against the faded wallpaper. "They're at the Rutting Bull. They've been there all along."

Chelsea's nose tickled. She chipped open an eye. Gossamer threads hung like doilies from the low rafter above her. Cobwebs. She pushed herself up on her elbows, the lumpy thing on which she lay scant protection against the hard floor.

Blood rushed her temples. The room spun. Small, mean, and windowless, it was a storage cellar of sorts. The pallet beneath her was the closest thing to furniture, unless one counted the barrels. A brace of candles set atop a keg a few paces away. The air was thick with the scents of cedar and mildew and dust.

Her nostrils tingled, the back of her throat scratched, and her eyes filled with water. She covered her mouth in anticipation of a sneeze and realized her wrists were bound. The same sturdy hemp lashed her ankles. This once she followed the advice of her former governess and tickled the roof of her mouth with the tip of her tongue, trying to ward off the inevitable.

She sneezed anyway. Invisible fists, hundreds of them, pummeled the base of her skull. Dazzled by the pain, she braced her back against the stone wall, closed her eyes, and willed her treacherous stomach to settle.

"God bless you."

Her eyes snapped open just as he slipped from the shadows.

Cloaked in evil and black serge, Squire Dumfreys dropped back his hood and smoothed a hand over his dark hair. In the dim light, she could see the flecks of silver that winged his temples. Was there perhaps more gray than when she'd last faced him, less than a month ago, in his study?

"I trust you slept well?" he asked, as solicitous as if she'd awoke from a feather bed instead of a straw pallet on a dirt floor.

She was in no condition to fight him. Her head felt too heavy for her shoulders, her tongue too thick for the cottony confines of her mouth. Even so, she tried to match his jauntiness.

"These are mean lodgings for a man of your station. Or are these merely the guest quarters?"

He smiled. "Your brother expressed similar reservations at first, but I believe he has settled in."

At the mention of Robert, her bravado cracked. "I want to see him."

He came down beside her and fingered the rope at her wrists, already rubbed raw. "My dear, I do admire your spirit but even you must allow that you are in no position to be making demands. You are here at my bidding. My command."

The vicious yank to the yoke knocked the breath from her lungs. When her head stopped reeling, she was on her knees, facing him. She tried not to look at his mouth, slick with slime, the upper lip coated with perspiration. Instead she focused on his eyes, liquid pools of lust and lunacy. Somehow they frightened her less.

Distract him. Keep him talking. Above all, conceal your fear.

"He is nearby, then?"

He held her head between his palms. Gently, as though they were lovers, his thumbs flicked over her jawline.

"He is safe . . . for the moment. That is all you need know. Whether or not he remains so depends upon you."

There it was—the threat. It was almost a relief to have it out in the open. "What do you want of me?"

"You have a beautiful mouth," he answered instead, moving to trace her bottom lip with his forefinger. " 'Tis made for giving pleasure."

"What do you want of me?" The beginnings of hysteria bubbled inside her, trebling the even tones she'd meant to use.

Holding her head with one hand, he forced the thumb of his other between her closed lips and pumped her tongue. "Everything."

She considered biting him, but only briefly. Trussed like a chicken, she was completely at his mercy. And the look in his eyes told her she could expect precious little of that.

"Why me?" she asked after he withdrew.

His eyes glittered. "Ever since I first saw you, I knew you were the one for me. You were only twelve, but how I wanted you." A muscle in his jaw twitched. "I would have had you too, found a way, but I could never get close enough. That fawning family of yours was always underfoot, keeping you from me. So I waited, feeding myself with the promise that I would be your first, your only."

His rapid breaths matched Chelsea's racing heart. He let her go and pulled a handkerchief from the folds of the cloak. She dropped back on her haunches against the wall. Watching him blot his forehead, she told herself that somehow she would manage to get both she and Robert out of this alive.

"But then you grew up and so . . . so beautiful. Every lad in the neighborhood was panting after you like hounds scenting a bitch in heat. It was only a matter of time before one of them caught your fancy, took you from me. I knew I could wait no longer, that I had to declare myself. I asked your father for permission to court you, but he refused. Said the difference in our ages was too great. That marriage between us would be *unnatural*." His face puckered.

"He never told me." A terrible foreboding stole over her. She had hoped talking would divert him, unravel him even, but it seemed she was the one about to come undone.

Dry-eyed, he continued, "He never had the chance. The next day he and your mother were leaving for Bath, a holiday to celebrate their wedding anniversary. There'd been a terrible storm the night before. The roads were bogs, do you remember?"

"Yes." Horror, fascination, fear crowded her senses. She thought of her kind father, her beautiful mother, smiling reassurances at her from beneath the big black umbrella. Had it been some premonition that had driven her to follow them outside and beg them to hold off until the weather cleared?

"Tampering with the coach was child's play," he told her, twining a lock of her hair around his forefinger. "With roads that bad, a loose carriage wheel might have sufficed but, to be safe, I sored the lead horse—drove nails into his front hooves."

So that explained why gentle Jasper had appeared to go berserk. No one, especially Chelsea, had understood why their trusted carriage horse had crashed, at full gallop, into the downed tree.

"You killed Father and Mother." The declaration emerged as a barely audible whisper, but the voice inside her head screamed, *Murderer! Murderer!*

"They were a . . . necessary sacrifice."

Her eyes fixed on his face and, for the first time in her life, she knew what it meant to hate. "Did you really think I would marry *you*, even then?" she asked, past caring how her contempt inflamed him.

Her barb found its mark. Scarlet splotched his cheeks. "Of course, of course," he answered, head jerking. " 'Twas unthinkable that a slip of a girl could run an estate on her own. Alone, you'd have no choice but to seek my counsel, my comfort. Or so I thought." His eyes hardened. "You were stronger than I'd credited."

But not strong enough.

He moved over her, straddling her thighs. His cape billowed over them. His hard sex pressed against her. Behind her was the wall, grinding against her spine. Dread, disgust, helplessness overwhelmed her. *I'm trapped.*

Desperate to divert herself from the horror, to postpone the inevitable, she asked, "Why bother with kidnapping Robert if it was me you wanted?"

He slid a hand between them, palming her breasts, her belly, the front of her trousers. Nausea rolled over her. The only thing that kept her from screaming was knowing that he craved her fear even more than her body.

"Believe me, I thought of it, dreamt of it. But you would have been missed and then there would have been a search. I wouldn't have been able to hide you for long. But everyone knew Robert had bought colors. No one expected him to return from abroad for years, if ever. A useful turn of events because I had to devise a way to get you to come to me. The usual bribery—gowns, jewels, trips to London—wouldn't work with you. No, to get you to submit, I would have to appeal to your self-sacrificing nature. To take something—someone—you loved very much."

The effort to hold back the tears was blurring her vision. "I hate you."

He stilled his hands, a temporary reprieve. "Not yet, but you shall. Before this day is over, you shall hate me just as passionately as I love you."

The dawning knowledge of the atrocities of which he was capable chilled her. She started to shake from cold and nerves. Her nipples, erect beneath her lawn shirt, were easy marks. He rolled one between his thumb and forefinger, squeezing until her eyes watered and she cried out.

He stopped, patiently waiting for the pain to ebb. "One day Robert came to me, shamefaced. The young scamp had been lured into deep play in a misguided attempt to win enough to set Oatlands to rights. He lost, of course—badly. And after the debacle at university, he couldn't very well come to you, now could he?" His eyes bored into her, daring her to refute him.

She couldn't. Losing her parents, struggling to save Oatlands, taking on the role of parent to Robert—all had hardened her. Over the past year, she'd grown short-tempered, even shrewish. The result—her own brother had been afraid to come to her, to admit his mistake, to share his burden. Regret, bitter as gall, tightened her throat. Tears gathered, but she swore she'd not give him the satisfaction of seeing her shed them. She'd wait until she was alone. He'd leave her eventually, after he'd finished with her. Assuming he didn't kill her.

His smile was beatific, his eyes pure evil. "Of course I agreed to advance him the sum. Even though he had no choice but to take it, it wasn't easy for him to accept. As you know, the Bellamy pride can be heady stuff. He insisted that it was only a loan, that he would repay me with interest once he'd made his fortune. To appease him, I agreed to hold his papa's ring as collateral. Then, slowly, the idea began to take shape in my mind."

"So you hired Stenton and Luke to kidnap him, then sent the ransom note along with the ring." It was so much easier to focus on minutia rather than the fear clawing at her. "You knew I hadn't any money, let alone five hundred pounds."

He inclined his head. "It was only a matter of time before you came to me. And what a charming supplicant you made. So grateful . . ." His eyes lost their mirth. "But not nearly grateful enough. Even after you left, I told myself you'd be back. I hadn't counted on you turning to thievery."

"You knew!"

He snorted. "One-Eyed Jack—hardly original, borrowing your butler's moniker. 'Twas I who came up with the plan for his—your—capture. I had the devil of a time convincing that lily-livered magistrate that it would work."

Her head swam as she struggled to make sense of it all. "So you could see me hang?"

He shook his head. "I wouldn't have let that happen. I would have offered myself as your guardian. With Oatlands confiscated, you would have had no choice but to come into my home . . . and my bed. If you'd allowed me, I'd have shown you gentleness, consideration. In time I might even have married you."

"How generous. And now I suppose you are going to kill me?"

His fingertips played on her bruised cheek. "Kill you! Never! Your corporal self shall be disciplined but preserved to soar to new, glorious heights of degradation."

Defiance blazed through her, burning away her fear. "You will have to kill me, then."

"Oh, I don't believe that shall be necessary. I have no doubt that you will prove an apt pupil. I trow Montrose taught you a few tricks last night that will serve you well."

With one swift motion, he tore open her shirt. She gasped. Buttons popped. He trailed his finger from the hollow of her throat to the valley between her breasts to her belly.

She ground her back teeth. *Just rape me and be done with it, damn you!*

"Such beautiful skin." His tongue slipped over his bottom lip, and perspiration pricked the back of her neck. "So white and unblemished."

"You cannot hold me forever against my will."

He smiled down at her as though she had said something highly amusing and hopelessly naive. "We shall see. I shall visit you often and when I return to Upper Uckfield, I shall leave you well-guarded."

"One day I shall escape. When I do, you will hang."

He chuckled. "Oh, I think not. What chance for a career and respectable life do you think young Robert would have if it were to get out that his sister was a thief and a whore?"

Did he intend to release Robert after all? If so, her ruin,

this degradation, would have a purpose. And yet she was not prepared to surrender. Not yet.

"I will explain everything," she said. "People will understand that you forced me."

He cocked a graying brow. "Did I force you to rob innocent travelers, to lie with the most notorious rake in London a week before his wedding? I think not. No, I doubt you'd win much sympathy were your sordid history made public. Who in their right mind would take the word of a thief and a trollop over mine?"

A knock on the door provided her reprieve.

Cursing, he got to his feet. "Damn you, Bess. I told you I didn't want to be disturbed."

The door cracked open. A big-boned blonde entered in a swish of cheap taffeta and even cheaper perfume.

"Beggin' yer pardon, but ye said I was to watch for Tony . . . I mean Montrose. 'E's above stairs, wi' the big bloke."

Anthony, here? Chelsea's heart leapt. Then she glimpsed the triumph in Dumfreys' eyes, and panic seized her.

"Is he? Well, the more the merrier." He turned back to Chelsea. "I'm afraid I must leave you for a time. I must not neglect my other guests." He withdrew a pistol from the lining of his cloak and held it up to the light. "I shall have to postpone our reunion while I make them *welcome*."

He followed Bess to the door.

As soon as the door closes, scream. Scream loud and long. Don't dare stop until Anthony finds you.

As if reading Chelsea's mind, he turned back. "Oh, and by the by, please do feel free to scream. It would save me a great deal of trouble if you could manage to draw Montrose below. By now, I know these catacombs like the palm of my hand." He closed the door behind him.

A moment later, she heard the lock click.

Chelsea fell back against the wall. Even though the cellar was cold as a tomb, perspiration pricked her forehead and rolled down her back. Should she scream or remain silent? Beat her bound fists against the door or cower in the dark?

Which course would do Anthony the greatest good? Or the greatest harm?

Feet, several pair, pounded down the hallway. Something heavy crashed. Whatever had fallen must be rounded on the sides, for she heard it rolling down the corridor toward her door. It bumped something and, seconds later, a man cried out. Anthony or Dumfreys?

She tried to break the rope at her wrists by prying them apart but all her efforts won her was bloodied flesh. A shot rang nearby. The acrid odor of gunpowder drifted inside her small chamber.

Oh God, Anthony!

Feral with fear, she gnawed at the knots.

It was no use. She spat bits of hemp and dropped to her elbows and knees, dragging herself to the door. Panting, she pressed her ear against the wide planks.

The silence rang with the finality of a funeral dirge. If Anthony were all right, surely he would already be here, releasing her. She hung back so the door wouldn't hit her when it opened.

It didn't budge. Eyes trained on the handle, she muttered snippets of prayers. With every passing second, she grew a little colder, a little number inside. Soon she stopped praying altogether.

Anthony lay wounded. If he wasn't dead already, he shortly would be. She waited, mentally calculating the time it would take Dumfreys to reload.

To keep her sanity, she counted to ten and back again, first in French, then in Latin. Still no second shot. That must mean the first bullet had hit home. That Anthony was dead. She crawled back to the pallet. Exhausted, she eased onto her side, drew her knees to her chest, and closed her eyes.

In murdering Anthony, Dumfreys no doubt believed he had removed the last obstacle to her complete surrender. He wanted to break her, to dominate not only her body but her mind. Her soul. But she would thwart him. Physical resistance would be futile, but there were other tactics, far subtler and infinitely more potent.

She would take her spirit, her soul, and bury it amidst the

rich velvet blackness. So deep that he'd never be able to find it, let alone claim it for his own. All he'd have of her would be her body—the empty, vapid shell.

It would be easy to accomplish, really.

Her heart was dead already.

Chapter Nineteen

Anthony looked down at the kidnapper, lying prone in a pool of whiskey, legs buried beneath the overturned barrel. He knew firsthand how it felt to lay helpless at the heel of the foe. It was a damnable state, one that he'd not wish on his worst enemy. Until now.

"Who are you?" His drumming boot set off ripples in the spillage. Kicking an already beaten foe violated every precept of a gentleman's code, yet Anthony was tempted. Sorely.

Sweat beaded an unrepentant face. "Go to hell, Montrose. I'll be damned if I'll answer to you."

Heavy footsteps pounded toward them. Anthony whirled, his pistol at the ready. Seeing it was Jack, he relaxed. "Everything under control?"

Jack nodded. "Aye. Stenton's tied up, and Luke's sleepin' like a wee babe. I left Master Robert to stand guard o'er them . . . and to care for your lady. Mugglestone's gone for the magistrate." Lifting his lantern, he glanced down at the kidnapper. "Lud, 'tis the squire," he exclaimed, his good eye popping.

One of the local squires was willing to make me a loan, but I found his terms for repayment . . . unacceptable.

Chelsea's admission pushed to the forefront of Anthony's mind. Was this her neighbor, the same squire whom, he suspected, had all but raped her? He hadn't pressed her for details at the time, not wanting to embarrass her. God, how much misery might have been saved if only he had.

If, indeed, this was the man.

Before he could ask, Jack supplied the answer. "His name's Dumfreys. Squire William Dumfreys. He's known Miss Chelsea and Master Robert since they was born." Shaking his head, he looked down at Dumfreys. "Why'd ye do it, man? Ye was like an uncle to her."

Dumfreys's face crumpled. A tear slipped down his cheek. "I wanted to be more. So much more."

The man was mad, but Anthony couldn't pity him. He thought of Chelsea, happy and sated as he'd left her that morning. What had she suffered since? How would he find her now?

Hatred gnawed at his entrails like a cancer. He went down on his good knee and pressed the barrel of his cocked pistol to one silvered temple. "Save the rest of your confession for the magistrate. Only answer me this—what have you done with her?"

"I'll tell you nothing." The kidnapper glared at him through silent tears. "You might as well pull the trigger. Go on." His voice dropped to a hiss. "Or haven't you the stomach for it?"

Fresh anger, bright and lethal, blasted Anthony. *I'm being goaded*, he told himself, but he no longer cared. His finger found the trigger. He had only to pull back and then . . .

Jack's hand landed on his shoulder. "Don't do it, lad. 'E's not worth the waste o' good shot. Leave him for the hangman."

Sweat pricked Anthony's palms. He looked from the squire to Jack's earnest face.

Trembling, he lowered the pistol and gained his feet. "I believe you have a point." Sending Jack a shaky smile, he secured and pocketed his firearm. "Why should I deprive myself—and Chelsea—of the pleasure of seeing this filth hang?"

He was lying, of course. He'd never subject Chelsea to such a spectacle. She'd already experienced enough violence to last several lifetimes.

From the floor, the venomous voice rang out, "Damn you, Montrose! Damn you to hell!"

Anthony started toward Dumfreys, but Jack stepped between them. "Miss Chelsea's waitin' fer ye. She's sure to be behind one o' these doors." He handed Anthony a ring of keys. "Go to 'er. I'll bide 'ere."

Anthony moved along the torchlit corridor, trying doors to his left and right. Chelsea was behind one of them—that much he knew. What he didn't know, was afraid to find out, was in what state.

There'd been an ensign in his company who'd been captured at Barrosa. He'd been tortured—even sodomized—until he revealed the location of the new Allied supply route. His torn flesh eventually had mended. But his mind, unhinged, had never repaired itself. The boy's senseless gaze still haunted him. Would he find Chelsea in a similar state, her lovely blue-green eyes blank and staring?

Stop it. You can't help her if you're like this.

He pressed on. Only two more doors to try. He slid back the bolt of the second to last. Whatever Chelsea had endured since he'd left her, he would find a way to make her forget, to make her eyes smile again. He'd not fail her. Not this time.

The rusted hinge shrieked when he pushed. He slipped inside. Eerie quiet thrummed and shadows crowded him. A puddle of candlelight splashed across the earth floor. Claret-colored stains trailed to a heap of rags in the distant corner.

The heap shifted. Wide, frightened eyes met his.

Chest tight, Anthony crept closer. "Chelsea?"

Chelsea's shriek jellied his blood and sent his feet flying from under him. As soon as his soles reconnected with the floor, he swooped down beside her, tore off his coat, and draped it around her quaking shoulders.

"A-anthon-y." Hair tangled, eyes feral, and shirt torn, she spoke his name through chattering teeth.

God, I'm too late. He cupped her cheek. It was cold, like marble. Cold like the faces of his dead friends and nearly as white.

But Chelsea was alive. Her head dropped to her chest. She

started to cry, soundlessly at first but soon the sobs intensified. He lifted her chin. Big, fat tears rolled down her mottled cheeks. Relief wrenched him. The ensign, he remembered, had shown no emotion.

"I thought you were a ghost," she sobbed into her steepled fingers. "I thought he'd . . ."

"And I thought . . ." Tears clogged his throat, wet his cheeks. Too grateful to bother hiding them, he searched her face. "I thought I'd lost you."

"He s-said he was going to k-kill you like . . . Oh, Anthony, he was our neighbor, a friend of my father's. And yet he killed him—and Mother. He k-killed m-my parents." She tried to bury her face in her tied hands.

"Hush, love. He won't harm you or anyone you love ever again."

He drew her hands down and kissed the salt from her palms. He'd deal with the ropes in a moment, after she'd calmed.

She looked up, eyes wary. "Is he dead, then?"

He shook his head. "Injured. Jack is guarding him."

He thought of how close he'd come to doing murder, and a chill blew across his back. To divert himself, he pulled out his pocket knife.

"Hold still," he cautioned when she shied away.

He slipped the blade beneath the ropes at her wrist and carefully cut. The hemp fell away, leaving only the braiding burned into her skin. *Bastard*. A pity that drawing and quartering was no longer sanctioned by the Crown, he reflected, shifting to cut the rope at her ankles.

Freed, she still shivered with cold and nerves. He drew her against him and lay down, pressing her back against his chest.

When he saw the patch of matted hair at the back of her head, rage knotted his insides. Subduing it, he pulled himself upright. Combing back the crust, he probed the bump.

"Does it hurt?"

Chowderhead. Of course it must throb like the very devil. The skin was broken, and the raised flesh was the size of a robin's egg.

She shook her head, then winced. "It did at first. Now I mostly feel muzzy."

He braced himself, every muscle tensed. "Did he . . . hurt you anywhere else?"

Turning away, she chewed her bottom lip. "He taunted me, promised to make me take part in all manner of degrading acts. But if you mean did he rape me, no."

He released the breath he'd been holding.

"It was a near thing," she admitted. "If it hadn't been for some woman—Bess was her name . . ." She turned onto her back, gaze fixed on the ceiling. "I collect you er . . . persuaded her to help you?"

Caught off-guard, he hesitated. Might she be . . . *jealous?*

Giddy at the prospect, he replied, "He owns this tavern, where she works. I promised to do everything in my power to see that the deed falls to her."

She sat up, eyes flying to the door. "But Anthony, what about Stenton? And Luke? At least one of them was here when I arrived. He hit me from behind."

He pressed her back down. "We found Luke in the kitchen upstairs. Without Stenton to think for him, he was easy enough to subdue." He winked. "You know what they say about brawn versus brains."

This time the smile reached her eyes. "Lucky for me, you have both."

He grinned, absurdly pleased. Women had been heaping flattery upon him for years, but compliments had never meant much. Until now. He took her chin between his thumb and forefinger and asked himself if it was too soon to kiss her.

Her eyes stayed him. "And Stenton?"

"Hm? Oh, yes." His fingers fell away. "We came upon him in the tunnels. With a pistol to his head, he was only too willing to lead us to Robert." *And Phoebe*, he nearly added, then thought better of it. Now was not the time to address that topic.

Relief shone in her eyes but almost immediately the clouds rolled in. "Robert?"

With his thumb he traced small circles on her soft cheek.

It was probably wrong of him, but he couldn't stop touching her.

"We found him in a room very much like this one. He's a bit worse for wear, but he looks to be a sturdy fellow. With some sisterly nursing, he'll soon recover his strength. The important thing is that he's safe—as are you."

"Safe." She closed her eyes and sighed. "I'm almost afraid to believe it."

He braced a palm on either side of her head. "Believe." Craving her lips, he settled for her forehead.

She opened her eyes. "Where is he now?"

Damning himself for a lout, he started up. "You're anxious to see him, of course." Ridiculous to be jealous of a brother and yet he was. Dreadfully so. He wasn't ready to share her.

She looped a hand about his wrist and tugged. "Yes, but in a moment. For now, just hold me . . . *please.*"

Pride and love. They swelled his chest until he thought surely his sternum would crack. She wanted him to comfort her. She wanted *him.*

He dropped down beside her, tucked an arm beneath her, and lifted her onto his lap. Her slight body trembling against him shredded the remnants of his reserve.

"Yes, I'll hold you. I'll hold onto you forever if only you'll let me."

He kissed the top of her head, buried his face in her hair, dragged his stubbled cheek across her smooth one, tasted a wayward tear winding down her cheek. He was about to claim her lips when a cough sounded.

He followed her wide-eyed gaze over his shoulder to the open door.

Reggie, Lord Tremont, Robert Bellamy—and Phoebe—crowded the archway, eyes wide and mouths agape.

Chelsea pushed at his chest. He thought she mouthed the words, "What have we done?" but couldn't be sure. To avoid a scene, he let her up. She stumbled to her feet, and he had no choice but to follow.

Lord Tremont's eyes snapped. "You didn't really expect I would stand idly by and leave the rescuing of my daughter solely to you, now did you?" His gaze shifted to Chelsea, and his scowl deepened. "But I vow, Montrose, when Reginald and I followed you here, I didn't expect to find . . . *this*."

"Montrose?" Robert Bellamy, gauntness lending inches to his moderate height, turned to Phoebe. "Your fiancé?"

Phoebe's face crumpled. "So I believed him to be." She backed away, turned, then fled.

"Phoebe, wait." Robert started after her, swayed, and clutched the door post. His hazel eyes, haunted and angry, fixed on Chelsea, then Anthony. "I'll deal with you later, Montrose." He pushed away from the door and left.

Tremont and Reggie moved to close the gap. Reggie's gaze settled on Chelsea, who had retreated to the back of the chamber.

"You're the redhead from Vauxhall, aren't you?" He started across the threshold. "The one he *deserted* my sister for."

Anthony blocked him. He wished he could shield Chelsea from the scathing words as easily as he could shield her body.

"Your quarrel is with me, Tremont. Leave her the hell out of it." He advanced. Another pace and he would tread on Reggie's toes.

Lord Tremont braced a stubby hand on his son's shoulder. "Stand aside, Reginald. You can have at him after I've done."

He stripped off his coat and shoved it at Reggie, then headed to the center of the room.

Red-faced, he tucked his stubby fingers into fists. "I don't suppose anyone has chalk?"

Anthony shook his head. "Lord Tremont, I am *not* going to fight you."

"Hah! Think you're too good to fight an old man, eh? Well, I'll have you know I was accounted quite the pugilist in my Oxford days. Still remember a thing or two." Intricate footwork brought him within inches of Anthony.

"Really, milord, this is absurd." Hands at his sides, Anthony stepped back. A blow stirred the air about his midriff.

"Think you can dupe my gel and get away with it," Lord Tremont huffed. Sweat streaming, he moved in to take another jab. "I'll teach you a thing or two about honor, you scalawag."

Anthony looked over Lord Tremont's head to Reggie, who still held his father's coat.

"Reggie, for God's sake, talk some sense into your father. Or are you just going to stand there and watch him have an apoplexy?"

Reggie hesitated. Suddenly his vague gaze sharpened. He pushed away from the wall and squared his shoulders.

"As a matter of fact, I'm not," Reggie said with more conviction than Anthony had ever heard him apply to any topic other than cards.

He draped his father's coat over a dusty barrel, removed his own cherry-colored outer garment, and folded it atop the other. He came forward and nudged his father out of the way.

Lord Tremont frowned. "But I was just warming up."

"Sorry, Papa, but the family honor is at stake." He drew back his gloved fist.

The next thing Anthony knew, he was tasting the most expensive kid leather. Bracing his back against the wall he'd just befriended, he shook his head, packed with wool and swimming with stars.

"Bravo! That'll teach him." Tremont beamed at Reggie. "Wouldn't have thought you had it in you. Seems you're my son after all."

His lordship's voice echoed inside Anthony's skull as if from a cavern. The gentleman wore two heads, both beaming with paternal pride.

Anthony bent and spat into a corner, grateful when no teeth accompanied the blood. "I wouldn't have thought you had it in you, either," he agreed, gathering himself.

Reggie flexed his right hand. "After that last bout on the bridge, I started working out at Gentleman Jackson's. Practice just about every afternoon." He grinned. "Never thought I'd best you, though. You look bloody awful, old boy."

Anthony smiled back. Blood oozed from his split lip, but

his head was beginning to clear, leaving plenty of room for rage. Reggie had all but called Chelsea a whore. That alone would earn him a second black eye.

"I'm glad to hear it." He pushed away from the wall.

"You are?" Reggie paused in retrieving· his coat. "W-why?"

"Because we're not finished."

Anthony launched forward.

The next minutes dissolved into pummeling fists, gasping breaths, and swashing blood and saliva—Reggie's. Anthony hadn't slept in more than twenty-four hours and his body, still sore and bruised from the tangle with Lord Ambrose, groaned in protest as he pushed it to its limit. Reggie's first attack had caught him off-guard. But, with his attention focused, he easily bested the younger, less experienced fighter. He softened some of his blows—but only some.

A pistol's deafening report caused the two·combatants to break apart. Jack scowled from the doorway, plaster raining on his head and shoulders.

"Mugglestone's back wi' the magistrate. They're waitin' upstairs." His scowl deepened. "Oh, and just so's ye know, while ye've been brawlin', Squire Dumfreys killed hisself."

Anthony combed the damp hair from his eyes with bruised fingers. He searched the narrow cell for Chelsea. How was she taking the news that her parents' murderer, her brother's kidnapper, her would-be ravisher was dead?

He would have to wait to find out.

Chelsea was gone.

As soon as the Tremonts moved from the door, Chelsea started toward it. She felt like a snared rabbit—suffocated, panicked, doomed. The only difference was that the rabbit was innocent.

She, on the other hand, was entirely culpable. The night before she'd knowingly made love with another woman's fiancé. That morning, she'd awoke, prepared to repeat the act. Just moments before she'd all but thrown herself at Anthony's head, shamelessly begging him to stay with her, to hold her. And he had, at great personal cost. She'd probably ruined his life.

She slipped into the hallway. At one end was Jack's unmistakable silhouette, carved in torchlight along with the overturned barrel at his feet. A black cape obscured all but the head and shoulders of the man trapped beneath, but she knew it was the squire.

Sickened, she took off in the opposite direction until the hallway ended in a set of rough wooden stairs. Knees shaking, she grabbed the banister and climbed.

She gained the top step. Opening the door, she found herself in the kitchen. An iron poker lay in the center of the cobbled floor. Nearby Luke was curled on his side, powerful limbs trussed. He looked so peaceful that, were it not for the pool of blood beneath his head and the ugly gash above his left eye, Chelsea might have thought he slept.

Stenton, tied to a nearby chair, lifted his chin from his bony chest and glared. "So, it *was* you, Ginger."

She shivered and hurried into the public room. What she needed was air. A great deal of it.

She yanked open the heavy front door and stepped outside. A fall breeze nipped her cheeks. Throughout the city, fireplaces burned and chimneys pumped coal dust into the chalky sky. She closed her eyes and took several deep, calming breaths, imagining that the air was clean and fresh like that of home.

"Chelsea."

Her eyes snapped open. She peered down the street and sighted Robert, rising from a bench set beneath a street lamp. And, with him, Anthony's fiancée.

Blast. She'd walk home before she'd face either of them. Seeing Robert so emaciated and filthy wrenched her, but not half as much as the disgusted look he'd lanced her when he'd found her in Anthony's arms. Being on the receiving end of her sibling's wrath would be a new, character-building experience. And one she was determined to avoid at all costs.

She directed her shaking steps to the opposite end of the street, praying she'd find her horse before Robert intercepted her.

Her brother's hand clamped down on her shoulder like a nutcracker. *Double blast.* Caught, she turned to him.

"Christ, Chels, it's good to see you." His tentative smile dissolved her dread. He held out his arms, and she walked into them.

"Don't blaspheme," she reproved, straining to see him through happy tears.

Giving up, she squeezed her eyes closed and returned the hug. Sharp ribs sliced through his shirt.

She stepped back and surveyed him. He'd definitely grown up over the past month. Gone was any hint of boyish mischief. In its place was an adult seriousness she wasn't certain she was ready to deal with.

"You feel as though you've lost two stone," she managed at length, "but we'll remedy that when we get you home. I'll have Cook prepare nothing but your favorites." She touched his chin and frowned. "Provided you shave off this monstrosity."

"No argument there. It's likely as lice-riddled as the rest of me."

She looked beyond Robert to Phoebe, who had risen and was silently observing their reunion. The girl looked genuinely miserable. Even at this distance, Chelsea could see that her light blue eyes were red-rimmed and swimming in tears.

What have I done?

These past few weeks, she'd been absorbed with Anthony and her deepening feelings for him. It had been easy, too easy, to forget that another person was involved. One who, like herself, had feelings and hopes and dreams.

Guilt flailed her. With it came the need to be punished. At minimum, she shouldn't deny Phoebe the chance to spit in her face.

Girding herself, she turned to Robert, who appeared to be studying Anthony's fiancée just as closely as she was. "Perhaps you should introduce us?"

Robert turned a telltale red, a family trait they shared. "All right." Taking Chelsea's hand, he led her back to the bench. "This is Phoebe." The blush deepened and his grip on her hand tightened until she thought the bones would snap. "I mean Lady Phoebe." He inclined his head toward Chelsea. "My sister, Chelsea."

Chelsea tensed. Any second now, vile accusations—perhaps even gouging fingernails—would fall on her like pelting rain.

"Miss Bellamy." Phoebe regarded her. Her expression was cool and openly curious but by no means vicious. "I've the strangest feeling we've met before. Before today, that is. We have, haven't we?"

With one word, Chelsea could destroy every girlish, romantic fantasy that Phoebe had ever entertained about her intended. A few more well chosen words would ensure that there would be no wedding on Thursday.

She had the power to ruin two lives. Or repair them.

Loving Anthony as she did rendered the choice both ridiculously easy and unspeakably hard.

Chelsea sat in the middle of the bench and patted the space on either side of her. "Make yourselves comfortable. I'm afraid it's rather a long story—and an outrageous one."

Breathing hard, Anthony stepped back from the undertaker's wagon where he and Jack had just deposited Squire Dumfreys's stiff and rather weighty remains. "By the by, thank you for keeping me from killing him."

Now that Chelsea was safe—and his blood had cooled—it chilled him to think of how close he'd come to doing murder.

"Anytime, milord." A lopsided grin split Jack's craggy countenance.

Anthony extended his hand. "I'd be honored if you'd call me by my Christian name—Anthony." He winked. "Or Toeless Tony, if you'd prefer it."

Grinning even wider, Jack grasped Anthony's hand in a grip that bordered on bone-crushing. "Anthony'll do just fine, mi—." Chuckling, he added, "Wants fer a bit o' practice."

They stood in silence, watching until the black-draped vehicle disappeared from view. Out of the corner of his eye,

Anthony spied Chelsea huddled on a bench with Robert and Phoebe. They were too far away for Anthony to overhear but, whatever it was that Chelsea was saying, she obviously held her two listeners in thrall. His heart drummed. Dare he hope she was revealing the whole, if unflattering, truth about his activities of the past weeks? If so, surely Phoebe would have no choice but to cry off their engagement? It would be a while before he found out.

"Justice—and the magistrate—awaits," Anthony said, gesturing toward the tavern. "Shall we?"

Thanks to Mugglestone, Anthony's second interview with the magistrate was blessedly brief. Although his hands were bound, the squire had managed to lift the lid off his signet ring using his teeth. An inner compartment contained the deadly poison that he carried in the event that his carefully crafted schemes should fail. According to Jack, who had watched his prisoner writhe, the end had been agonizing but brief. Everyone agreed that the best course would be to record the gentleman's death as a suicide. Stenton had been on the lam for years now. He would be tried—and hung— for his previous crimes, too copious to count. As for Luke, there was a cell in Bethlehem Royal Hospital—Bedlam— that would suit him splendidly.

That left only the matter of Anthony's own future to address. He came out onto the tavern steps along with Jack, Reggie, and Lord Tremont. Together, they watched Mugglestone prod his two prisoners toward the magistrate's waiting carriage.

"I suppose it's over then," Lord Tremont said, speaking their collective thoughts aloud. Turning to Reggie, he added, "Time we collected your sister and were on our way." His gaze, yet to thaw, angled toward Anthony. "Coming, Montrose?"

"Yes, I suppose so," Anthony replied, distracted by the sight of Chelsea still perched between her brother and Phoebe.

Chelsea looked up. Their gazes met and melded. Anthony saw the yearning in her eyes and knew that it matched his own. His self-control, drawn taut as a bowstring, very nearly snapped. Leaving the others behind, he rushed toward her, his gait skirting a run.

Phoebe, not Chelsea, rose to meet him. She flew to his side, blocking his path. He dug in his heels and prepared to be slapped—or worse. And yet there Phoebe stood, *smiling*.

"Oh, Anthony, Miss Bellamy has explained everything." She launched herself into his arms.

"She has, has she?" His gaze fell on Chelsea, who colored and looked away.

Phoebe nodded vigorously. "Yes. And to think these last weeks you've been engineering Mr. Bellamy's rescue. Really darling, you might have said something. I was halfway to believing that there was—" Blushing profusely, she finished in a small voice, "Well, that is to say, someone else. Can you ever forgive me?"

Anthony couldn't meet Phoebe's eyes. He stared over her shoulder at Chelsea, who stood between Jack and her brother. He wanted to shrug Phoebe off and go to her, but the steely look in Chelsea's turquoise eyes stayed him. He might have been a stranger instead of the man who only last night had shared her bed.

"You do forgive me, don't you?"

He looked down at Phoebe and mumbled, "Of course."

Lord Tremont slapped Anthony on the back. "Seems I misjudged you, my boy." He held out his hand. "Bygones?"

Wishing he might sink beneath the sidewalk, Anthony took Lord Tremont's hand. "Of course, sir."

Lord Tremont turned to Chelsea. "And to you, Miss Bellamy, I offer my deepest apology. Inadequate as it is, I hope you will accept it?" He elbowed his son, who mumbled his own regrets through bloodied lips.

"You have nothing for which to apologize, your lordship." Chelsea's expression was funerary, her voice disconcertingly earnest.

Trying to catch her eye, Anthony caught Robert Bellamy's glower instead. It was obvious that Chelsea hadn't managed to convince everyone that Anthony had spent the past weeks engaged in nothing but heroic deeds. The young man's eyes blazed with a dislike that bordered on hatred. Then they fell on Phoebe and softened.

Anthony looked to Phoebe, who had finally stepped out of his arms. Bedraggled and flushed, she appeared more vibrant than he'd ever seen her. Had captivity bred a *tendre*? The boy was obviously smitten. Dare he hope that Phoebe's heart might be likewise engaged?

Before he could explore that tantalizing possibility, an elegant town carriage drew up alongside their party.

Lord Tremont hailed the driver. "My carriage. Shall we?"

Phoebe linked her arm through Anthony's. She smiled up at *him*, and his heart plummeted. "Yes, do let's leave this dreadful place. I want a bath and a nap—and *food*. I'm far too ravenous to wait until tea. Perhaps afterwards, you can take me for a ride in the park? I want to hear all about your exploits over the past weeks, every thrilling detail!"

Anthony swallowed. Hard. "Yes, well, we'll have to see." He looked beyond Phoebe to Chelsea, who was distancing herself from them. From him. If he could prolong contact, perhaps he could contrive a moment alone with her?

"Miss Bellamy, may we offer you and your brother a ride?"

She flinched as though he'd struck her. "No thank you, Lord Montrose. My horse is nearby. My brother can ride pillion, and Jack has his own mount."

She was dismissing him. Worse, she was saying farewell.

Desperate, he persisted, "But you're injured. My physician really should have a look at that bump on your head."

She pressed her lips together. "Good-bye, Lord Montrose."

Their gazes met and held. The others drifted away, and it was as though Chelsea and he stood alone, facing one another across the abyss. The abyss that he'd dug a bit deeper every time he'd tried to beguile her into becoming his mistress.

And now she was leaving him. Or rather she'd engineered events so that he had no choice but to leave her.

I love you, Chelsea. "Good day, Miss Bellamy."

He couldn't, he wouldn't say good-bye. But it was good-bye, and he knew it. He could see it in her eyes, in the way she worried her bottom lip.

Phoebe looked about, face bright. "Gracious but you all sound as though this is *adieu* rather than *au revoir*." She turned to her father and tugged his sleeve. "Certainly we'll invite the Bellamys to the wedding, won't we, Papa?"

Lord Tremont began an intense examination of his shoes. "Perfectly fine by me, of course, but we'll have to talk to your mother. Guest list all planned. Invitations already sent. Could cause quite a to-do."

"What fustian." Phoebe stamped her slipper on a cobble. "Of course Mama will agree once we tell her how delightful they are." Her gaze settled on Robert. "That is, if you and your sister are available on the thirtieth?"

Chelsea opened her mouth, then closed it. Anthony wondered if he was the only one to see her eyes fill with tears.

Robert offered Phoebe a low bow. Averting his gaze from Anthony, he replied, "I'm afraid we must decline, Miss Tremont. My sister and I have been absent from our home overlong. So, we must bid you farewell and wish you happy all at once."

Phoebe's face fell. "I see. Well, safe journey then." She gave Anthony her hand.

He helped her up the carriage steps. A frozen feeling crept over his chest. He looked back at Chelsea, but she only shook her head and turned away. He started up the steps. The coldness spread, settling in the pit of his stomach. He stopped, right foot poised on the top step.

Chelsea! Grief gripped him. He was about to lose her as surely as if she had died. If only she would stop being so damned noble! Frustration stabbed through the frozenness, chipping it away. Raw feelings washed over him. He wanted to shout, swear, fall to the ground, rend his clothes.

He started to climb down, but Lord Tremont was at his back. "I say, Montrose, need a hand after all that knocking about?"

"No, I'm fine," he lied.

He ducked inside and collapsed against the velvet seat across from Phoebe. They were a week from marriage, and no one would have taken it amiss if he'd positioned himself more intimately beside her. As it was, Lord Tremont and Reggie had to step over him, for he wasn't about to relinquish the window.

It afforded him one last view of Chelsea as she turned and walked out of his life.

Chapter Twenty

One Week Later

It had been the week from hell.

From the window of his bedchamber, Anthony watched gray drizzle fall from chalk white skies and wondered if it was cold enough for snow. Snow in September? Why the devil not? If London's most renowned rogue could spend a week tearing his heart out over a woman who'd spurned him, then anything was possible.

Turning his back on the uninspired vista, he crossed the room to his dresser. On the way, he kicked aside an overturned brandy decanter, one of several empties littering the carpet. He'd been drinking hard and heavy every night for the past week. Brandy mostly although the port and claret had gone down almost as smoothly. He'd finally stopped around midnight the night before after he'd acknowledged that the pain was growing sharper, not duller, with each emptied glass.

He stared into the mirror above the bow front dresser. It was the first time he'd looked at himself—*really* looked—in a week. A brown beard hid most of his face, but the skin stretched over his cheekbones was sallow as a Spaniard's. His hair, untrimmed, curled around the velvet collar of his dressing robe. And his eyes, world-weary and shot with red, belonged to a man twice his age.

What had he expected? He'd been living on liquor and

false hope for a full week. He dropped his gaze to his dresser top. Seven dead roses—one for each day—lay alongside a stack of unopened letters. His letters. Chelsea had returned them along with the flowers. Except for the seventh. That letter she'd exchanged yesterday with a note of her own. In it, she'd told him to forget her.

Forget her. As if he ever could. Did the heartless wench think he chose to feel this dull, omnipresent ache? Did she imagine he spent his every waking moment scheming to get her back because he had no other occupation?

Last night, after he'd emptied the liquor cabinet, he'd spent the predawn hours pacing. Self-reflection could be a heinous thing. It peeled away his pride, layer by layer, like the skin of an onion until only the inner bulb remained, shriveled and sickly. He'd finally seen what others saw—a spoiled, conceited dilettante. A wretch who cared only for pleasure—his own. Such a man didn't deserve to be happy, but Chelsea did. And so did Phoebe.

The knock at his door jarred him. He swung around. "Enter," he called out, remembering that he'd rung for his valet only moments before.

"Good morning, milord." Yawning, Tobias crossed the threshold with a steaming basin of water and a towel draped over one arm. "I didn't expect to find you up and about for an hour or more but, like they say, 'tis the early bird that catches the worm."

Anthony folded his arms across his stained robe front. "Indeed? I'd only hoped to catch a shave."

"Coming up, milord." Oblivious to his master's sarcasm, Tobias carried the basin to the washstand. Slanting Anthony a sidelong glance, he began laying out the shaving things. "'Tis good to see you looking so, uh . . . chipper."

Chipper. Anthony had never felt less chipper in his life, but he cracked a smile at such an early morning display of cockney optimism. "Well, it is my wedding day after all."

Tobias dropped the pot of shaving soap into the basin. Water lopped over the sides. He fished out the soap and glanced at Anthony over his shoulder. "Yes, well, er, looks as if you've come through the wedding jitters."

Wedding jitters. So that's what they were calling it be-lowstairs. Personally, he'd thought he was going mad.

"Indeed. I feel far less *jittery* than I have for some time." He came up beside Tobias and reached for the razor. "Quite calm, really."

Tobias snatched it away. "Allow me, milord." He motioned Anthony to a chair. "Do sit, if you please."

Anthony complied, amused that his valet didn't trust him with sharp objects. Trying not to smile, he angled his face upward and held still while Tobias draped the towel over his shoulders and used a soft-bristled brush to slather soap over his face and neck.

"That has it," Tobias announced at length, toweling him dry. He slapped cologne on Anthony's stinging cheeks and moved to the wardrobe.

"The canary jacket and gray trousers, milord? Or will it be the burgundy frock coat?"

Anthony shook his head. "Neither. The black."

"Are you certain, milord? 'Tis your wedding day."

"Quite."

The valet stared at him but knew better than to countermand an order. He removed the required articles and helped Anthony dress with a minimum of fuss.

Anthony turned to face the mirror. Raccoon-eyed, hollow cheeked, and dressed in unrelieved black, he looked more like an undertaker than a bridegroom, but the shave had restored him to respectability. The hell with that. He picked up one of the withered roses from his dresser, snapped off the stem, and tucked it in his button hole.

He caught Tobias staring at him in the mirror. Turning, he schooled his features to innocence and asked, "How do I look?"

Speechless, Tobias handed him his beaver hat and cane.

It was getting more and more difficult to retain servants with any sense of humor, he reflected, heading down the stairs. Peering over the balustrade, he saw that his entire staff awaited him in the front hall. Bloody hell.

Chambers stepped forward. "On behalf of the staff, milord, allow me to wish you happy."

"Thank you, Chambers. I shall endeavor to try." Inclining his head, he gritted his teeth as each servant stepped forward in turn to congratulate him.

By the time he made it through, he was drowning in well-wishes. Chambers helped him into his greatcoat and opened the front door. Outside rain swelled the gutters and the patch of front lawn was a mud pit.

The butler shook his grizzled head. "A pity about the weather, your lordship, and on your wedding of all days."

The damp misery of the day suited Anthony, but he made an effort to appreciate the sentiment. "Indeed," he murmured, stepping outside.

Masters waited on the other side of the door, a large black umbrella held aloft and a daisy in his hat in honor of the day.

"Do let me see you to the carriage, milord," he insisted, after Anthony waived the umbrella aside. "You'll be soaked through if I don't. And 'tis your wedding day."

"Yes, yes, I know." Anthony growled as the umbrella resurfaced over his head. "You must be the twentieth person to remind me of it."

"Mind that puddle, milord." Unflappable, the driver steered him down the path, circumventing each and every watery pitfall. "Not to fret. I'll make the church before the bridge floods. You can depend upon it, milord."

Anthony ducked out from the covering and smiled up at the dark, angry sky. "We've a stop to make first."

Eyes closed, he held his face up to the deluge. The rain falling on his face felt so good, so *cleansing*, that he took off his hat and let it lave his bare head.

Masters's eyes bulged. "Milord!" He opened the carriage door and almost shoved Anthony inside.

Anthony tossed his soaked hat on the seat, then climbed in. Combing wet hair from his forehead, he settled back against the squabs. "Nine Grosvenor Square."

"Lady Phoebe's direction?" At Anthony's nod, Masters hunkered inside the open portal. "But milord, 'tis ill luck for the groom to see the bride before the ceremony."

"Hm," Anthony replied. Turning to gaze out the window

on the opposite side, he left the driver no choice but to close the door and climb atop the box.

No more running, he vowed as they clattered through Mayfair's gray, rain soaked streets. He'd spent the better part of his life shirking his duty. Running away, never to. Plunging headfirst into pleasure had seemed so much easier than asking for his father's respect, his mother's love, his dead friends' forgiveness. Now that he'd finally stopped, he realized it felt good to pause and savor the moment.

Even if it was the darkest one of his life.

"Look, Chels, a rainbow." A clean-shaven Robert beckoned Chelsea to the parlor window.

She glanced up from the pile of clothing she'd been folding on the dining room table. "A rainbow in London. I don't believe it."

"Believe it—and hurry before it vanishes."

Chelsea dropped the shirt she'd been trying to wrap and joined him.

He moved over to make room. "Above that stand of trees. Over there."

In profile, Robert still resembled her baby brother, but captivity had changed him. His sad eyes held a newfound wisdom, and his gauntness made him look years older. He wasn't yet twenty, but he might have been Anthony's age.

Anthony. *Blast*. Today was his wedding day. It was nearly ten o' clock. By now, the vows had been taken, the rings exchanged, the blessing given. The deed done. Even now Anthony might be seated at his wedding breakfast, toasting his bride.

She forced back tears. She was getting better and better at mastering her misery. *Life goes on*, she told herself firmly. There was even a rainbow outside. Stripes of pale pink, soft yellow, and green arced above the treetops.

"You're right." She forced a lilt into her voice. "I wouldn't have believed anything could cut through this fog."

Jack's footsteps clanked from the stairs. He passed through the hallway, a portmanteau dangling from either hand. "Enough woolgatherin', you two. At this rate, we'll never make the first posting inn afore dark."

Despite the reproach, he whistled as he carried their luggage outside to the wagon. He was looking forward to going home. She wished she could capture some of his enthusiasm.

Staring back outside, Chelsea said, "It hurts, doesn't it?"

"Like the very devil. But what about you? I'll never forgive Grenville for—"

"I'm going to be fine and so are you." She pushed away from the sill, determined to stop brooding. "Once we clear the London coal dust from our lungs and breathe the fresh Sussex air, we'll be back to our old selves. You'll see."

Robert's somber face told her he didn't believe her for an instant. But then, neither did she.

"Packing can wait." She held out her hand. "Come, take a walk with me. Now that the rain's stopped, it's lovely outside. We've both been cooped up far too long."

He shook his head. "You go. I'll finish up." He attempted a smile. "You bought me all these clothes. The least I can do is help pack them."

She sighed. "Only too true, but won't you come anyway? We're leaving in a few hours, and you've yet to see London. We can hire a hackney to drive past the sites."

He walked into the dining room. "I've seen all of London I care to. You go on."

Chelsea studied the rigid set of his thin shoulders and shook her head. Robert's new adult wisdom could be a discomfiting thing, but she could still read his thoughts. His animosity toward Anthony was not entirely on her behalf. She'd seen how dejected he'd looked when Phoebe had stepped inside that carriage.

Robert was in love with Phoebe, she with Anthony. Phoebe and Anthony were wed. The situation reminded her of *As You Like It*, her favorite Shakespearean comedy. Except that London was no Forest of Arden. And none of the "players" were laughing.

"I'm going to pay one last visit to Hyde Park then. I'll be back inside of an hour."

She grabbed her shawl from the peg by the front door and picked up her basket. Then she hurried outside to where Jack was hoisting a heavy trunk atop the others.

The mail coach would have gotten them home faster, but then she wouldn't have been able to bring Autumn. Saving the gentle horse from the glue factory had been a splendid use of her ill-gotten gains.

The mare, hitched to the wagon along with Jack's horse, whinnied when she approached. "No sugar cones left but here's a carrot." She plucked the root from her basket and offered it.

Jack stepped away from the load he'd just balanced. "Goin' somewhere?"

"I know I'm a wretch to leave the rest of the packing to you and Robert, but I've got to get away for an hour. The truth is, I need some time to myself. Forgive me?"

He pulled on one of her curls that had escaped the lace edged cap. "What do I tell 'im if . . ."

She silenced him with a look. "He won't."

He shook his head. "'E's come every day now."

She folded her arms across her thundering heart. "Today is his *wedding* day."

Jaw set, Jack tested the rope he'd just tied across the stacked trunks. "I b'aint givin' up on 'im yet."

"Well, I am." She scratched Autumn on the withers, then started down the street.

She'd intended to hire a carriage, but the bracing air buoyed her spirits and the sun felt wonderful on her face. By the time she reached the park, the sky was a brilliant blue, birds chirped, and carriages and men and women on horseback thronged the main gate.

Avoiding the more popular walks, she found an unoccupied bench overlooking the Serpentine. As soon as she sat, ducks and geese crowded her. She took out the loaf of stale bread she'd brought, broke it into bits, and tossed it to them, smiling at their silly antics and greedy machinations.

A young mother pushing a pram settled on the next bench. Sighting greener pastures, Chelsea's feathered friends moved on.

Inconstant creatures, waterfowl. So like . . . men.

Deprived of her diversion, she took out the letter she'd brought and broke the seal.

"Come live with me and be my love, and we will all the pleasures prove."

Marlowe had certainly known how to cut to the core of a woman's heart. And so did Anthony. He'd followed Marlowe's sonnet with his own eloquent plea, begging her to reconsider.

She lifted streaming eyes from the paper. His previous six letters she'd returned unopened. Yesterday she'd weakened and kept this one. Common sense told her to burn it the moment she got back, but she was more likely to hold onto it, perhaps forever.

Forever. What a dreadfully long time that seemed. She reached inside her pocket for a handkerchief. Miraculously, she'd remembered to put a fresh one inside. She dabbed her eyes.

She was pathetic. If Anthony's scribbling could reduce her to such a state, what would happen if she were to come face to face with him? She knew the shameful answer all too well. Her resolve would melt like butter beneath a summer sun. Which only confirmed she'd been right to refuse his visits. Like a confirmed drunkard, complete abstinence was her only hope of a cure.

She pocketed the note, reminding herself that Anthony's invitation didn't extend to marriage. Aristocrats didn't wed the daughters of obscure country squires.

And Bellamys didn't become mistresses. But beyond pride, beyond morality, lay fear. Sharing Anthony with Phoebe—with any woman—would probably turn her into a jealous shrew. And Anthony would grow to despise her. Even if she managed to conceal her jealousy, he would tire of her eventually. To watch his warm regard sour into disinterest, perhaps even dislike, would be a living death, to be pensioned off the most humiliating of fates.

"Pardon me, but is this seat taken?"

She started. She'd recognize the rich timbre of Anthony's

voice anywhere. Her head snapped up just as he rounded the bench. Without waiting for her permission, he sat beside her.

"How did you know where to find me?" she asked, gaze trained on a large mallard gobbling the last of the bread.

"I've just come from your house." He put an arm around her and drew her against him. "Your brother wouldn't tell me where you'd gone, but fortunately I came across Jack." His eyes narrowed. "He was loading your baggage into a wagon. You were going to leave without saying good-bye, weren't you?"

Sitting in the circle of his arms, it was impossible to lie. "Yes. I thought it would be easier."

His eyes widened, accentuating the dark crescents chiseled beneath. "Easier for whom?"

"For both of us." She hesitated, picking at one of the ornamental rosebuds sprigging her skirts. Who did she think to fool? "For me, especially." She folded her hands in her lap to keep from touching him. "In case I forgot to mention it before, thank you for saving me and for rescuing Robert. We shall always be grateful."

He cocked a brow. "Grateful, is he? He has a rather odd way of showing it. Unless, of course, fisticuffs is a family custom."

She turned to him. "Oh, Anthony, he didn't . . . You didn't . . . ?"

"Fight him?" He shook his head. "Of course not. He's still weak as a kitten. And I'm . . . tired of fighting. Especially with you."

She sighed. They'd covered this ground so many times before. "It's no use, Anthony. I love you, but I won't live as your mistress."

To her surprise, he nodded. "I suppose deep down I've known from the first that you wouldn't change your mind, but I wasn't prepared to face the truth until today. It was wrong of me to ask you in the first place, but then we rakes are notorious for allowing our desires to overcome our better judgement." He smiled, and her heart caromed. "I suspect there may be a rule book somewhere that says so." His smile thinned. "It was, above all, unmitigatedly selfish of me to expect you to abandon your principles simply to make my life easier."

She thought of Lady Phoebe, the woman she'd wronged. Perhaps, if Chelsea hadn't interfered, Anthony might have spent more time getting to know the woman who was now his wife.

Head bowed, she murmured, "I think we've both been guilty of selfishness along the way."

"Will you forgive me mine, then?"

"Most definitely." His sudden vulnerability tugged at her, tingeing the moment with bittersweet regret. "It's just as well, really. I should have made a very poor mistress." She tried to laugh, but the sound died in her throat.

He shrugged. "It no longer signifies. I've come to realize that I don't really want a mistress."

Chelsea's heart dove. Even though she'd resolved never to see him again, hearing that he no longer wanted her was more painful than she could have imagined. Tears welled, making a blur of the lake, the waterfowl, and Anthony's face. The first tear splashed her cheek. He reached out and caught it on the edge of his thumb.

"Anthony . . . don't, please. I can't bear it."

His voice trembled, but his eyes blazed. "And what makes you think I can?"

Rather than answer, she started up. "I should be getting back." Belatedly she realized that part of her gown was caught beneath him. Tugging the errant fabric, she sent him a beseeching look. "Anthony, *please*. Robert and Jack will wonder where I've got to."

"Robert and Jack can bloody well wait." Jaw clenched, he grabbed her wrist and pulled her back down beside him. "This can't."

His mouth, hot and demanding, came down hard on hers. She matched his intensity, kissing him back with all the passion she'd shored up over the past week of loneliness and self-denial. When they pulled apart, they were both panting.

He rested his damp forehead against hers and cupped the side of her face. "What I want is a wife, but only if she can be you."

I must be dreaming. Or hallucinating. "Anthony, I don't understand. You're . . . you're already married."

He released her. "No, no, I'm not." His eyes flashed with a fierce tenderness.

She stared at him, dumb. If this was a dream, she never wanted to wake.

He took her hand. His thumb swept her palm with reassuring strokes. "I may be a rake, but I'm not a coward. I wasn't about to leave Phoebe at the altar. I went to her house early this morning and called off the wedding."

Chelsea found her voice at last. "What did she . . . that is to say, how did she take it?"

A smile tugged the corners of his mouth. "She thanked me."

"Thanked you!"

"Indeed, she said that she'd met someone else—someone *younger* than I—but that she hadn't mustered the nerve to cry off and was grateful I had." He grinned. "I don't mind admitting it was a damnable blow to my pride."

"Oh, Anthony. It must have been awful." She tried to sound sympathetic but ended up laughing. Giddy with happiness, all she wanted to do was laugh and dance and kiss. Mostly kiss.

"We called in her family and made the announcement together. Afterwards Lord Tremont threatened to run me through. Lady Tremont fainted, of course, which diverted most of the attention from Phoebe and I."

"Does Robert know that er . . ." She hesitated. How to put it delicately?

"That Phoebe's a free woman? He does now." He winked. "I shouldn't be surprised if he isn't making haste to Muttonsford with a bouquet and words of undying devotion even as we speak."

She gripped his sleeve. "Oh, Anthony, do you think the Tremonts will accept him? He's poor as a church mouse. We'll be lucky if Oatlands isn't falling on our heads when we return."

He shrugged. "Oh, they'd prefer someone with a title, to be sure, but after word gets out that their daughter was a happily jilted bride, they'll be willing to settle for respectability—and quickly. Phoebe's a considerable heiress, so there's no need for her to marry money. If anything, hers will go a long way in setting Oatlands to rights."

"You seem to have everything arranged."

His smile dimmed. Stiffly, he dropped down onto one knee on the bridle path. "Not everything. Not . . . us."

He reached into his pocket, pulled out a small velvet-covered box, and opened the lid. A brilliant emerald, surrounded by diamonds, winked at her.

"Marry me, Chelsea. Be my wife." Looking into her eyes, he slipped the emerald onto her ring finger. "I'd say I love you, but love is a paltry word for what I feel." His voice, usually so sure and steady, shook.

Wetness slid down her cheeks, and she realized she was crying again. For a woman who prided herself on never crying in public, she'd done a great deal of it over the past weeks.

"I love you too, Anthony, so very dearly."

Wincing, Anthony shifted to his other knee. "Then say 'yes' and quickly unless you have a strong desire to see me permanently ensconced in a bath chair."

She grinned. "Sure of yourself, aren't you?"

He sobered. "Never less so than at this moment."

With nothing and no one to keep them apart, Chelsea scooted off the bench and into Anthony's arms. He fell back, and she landed atop him.

"Yes, yes, *yes!*" She kissed his closed eyes, the tip of his arrogant nose, the corners of his mouth, his neck.

Sprawled on the damp ground, they drew scandalized stares from several passersby as well as squawks from a number of displaced ducks.

She might have stayed like that the rest of the day, but Anthony gained his feet and brought her with him. He lifted her high in his arms and twirled until the sky and ground changed places. When he finally set her on her feet—seconds, or was it hours later?—Chelsea clutched his waist to keep from falling.

He didn't seem to mind. "I love you, Lady Montrose."

She tilted her head upward and brushed a feather from his silky hair. "That's a bit premature, don't you think? We won't be man and wife for months yet."

He flashed the rogue's smile she'd come to love. "I've the special license in my pocket. We can be married in two days."

She sighed. He was completely incorrigible. Completely . . . perfect. She hoped he never changed. "You were that sure of me!"

He winked. "Frankly no, but then the first rule of rakehood is to always come prepared."

Turn the page for a preview of . . .

My Lord Pirate

Coming in January from Jove Books!

Chapter One

September 1690
Jamaica

"**D**raw no blood, men. Remember, this is to be a wedding party."

"Aye, cap'n. It be some kind of party by the sound of it."

Over the crash of waves breaking against the rocks, strains of a minuet drifted through the darkness. The pale moon lit a desolate landscape barely visible in the heavy salt mist. Tormented vegetation clung to the lifeless hillside, which rose from a boulder-strewn inlet where only a suicidal fool would take refuge.

They called him Pirate. Plunderer. Dark Lord of the seas. No nation controlled him. Vengeance drove him. It ruled him now, colder and harder than the iron that had once shackled his limbs.

Talon Drake stood with his feet apart, the scuffed soles of his jackboots half buried in the debris littering the shore. Hands braced on his hips, his eyes fastened on the pillared residence stark white against the pall of a blackened sky. Its extravagance was a sickening mockery to the impoverished village it overlooked.

"Will the house be heavily guarded, milord?"

"You can wager the crown jewels it is, Sulley. You know how His Excellency, the governor, values his worthless neck."

A burst of wind caught in the silken folds of Talon's black shirt made damp by sea spray. More than the hint of bad weather clawed at his control. Ribbed with sharp rocks, the cliff shaped itself into a stone escarpment. No visible trail would guide him. He was about to make a raid. All to snatch the governor's precious betrothed from beneath the popin-jay's very nose.

"I hear she's a rare beauty, milord."

A knot of loathing tightened his chest. "She's a Welles."

"She's barely more than a child. Innocent of her family's crimes, milord."

Talon dropped his arms to his side, his cutlass scraping the rocks as he faced the needle-thin man beside him. Silver eyes narrowed on the crop of white hair. "Sulley, I told you to cover that grizzled head of yours. You'll get the lot of us hanged for your carelessness."

"Aye, sir!" Sulley's jaw worked nervously as he fumbled with the black sash tied at his waist. "I'm not as remember-in' as I used to be, milord. I don't know why ye brought me along."

Talon felt himself grin. "You've a fatherly look about you. An English lass facing the devil's own might be more coop-erative with you watching over her."

"If you say so, sir. It's good to see you so considerate of the lady."

Talon snorted at Sulley's absurd tenderness. Being good to the lady wasn't what he had in mind. "This is a raiding party, Sulley." Talon's gaze raked the six battle-hardened men standing at arms behind his dead father's loyal steward. "Consideration only works if it doesn't get us killed. Re-member that, old man. Or you'll cost us all our lives."

Regan Welles stepped from the elegantly decorated ball-room into the fresh air. Lifting her face into the plumeria-scented breeze, she gazed at the stars scattered across a black sky. Sirius was visible. And the Orion belt. Their beauty was like a benediction after the past few hours of cloying chatter. The pomp and splendor of her half brother's life left her winded.

At her approach, four stout seamen in formal dress snapped to attention. Each held lanterns that contributed to the glow surrounding the gardens below the verandah. Regan walked past them, her limp more noticeable with her exhaustion.

"Is this not the most beautiful night?"

The musical voice summoned Regan's attention. She turned back to the ballroom, smiling at her cousin running with unladylike grace toward her. Arabella's tabby petticoat flowered beneath a rich buff silk gown. Her blond ringlets bounced prettily around a face flushed with excitement.

Their fathers were brothers, but she and Arabella were more like sisters than cousins. "Leaving your engagement party?" Regan chastened. "Won't Harrison be looking for you?"

"His Excellency is a busy man."

Arm in arm, she walked with Arabella into the garden. Moisture in the grass dampened Regan's slippers. "As the governor's wife, I expect you'll be just as busy once you've married."

Arabella whirled with childlike abandon. "Isn't he the most handsome man you've ever seen?"

Ten years Regan's senior, her half brother would forever possess that distinction in her heart. Harrison Kendrick had been nine when their newly widowed mother married William Welles. Regan was born a year later. Since her first steps, she'd adored the man her father had accepted as his own son. The stepson who would one day become the youngest governor of Jamaica.

"You're happy then?" Regan needed to know.

"Oh, yes." Arabella faced her, blue eyes reflecting like sapphires in the warm glow of lantern light. "I'm living a dream. A wonderful glorious dream."

She was like a doll with her porcelain-blond curls and delicate heart-shaped face flushed with excitement. Regan oft wondered what life would have been like had she possessed such fine coloring and features. With dark brown hair and eyes the odd color of island cinnamon, she felt decadent compared to Arabella's aristocratic beauty. At eighteen, Arabella was only two years younger than Regan. Yet, Regan felt like an old maid in the wake of her cousin's impending marriage.

Suddenly, she wanted to hug her cousin, tell her how much she loved and missed her over the years. How glad she was to be back among the family, if only temporarily.

"Harrison will make you a fine husband despite what your father thinks."

"Mother was right to honor the marriage contract." Arabella lifted her dainty nose in disdain. "I don't know what has gotten into Papa. I shall never forgive him for not attending tonight. His actions have put a blight on the Welles name and insulted Harrison terribly."

"Your handsome prince seems unaffected by the slight."

"You're always so calm about these things."

"Only because you're so dramatic."

"And nervous. I can't breathe." She gripped her waist and laughed. "How can you breathe?"

"Because I refuse to be trussed in this sweltering heat for the sake of fashion." Besides, Regan reasoned, she could be a shriveled corpse and still never have a stylish seventeen-inch waist.

"Mother would have the vapors."

Which was normal. Regan's aunt had a permanent case of the vapors. "You should suggest she loosen her stays."

Arabella stifled a fit of giggles. "You're as naughty as you always were. How have you survived convent life all these years?"

Regan fingered a pale pink hibiscus bloom. "It hasn't been so bad, really." She plucked the flower and slid it behind Arabella's ear. Their eyes met. Regan felt the burn of tears. Next to her half brother, Arabella was the only family left alive that she truly loved. They'd shared a trunk load of correspondence over the years.

"I can't believe you'll be taking your vows with the church soon." Arabella's voice softened. "Why, I remember you were always getting into trouble when we were children. I think your father wanted a boy." She laughed. "You used to climb everything. Little Monkey. That's what your mama called you."

Fidgeting with the lace on her sleeve, Regan's mood dampened. Very few people knew her by that name.

"Maybe, if I'd had the courage to follow you just once—"

"Please, Arabella. I'm not that person anymore."

Arabella flung her arms around Regan, mussing her stubbornly coifed hair. The curly mass tumbled down her back.

"Thank you for allowing me to steal you away from Martinique. I know it's been hard on you, returning to Jamaica . . ." She shivered. "Making the trip from London frightened me after what happened to your parents. With the piracy and the terrible threats against our family, I didn't know what to expect."

The past few years almost every ship in the family's once profitable fleet had met disaster at the hands of the infamous Talon Drake. Arriving unscathed in Jamaica had been something of a miracle. Regan chose to think it was because the notorious pirate met his deserved fate at the bottom of an unforgiving sea; the very same grave where her parents lay buried. Or better yet, dangling at the end of a rope from the King's gibbet.

"Arabella!"

Arabella leaped back. "Mother's calling!" Her mortified gaze dropped in a panicked inspection of her gown. "They must be getting ready to make the announcement. I look a dreadful mess."

"You look beautiful."

"My lace fan!" Arabella lifted stricken eyes. "I must have my fan. A lady doesn't appear in front of an audience without her fan."

Indeed, to make such a fashion *faux pas* could prove an unfortunate blunder for the governor's debutante bride. Regan's pale blue fan would not substitute for the elegant pearl encrusted one Harrison had presented to Arabella earlier that evening.

"Where did you leave it? I'll fetch it," Regan offered, leading her cousin out of the exotic garden back onto the marble verandah.

"I must have left it in my bedroom when I went up with Mother earlier. Please hurry."

"Breathe, Arabella—" Regan squeezed her cousin's hand."—or you'll pass out."

Making an attempt at composure, Arabella nodded. "My room is well lit. You'll see it on the dresser—"

"Look at you, child." Arabella's mother swooped down on her despondent daughter with the cranky disposition of a nasty owl. "How many times have I told you not to come out in this horrid night air? And what nonsense is this?" Tearing the flower from Arabella's hair, she pierced Regan in accusation. "Hurry, child," she clucked as if Arabella were a two-year-old. "His Excellency is waiting."

Forgotten on the huge verandah, Regan watched them go. A familiar pang of loneliness knocked against her ribs. The old feeling annoyed her. Years ago, she'd ceased questioning the reasons her aunt disliked her so. Jealousy definitely wasn't the issue. Arabella possessed incomparable beauty and grace. She'd attended the best schools offered young ladies of good standing. Perhaps it was because Regan was an oddity. A cripple. An embarrassment.

Ignoring the subtle ache in her hip, Regan entered the stately residence through another set of French doors. Her slippered feet carried her swiftly over the polished marbled hallway of her brother's palace, as she referred to his residence. His extravagance these days bordered on the eccentric.

She followed the wide mahogany staircase past beautiful paintings worthy of a king's fortune. At the top of the stairs, she slowed beside one particularly priceless piece. It looked strangely familiar. She'd seen its like presented to a visiting French emissary by her father while he was chief justice of Jamaica.

"Milady."

Regan's heart gave a start. She knew that voice, and felt her face warm. "Captain Roth." She smiled.

He stepped from the governor's private library. "You've wandered far from the festivities."

Flashy gold ribband ornamented his green doublet. Wear-

ing a full bottomed periwig to which burnt alabaster had
been added to give it body, he was almost unrecognizable as
the captain of the *Viper*, who brought her here from Martinique. With considerable flourish, he swept his ostrich-
plumed hat from his head.

"Do I sense your approval, Lady Regan?"

"Captain Roth, you look like a true gentleman."

Black currant eyes flashed over the pale curves of her
breasts, sending nervous tendrils over her skin. "Milady—"
He closed the short distance between the them."—I've been
remiss."

"Have you?"

"I've not asked you to dance as I promised."

Surely, he knew her limp made it impossible to dance. It
was unseemly, as her aunt would say, for someone who
couldn't walk gracefully to take up the minuet. "I can't. Arabella needs—"

He casually placed his hand on the wall, almost touching
her face. "And I insist you take time for yourself, milady."

While sailing from Martinique on board the *Viper*, she'd
accepted his flirting as a matter of course because Arabella's
presence always inspired such foppish behavior from men.
Now, with her cousin nowhere to be found, Regan's usual
wit mutinied. A need to tactfully change the subject was at
hand.

She looked around him into the library shadowed in darkness. "If His Excellency catches you in there, he'll have
your handsome periwig for breakfast, Captain Roth."

"Rest assured, I've no need of state secrets." He stepped
away and closed the door. "My men and I are checking the
grounds."

"Is anything wrong?"

"False alarm, I'm sure. The governor's guard watches
over the front. And the back . . . well, the back overlooks the
cliff." He grinned. "Perhaps you would care to view the
scenery?"

"If it's the landscape you really wish to view, Captain
Roth," she replied in her most dulcet tone, " 'tis better seen
in daylight."

Roth stepped back and bowed in acquiescence. "Touché, milady."

Regan recognized that she'd just successfully flirted. "Are you always so bold with the ladies, Captain?"

"Only with those who don't bite."

Suddenly very pleased, she laughed. "I'll remember that."

"I shall await your pleasure downstairs, Lady Regan."

She watched him descend the stairs, listening until his steps faded on the marble floor. A fierce need to forget logic just once and indulge in her own femininity overtook her. Perhaps 'twas the music in the air that stirred the air around her. This was a happy celebration, after all. There should be nothing wrong with enjoying herself for once.

Heady with a sense of purpose, Regan whirled on her heel and hurried down the hallway. Reaching her cousin's room, she started to open the heavy door. Her hand stilled on the brass latch. A draft curled around her feet and slithered up her stockings. The smell of smoking flax tasted acrid in her mouth.

Regan eyed the dim hall behind her. Some of the wall sconces were out as if a burst of wind had extinguished the flame.

Refusing to heed her childish fear of the dark, she opened the door and hurried inside. Her heart grounded to a stop. Arabella had reassured her the room was lit. Light from the hallway pooled around her feet, framing her protectively within its faded golden circumference.

Regan felt utterly alone in a world bereft of human life. Then sensed she wasn't. The door slammed shut, shrouding her in darkness.

A hand clamped across her mouth, choking her scream into a muffled squeal. She bit down.

"Bloody hell!" The oath split the darkness.

A man's powerful arm encircled her ribcage beneath her breasts. Her breath exhaled in a rush as he lifted her off the floor, kicking wildly, her cries muted and weak against his hand. A table crashed to the floor shattering the crystal lamp. A glass jar of lavender-scented powder exploded in a choking cloud of dust.

Regan pounded her fists into her captor's hips. She tried to scratch his face, then went down onto the soft bed beneath his weight. The air expelled from her lungs. Pressed against the intruder's chest, his threatening size came to mind. The smell of salt spray assailed her senses.

This man had climbed over Arabella's balcony from the cliff! Only a madman scaled a rock, better suited for the winged creatures that nested within its shadowed crevices? That he dared the impossible—a raid on the governor's residence—made him extremely dangerous.

A ragged whisper ruffled the hair on her cheek, and she felt the scratch of a jaw that hadn't seen the sharp side of a razor for at least a week. "I haven't come all this way to be unmanned by a slip of a girl." The rich baritone voice and hardened body belonged to no local fop. He flipped her easily on her back. Pressing a muscled thigh between hers, he subdued her struggles. His shirt was damp. His body warm. She felt the hilt of his cutlass heavy against her hips.

Pinning her wrists above her head with one hand, he gripped her chin with the other. "Especially when I have much to offer to our future, Lady Welles."

Dear Lord! Regan couldn't believe this was happening. "How . . . do you know my name?"

"The cut of your gown tells me you're no servant." His hand boldly made his point. "Who else would venture into her own room, but the lady herself?"

Regan started to scream.

"You open your mouth any wider, you won't like what I stuff into it." His breath was hot against her face and smelled oddly of mint. "Rags are nasty things, especially when you don't know where they've been."

"What do you want? Who are you?"

"I assure you, this isn't a social call."

"How foolish of me to think otherwise."

"Ahh—" A hint of white flashed against a face shadowed by darkness."—a woman with spirit. How refreshing. Sulley! Strike the flint. I have a hankering to see just what I've bargained the devil for this night."

"You'll not get away with this." The threat lacked the

force she intended. Her heart thundered in her ears. Regan heard the snap of movement somewhere behind her.

The dull light of a candle filled the tight space over the bed. Her captor's face, so close to her own, came to life. Silver eyes probed hers with fatalistic indifference. And to her horror, her heart leapt with more than the heady rush of panic. A black scarf covered his head, accentuating the lethally handsome features of his face. With the exception of Captain Roth, she'd never seen anyone so unfashionably tanned. His gaze invaded her senses, hesitating a fraction on her mouth before moving to the swell of her breasts. All she could hear was the pounding of her own wild heart. Against her will, heat settled in the nervous pit of her belly.

"You're not what I expected." His slight English accent was aristocratic, sculpted like the man, and to Regan's ears not without a hint of disappointment.

"Really!" She'd yield nothing to this miscreant. Least of all her pride. "And does slinking about a lady's bedchamber qualify you to form such an opinion?"

With one hand clamped to her wrist, he wrenched her to her feet. Her knees felt rubbery, and she stumbled against the firm wall of his chest. A dark shirt with billowing sleeves, opened to his waist, baring his chest. Vibrant heat licked her.

Sakes alive! She was nearly a nun. What was she doing reacting with lascivious thoughts to a dangerous prowler? A lice-ridden knave, no doubt, intent on thievery and mayhem. Mayhaps, even murder!

"A child, you said." The disgruntled snort seemed aimed at someone behind her. "Of docile temperament and beauty?"

"That's what he said, sir," the unseen man replied.

"When a man doesn't know his own daughter, I question his wit, Sulley."

Daughter? What did he mean? Her father was dead.

It took a frayed minute to realize he spoke to yet another man on the balcony. Dizziness fell over her. Regan wanted to scream, needed to scream if she were to warn her brother.

But it was her captor's presence that commanded her silence. He loomed like a shroud over her will.

Standing eye-level to the expanse of bronzed flesh, she caught the flash of metal, a necklace, hanging around his neck. Her gaze dropped to the black sash knotted at his waist. It held the heavy hilt of a cutlass, the size a sure testament to this man's formidable strength. But as her eyes narrowed on the fingers that still restrained her hand, her stomach knotted.

She could do nothing but stare at the harrowing scars that banded his wrist. This man bore the cruel mark of bondage. Compassion assailed her. Nay, terrified her. Only the most tortured victims or slaves endured manacles long enough to viciously scar a man's flesh.

Her attention shifted abruptly to his face. Silver eyes were fastened on her, and froze the chaotic beat of her heart.

"Are you satisfied with what you see, milady?" He seemed amused by her gaping perusal.

Her flush deepened. "Who . . . are you?"

He bowed over her hand. His fingers were warm against hers, intensifying her own confusing reaction to his touch. Her skin tingled and shivered.

"Talon Drake at your service, milady."

"Drake!"

His atrocities against her parents joined his name with the devil! She snatched back her hand and as if that alone would cast away the fiery remnant of his loathsome touch.

"And I have the pleasure of informing you that you're coming with me."

"Never!" She struck out at him and found her hand snatched from its purpose. The air between them sparked with the violence of a hurricane and churned her belly.

His eyes glittered when they again plundered hers. "Never is a long time, milady."

"I'll be no prisoner of yours, Talon Drake," she whispered, fighting to keep hold of her courage.

Her nails cut his flesh. Dark drops of blood beaded his skin. His grip on her wrist never tightened. Yet, his power over her was as complete as the darkness beyond the swirling light of the candle.

"Sulley," Drake called without taking his eyes from hers. "I need to check our way."

Her chin lifted slightly. "Do you intend to kill me?"

"The idea certainly has merit, milady. But fortunately for you, I need you alive." His mouth lifted in a grin. "For now."

The rogue mocked her fear. "I've not the money to pay a ransom if that's what you're after."

"Rest assured, you're more valuable to me than any ransom."

An awful lump rose in her throat. "Tell me what you want then?"

Flashing her a white smile, Talon Drake released her and stepped back into the scant light. In a showcase of masculine gallantry, he raised his cutlass in a mockery of a salute and damned her with eyes as silver as the finest sterling.

"Why nothing less than to marry you, Lady Arabella."